USA Today bestselling author **Nancy Robards Thompson** has a de.... ... newspaper reporter ... ...the facts' was boring. H... ... report to her muse, Nancy writes women's fiction and romance full-time. Critics have deemed her work, 'funny, smart and observant'. She lives in Tennessee with her husband and their crazy corgi. For more, visit her website at NancyRobardsThompson.com

Jessica Hart had a haphazard early career that took her around the world in a variety of interesting but very lowly jobs, all of which have provided inspiration on which to draw when it comes to the settings and plots of her stories. She eventually stumbled into writing as a way of funding a PhD in medieval history, but was quickly hooked on romance and is now a full-time author based in York. If you'd like to know more about Jessica, visit her website: jessicahart.co.uk

USA Today bestselling author **Cassie Miles** lives in Colorado. After raising two daughters and cooking tons of macaroni and cheese for her family, Cassie is trying to be more adventurous in her culinary efforts. She's discovered that almost anything tastes better with wine. When she's not plotting Heroes books, Cassie likes to hang out at the Denver Botanical Gardens near her high-rise home.

Friends to Lovers

June 2024
One Kiss

September 2024
A Little Surprise

July 2024
Pretend

January 2025
Something More

August 2024
Always You

February 2025
Better Together

Friends to Lovers:
Better Together

NANCY ROBARDS THOMPSON

JESSICA HART

CASSIE MILES

MILLS & BOON

All rights reserved including the right of reproduction in whole or in part in any form. This edition is published by arrangement with Harlequin Enterprises ULC.

This is a work of fiction. Names, characters, places, locations and incidents are purely fictional and bear no relationship to any real life individuals, living or dead, or to any actual places, business establishments, locations, events or incidents. Any resemblance is entirely coincidental.

This book is sold subject to the condition that it shall not, by way of trade or otherwise, be lent, resold, hired out or otherwise circulated without the prior consent of the publisher in any form of binding or cover other than that in which it is published and without a similar condition including this condition being imposed on the subsequent purchaser.

® and ™ are trademarks owned and used by the trademark owner and/or its licensee. Trademarks marked with ® are registered with the United Kingdom Patent Office and/or the Office for Harmonisation in the Internal Market and in other countries.

First Published in Great Britain 2025
by Mills & Boon, an imprint of HarperCollins*Publishers* Ltd
1 London Bridge Street, London, SE1 9GF

www.harpercollins.co.uk

HarperCollins*Publishers*
Macken House, 39/40 Mayor Street Upper,
Dublin 1, D01 C9W8, Ireland

Friends to Lovers: Better Together © 2025 Harlequin Enterprises ULC.

How to Marry a Doctor © 2015 Nancy Robards Thompson
Mr (Not Quite) Perfect © 2014 Jessica Hart
The Girl Who Wouldn't Stay Dead © 2018 Kay Bergstrom

ISBN: 978-0-263-39781-9

This book contains FSC™ certified paper and other controlled sources to ensure responsible forest management.

For more information visit: www.harpercollins.co.uk/green

Printed and Bound in the UK using 100% Renewable Electricity
at CPI Group (UK) Ltd, Croydon, CR0 4YY

HOW TO MARRY A DOCTOR

NANCY ROBARDS THOMPSON

This book is dedicated to everyone
who believes in happily ever after.

Chapter One

Anna Adams parked her yellow VW Beetle in Jake Lennox's driveway, grabbed her MP3 player and took a moment to make sure it was loaded and ready to go.

She was about to hold an intervention and music—just the right song—was the key component of this quirky job.

Today, she was going to save Jake, her lifelong best friend, from himself. Or at least from drowning in the quicksand of his own sorrow.

This morning, Celebration Memorial Hospital had been abuzz with rumors that Jake's girlfriend, Dorenda, had dumped him. Anna might've been a little miffed that she'd had to hear about his breakup through the nursing staff grapevine, but the sister of one of Dorenda's friends was an LPN who worked the seven-to-three shift at the hospital and she'd come in positively brimming over with the gossip.

Jake had been scarce today. He hadn't been around for lunch. Another doctor had done rounds today. When she'd tried to phone Jake after work, the call had gone to voice mail.

The radio silence was what made Anna worry. She hadn't realized that he'd been so hung up on *Miss Texas*. That's what everyone called Dorenda, even though no one was sure if she'd actually held the title or if she'd gotten the nickname simply because she was tall and beautiful and looked like she should've worn a crown to her day job. Poor schlubs like Anna did well to make it to their shifts at the hospital wearing mascara and lipstick.

Anna wasn't sure what the real story was. When Jake had a girlfriend, he tended to disappear into the tunnel of love. Or at least he never seemed to bring his girlfriends around her. And Dr. Jake Lennox usually had a girlfriend.

Anna didn't celebrate Jake's breakups, but she had to admit she did relish the intervals between his relationships, because, for as long as she'd known him, that was when she'd gotten her friend back. Sure, they usually saw each other daily at the hospital. It was not as if he completely disappeared. But in those times between relationships, he always gravitated to her.

She would take the spaces in between any day. Because those spaces ran deeper than the superficial stretches of time he spent with the Miss Texases of the world.

Anna rapped their special knock—*knock, knock-knock, knock, knock*—on Jake's front door, then let herself in.

He never locked the door, but then again, they never waited to be invited into each other's homes. "Jake? Are you here?"

Really, she wasn't surprised when he didn't answer. In fact, she had a pretty good idea of where he was. So, she closed the door and let herself in the backyard gate and followed the mulch path down to the lake, the crowning jewel of his property.

Yep, if he was back here brooding, it clearly called for an intervention or, as they'd come to call it over the years, the Sadness Intervention Dance.

It was their private ritual. Whenever one of them was blue about something, the other performed the dumbest dance he or she could come up with for the sole reason of making the other person smile. The dance was always different, but the song was *always* the same: "Don't Worry, Be Happy" by Bobby McFerrin.

Jake had invented it way back in elementary school. Gosh, it was so long ago—back when the song had just hit the airwaves—she couldn't even remember what she'd been upset about that had compelled him to make a fool of himself to jolt her out of it. But it stuck and stayed with them over the years and now, even though they were both in their thirties, it was still their ritual. The SID was as much a part of them as all those New Year's Eves their families had rung in together or all those Fourths of July at the lake they'd shared. Back in the day, the mere gesture was always enough to push the recipient out of his or her funk. Or, on the rare occasion that it didn't, the SID was the kickoff of the pity party and the guest of honor was officially put on notice that he or she had exactly twenty-four hours to get over whatever was bringing him or her down. Because whatever it was, it wasn't worth the wasted emotion.

Nowadays, it was usually performed at the end of a love affair, as was the case today and the time that Jake had basically saved her life when her marriage had ended—metaphorically speaking, of course. But then again, he was a doctor. Saving lives was second nature to him.

Love was no longer second nature to Anna.

Sure, once upon a time, she'd believed in true love.

She'd believed in the big white dress and the happily-ever-after. She'd believed in spending Saturday nights snuggling on the couch, watching a movie with her husband. She'd believed in her wedding vows, especially the part where they'd said *'til death do us part* and *forsaking all others*. From that day forward, the promises she and Hal had made were etched on her soul.

Then it all exploded right in front of her face.

After nearly four years of marriage, she discovered Hal, who had also looked her in the eyes and made the same vows on their wedding day, had been sleeping with his office manager.

That was when Anna had stopped believing in just about everything. Well, everything except for the one person in the world who had ever been true to her: Jake Lennox.

Jake had been her first friend, her first kiss, and the

first guy to stick around after they realized they were much better friends than anything more.

He'd never stopped believing in her.

After finding out about Hal's infidelity, the only thing Anna had wanted to do was to numb the pain with pints of Ben and Jerry's and curl up into the fetal position in between feedings. Jake, however, was having none of that. He'd arrived on her doorstep in San Antonio and pulled her out of her emotional sinkhole and set her back on her feet. Then one month ago, after the divorce was final, he'd come back to San Antonio, single-handedly packed Anna's belongings and moved her to Celebration. He'd even helped her find a house and had gotten her a nursing job at Celebration Memorial Hospital.

But before he'd done any of this, he'd done the SID.

There he stood: a tall, handsome thirty-four-year-old man doing the most ridiculous dance you could ever imagine to "Don't Worry, Be Happy."

Was it any wonder that Anna felt duty-bound to be there for him on a day like today?

It was her turn to perform the SID. As humiliating as it was—well, that was the point. Anna was fully prepared to make a colossal fool of herself.

The gardenia bushes were in full bloom. Their heady scent mixed with the earthy smell of the lake perfuming the humid evening air. She swatted away a mosquito who had decided she was dinner.

Instinct told her she'd find Jake on the dock, most likely sitting on the ground with his feet in the water and a beer in his hand. Her intuition didn't let her down.

There he sat, with his back to her, exactly as she had imagined. His lanky body was silhouetted by the setting sun. She could just make out his too-long brown hair that looked a little mussed, as if he'd recently raked his fingers through it. He was clad in blue jeans and a mint-green polo shirt. A symphony of cicadas supplied the sound track to the sunset, which had painted the western sky into an Impressionistic masterpiece in shades of orange, pink and blue.

A gentle wind stirred, rippling the lake water and providing welcome relief to the oppressive heat.

Obviously, Jake hadn't heard her coming.

Good. The element of surprise always helped with the SID.

She took advantage of the moment to ready herself, drawing in a couple of deep breaths and doing some shoulder rolls. With one last check of the volume on her MP3 player, she pushed Play and Bobby McFerrin's whistling reggae strains preempted the cicadas' night song.

Jake's head whipped around the minute he heard the music. Then he turned the rest of his body toward her, giving her his full attention.

Anna sprang into action attempting to do something she hoped resembled the moonwalk. Thank goodness she didn't have to watch herself and the shameless lengths she was going to tonight.

Once she'd maneuvered off the grass and was dancing next to him on the dock, she broke into alternate moves that were part robot and part Charleston and part something...er...original.

As she danced, trying her best to coax a full-on smile from him, she tried to ignore the sinking feeling that maybe he'd been more serious about Dorenda than the others. That his most current ex had sent him into a Texas-sized bad humor.

She reminded herself that was exactly why she was here today. For some quality time with her best bud. To bring him out of his post-breakup funk. She knew she looked ridiculous in her pink nurse's scrubs that were slightly too big and clunky white lace-up shoes, but Jake's initial scowl was beginning to morph into a lopsided smile, despite himself. She could actually see him trying to fight it.

Oh, yeah, he was fighting it, but he couldn't fool her. She knew him much too well.

In fact, it only made her unleash the most ridiculous of her dance moves: the sprinkler, the cotton-swab, and the Running Man. Dignity drew the line at dropping down onto her stomach and doing the worm. Although that move hadn't been below Jake a month ago when he'd been there after she'd signed her divorce papers.

That intervention had been a doozy and a true testament to the depth of their friendship.

But he wouldn't have to perform another intervention for her anytime soon.

After losing herself and getting burned so badly, Anna wasn't in any hurry to get involved again.

For now, she was happy to serve as Jake's intervener.

Sprinkler-two-three-four, *cotton-swab*-two-three-four, *Running Man*-two-three... She was just getting into a groove, ready to transition from the Running

Man back to the robot when, in the middle of possibly the best sequence yet, her foot hit an uneven plank on the dock, causing her to lose her balance.

She saw the fall coming in slow motion and she would have face-planted if not for Jake's quick reflexes. Instead of kissing the dock, she found herself safe in the strength of his strong arms, looking up into his gorgeous blue eyes.

Anna smelled good.

The kind of *natural good* that made him want to pull her closer, bury his face in her neck and breathe in deeply.

But this was *Anna*, for God's sake.

He couldn't do that.

He respected her too much and owed her so much more than that.

Especially after she'd gone to such crazy lengths to cheer him up. Did he dare tell her that he really didn't need cheering up? Not in the way she thought he did. Sure, Dorenda had ended things, but the breakup had come as more of a relief than anything.

Before he did something stupid that would be awkward for both Anna and him, he set her upright and took a step back, allowing both of them to reclaim their personal space.

"That was graceful," he said, hoping humor would help him regain his equilibrium.

"You know me," Anna said. "Grace is my middle name." Actually, it really was. "I aim to please. How are you doing, Jake? You okay?"

Her long auburn hair hung at her shoulders in loose waves. Her clear, ivory skin was virtually makeup-free. She had this look in her blue eyes that warmed him from the inside out.

He tried not to think about the strange impulse he'd had just a minute ago, an impulse that lingered even if he was trying not to acknowledge it.

"I'm great," he said. "Want a beer? I'd like to toast your latest choreography. You're getting really good at it. I'll give your Running Man a nine-point-five. I have to take off a half point since you didn't stick the landing."

She swatted him and quickly crossed her arms in front of her.

"Yes, I'd love a beer. Thank you. I need one after that."

He smiled. "Come on. Let's go back up to the house. I have five of a six-pack in the fridge."

She was eyeing him again. "Well, good. I was afraid that maybe you'd been at home all day drowning your sorrows."

"I was seeing patients all day. In case you haven't noticed, I usually don't take off midweek to go on a bender."

He and Anna both worked at Celebration Memorial Hospital, but she was an OB nurse on the third-floor maternity ward and he was a hospitalist on the general medical-surgical floors. Unless they sought each other out, their paths usually didn't cross at work.

"I must say, you're taking this awfully well," she said.

"What?"

"The breakup. If I didn't know better, I'd swear that you were fine."

"Do I act like I'm not fine?"

"Well, no. That's what I just said. You seem remarkably unfazed by Miss Texas's departure. Sorry, by *Dorenda's* breaking up with you."

He pulled open the back door for her and stepped aside so she could enter the house first.

"Dorenda was a great woman, but our relationship had run its course. I'll miss her, but it was time to move on."

He shrugged and stepped inside behind her.

"Are you telling me that *you* broke up with *her*?"

Throwing her a glance over his shoulder as he walked toward the kitchen, he said, "No, she's the one who dropped the bomb. Actually, it was more of an exploding ultimatum. I saw it coming a mile away."

He reached into the fridge, grabbed a beer and twisted off the bottle cap.

"She gave you an ultimatum? Really? Well, but then again, how long were the two of you together?"

"Four or five months or so. Do you want a mug? I have some in the freezer."

"Yes, please. Had it really been five months? I mean, I've only been back a month."

He nodded as he poured the beer down the inside of the mug, careful to create just the right amount of foam on top. "She reminded me of that more than a few times last night. She was talking five-year plans that involved marriage and kids and bigger houses. She kept saying she needed some assurance about our future, needed to know where we were going. I'm not going to lie to her. I enjoyed her company, but I wasn't going to marry her."

He handed the beer to Anna.

"Why not?" Anna asked. "She was beautiful. You seemed like you were really into her."

Jake nodded. "She was nice. Pretty. But…I couldn't see myself spending the rest of my life with her. That's the bottom line."

Anna squinted at him, her brows drawn together, as she sipped her beer.

"What's wrong? Is the beer not good? You don't have to drink it if you don't like it."

She set down the mug on the kitchen counter. "No, I like it. But I have two questions for you."

"Okay. Shoot."

"First question. If you're *fine* with everything, how come you let me keep dancing and make a fool of myself?"

Her voice was stern.

He laughed out loud. He couldn't help it. "Are you kidding? Watching you was the most fun I've had in months. No way was I going to stop you. For the record, you didn't make a fool of yourself. You're adorable. In fact, you'd been away so long down there in San Antonio, I'd almost forgotten how adorable you are."

She rolled her eyes, but then smiled.

"So happy to have cheered you up," she said.

"What's the second question?" he asked.

She looked at him thoughtfully for a long moment.

"Why, Jake? Why do you keep dating the same type of women? I don't mean to be judgmental and I know I haven't been around for the last decade or so. But think of this as tough love. You keep dating the same type of women, expecting to get different results, but it always turns out the same way. Always has, always will."

He crossed his arms, feeling a little defensive, but knowing she was right. Sometimes her friendship felt like the only real thing in the world. But still, he didn't want to get into this right now.

"I don't exactly see you out there blazing trails in the dating world," he countered.

She sighed. "The divorce has only been final for a month."

"But you were separated for nearly two years."

"This isn't about me, Jake. This is about you. What are you looking for?"

He shook his head.

"*Company*. Companionship? That's why, when I know the relationship has run its course, I end it. Or in today's case, I let Dorenda do the honors. I don't string them along."

"But you do sort of string them along. You dated Dorenda for four months. That's a significant amount of time in the post-twenties dating world."

Overhead, the fluorescent lights buzzed. He glanced out the kitchen window. Inky dusk was blotting out the last vestiges of the sunset.

"I don't know what you want me to say, Anna."

"Say that you'll let me fix you up with a different type of woman."

Different?

"Define *different*."

"Don't take this the wrong way, but maybe you should consider women who are a little more down-to-earth than the Miss Texases of the world."

He knocked back the last of his beer and debated grabbing another, but his stomach growled, reminding him he really should think about getting some food into his system first.

"Down-to-earth, huh? I wouldn't even know where to begin to look for someone down-to-earth."

"Exactly. That's why I want you to let me fix you up."

"I don't know, Anna. Blind dates aren't really my thing."

He returned to the fridge, pulled open the door and surveyed the meager contents.

"When was the last time you went on a blind date?"

"Better question," he countered. "When was the last time *you* even went on a date?"

He looked back over his shoulder to gauge her reaction. She didn't seem to like being in the line of fire any more than he did.

"This isn't about me, Jake."

"It's been nearly two years since you and Hal broke up. So, while we're on the subject, it's high time for *you* to get back in the saddle and try again."

She put her hands on her hips and shook her head, looking solemn. "Okay, you're changing the subject, and I don't know if I even want to date. You, on the other hand, obviously do like getting involved. I know you so well, and if you'll just let me help you, I'll bet I can make it a much more rewarding experience for you. Or at least one that has the potential to last, maybe even change your mind about marriage. Come on. Be a sport."

"Why are women always trying to change me?"

"The right woman wouldn't change you, but she might make you want to see other possibilities.

He took out a carton of eggs, some butter, various veggies and the vestiges of a package of turkey bacon. It was all he had. When all else failed, breakfast for dinner always worked. It was his favorite go-to meal when the pickings were slim. He really should go to the grocery store later tonight. The rest of his week was busy.

"You'd really wager that you could fix me up with someone who is better for me than my usual type?"

She raised her chin. "You bet I could. In fact, I'll bet I could introduce you to your soul mate if you gave me a fair chance."

He chuckled. "You are the eternal optimist. Do you want to stay for dinner? I'll make us an omelet."

She put her hand on her stomach. "That sounds great. I'm starving. We can talk more about this wager. How can I help with dinner?"

"You can wash and dice the onions and red peppers."

She stepped up to the sink to prep the peppers, but first she began by putting some dirty dishes into the dishwasher and hand-washed several pieces of flatware.

"You don't have to do that," he said. "I didn't have time to clean up this morning before I left for work. I'll do those later when I clean up the dinner dishes."

"Actually, it's sort of hard to wash the peppers with dishes in the way. I don't mind, really. You are fixing me dinner. And we're going to need forks to eat with."

Jake left her to do what she needed to do because God knew she would anyway.

He took a bowl out of one of the cupboards and began cracking eggs into it. "Since when did you become a matchmaker? And what makes you think you can find me the right woman? I've been trying all these years and I haven't been successful."

"That's easy. A—I know you better than you know yourself, and B—you are attracted to the wrong women. Your judgment is clouded. Mine is not."

She might've had a point. But after just getting out of a relationship, he wasn't very eager to jump back into anything serious. So looking at it from that perspective, what harm would a few dates do? Other than take up what little free time he had away from the hospital. He could indulge Anna. She meant that much to him. Then again, could he ever really expect to find his soul mate or anyone long-term when he never wanted to get married?

That was something he'd known for as long as he'd had a sense of himself as an adult. He did not want to get married. Marriage was the old ball and chain. It took something good, a relationship where two people chose to be together, and turned it into a contractual obligation. He'd witnessed it firsthand with his parents. All he could remember was the fighting, his mom leaving and his father's profound sadness. Sadness that drove him to seek solace in the bottle. Anna knew his family history. Sure, she'd have good intentions. She'd think she was steering him toward someone who made him happy, but what was the point?

Jake vowed he'd never give a woman that much power over him.

So he said, "Before we go any farther, I have a stipulation."

"Jake, no. If we're going to do this and do it right, you have to play by my rules. You can't give me a laundry list of what you want. That's where you get into trouble with all these preconceived notions. Maybe we can talk about deal breakers, such as must not be marriage-minded or must not want kids, etcetera, but we're not getting into the superficial. You're just going to have to trust me."

He poured a little milk into the eggs, a shake of salt, a grind of black pepper and began to beat them. Even though they'd spent a lot of time apart, Anna still knew him so well. A strange warmth spread through him and he whisked the eggs a little faster to work off the weird sensation.

"I wasn't going to get superficial. In fact, my stipulation wasn't even about me. I want to propose a double wager. Since we both need dates to the Holbrook wedding, I'll let you fix me up, if you'll let me fix you up."

The daughter of Celebration Memorial Hospital's chief executive officer Stanley Holbrook was getting married in mid-July. Jake had his eye on a promotion and attending his boss's daughter's wedding was one of the best ways to prove to the man he was the guy for the job. Since Holbrook was a conservative family man, Anna's offer to fix him up with a woman of substance wasn't a bad idea.

She was looking at him funny.

"Deal?" he said.

She opened her mouth, but then clamped it shut before saying anything. Instead, she shook her head. "No. Just...*no*."

"Come on, Anna, fair is fair. I know Hal hurt you, but you're too young to put yourself on a shelf. You want to get married again. You want to have kids. There are good guys out there, and I think I know one or two who would be worthy of you."

She stopped chopping. "Worthy of me?" Her expression softened. "That's the sweetest thing anyone has said to me in a very long time."

"Case in point of why you need to get out more, my dear. Men should be saying many *nice* things to you."

She made short order of chopping the peppers, scraping the tiny pieces into a bowl and then drying her hands.

"Okay, I'll make a deal with you," she said. "We'll do this until Stan Holbrook's daughter's wedding. Between now and then, I'll bet I can match you with your soul mate and cure you of your serial monogamy issues."

He winced. "What? As in something permanent?"

She shrugged. "Just give me a chance."

"Only if you'll let me do the same for you. Do we have a deal?"

She nodded.

"So what are we betting?"

She shrugged. "I didn't really mean it as a serious bet."

"I think making a bet will make this more interesting. We don't have to decide the prize right away. Let's just agree that the first one who succeeds in making a match for the other wins."

Anna wrinkled her nose. "Knowing you, you'll let a good woman go just to win the challenge. You're so competitive."

"But if you think about it," he said, "who will be the real winner? One will win the bet, but the other will win love."

"That's extremely profound for a man who has such bad taste in women." She gave him that smile that always made him feel as if he'd come home. He paused to just take it in for a moment.

Then Jake shook her smooth, warm hand, and said, "Here's to soul mates."

Chapter Two

Soul mates.

Why did hearing Jake say that word make her stomach flip? Especially since she wasn't even sure if she believed in such a thing as *soul mates*. After all she'd been through with Hal, she still believed in love and marriage enough to try again…someday. But *soul mates*? That was an entirely different subject. The sparkle had dulled from that notion when her marriage died.

"I'm done chopping." Anna set the bowl on the granite counter next to the stove where Jake was melting butter in a frying pan. Then she deposited their empty beer bottles into the recycle bin in the garage.

"Now what can I do?" she said when she got back into the kitchen.

"Just have a seat over there." With his elbow, he gestured toward the small kitchen table cluttered with mail and books. "Stay out of my way. Omelet-flipping is serious business. I am a trained professional. So don't try this at home."

"I wouldn't dream of it," she said, eyeing the mess on the table's surface. "That's why I have you. So you can fix me omelets. Apparently, I will repay you by setting the table for us to eat. And after I've excavated a space to put the plates and silverware, then I might clean the rest of your house, too. I thought you had a housekeeper. Where has she been?"

"Her name's Angie and she's been down with the flu. Hasn't been available to come in for two weeks."

Anna glanced around the room at the newspapers littering the large, plush sectional sofa in the open-plan living room. There were mugs and stacks of magazines and opened mail on the masculine, wooden coffee and end tables. Several socks and running shoes littered the dark-stained, hardwood living room floor.

"Wow. Well…" In fact, it looked as if Jake had dropped everything right where he'd stood. "God, Jake, I didn't realize you were such a slob."

Jake followed her gaze. "I'm not a slob," he said. "I'm just busy. And I wasn't expecting company."

Obviously.

Anna thought about asking why he didn't simply walk a few more steps into the bathroom where he could deposit his socks into the dirty clothes hamper rather than leaving them strewn all over the floor. Instead, she focused on being part of the solution rather than nagging him and adding to the problem. She quickly organized the table clutter into neat piles, revealing two placemats underneath, and set out the silverware she'd just washed and dried.

"Where are your napkins?" she asked.

He handed her a roll of paper towels.

This was the first time in the month that she'd been home that they'd cooked at his place. Really, it was just an impromptu meal, but it was just dawning on her how little she'd been over at his place since she'd been back. That was thanks in large part to Jake's girlfriend. She wondered if Dorenda had seen the mess—or had helped create it—but before she could ask, she realized she really didn't want to know.

"It must be a pretty serious case of the flu if Angie has been down for *two* weeks. Has she been to the doctor?"

Jake gave a one-shoulder shrug. "She's fine. I ran into her at the coffee shop in downtown the other day. She looked okay to me. She'll probably be back next week."

Anna balked. "Why do you keep her?"

She crossed the room to straighten the newspapers and corral the socks. She couldn't just stand there while Jake was cooking and the papers were cluttering up the place and in the back of her mind she could hear him toasting soul mates.

Even that small act of picking up would help work off some of her nervous energy.

"I don't have time to find someone else," he said. "Besides, it's not that bad around here."

She did a double take, looking back at him to see if he was kidding.

Apparently not.

But even if it looked as if Jake had simply dropped things and left them where they fell, the house wasn't dirty. It didn't smell bad. In fact, it smelled like *him*—like coffee and leather and something else that bridged the years and swept her back to a simpler time before she'd married the wrong man and Jake had become a serial monogamist. She breathed in deeper, wondering if they were still the same people or if the years and circumstances had changed them too much.

She bent to pick up a dog-eared issue of *Sports Illustrated* that was sprawled on the floor facedown. As she prepared to close it back to its regular shape, she nearly dropped it again when she spied the tiny, silky purple thong hidden underneath. Like a lavender spider. Only it didn't get up and crawl away.

"Eww." Anna grimaced. "I think Miss Texas forgot something."

Jake gave a start as his gaze fell to where Anna pointed.

She reached over and grabbed the poker from the fireplace tool set on the hearth and used it to lift the thong off the ground.

"This is classy. How does a woman forget her underwear?"

He smiled that adorable lopsided smile that always suggested something a little bit naughty. There was no doubt why women fell for him. Heck, she'd fall for him if he weren't her best friend.

"She carried a big purse," Jake said. "It was like a

portable closet. She probably didn't leave here commando." His gaze strayed back to the panties. "Then again, maybe she did."

Anna raised the poker. The thong resembled a scanty purple flag, which she swiftly disposed of in the trash can.

"She might want that back," Jake protested.

"Really? You think she's going to call and ask if you found her underwear?"

They locked gazes.

"If she does—" Anna scowled at him and pointed to the garbage "—it's right here."

He was quiet as he pulled out the toaster and put in two slices of whole wheat bread.

Anna returned the poker to its stand.

"Jake, this is why we need to have a heart-to-heart talk about what you want in a woman. It's no wonder you can't seriously consider spending the rest of your life with a woman who leaves her panties on your living room floor. Even if she lived here, *leaving* her panties lying around in the living room wouldn't be a good sign."

"I leave my socks on the floor," he said as he transferred the omelet from the frying pan onto the two plates Anna had set out.

"Yeah, and it wouldn't take that much more effort to put them in the laundry hamper," she said. "Do you want orange juice? I need orange juice with my eggs."

"Sorry, I'm out. I have coffee and there's more beer. I need to go to the grocery store. I really should go tonight because I'm not going to have time to go later with everything going on this weekend."

She passed on the beer. Not her favorite thing to drink with eggs. Even if it was dinner. It was one of those combos that just didn't sound appetizing. She opted for making herself a quick cup of coffee in his single-serving coffee brewer. As she pushed the button selecting the serving size, it dawned on her that even if they had been apart for a long time, she still felt at home with Jake. She could raid his K-Cups and brew herself a cup without asking. Even in the short amount of time that she'd spent here, she knew which cabinet contained the coffee, and that he stored his dinner plates in the lower cabinet to the right of the sink because they stacked better there.

"I need some groceries, too," she said. "How about if we shop together after we do the dishes? We can talk as we shop and figure out where the happy medium is between the nice women you *should* be dating and the ones who leave their underwear all over town."

Jake's brows knit together as he set the dinner plates on the table.

"Don't look at me like that," Anna said as she slid into her seat at the table. "You know I'm right. If you keep doing what you're doing, you'll keep getting what you're getting and you'll keep repeating the same pattern. You need to look a little deeper than a pretty face."

He sat down, speared some of the omelet and took a bite, watching her as he chewed. She wished he'd say something. Not with food in his mouth, of course. But that was the thing about Jake—he may be a manly guy's guy who didn't know how to pick up after himself, but he still had manners. He didn't talk with his mouth full, he said please and thank-you; Jake Lennox was a gentleman.

He knew how to treat a lady. He just didn't know how to choose the right lady.

"So what are the deal breakers, Jake?"

"Deal breakers?"

"You know, the qualities in a woman that you can't live with."

"Why don't we focus on the good? The attributes that I'm attracted to?"

"Because attraction is what gets you in trouble. Attraction is what caused Miss Texas to leave her thong on your living room floor."

Ugh. She sounded like such a harpy. She knew that even before she saw the look on his face and consciously softened her tone.

"I don't mean to be a nag. Really, I don't. It's just that sometimes it helps if you work backward."

She wasn't going to pressure him. That was the fastest way to suck all the fun out of the bet. This was supposed to be *fun*, not an exercise in browbeating.

She was prepared to change the subject when he said, "Anyone I date has to be comfortable with the fact that I don't want to get married and I don't want kids. I don't want anyone who thinks they can change my mind. That's a deal breaker. It's what started things going south with Dorenda. She was Miss Independent for the first couple of months. Then she started in with the *five-year plan*, which eventually turned into an ultimatum."

Anna realized it was the first time she'd ever been on Dorenda's side. Who could blame her for wanting more? Especially when it involved more Jake. But she wasn't going to argue with him. This anti-marriage/anti-family stance was new. Or at least something that had developed during the time that they were apart. Probably the reason he'd been involved in his string of relationships. Jake had grown up in a single-parent household. His mom had left the family when Jake was in first grade.

One night before they left for college, when she and Jake were having one of their famous heart-to-hearts, he'd opened up about how hard it had been on him and his brothers when their mom left the family.

Yet he'd never mentioned that he didn't want to get married.

Actually, though, when she thought about it, it was a good thing he was being so up front about everything. That's just how Jake was. He knew himself, and he was true to himself. Maybe if Hal had been more honest with both of them, they might have avoided a world of hurt.

So yeah, considering *that*, Jake's candid admission was a good thing.

Now, her mind and its deductive reasoning just had to convince her heart that was true, because she hated the thought of Jake ending up alone years down the road.

"So you want someone who is family-oriented, funny, kind, honest and smart," Jake recapped as he pushed the shopping cart down the canned goods aisle in the grocery store. "You don't want to date a doctor, because of Hal. So what about looks? What's your type?"

Anna stopped to survey a row of black beans lined up like soldiers on a shelf.

"I thought we agreed that we weren't going to concentrate on the physical. That's where we get into trouble. We need to get past that."

"What? Should I disqualify a guy if he is good-looking?"

She quirked a brow at him as she set two cans in the otherwise empty cart. "I'd love to hear your idea of a good-looking guy."

He scowled back at her. "I don't know. Beauty is in the eye of the beholder, as they say. I have no idea what makes a guy attractive to a woman."

"I was just teasing, Jake. You know you're my ideal. If I can't have you, then…"

She made a *tsk*ing sound and squeezed his arm as she walked farther down the aisle to get something else on her list.

If he didn't know her so well, he might've thought her harmless flirtation had started a ripple of *something* inside him. But that was utterly ridiculous. This was *Anna*, and that's why he couldn't put his finger on the *something* she'd stirred. Maybe it was pride, or actually, more like gratitude that pulled at him. He looked at her in her scrubs that were a little too big for her slight frame. Her purse, which she'd slung across her body, proved that there were curves hidden away under all that pink fabric.

He averted his gaze, because *this was Anna*. Dammit, he shouldn't be looking at her as if she was something he'd ask the butcher to put on a foam tray and wrap up in cellophane. As the thought occurred to him, he realized his gaze had meandered back to where it had no business straying.

He turned his body away from her and toward the shelf of black beans Anna had just pored over. He didn't know what the hell to do with canned black beans, but he took a couple of cans and added them to the cart as he warred with the very real realization that he didn't want to fix her up with just anyone. Certainly not most of his buddies, who if they talked about Anna the way they talked about other women he'd have no choice but to deck.

"Excuse me." Jake looked over to see a small, silver-haired woman holding out a piece of paper. "Your wife dropped this list." The woman hooked her thumb in Anna's direction at the other end of the aisle. "I'd go give it to her myself, but I'm going this way."

My wife?

Jake smiled at the woman and started to correct her, to explain that he and Anna weren't married, but the words seemed to stick in his throat. He found himself reaching out and accepting the paper—a grocery list—and saying, "Thanks, I'll give it to her."

She nodded and was on her way before Jake could say anything else.

Hmm. My wife.

He tried to see what the woman saw—Anna and him together…as a couple. But in similar fashion to not being able to look at her curves in good conscience, he couldn't fully let his mind go there.

It wasn't that the thought disgusted him—or anything negative like that. On the contrary. And that brought a whole host of other weirdness with it. The only way around it was to laugh it off.

"You dropped your list," he said as he stopped the cart next to her. "The nice lady who found it thought you were my wife."

Anna shot him a dubious look. "Oh, yeah? Did you set her straight?"

She deposited more canned goods into the basket and then took the list from his hand.

"No. I didn't. I need bread. Which aisle is the bread in?"

She let the issue drop. He almost wished she would've said something snide like, *That's awkward.* Or, *Me? Married to you? Never in a million years.* Instead, she changed the subject. "Do you want bakery bread or prepackaged? And why don't you know where the bread is?"

He certainly didn't dwell on it.

"I don't know. I guess I don't retain that kind of information. Grocery shopping isn't my favorite sport."

"I can tell," she said. "And if you don't pick up the pace, you're going to get a penalty for delay of game. I'm almost finished. Where's your list? Let me see if I can help move this along."

"I don't have a list," he said. He knew he should make an off-the-cuff comment about her, his pretend wife, being the keeper of the list for both of them, but it didn't feel right.

Since when had anything ever not felt right with Anna?

"I keep the list in my head," he added.

"And of course, you're out of everything. Here, I can help. We'll just grab things for you as we go by them."

She pulled the shopping cart from the front end and turned the corner into the next aisle.

"Do you want cereal?" she asked.

Before he could answer, a couple a few feet away from them broke out into an argument that silenced both Anna and him.

"Look, I'm an adult," said the guy. "If I want to eat sugary cereal for breakfast, I will. In fact, if I want to eat a bowl of pure sugar, I will. You get what you like and I'll get what I want."

"Breakfast is the most important meal of the day, honey." The woman took a cereal box—the bright yellow kind with fake berries—out of the shopping cart and put it back on the shelf. "This won't hold you. You need something with fiber and protein. If you eat this, you'll be raiding the vending machine by ten o'clock."

The guy took the cereal box off the shelf and put it back in the cart. "I grew up eating this stuff. You're my wife, not the food police. So hop off."

Anna and Jake quickened their pace as they passed the couple. They exchanged a look, which the couple obviously didn't notice because now insults were inching their way into the exchange and tones were getting heated.

"We'll come back for cereal," Anna said.

Jake nodded. "When we do, are you going to mock my cereal choice?"

"Why would I do that? I'm not your wife."

There. Good. She said it. The dreaded w word.

"Are you saying it's a wife's role to mock her husband's cereal choice?"

"Of course not. I never told Hal what he could and couldn't eat. Then again, since I was the one who cooked in that relationship, he didn't have much say. But he was completely on his own for breakfast and lunch, free to make his own choices. And you see where that got me. Do you think we would've lasted if I had been more concerned?"

"No. Hal was an ass. He didn't deserve your picking out healthy cereal for him."

"So you're saying the woman picking out the cereal rather than leaving him to his own devices was a good thing?"

"Well, yeah. For the record, in the couple we saw back there, the wife was right. He may have wanted that crap, but he didn't need it. So I'll side with her. Do you want me to go back over there and tell her I'm on her side?"

"Better not. Not if you want to keep all your teeth."

Jake laughed but it sounded bitter—even to his own ears. "Why does that have to happen in relationships? People get married and end up hating each other over the most ridiculous things. They fight and tear each other apart and someone leaves. That marriage is in trouble over Much-n-Crunch and its artificially flavored berries. That's exactly why I don't want marriage."

"So you're saying that the guy should've gotten the cereal he wanted?"

"No. I already said I thought the wife was right. Junk like that *will* kill you. I agree with her. Healthy eating habits are good."

As they strolled past the dairy section, Anna studied him for a minute. "I've just figured out who I'm fixing you up with on your first date. She's a nutritionist. I think the two of you will have a lot in common. I can't believe I didn't think of her until now."

Her response caught him off guard.

"What is she like?" he asked.

Anna raised her brows. "You'll just have to wait and see."

"Okay. Two can play that game," he said. "You'll have to be surprised on your first date, too."

She grimaced. "Go easy on me, Jake. I'm so out of practice. You know how I am. I'm casual. I haven't been out there in so long."

"That's why you need me to fix you up."

He had no idea who he was going to pick for her first date. Who would be worthy of her? Maybe the best place for him to start would be to rule out anyone who was remotely similar to himself. Because Anna deserved so much better.

Chapter Three

"Try this one." Anna's sister, Emily, shoved a royal blue sundress with a white Indian motif on the front through the opening in the fitting room curtain in the Three Sisters dress shop in downtown Celebration. "It looks like the basis of a good first-date outfit."

Anna still wasn't sure who her date was or where they were going, but one thing she did know was they were getting together on Wednesday and she had nothing to wear. It had been so long since she'd worn anything but jeans or hospital scrubs, she didn't have a stitch appropriate for a...date. Plus, she had a busy week ahead and this was Emily's night off. So Anna figured she might as well seize the moment and bring her sister along to help her pick out something nice. If she felt good with what she was wearing, she might feel less nervous on the date, thereby eliminating one potential avenue of stress…or disaster.

She held up the dress her sister had chosen and looked at herself in the mirror. The white pattern running up the front of the dress had a design that might've made a nice henna tattoo. It was a little wild for her taste.

"I don't know, Em, this one looks a little low cut."

"Try it on. You never can tell when it's on the hanger."

Wasn't that the truth? The same rule could apply to men, too. You had to try them on—well, not literally, of course. She couldn't fathom getting intimate with a man. Even if it was a man Jake had picked out for her. Not that she was contemplating life as a born-again virgin. It was just too much to contemplate right now. First, she'd meet the guy or guys—Jake did have until the wedding—and see how she got along with him or them. Then she'd think about…more.

The thought made her shudder a little.

She slipped out of the dress she'd just tried on and hung it up—it was a prim flowery number in primary colors. It was too dowdy—too matronly—too…*something*. Anna couldn't put her finger on it. Whatever it was, it just didn't feel right.

"Who did you fix Jake up with?" Emily asked from the other side of the fitting room curtain.

"Her name is Cheryl Woodly. She's a freelance nutritionist who works with new mothers. I met her at the hospital."

"Oh, yeah? What's she like?"

Anna slipped the dress over her head.

"Nice. Smart. Pretty."

"How is she different from Jake's past girlfriends?"

"Did you not hear me say she's *nice* and *smart*? Miss Texas possessed neither of those qualities."

"Me-ow," said Emily.

"I'm only speaking the truth."

"When are they going out?"

"Friday."

Anna stared at herself in the mirror, tugged up on the plunging halter neckline, trying to give *the girls* a little more coverage. She wasn't so sure she wanted to put everything on display on a first date. The dress was great, but it was decidedly not *her*.

"Anna? Did you try on the one I just gave you?"

"Yeah, but—I don't know."

"Come out. Let's see it."

"Nah. Too much cleavage. Too little dress."

Anna hesitated, turning around to check out the back view. She had to admit it was a snappy little number and it looked great from behind. But the front drew way too much focus to the cleavage and that made her squirm.

"Let me see." Before Anna could protest, Emily's face poked through the split in the curtain.

Anna's had flew up to her chest.

"It looks great," Emily said. "The color is out of this world on you. It brings out your eyes. And move your hand."

Emily swatted away her sister's hand from its protective station.

"I don't know what you're afraid of. It accentuates your tiny waist and you're barely showing any cleavage at all. It's just-right sexy. A far cry from those scrubs you hide in every day."

"My scrubs are for work. They're my uniform." Anna turned back to the mirror and put her hands on her hips. She turned to left and then to the right. "You're just jealous that you don't ever get to dress so comfortably at work."

By day, Emily worked in a bank in Dallas and wore suits to work. Because she was saving for a house, two or three times a week she worked as a hostess at Bistro St. Germaine, where she had to dress in sleek, sophisticated black to fit in with the timeless elegance of the downtown Celebration restaurant. Emily had great taste in clothes. Anna would've asked if she could borrow something from her younger sister—and Emily would've graciously dressed her—but it was time for Anna to add a couple of new pieces to her own wardrobe.

"Scrubs are like wearing jammies to work every day," Emily said.

"You know you would if you could," Anna said.

Emily rolled her eyes. "I think you should buy that dress. If not for a date, for you."

"I'll think about it. Now let me change."

Emily stepped back and let Anna close the curtain. Before Anna took off the dress, she did one last three-sixty. It really was cute, in a boho-sexy sort of way.

"Do you really think Jake has some good prospects in mind for you?"

"Who knows? We just talked about this a couple of days ago."

She slipped off the dress and put it with a cute red dress with a bow that tied in front. As she pulled on her jeans and plain white T-shirt, Emily said, "You don't sound very enthusiastic. Are you sure you want to do this?"

"The ball is already rolling. It's just until the wedding. I'll be surprised if it's even five dates. We'll see what happens."

When Anna opened the curtain, she noticed a certain look on her sister's face.

"What?" Anna asked and gathered the clothes, keeping the red and blue dresses separate from the things she didn't want.

"I have to be honest," Emily said. "I always thought you and Jake would end up together."

Her stomach clenched in a way that bothered her more than her sister's words.

"Emily, why would you say that? Jake and I are friends. Good friends. Nothing more."

"Because for better or worse, you two have always stuck together. I mean, I grew up with him, too, but you don't see him hanging out with me. The two of you have always had a really strong bond. Think about it. You and Jake outlasted your marriage. Why the heck are you fixing him up with someone else?"

"Emily, don't. That's not fair."

Anna walked away from her sister.

"Yes, it is. Why is it not fair?"

Anna set the two dresses she wanted to buy on the counter and handed the hanging clothing she didn't want to the sales clerk. After she paid for her purchases and they were outside the Three Sisters shop, Emily resumed the conversation.

"What's not fair about it?"

"You know I can't date Jake. He's my *friend*. He's always been my friend and that's all we will ever be."

Anna felt heat begin to rise up her neck and bloom on her cheeks.

"Then why are you blushing?" Emily asked.

Anna turned and walked to the next storefront, the hardware store, and studied the display as if she'd find the perfect pair of sandals to go with her first-date dress hidden somewhere among the tool kits, ladders and leaf blowers showcased in the window.

Of course, Emily was right behind her. Anna could see her sister's reflection in the glass. She couldn't look at her own as she tried to figure out exactly what was making her so emotional. It wasn't the fact that she was fixing Jake up with someone who could potentially change his mind about marriage being the equivalent of emotional Siberia. Good grief, she was the one who came up with a plan in the first place.

Now Emily's arm was on Anna's shoulder.

"Hey, I'm sorry. I didn't mean to upset you. I'm just a little puzzled by your reaction. I was half teasing, but you're upset. You want to talk about it?"

Anna ran her hand through her hair, feeling a bit perplexed herself.

"I guess it's just the thought of the dating again. You know, starting over. I'm thirty-three years old. This is not where I thought I would be at this age. Em, I want a family. I want a husband who loves me and kids. I never thought I'd be one of those women who felt her biological clock ticking, but mine feels like a time bomb waiting to explode."

The two sisters stood shoulder to shoulder, staring into the hardware store window.

"Well, I guess that eliminates Jake, since we know his thoughts on marriage. Even if he is the hottest guy in town, you don't need to waste your time there."

Anna drew in a deep breath, hoping it would be the antidote to the prickles of irritation that were beginning to feel as if they would turn into full-blown hives.

"Even if he was the marrying kind, he's my best friend, Emily. There are some things you just don't mess with and that's one of them. Hal used to go on and on about how Jake and I secretly wanted each other. Once he even swore there was something going on between Jake and me. But Hal was my husband. I loved him. I loved our marriage and I never cheated. He couldn't get it through his head that a man and a woman could be friends—that there was nothing sexual about it."

"That's probably because in his eyes he couldn't look at a woman without thinking about sex," Emily said. "You know what they say, people usually yell the loudest about the things they're guilty of themselves."

"So, could you just help me out please and not talk about Jake and me in those terms? He's my friend. End of story. Okay?"

Jake had heard a lot of excuses for getting out of a date, and tonight's ranked up there with the best. Cheryl Woodly had called him thirty minutes before he was supposed to pick her up at her place in Dallas for dinner. Her reason for begging off? Her cat, Foxy, had undergone emergency surgery that day and she wasn't comfortable leaving it alone.

He could understand that. He knew people were as crazy about their animals as they were about their children. In some cases, people's animals were their children.

As he turned his 1969 Mustang GTO around and headed back toward Celebration, he realized he wasn't a bit disappointed that Cheryl Woodly had canceled. In fact, from this vantage point, getting out of the blind date seemed like a blessing in disguise. Cheryl had halfheartedly mentioned that maybe they could have a rain check, and he'd made all the right noises and said he'd call her next week to see if they could get something on the books. He wasn't sure if she was preoccupied with her animal or if she was only being polite in suggesting they reschedule. Either way, she didn't seem very enthusiastic. So he wished Foxy the cat well and breathed a sigh of relief.

Still, there was the matter of what to do with the two tickets he'd bought to the Celebration Summer Jazz Festival. He didn't want them to go to waste. Five minutes later, he found himself parking his car in the street in front of Anna's house.

She lived in a Key West–style bungalow two blocks away from downtown Celebration's Main Street. Jake had helped Anna pick out the house after she'd moved to Celebration and her divorce was final.

The place had been a fixer-upper in need of some TLC. Anna had said it was exactly what she wanted—

a project to sink her heart and soul into while she was getting used to her new life. She'd done a great job. Now the house was neat and a little quirky with its fresh island-blue and sea-green paint job. Its style reflected Anna's unique cheerful personality and it always made Jake smile. The lawn was neatly manicured. She must've recently planted some impatiens in the terracotta pots that flanked the porch steps. The flowers' vibrant pinks, fuchsias and reds added another well-planned accent to the already colorful house.

That was the thing about Anna; she put her heart and soul into her home and the place radiated the care she'd invested.

Her Beetle was in the driveway. He could see the inviting faint glow of a light through the living room window.

Good. She was home.

He was going to razz her about her matchmaking skills being a little rusty, since the first date she'd arranged had essentially stood him up. Technically, Cheryl hadn't left him hanging. But Jake was realizing he could get some mileage out of the canceled date and he intended to use it as leverage to get Anna to go to the jazz festival with him tonight.

He'd have a lot more fun with her anyway.

Jake let himself out of the car and walked up the brick path that led to Anna's house. He rapped on the door. *Knock, knock-knock, knock, knock*, their traditional signal that announced they were about to let themselves inside. Really, the knock was just a formality, to keep the other from being surprised. In case she was having sex in the kitchen or something.

Actually, he hadn't been concerned about walking in on Anna having sex because she'd been living like a nun since her divorce. And funny, now that he thought about it, Anna never seemed to come around as much when he was in a relationship.

Hmm. He'd never realized it until right now.

He tried the handle and her door was unlocked. So he let himself in the side door.

"Hey, Anna? It's me."

He heard a muffled exclamation from the other side of the living room. Then Anna stuck her head out of the bedroom door.

"Jake? What are you doing here? Why aren't you out with Cheryl?"

She was hugging the doorjamb and clutching something to her chest as if she were hiding. It looked like she was wearing a dress.

When was the last time he'd seen Anna in a dress?

"She stood me up. What are you all dressed up for? Don't tell me you have a date."

Anna straightened, moving away from the doorjamb, cocking her head to the side.

"She stood you up? Are you kidding me?"

Whoa. She was definitely wearing a dress and she looked *nice*. He'd never realized she had so much going under those scrubs...so much going on *upstairs*. How had he never noticed that before?

The fact made him a little hot and bothered.

He had to force his gaze to stay on her face. Or on her bare feet. Her toenails were painted a sexy shade of metallic blue that matched the dress. Her legs—how had he never noticed her legs before? They were long and lean and tan and looked pretty damn good coming out of the other end of that skirt, which might've been just a hair short...for Anna.

Damn. She sure did look good. No. She looked *hot*.

If she looked like that, why did she cover herself up?

Because this was *Anna*.

He cleared his throat. "Well, she didn't technically stand me up. She called me when I was on my way to get her to say her cat had surgery today and she didn't feel right about leaving it alone."

Anna put her hands on her hips and grimaced. The movement accentuated the low neckline of her dress and the way her full breasts contrasted with her tiny waist that blossomed into hips... Jake forced himself to look away.

"So you didn't shave before you went out? Are you trying to look cool or are you just too lazy?" she asked.

"What?" He rubbed his hand over the stubble on his jaw. "I'm trying to look cool. The ladies like a little five-o'clock shadow."

She quirked a brow and smiled. "Okay, I'll give you that one. It does look pretty...hot."

Something flared inside of him.

"Well, I mean it would be hot if it wasn't *you*."

"What do you mean *if it wasn't me*?"

She shot him a mischievous smile that warmed up her whole face.

"You're messing with me, aren't you?" he said.

"Yeah. I am. It's fun. Oh, I forgot to tell you that Cheryl is a major animal lover. I'm not surprised she wanted to stay home with the cat, but it would've been nice if she could have given you a little more notice."

"Ya think? Where are you going, dressed like that?"

Anna blushed and crossed her arms in front of her, suddenly seeming self-conscious again. It was one of the things he found most endearing about her.

"I'm not going anywhere. I bought some new clothes and I was trying them on so I could figure out what I wanted to wear on my date with Joseph. He texted me today and asked what I was doing next Wednesday. So I figured I needed to decide what I was going to wear. What do you think of this dress? I wasn't so sure, but Emily talked me into getting it."

She put her hands back on her hips and struck a pose. The tags were dangling under her arm and he had an urge to suggest she take it back and exchange it for something a little more modest. Something that didn't make her look like such a knockout.

"It's, uhh… It looks great."

Maybe a little too great for a first date with a guy like Joseph Gardner. He and Joe had been roommates in college while Jake was doing his undergraduate work. Joe lived in Dallas now. He was a friend, a good guy, really. That's why he'd decided to fix him up with Anna.

And that was why his own attitude about the dress confused him.

"In fact, since you're dressed, why don't you give it a test run and wear it to the jazz festival with me tonight?"

Anna groaned and shook her head. "No, Jake, I really wasn't up for doing anything tonight—"

"God, you're so boring." He smiled to let her know

he was just kidding. "Besides, since you fixed me up with a dud, don't you think you owe it to me to not let this extra ticket go to waste?"

She sighed and cocked her head to the side. She smiled at him. He could see her coming around.

"In fact, if we leave now, we will have just enough time to grab something to eat and get over to the pavilion for the first act."

She shook her head. "Jake, I took my makeup off when I got home from work. Can you give me a couple of minutes to fix myself up?"

She looked so good he hadn't even realized she didn't have any makeup on. Her skin was clear and her cheeks and lips looked naturally rosy. Standing there with her auburn hair hanging in loose waves around her shoulders... And with just the right amount of cleavage showing, he couldn't imagine that she could make herself any more beautiful.

Something intense flared inside him. It made him flinch. His instinct was to mentally shake it off. When that didn't work he decided to ignore it, pushing it back into the recesses of his brain where he kept all unwelcome thoughts and memories and other distractions that might trip him up or cause him to feel things that were unpleasant.

It was mind over matter.

Right now, what mattered was him getting his head on straight so that they could get to dinner and the jazz festival.

"You look fine," he said. "Besides, it's just me."

"Yeah, you and the hundreds of other people that will be at the jazz festival. You don't want them looking at you and wondering, Who's that homely woman with Jake Lennox?"

Homely? How could she see herself that way? It didn't make sense.

"Darlin', you are a lot of things, but homely isn't one of them."

She rolled her eyes at him. "Okay. Okay. You don't have to lay it on so thick. Let me get my sandals and we can go."

When she turned around to walk back into the bedroom, his eyes dropped to her backside which swayed gently beneath the fabric of her dress.

What was wrong with him?

Nothing.

Just because Anna was his friend and it had never really registered in his brain that she was an attractive woman, didn't mean she wasn't or that he couldn't appreciate her...from afar.

From very far away. If he knew what was good for him.

But why now?

Why, in the wake of this bet, did it feel as if he was seeing her for the very first time?

Chapter Four

One of the things Anna loved most about Jake was his ability to surprise her. Like tonight, for example. When she'd gotten home from work, she thought she would try on her new dresses, figure out which one she wanted to wear on her date with Joseph, then put on her sweats, make a light dinner and settle in with a good book and a cup of tea.

The last thing she thought she'd be doing was sitting on a red plaid blanket in the middle of downtown Celebration at a jazz festival waving at people she knew, talking to others who stopped by.

But here she was.

And she was enjoying herself.

Who knew?

It was a nice night to be outside. As evening settled

over the town, a nice breeze mellowed the heat of the late June day, leaving the air a luxuriously perfect temperature.

Leave it to Jake to completely turn her plans upside down—and she meant that in the best possible way. He was her constant and her variable. He was her rock and the one who challenged her to leap off the high dive when she didn't even want to leave her house. Like with these dates they were fixing each other up on. The prospect of spending the evening with blind dates felt like a huge leap into the unknown. Without the assurance of a safety net. Yet somehow she knew Jake wouldn't steer her wrong.

She trusted him implicitly.

That's probably why spending the evening with him and his five-o'clock shadow at an event like this—which could actually be quite romantic with the right guy—seemed more appealing than being here with...another guy.

They'd staked out a great place on the lawn in downtown Celebration's Central Park—close enough to the gazebo that they could see the members of the various bands that would be performing tonight, but not so close that they wouldn't be able to talk. Jake had purchased tickets for the VIP area that allowed for the best viewing of the concerts. Leave it to him to do it first-class.

The area was packed with people of all ages: couples, families, groups of friends. All around them, people were talking and laughing and enjoying picnic suppers. There was a happy buzz in the air that was contagious. Suddenly, Anna knew she didn't want to be anywhere else tonight except right here in the middle of this crowd, holding down the fort while Jake went to get them a bottle of wine and their own picnic supper from Celebrations Inc. Catering Company, which had set up a tent at the back of the park.

She'd almost forgotten what it was like to feel like part of a community. Living in San Antonio with Hal had been completely different. Houston was a thriving metropolis; Hal had been kind of a stick-in-the-mud, actually. Picnics and jazz festivals weren't his gig. He was more the type to enjoy eighteen rounds on the golf course, dinner at the club with his stuffy doctor friends and their wives. If the men weren't playing golf, they were talking about it or some scholarly study they'd read about in a medical journal. Anna had tried to join in their conversation once when they were discussing risk factors for major obstetric hemorrhage—after all, she was an OB nurse—but they'd acted as if she'd wanted to discuss the merits of Lucky Charms with and without marshmallows.

Later, Hal had been furious with her. He'd claimed she had embarrassed him and asked her to just do her part and entertain the wives. Never mind that she had zero in common with any of them. She worked, they lunched. She didn't know the difference between Gucci and The Gap—and frankly, she didn't care. Still, she was forced to sit there and listen to them prattle on about who had offended whom on the country-club tennis team and who was the outcast this week because she was sleeping with someone else's husband.

Of course, Anna made the appropriate noises in all

the right places. She'd become an expert at smiling and nodding and sleeping with her eyes open as the women went on and on and on about utter nonsense. Funny thing was, it didn't seem to matter that she had nothing to contribute. They were so busy talking and not listening—too busy formulating what they were going to say next while trying to get a foot in on the conversation—that it didn't even matter that Anna sat there in silence.

Until the last dinner. Anna had sensed the shift in the air even before they sat down to order. The women were unusually interested in *her*. Their eyes glinted as they asked her about her job, the hours she worked. Did she ever work weekends? Nights? How long had she and Hal been married now? How on earth did they make their two-career marriage work?

It reminded her of those days back in elementary school when one kid was chosen to be the student of the week and all the bits and pieces of their lives were put on display for all to see. Of course, the elementary school spotlight was kinder and gentler. The interest was sincere, even if the others really didn't have a burning desire to know.

This sudden interest in her personal life was downright creepy. And she'd left the club that night with the unshakable feeling that something was up. Something was different. They knew something, and like a pride of lionesses, they were going to play with their prey—get maximum enjoyment from the game before the kill.

On the way home Anna had tried to talk to Hal about it, but as usual he wasn't interested.

Exactly one week to the day later—after the niggling feeling that something was *different* grew into a gut-wrenching knowledge that something was very wrong, something that everyone but her seemed to know about—she'd checked Hal's email and everything was spelled out right there. Sexy messages from his office manager. Plans for hookups and out-of-town getaways. The jackass had been so smug in his cozy little affair that he'd left it all right there for her. All she had to do to learn what was really going on was type in his email password, which was the month, day and year of their wedding anniversary.

And Hal had had the nerve to accuse her of being more than just friends—or wanting to be more than just friends—with Jake.

Anna's gaze automatically picked out Jake in the midst of the crowd. As he walked toward her carrying a large white bag in one hand and a bottle of wine in the other, she shoved aside the bad memories of Hal, refusing to let him ruin this night.

She watched Jake as he approached. He was such a good-looking man—tall and broad-shouldered, with dark hair that contrasted with blue-blue eyes. But what mattered even more was that he was a good man, an honest man. He might be a serial monogamist, but he broke up with a woman before he began something with someone else. That was more than she could say for her ex-husband.

It hit her that she was luckier than any of Jake's past girlfriends. They had a connection that went deeper than most lovers. As far as she was concerned, she would do whatever it took to keep their relationship constant.

"They had this incredible-looking bow-tie pasta with rosemary chicken, mushrooms and asparagus," Jake said as he lowered himself onto the blanket. "I got an order of that and they had another type with a red sauce. I picked up a couple of salads and some flatbread. And they had tiramisu. So save room for dessert. Unless you don't want yours. I'll eat it."

"I'll bite your arm if you try to take my dessert."

He held up his hands. "Never let it be said that I came between you and your tiramisu."

"You're a smart man."

Yes, he was.

She took the feast out of the bag and set the containers out on the blanket as Jake opened the red wine and poured it into two plastic cups. He handed one to Anna and raised his, touching the rim to hers.

"Thanks for being such a good sport and coming out here with me tonight," he said. "I would've hated for the tickets to go to waste. Cheryl doesn't know what she's missing."

"Poor Cheryl," Anna said. "No, actually, not poor Cheryl. I understand that she needed to take care of her cat. I wish she could've given you a little more notice."

"No problem," said Jake as he began dishing up pasta on two plates. "I'll probably have a better time with you anyway."

"Are you going to give her another chance?"

Jake gave a noncommittal shoulder roll. "We talked about it, but she didn't sound very eager. If I didn't know better I'd think she changed her mind about the date altogether. But hey, that's fine."

Anna tasted a bite of the bow-tie pasta. It was delicious. She hadn't realized how hungry she was until now, and she had to force herself to chew her food slowly to keep from eating too fast. As she chased down the bite with a swallow of wine, she noticed a couple of women who were sitting in lawn chairs a few feet away from them blatantly looking at Jake and talking to each other. Clearly, they were talking about him.

Really?

She wanted to tell them that they were being obvious.

What if he was on a date tonight? For all they knew, she could've been his girlfriend. They were being so obvious it was rude. Through it all, Jake seemed to be oblivious.

Anna reminded herself that she wasn't his girlfriend. She had no right to feel territorial.

Yeah, what was with that anyway?

She may not have liked Miss Texas—er Dorenda— but she never felt...like *this*.

Then again, she'd always done her best to give Jake and his women plenty of space.

Now that he was free, what was she doing? Why was she meddling? Jake certainly did not want for female attention. And he really wasn't looking to settle down into anything permanent. Maybe Cheryl's canceling was a sign that she needed to back off.

Maybe she should simply enjoy this time with him before he got involved with somebody else—maybe she shouldn't be so quick to pair him up with someone new.

Right. But how was she supposed to get out of the bet now?

* * *

"Is that the blind date you're with?" asked Dylan Tyler, an orthopedic doctor who was brand-new to Celebration Memorial Hospital. He'd come over to say hello after Anna had excused herself to find the ladies' room before the music started.

"No, I'm here with my friend Anna Adams. Do you know her? She is a nurse at the hospital. Works up in OB."

"How did I miss her?" Tyler asked. "You're not going out with her?"

Jake shrugged off Dylan's question.

"If not, introduce me. It's nice to meet new people. I'd certainly like to get to know her better."

I'll bet you would.

Since Tyler had moved to the area, Jake got the feeling the two of them might occasionally *fish in the same pond*. He hoped his colleague wasn't the kind of guy who would poach. Because his interest in Anna encroached a little too close to home.

"I don't think so."

"So you are interested?" Tyler asked. "If so, I'll back off. No problem."

No. He just didn't want someone like Tyler messing with Anna.

Still, Jake nodded.

Dylan Tyler was a good doctor, but he was the last person he'd fix up with Anna. Or one of the last. There were others who were probably worse, but Dylan's overenthusiasm had helped Jake make an instantaneous decision that he wanted to keep the hospital a dating-free zone—for both of them. He'd have to talk to Anna about that as they continued to work out the parameters of this bet they had going on.

Besides, she didn't want to date a doctor anyway. So that automatically ruled out Dr. Dylan Tyler and any lecherous ideas he might have in mind as he tried to get his hands on her.

"No problem, bud. I can take a hint. Anyway, here comes your lady. I'll let you get back to business. You're welcome to join us." With a jerk of his head, Tyler gestured to his party of at least fifteen people, who had set up camp a few yards away from Jake and Anna's blanket for two. "Or if you'd rather be alone, have fun *not dating* her."

Tyler smirked and gave Jake a fist bump before he walked away.

"Who was that?" Anna asked, watching Tyler still watching them—or her. Was the guy blatant or what? She waved at him, obviously wanting to let him know that she was aware of him. It wasn't exactly a flirty move, as much as it was an I-see-you-there act of self-assurance. Even though she had a shy side, when it came to things like this she had a wit that Jake loved.

"That's Dylan Tyler. Orthopedics. He's the new kid in town. Only been at the hospital for about ten days. You haven't met him?"

He knew she hadn't. He just wanted to see what she'd say.

"No. I haven't had the pleasure. He's cute."

Something strange and possessive reared inside Jake. "I thought you said you didn't want to date a doctor."

Anna dragged her gaze from Dylan back to Jake. In the evening light, her blue eyes looked like twin sapphires. "Yes. I did say that, didn't I? Maybe I need to reconsider my criteria. Or at least make an exception. Why let Hal...rob me?"

"What? Rob you of that guy?" Jake asked.

"You look like you smell something gross. Is he that bad?"

Dr. Tyler wasn't really *bad*, but Jake wasn't convinced he was good enough for Anna. Hmm...maybe he identified with Tyler just a little too much? That's why he understood his game.

"Look, you can't keep changing your list of deal breakers," Jake said. "If you do, how am I supposed to know what kind of guy to fix you up with?"

He lowered himself onto the blanket and Anna did, too, gracefully curving her legs around to the side and positioning her dress to cover her thighs. Even so, there was still a whole lot of pretty leg showing.

"Who said anything about not being able to change criteria? The list shouldn't be set in stone, Jake. What if we go out with someone and we realize that something else is a deal breaker, or maybe there's a quality we originally thought was a deal breaker that turns out to not be such a bad thing after all?"

It irritated him the way she glanced in Tyler's direction when she said that.

"If you want me to introduce you to him, I will." He hadn't meant for his voice to hold that much edge.

"Someone's a little touchy tonight." She raised a brow at him.

"I'm just saying, how am I ever going to win this bet if you don't know what you want?" With that, he took care to infuse humor into his tone.

"I don't think either of us knows what we want. If we did, there would be no bet."

Touché.

The first musical group up, a Rastafarian reggae-jazz fusion band, took the stage and preempted their conversation. After a short warm-up, they got the party started with a Bob Marley tune, which got most of the crowd to its feet. Some people swayed, while others sang along.

After the first song ended, the singer in his smooth Jamaican accent shouted, "Hello, all of you beautiful people. We are so happy to be here tonight. How are you all feeling?"

As the crowd cheered, Jake and Anna exchanged glances that seemed to call a truce to the discussion they'd had a moment ago.

"We are releasing our first CD next month and we would like to introduce you to the first single from that album. It's all about feeling the love and sharing it. Isn't that a great thought? Wouldn't you like to fill the world with love?"

As the band broke into the first strains of their song, the singer said, "I want to see everybody on their feet. Let's all dance and sing and fill the world with love. I don't want to see anybody sitting down looking sad."

Jake took her Anna's hand and pulled her to her feet.

"Oh, no, you're not—"

"Oh, yes I am."

He pulled her in close, holding one of her hands

down at their sides as she placed her other hand on his shoulder and he placed his hand on the small of her back and sent her out for a twirl. Back in middle school, they had learned to swing dance in PE. It was something that the two of them still loved to do, though he couldn't remember the last time they had gone dancing. Anna's husband, Hal, hadn't been very understanding. So Jake had let it go so as not to rock the boat.

Other than their Sadness Intervention Dance, it had been far too long since they'd done that. They weren't the only ones dancing; it seemed a good part of the crowd had been inspired by the Rastafarian singer as he sang his song of spreading joy and love.

It was funny how even after all these years the steps moved through him and into Anna and back to him, the steps and twirls pulling each other together and breaking them apart, but ultimately reeling them back in.

Maybe it was the wine or the music, or it could have even been the setting sun that was sinking lower in the evening sky and bathing everything in a warm golden glow, but for the first time in a long time Jake felt as if he didn't have a care in the world.

As the song wound down, the Rastafarian hopped down off the bandstand into the audience and was encouraging people to fall in love, "at least for tonight. Love the one you're with and send a message of love and good energy out into the world."

Jake gave Anna one final flourishing spin and reeled her back in so that they stood face-to-face, still in each other's arms. Jake's hands moved slowly up her back and over her shoulders until his fingers cupped her face.

His body knew what he was going to do before his mind could stop him.

He bent his head and covered her lips with his.

She didn't pull away. She accepted the kiss like a gift. A gift that was as much for him as it was her.

Her mouth was soft and yielding.

She sighed, a feminine little shudder of a breath, and he pulled back the slightest bit to allow her to object.

But she didn't.

So, he took that to mean that she had accepted his gift and leaned in and kissed her with hunger, and conviction and a need that made the axis of his world shift.

And she kissed him back.

He didn't care that they were in the middle of downtown Celebration in Central Park where anyone could see. Hell, for all he knew, her parents and sister or his brothers might be watching him kiss his best friend, Anna Adams. But he didn't care. Because, for that moment, they were the only two people in the world.

It was just him wanting her and her kissing him back.

Chapter Five

Jake wasn't avoiding Anna.

But he wasn't at all positive she wasn't avoiding him.

He had no idea what had gotten into him Friday night. One minute they'd been dancing and having a great time, and then they were kissing. He wasn't sure who had started it—or if it even mattered. The thing was, he'd kissed his best friend, and at the time neither of them seemed to mind. In fact, it felt good...as if it worked.

Would they work? The two of them...?

It should've felt like kissing his sister. But it hadn't. It felt warm and ripe and *right*. At least in the moment. Then they had done a damn good job of settling down and pretending as if nothing had happened. They'd watched the rest of the concert with a respectable amount of space between them on the blanket. He'd taken her home, walked her to the door and they'd wished each other a platonic good-night.

To the untrained eye, it might've looked as if nothing had happened between them. But then they'd gone all weekend without talking to each other. Proof positive that all was not well and it simply shouldn't have happened.

Jake couldn't remember the last time he and Anna had gone two days without talking. Not since she'd moved back to Celebration. Even when he'd been dating Dorenda and the women who had come before her, he and Anna had talked. They may not have seen each other every day, but they'd talked. Now everything felt off balance and he knew it would stay that way until one of them broke the ice. And that was exactly what he intended to do.

It was eleven-thirty on Monday morning and he'd be damned if he was going to let this weirdness go on a moment longer. He did his best to isolate the kiss, to box up the memory of it and relegate it to the places in his mind where he kept things he didn't want to think about, the things that got in the way.

With that done, he realized that on a normal day by now, he probably would have already seen her—razzed her about whether or not she'd seen Dr. Dylan Tyler today and probably asked her if she had plans for lunch.

He might've been a little behind schedule, but it wasn't too late to man up and get up to speed.

The elevator opened on the maternity ward on the third floor of the hospital. It wasn't his usual territory.

He generally stayed one floor below on the second floor. But every so often—mostly when he wanted to see Anna—he'd find his way up here.

It must've been a slow morning, because three nurses stood talking behind the main desk. They looked up and one blushed as he approached.

"Hi, Dr. Lennox," said one nurse. Her name was Marissa. He knew that because Anna always spoke highly of her. "How can I help you?"

Jake glanced down the empty hallway toward the patient rooms, but didn't see any sign of his friend. The sound of a newborn crying cut through the air.

"Hi, Marissa, ladies. Is Anna around?"

On the wall behind the desk a bulletin board was full to overflowing with baby and family pictures, thank-you notes and pictures drawn in crayon. A call light came on, signaling that a patient needed help and one of the nurses—he wasn't sure of her name and she wasn't wearing a name tag—excused herself to tend to the woman.

"No, we're pretty slow up here today. But I hear you're hopping downstairs. The chief asked if Anna would come down there and help until y'all are caught up. I'm surprised you didn't see her since that's your floor."

"Really? How long had she been there?"

The two nurses exchanged a glance. "Probably since about ten o'clock," said the one whose name tag read "Patty."

So Anna had been on his floor for an hour and a

half and she hadn't said anything. Okay, this definitely called for an intervention.

"I guess that just shows you how busy we've been," said Jake. "Thanks, ladies."

As he turned to walk away, Patty said, "Did you have fun at the jazz festival Friday night? I saw you there and I wanted to get over to say hello, but..." Patty and Marissa exchanged another look. "You saw for yourself how crowded it was and, well, I didn't want to interrupt. Y'all looked like you were having such a good time."

Patty's words were like a well-landed kick in the gut.

Great. Just great. All they needed was to become a rumor on the hospital grapevine. He should've thought of that before losing his mind Friday night.

He stared at the women for a moment, unsure of what to say. After all, what did one say to a comment so full of insinuation?

It's none of your business?
Quit gossiping?
Get back to work?

What an inappropriate thing for them to say. Celebration Memorial didn't have an uptight work atmosphere, but they still adhered to a certain level of professionalism.

They must've read his irritation on his face, because their smiles gradually faded. He hoped they hadn't been this out of line with Anna. But if Patty felt free enough to be that bold with him, he had a sinking feeling he'd better find Anna fast and make sure everything was okay.

"Ladies." He gave them a curt nod and turned back toward the elevator.

This was case in point of why it was a bad idea to date anybody he worked with. He was sure Anna would tell him the same thing once they had a chance to talk.

Relationships were complicated enough. Things like this made them worse. There may have been one day of gossip when he and Dorenda broke up, but it had faded and everyone went on about their business.

Honestly, he hadn't cared what everyone was saying.

But this was different.

Now every time he and Anna were together, people would be speculating. He didn't worry for himself; he worried about how it would make Anna feel.

The elevator dinged and Jake steeled himself to see someone else who might've been at the festival, someone who would give him a sidelong, raised-eyebrow look. But when the door slid open, a man holding a little girl in one arm and a giant vase of roses in another smiled at him as he stepped out into the hall. Jake smiled back and let them clear out before he got in and pressed the button for the second floor.

To hell with them. To hell with them all. Except Anna.

If he could have a do-over, Friday night would be it. Never in his life had he wanted to take back something so badly. Well, of course the other big do-over would be to go back and make things right with his mother. All those years that she'd lived with that secret and let her sons believe she was the culprit who caused the splintering of their family, when in actuality their dad had given her a very good reason to leave. And he'd been content to take the secret to his grave.

If Jake's indiscretion with Anna was his reason for not dating coworkers, his mom and dad's story was the case against marriage. Marriage could turn everything you believed in into a lie. You thought you knew someone, and it turned out they were a complete stranger. Then you had to wreck a lot of lives to get back to the truth.

Jake scrubbed his eyes with his palm, trying to scour away the regret. He had too much to do today to worry about things he couldn't change.

When he stepped out of the elevator on the second floor, Anna was at the nurses' station. She looked up and their gazes snagged. For a split second, she looked like a deer caught in headlights, but then the warm smile that he loved so much spread across her face and he knew everything was going to be okay.

"There you are," he said as he walked toward the nurses' station.

"Here I am," she said. "I didn't know I was lost."

"Actually, I'm probably the one who is lost. I had no idea you were working down here today. I just went up to three to find you."

Her smile froze and her eyes got large and she didn't have to say a word for him to know that Patty and Marissa had probably given her a more intense grilling than they had given him.

He wondered what she'd said, but this was not the time or the place to ask her.

He looked at his watch. "Hey, I was wondering if you wanted to grab a bite of lunch."

Anna's face fell. "I just got back from lunch. I only

took a half hour since we're so busy. I wish I'd known—I would've waited."

"Hey, no problem—"

"Excuse me, Dr. Lennox," said Cassie Davis, one of the surgical floor nurses. "The family of Mr. Garrity, who is in room 236, is here and they have some questions for you. I told them you probably wouldn't be able to meet with them right now, but I said I would ask. But if you're just getting ready to go to lunch, I can tell them you're busy."

Jake shook his head. "No, I can talk to them now. It's fine."

Cassie handed Jake the patient's chart. "Thank you," he said to her as she walked to the opposite side of the nurses' station. When she was out of earshot, he said to Anna, "Let's talk later. Okay?"

She nodded.

"Maybe tonight?" he said. "Do you want to grab a bite after work?"

Anna closed the computer file she had been working on. "Actually, I can't. I have a date. Over the weekend, Joseph Gardner, the guy you set me up with, texted and asked if we could move our date from Wednesday to tonight. We're going ice-skating."

Ice-skating in June? That was different. Good. It meant she would have to cover up. She'd have to wear something like jeans and a turtleneck. Multiple layers on top. Maybe even a scarf around her neck.

Anna gave a little shrug. She looked unimpressed. "Oh, okay. Have fun."

All Jake could think was, thank God she wouldn't be wearing that blue-and-white dress.

Have fun?
Oh, okay. Thanks.
Was that all he had to say?
Then again, what did she want him to say?
"Dr. Lennox is such a great guy," said Cassie. There was a dreamy note in her voice. "Why can't all doctors in this hospital be more like him?"

Anna followed Cassie's gaze and saw her watching Jake disappear into Mr. Garrity's room.

"Nice and so good-looking…" Cassie sighed, looking absolutely smitten. "A rare combination in these halls, wouldn't you say?"

"You've got that right."

Actually, truer words had never been spoken. Anna knew all about good-looking doctors who were not of the nice variety. Her husband, Hal, had been smart and handsome, but sometimes he could be the most insensitive, obtuse SOB you could have ever imagined. When he was irritated or bored, he let his feelings hang out there. He could be caustic and rude.

If he'd been on his way to lunch, the patient's family would've had to wait. His philosophy was, if you didn't set boundaries, coworkers and patients and their families wouldn't set them for you.

On paper, his argument was valid. The only problem was, he didn't seem to realize that other people had boundaries and feelings…and needs.

Jake always seemed to have a moment for anyone who asked, yet he never acted as if he felt compromised.

Anna hoped Friday night hadn't compromised their friendship.

There was no denying that the kiss had blown her mind. She'd never really given much thought to what it would be like to kiss Jake, but now she couldn't get it out of her mind.

All weekend long she'd felt his hands on her body, felt the phantom sensation of his lips moving on hers. He tasted wonderful, like red wine and chocolate-laced espresso from the tiramisu. Flavors that were rich and dark and delicious. Flavors that a girl might start craving once she got a taste.

And she couldn't even believe she was linking cravings and Jake Lennox in the same thought.

What's wrong with me? Am I in high school?

No, because in high school Jake had always been like a brother she'd never had.

Now she'd gone and kissed him. And he wanted to talk.

Talk. That couldn't be good. He hadn't kissed her at the door Friday night—would she have wanted him to? That needy, greedy part of her that could still taste him probably wouldn't have objected if he had. But the logical, sensible Anna knew they were flirting with disaster.

She knew what he was going to say. That the kiss had been a mistake. That they needed to pretend it never happened.

She bit her bottom lip.

They didn't need to discuss it. As far she was concerned it was forgotten.

Ha, ha! Now they'd satisfied that little curiosity, it was time to put it behind them.

She felt her phone vibrate in the pocket of her scrubs, signaling a text. She pulled it out and looked at it. It was from Joseph Gardner, her date tonight.

Maybe he was canceling. *God, wouldn't that be great.* But then she saw the message he left.

Looking forward to ice-skating tonight and seeing if we might fall for each other.

What?

She cringed. Oh, God, that was a bad pun. Ice-skating and falling.

No. Just no.

"Everything okay?" Cassie asked.

Anna hadn't realized Cassie had walked up behind her. The woman seemed to be the only one in the hospital who hadn't heard about her public display of... friendship with Jake.

"Yes. Fine."

She dropped her phone back into her pocket as if it was a hot potato and took a deep breath.

With her attitude, she probably had no business going out with this poor guy. Really, the text was sweet. Corny, but sweet. Despite the fact that she hadn't even met him in person, it showed that he had a sense of humor. It was the kind of gesture that a woman would find very endearing if she was into the man who'd sent it.

But for the woman who wasn't even looking forward to the date...

Stop it, Anna. What kind of horrible attitude is that?

Joseph Gardner had taken time out of his day to text her. She should consider it a good sign. She should be nice.

Or maybe she should save him the brunt of her bad humor and cancel...

She drummed her fingernails on the desk for a moment, contemplating what to do. Then she pulled her phone out of her pocket again and texted Joseph back.

Anna had insisted on meeting Joseph Gardner at the ice rink in Celebration. Even if this guy was a friend of Jake's and an established investment banker, she didn't know him. Besides, she liked the idea of having an escape in case she wanted to leave.

She arrived at the skating rink right on time, with her socks and her gloves and the determination to come into this evening with a better attitude than she had had today.

She wouldn't think of Jake and his lips and his taste of red wine and chocolate.

Nope. She wasn't gonna invite him along on this date.

She got out of the car and walked up to the window where they sold admission. She looked around, but she didn't see anyone who might remotely be Joseph.

Should she wait for him out here? Or should she go inside and get her skates?

But if she went inside, that meant she would pay for

herself. She had no problem with that; in fact part of her preferred it because then there would be no feelings of anybody owing anyone anything.

But it was awkward. Should she buy his ticket, too? No. That would be weird.

At heart, she was a traditionalist who enjoyed being treated like a lady. But it didn't necessarily mean she wasn't a lady if she paid her own way.

She really was so bad at this.

No. Not bad. Just a little rusty.

And he was late.

Anna got in line. The box office was manned by a lone teenage boy who didn't seem to be in a hurry for anything. It took about five minutes to get to the window.

"One admission, please, for the seven o'clock skating session. I'll need to pay for skate rental, too."

The teenager checked his phone and answered a text before he methodically punched numbers into the cash register. No wonder it was taking so long. But why should she be in a hurry?

"That'll be ten bucks. Four for the skates, six for admission."

As she was fishing her wallet out of her purse, she wondered if she should wait a few minutes longer. What if he didn't show? Did she really want to be stuck here all evening?

It's not like I have to stay if he doesn't show.

As she opened her wallet, someone behind her said, "Anna? Are you Anna Adams?"

She turned around and saw a tall, thin, blond man with sparkling brown eyes.

"Joseph?"

"The one and only. I'm sorry I'm late. You know, when longshoremen show up late for work they get docked."

She blinked at him. She might've even frowned because she had no idea what he was talking about.

"Longshoremen," he repeated. "They get *docked*. It's a joke."

"Oh!" Anna forced a laugh, even though it really wasn't funny. It was kind of sophomoric, actually. But she wanted to be a good sport. "I get it. You're a *punny* guy, aren't you, Joseph?"

His eyes lit up and he opened his mouth and pointed at her. "That was good. I think I'm going to like you. Put your money away. When I ask a woman out, I pay. So this is on me."

She held her breath, waiting for him to deliver another pun, but he didn't. So she stuffed the ten-dollar bill back into her wallet.

"Thank you, Joseph. Do you go by Joseph? Or should I call you Joe?"

He took their tickets and stepped away from the window, motioning toward the door. "Yeah, it's Joseph. And you can call me Joseph."

Umm? Oh. "Okay. Joseph."

"No, actually you can call me Joe. I'm just kidding you."

Was that supposed to be funny?

They waited while a family of four entered the building. Then Joseph held the door for Anna, allowing her to step inside first.

At least he was a gentleman.

Inside, the place was at least thirty degrees cooler than it had been outside; the smell of freshly popped popcorn and hot dogs mingled with the scent of dampness. The sound of video games warred with loud music. The rink was already buzzing with activity, but an uncomfortable silence had wedged itself between Anna and Joe. As they waited in line to get their ice skates, Anna could feel the nervous energy radiating off her date. She sort of felt bad for the guy.

She'd been anxious about meeting him, but now she wanted to take him by the shoulders, look him in the eyes and tell him to take a deep breath. He didn't have to try so hard.

Maybe *she* needed to try a little harder to take a little of the pressure off him.

"What do you do, Joe?"

"I'm an investment banker, but I'm starting to lose interest."

He laughed, then cleared his throat when he noticed that Anna was grimacing.

"So you're a nurse?" he said. "Did you hear about the guy whose entire left side was cut off? He's all *right* now."

Anna winced.

"You better slow down there, buddy. You don't want a use up your best material before they Zamboni the ice for the first time."

He looked a little embarrassed. "Too much, huh?"

Anna held up her thumb and index finger so that they were about an inch apart. "Just a tad."

She didn't want to be mean, but really, was there anything much worse than canned humor? Couldn't he hear himself? A horrifying thought crossed her mind—that he could hear himself, but just couldn't *help* this incessant need to make a joke out of everything.

Was there a name for that sort of disorder? Or was it a defense mechanism?

Either way, at this rate, it was going to be a long night. She sat down on the bench to put on her skates. She'd have to ask Jake if his pal Joe had been the class clown.

In all fairness, she'd told Jake that humor was high on her list. She loved to laugh. Who didn't? But no one liked to be pelted with nonstop rehearsed repertoire.

By the grace of God, Joe managed to contain himself as they finished putting on their skates.

After she put on her gloves, Anna stood, wobbling a little bit. Joe reached out a hand, which she grabbed to steady herself.

"It's been a long time since I've been ice-skating. Hope I can still do it."

She braced herself for another pun, vaguely fearing that she'd left herself wide-open by saying that, but either Joe was out of material or he was showing some restraint.

"Jake told me you were athletic. That's why I thought this would be fun."

Fun. Okay, that was a good sign. If he could stop

with the bad jokes, she could loosen up a little bit and have fun.

They made their way into the rink. He stepped onto the ice first, looking sure of himself and steady. He held out his hand and helped Anna. She wobbled again, but managed to grab the bar attached to the shoulder-high wall surrounding the ice. But soon enough, she found her balance and they began circling the rink. He seemed to understand Anna's need to hug the wall for the first couple of rounds. For the most part, he stayed next to her, but showed off a little bit, skating backward every now and then.

At least he didn't try to hold her hand.

Was it natural for a man in his thirties to be this good at ice-skating?

She gave herself a mental slap for being so judgmental.

When the music changed to a slow song and the DJ dimmed the light and turned on the disco ball, Joe turned around to skate backward and started to reach for her.

"I need a break," Anna said. "How about we sit this one out?"

They made their way to a table in the concession area. Joe got them hot chocolate and a tub of popcorn. Anna had to give him props for getting it to the table without dropping, sloshing or spilling. She wouldn't have been so adroit.

He set the drinks on the table and they sat quietly as they watched the skaters float by in pairs.

"Do you have any hobbies? Or do you play any sports?"

"I like basketball."

It made sense. He was tall and moved well. So, okay. Good. Now they were getting somewhere.

"When I'm playing, I always wonder why the basketball keeps getting bigger, and then it hit me."

She blinked at him. The guy just couldn't stop. She was going to kill Jake. Why in the world would he fix her up with an amateur comedian?

"So I imagine that right about now, you want to throw something at me, don't you?" he said.

Yes.

She smiled and shrugged.

"If you do, I hope you'll make it a soda—"

"Because it's a soft drink," Anna finished. She shook her head.

Okay. That's enough. There was being a good sport and then there was being a martyr. Was this the kind of guy Jake saw her with? Just what part of this did he think she would find attractive? No offense to Joe. He was a good guy and would make the right woman happy—hysterically happy. But he wasn't for her. Clearly, her heart was somewhere else.

"So, Jake told me you're divorced," Joe said. Even though this was a topic Anna generally wouldn't want to talk about with a stranger, and certainly not on a first date, it was Joe's first real attempt to make conversation that wasn't a setup for a pun.

"I am. The divorce was official a month ago, but we've been broken up for about two years now."

Joe stared at his hands for a moment.

When he looked up, Anna saw something that resembled vulnerability in his eyes.

"It's only been six months for me," he said. "Does it get easier?"

So that explained it—his nervousness, his need to cover up by making dumb jokes. Well, maybe that was just part of his personality. But she felt bad for the guy. He was obviously hurting.

"It does. It just takes time. If it makes you feel any better, you are my first date since my divorce."

And Jake was your first kiss.

Knock it off, Anna. Stay in the moment.

Joe's eyes lit up the way they did when he was about to bomb her with a bad joke. Anna held up her hand and he stopped.

"Joe, you're a nice guy, and I can't deny that you are just as rusty at this as I am. But the jokes and the puns... maybe use them like salt and pepper?"

He looked sheepish.

"I don't mean to be a bitch. Really, I don't. Can you just think of it as—?"

She started to say *tough love*, but she didn't want to give him the wrong idea.

"Think of it as a friend being brutally honest."

Had Jake planned on dishing out a heaping helping of brutal honesty when he'd asked her to lunch today?

"You're right," he said. "I appreciate your brutal honesty. I guess it might be a little too soon for me to be getting out there again. Obviously."

"You'll be a fun date when you are finally ready,"

said Anna. She wanted to add, *when you meet the right woman*, but she was sure he already knew that.

The couples' skate ended, the lights were restored to their earlier brightness and a faster, decidedly less romantic tune sounded from the speakers.

"Shall we head back out there?" he asked.

She stood. "I need to go to the ladies' room. How about if I meet you on the ice?"

As she scooted out of the booth, Joe stood—just like a gentleman should. But somewhere between scooting and standing, the toe of her skate connected with something hard and the next thing Anna knew she was pitching forward, sticking her hands out to keep from doing a face-plant.

Her wrists bore the brunt of her fall. As Joe pulled her to her feet, a white-hot pain shot down the fingers of her left hand and up to her elbow. She pulled her hand into her chest, cradling it, but trying to not draw any more attention to herself than she already had.

She must've been a lousy actress.

"Are you okay?" Joe asked, reaching for her hand. "Let me look at that. You didn't break it, did you?"

She could move her fingers, but the movement sent flashes of pain spiraling through her.

"I don't think it's broken, but it hurts."

"Let me get you some ice," he offered. "This place should have plenty."

He was almost to the concession stand before she could object. Then, by the time he returned, she knew the night was over.

"Thank you for the ice, Joe. But I think I should go. I'm sorry."

"Should we go to the hospital and get it x-rayed?" he said. "I'll go with you. I hate it that you got hurt."

"No, thank you for offering, though. I'm a nurse. I'm sure it's not fractured. It's probably just a sprain. But I think I should go and ice it down and take care of it. The last thing I need is to fall on it again. Given my graceful performance tonight, that's not so far-fetched."

Joe looked a little relieved. "Aren't we a pair? You with your sprained wrist and me with my bad jokes."

He didn't have to say any more for Anna to know that he wasn't really feeling the chemistry either. Despite everything, it made the night better. Sort of like negatives canceling each other out to make a positive.

"Let me drive you home, at least," he said. "I'll arrange to get your car tomorrow."

"No. But thank you, Joe. I don't live too far from here. Really, I'll be fine. Thank you for everything."

As she extended her good hand to shake his, she looked into his earnest brown eyes. There was a woman out there who would love Joseph Gardner's quirky sense of humor. He truly was a good guy. Sadly, he just wasn't the guy for her.

Chapter Six

"What did you do to your hand?" Jake wasn't calling Anna to check up on the date. In fact, he hadn't planned on calling her at all that night, but what kind of friend wouldn't have checked on her after learning she'd fallen at the ice-skating rink and had hurt herself?

"Jake? I'm fine. How did you know?"

He explained that Joe had called him and given him the scoop.

"What else is there to tell you?" Anna asked.

"Why don't you let me have a look at your hand?"

He knew what her reaction would be, and that's why he'd driven over before she could tell him not to.

"Jake, you didn't have to drive all the way over here. I'm sore, but I really don't think it's broken."

He got out of the car and started walking up the brick path.

"I was in the neighborhood."

"You and I do not live in the same neighborhood."

"Well, I'm here now. In fact, I'm standing outside your front door. Are you going to let me in or not?"

"Sure."

He would've let himself in like he always had, but now... Now that Anna was dating, he thought it would be best to respect her privacy. Although part of him was a little surprised when she did not comment on the fact that he'd knocked when he'd always let himself in in the past.

He glanced at his watch. It was nearly nine o'clock. She'd probably already locked up for the night. In fact, if she hadn't, he was going to say something. Insist that she be more careful. Celebration was as close to being a crime-free community as one could hope for, but she was a single woman living alone. Just to make sure she wasn't compromising herself, Jake reached out and tried the door.

It was locked. As it should be. *Good.*

The porch light flicked on, followed by the sound of the dead bolt turning and the big wooden door opening. His heart clenched when he saw her standing there with her left arm in a makeshift sling. She was wearing a soft-looking pink T-shirt with blue pajama bottoms patterned with white sheep—or they might have been cumulus clouds. He didn't want to look too closely; besides he was more concerned with the drawn look on her face and the dullness in her eyes that indicated that she was in considerable pain.

"What did you do to yourself?"

She stepped back and let him inside, closing the door behind them.

"I don't know why I thought I could escape tonight unscathed," she said as he followed her into the family room off the kitchen. There was a pregnant pause and for a moment he wasn't sure if she was talking about the date or the ice-skating. He decided to wait for her to continue rather than ask.

"I guess I'm not as young as I thought I was."

"Don't be ridiculous. You are one of the most athletic people I know."

"Obviously, I'm no Tara Lipinski."

She sat down on the couch and gestured for him to take a seat next to her.

"No medals?"

"Only if they gave awards for klutziness—I'd win the gold. I wasn't even on the ice when I fell. If I was going to walk away with battle wounds, at least I could've had a good story to tell—that I landed wrong when I attempted my triple Salchow sequence. But no, I tripped over the leg of the table in the snack bar. There's a story for my grandkids."

Jake knew it was only a figure of speech, but Anna did see grandkids in her future. She wanted them—like most normal, healthy women. And she should have a family—a husband who loved her, a house full of kids and even more grandkids.

He could never give her that.

Not that she was thinking about him that way, he hoped. Everything had just gotten so muddied since the kiss. At least it had for him.

"Let me take a look at that." He reached out and eased the scarf that she was using as a makeshift sling over her head. She smelled good. Like shampoo and that flowery perfume she wore. The closeness and the smell of her and the act of lifting the scarf off her body conjured visions of him leaning in and kissing her again and taking off her shirt—

What the hell was wrong with him?

He was here to help her, not mentally undress her.

Holding her injured hand, he moved his knee away from hers to put a little distance between them. He tried to ground himself firmly in the reality that he was holding her hand because he was a doctor. And she was in pain, for God's sake. Never mind that her fingers were long and slender and her wrist was fine-boned, despite the swelling. He could tell that when he compared it to the one that wasn't injured.

He'd known her all these years, yet he'd never noticed this? How had that happened?

"Can you move your fingers?"

"I can." She demonstrated slowly, but grimaced from the pain.

"How about your wrist?"

"Yep." She lifted her hand from his and circled it in the air. "Ouch."

She lowered her hand back into his, palm side up, and he lightly stroked her skin with his thumb. She was so soft, so—

"I know this hurts," he said. "I'm sorry. But just one more test. Can you make a fist?"

"I can, but I don't want to because it hurts."

"I think we should take you in and get an X-ray," Jake said. "Just as a precaution."

He was still cradling her hand in his. Now he was using his other hand to lightly caress the soft skin on her inner forearm.

"Would you let me take you to the hospital?"

She pulled her hand from his, holding it against her chest.

"No, Jake." She looked almost panicked.

"Why not?"

"Because if we come into the ER together at this time of night, it's just going to perpetuate the rumors."

Oh. God, that's right.

He raked his hand through his hair. "You know what? I don't give a damn what they think. I don't care what they're saying. We are none of their business."

We?

They weren't a *we*. Well, they were, but not *that kind* of we.

Anna sat back on the couch. "Yeah, that's easy for you to say because you don't have to hear what they're saying. Since you're a doctor, they talk about you, but not to you."

He frowned. "Oh, I heard about it all right, from Patty who works with you up in OB."

Okay, so she had a point about the gossip. Yes, if they came in together tonight, the rumors would be flying tomorrow.

"But, Anna, if you need an X-ray, you need an X-ray. As your attending physician, I am suggesting that you get this looked at just to be sure."

"You are not my doctor. You're my—" She shook her head. "You're my friend." She held up her hand. "If it were broken, I couldn't do this." She made a fist with her hand and shook it at him, but no sooner had she done it than she gasped from the pain.

Now he was shaking his head.

"You need an X-ray."

"Not tonight."

"You have to be one of the most stubborn women I've ever met."

She shrugged. "Well, the least you could do is go get me some ice. Even Joe was nice enough to do that. Before you called, I was using that bag of frozen peas." She nodded in the direction of a bag lying atop a magazine on the coffee table. "But I think it's spent. I could probably use a full-fledged ice pack. There's a box of zipper baggies in that drawer in the kitchen. You know where the ice is."

He gave her a look, but he spared her the lecture about refusing physicians' orders. She was right—he wasn't her doctor. And she was a smart woman. She knew her body. Then again, sometimes health-care workers were the worst when it came to taking care of themselves in situations like this.

"Jake. The ice? Please?" Then as if she were reading his mind she added, "If the pain gets any worse, I'll have it x-rayed when I get to work tomorrow."

He came back with the ice and handed it to her.

"Do you want me to go to the pharmacy and get you something for the pain?"

"No, thanks. You know I'm no good on strong meds. I took some ibuprofen when I got home. It's starting to take the edge off."

"Speaking of, how did you get along with Joe?"

He knew she might not be in the mood to talk about it, but it didn't hurt to ask. He was curious, and Joe had been a little tight-lipped on the phone, not really sharing much other than the fact that Anna had fallen and wouldn't let him take her to the hospital.

"He's a nice guy deep down. But did you really think he was my type? He kept cracking these really corny jokes. I mean it was rapid-fire, one right after the other. Did he act like that when you roomed with him in college?"

Had he?

"I guess he was a little annoying, but that was a while ago. Because if I were he, I would've grown up a little by now."

"I think he uses humor to deflect his pain. He hasn't been divorced for that long."

"I guess not. Maybe he's not over his ex. Maybe it was too soon."

"Why would you fix me up with someone who'd recently gone through a divorce?"

Jake rolled his shoulders. What was he supposed to say? *Because the two of you had that in common.* Obviously, he was not a matchmaker. Obviously, he didn't have a clue.

"Not your type, huh?"

"No." He wasn't sure if she was annoyed or if it was the pain bleeding through into her words.

His gaze fell to her bottom lip. He was irrationally relieved that Joe hadn't kissed her. He couldn't quite reconcile that feeling. He knew she was off-limits to him. He'd fixed her up with Joe, thinking they might get along. Or if he thought about it a little more, he realized that she and Joe probably had nothing in common.

"Good to know," he said. "Maybe it's not a bad idea to have a debriefing after each of the dates so that we can figure out what worked and what didn't work, so that the next time, we come closer to getting it right. What do you think?"

"If you'll actually go on the next date I set up for you, you might not need next time."

He had the strongest urge to ask her if she wanted to talk about what happened between them at the jazz festival. He realized it was completely out of context, but here she was still hell-bent on introducing him to the perfect woman.

A voice way back in the recesses of his brain challenged him to consider the possibility that the perfect woman was sitting right here in front of him.

But no. Oh, no. *Hell, no.* He wasn't about to go there. He couldn't.

He lowered himself onto the couch next to her face-forward so he wouldn't have to look at her.

"So, using Joe as a point of reference, what should I do differently when I arrange the next date?"

She thought about it for a moment. She laid her head back on the couch and stared at the ceiling.

"Well, I liked the fact that Joe acted like a gentleman. He got points in that area, but there was zero attraction."

Good.

"And of course there's funny, and then there's annoying. In that area, Joe bordered on annoying. So, next time maybe go with somebody perhaps a bit more intelligent, someone kind and someone who hasn't just come from signing divorce papers."

She sat up and rearranged the ice pack on her wrist inside the sling, then looked at him.

"I have an idea," she said. "One thing that might be making this difficult is that we've never seen each other in action out on a date."

"You saw me with Dorenda."

"I felt like I needed to avert my eyes when you and Dorenda were together. Either that, or tell you to get a room. The PDA was really unbearable."

"So what are you getting at?" he asked.

"For our next date, why don't we go on a double date? That way we can see each other in action. Of course, it will have to wait until I'm feeling better. But let's start looking at prospects."

"All right," he said. "That could be interesting. But I'm still unclear about something you said. Did you say you didn't want to date anyone who is divorced?"

"No, that's not what I meant. I understand that when you get into your thirties, most guys are going to come with some baggage. We're not spring chickens anymore. So, yes, divorced is okay—I'd be a bit hypocritical if I ruled out all divorced men. Actually, what scares me more at this point in the game is the ones who have never been married. There're usually issues with them, too."

He nudged her with his knee. "Need I remind you that I've never been married? I don't have issues."

"I hate to break it to you, but you have more issues than most guys."

He made a face as if he was offended. "I don't have issues. I just know what I want."

"You never want to get married."

They sat in silence for a moment, her words ringing in the air.

Finally, she turned to him. "Jake, I know your mom left your family and it was hard on you boys. I saw what you went through. I lived it with you. Even as bad as it was, you, your brothers and your dad were always close. I really don't understand how you can let her leaving your family rob you of one of the most wonderful experiences of life. It's made you so dead-set against getting married. Most women out there aren't going to be like your mother. They'll be faithful and loving wives. A wife is someone you can count on. It goes beyond the sex and having kids. A husband and wife are a team. Your spouse is someone you can count on when nobody else in the world has your back. Forgive me for saying this, because I know your mom is gone, but she was wrong. She took the easy way out. And you shouldn't have to keep suffering for her bad decision."

The day his mom left the family, she'd tried to take the kids with her, but of course his dad had put up a fight. His dad had told her, "It may be your choice to divorce yourself from this family, but I'll be damned if you're going to take my boys."

Two days after she'd moved out, his mom had crashed her car over on Highway 46. The police report indicated her car had drifted off the road and she'd overcorrected and lost control of her car. It had flipped several times.

She'd been pronounced dead at the scene.

Anna knew this part of the story. What she didn't know was the part Jake had learned three years ago, when his father died. It had changed everything.

"What?" Anna asked. "You looked so far away there for a minute. We were talking about how I'm sure the right woman can help you see that your family history shouldn't turn you against marriage."

He wasn't sure why he was going to tell her this, but how could he make her fully understand? But the words were spilling out before he could stop himself.

"When my dad died three years ago, you couldn't come for the funeral."

She frowned. "I know. I'm sorry, Jake. Hal was just so impossible when it came to you."

"God, he was obsessed with the notion that you and I had something going on. It was kind of crazy, huh?" He shook his head as he remembered the no-win situation. "I've never told you this, but after my dad died, I learned something that floored me. It changed me. In fact, it turned my entire childhood and upbringing into a lie."

Anna sat up, grimacing as she did so, but she turned her full attention on him.

"What was it, Jake?"

He took a deep breath, suddenly regretting opening up this line of conversation. But they'd come this far and Anna was the one person he'd always trusted with all his secrets. He'd managed to keep this one to himself for three years.

"My mom didn't simply leave our family out of the blue. She had a good reason—my father had been seeing Peggy for at least a year when my mom found out about their affair. He kept their relationship hidden for two years, or at least he kept her away from my brothers and me, but he married her. You know how she made our lives hell when we were growing up. And then after the funeral, she couldn't rest until she made sure that my brothers and I knew about her affair with our father."

Anna's jaw dropped.

"All those years, we thought my mom was the one who'd walked away from us, and my dad let us believe she was the villain, even after she died, when all that time our father had been living a double life. I just can't get over what a screwed-up situation it was, and then there's the added guilt of how my brothers and I vilified our mother because we believed she'd walked out on us.

"That's why I don't want to get married, because their bad marriage and my dad's deceit ultimately turned our childhood into one big lie."

She sat there watching him, taking it all in. "I'm so sorry that happened to you and your brothers. With both of your parents gone, I'm sure it must feel like a whole lot of unresolved business. But, Jake, I am imploring you not to let it continue to rob you of something that could be incredibly good for you."

* * *

The following week, Anna was definitely on the mend. Her sprained wrist was still tender, but it was feeling remarkably better. She'd done light duty to give it a chance to heal. Now she was nearly back up to speed. Since she'd only been at the hospital for a little over a month, she wanted to make sure she pulled her own weight. She didn't have time for an injury, but she was heartened when her coworker, Patty, had assured her that she and the others on the OB floor were happy to pick up the slack, such as carrying heavy supply baskets and equipment.

Even if they leaned a little heavy on the gossip sometimes, Anna believed that they truly had her back, even in the short time she'd been working at Celebration Memorial Hospital.

Of course, nothing came without a price. They were more curious than ever about what was happening with her and Dr. Lennox.

"Nothing is happening," Anna told them.

And Patty maintained that the jazz festival lip-lock certainly didn't look like *nothing*.

"Sorry to disappoint you, but he and I are just friends. I've known him all my life."

Patty and Marissa exchanged dubious glances. "Looks more like friends with benefits to me," Patty said.

"No. It's not like that. If you don't believe me, maybe this will change your minds—we both have dates tonight. In fact, we are double-dating."

"Are you dating each other and going out with another couple, or…" Marissa asked.

"Or. He has a date and I have a date. Since our dates are both this evening, we thought it would work if we all went out together. You know how blind dates are. Anything to make them easier."

Patty's eyes grew large. "Did you fix Dr. L up on a blind date?"

"I did." Anna had the sinking feeling she'd better steer this conversation in another direction. It was getting a little too personal; Jake wouldn't be very happy if word got out and he traced it back to Anna as the original source.

"If you're looking for candidates, keep me in mind," said Marissa.

"Hey, I have dibs," cried Patty.

"You're both crazy," said Anna. "But only in the best way."

That evening as they walked into the bar inside Bistro St. Germaine to wait for their dates, Vicki Bright and Burt Jewell, Anna was hyperaware of the light pressure of Jake's hand on the small of her back. It was more possessive than if he'd simply walked beside her, but not quite as intimate as if he held her hand or put his arm around her. But why was she even thinking about that kind of closeness?

The bistro—where Emily worked, but she was off tonight—was an upscale spot with floor-to-ceiling glass doors that folded open so that the bar and casual dining area spilled out onto the sidewalk outside the restaurant. The more formal dining room had tables in the back that were covered with crisp white linen tablecloths and sported small votive candles and vases hosting single red rosebuds.

As they approached the maître d' stand, the soft strains of a jazz quartet and muted conversation buzzed in the air.

Anna was glad she'd worn her black dress—it wasn't too dressy, but it still had an air of sophistication.

They were meeting their dates at the restaurant. The one thing to which Anna had held firm during this bet with Jake was that she would meet her blind dates at the location. She didn't want strangers picking her up. What if the guys were real duds? Or turned out to be stalkers? Still, Anna made no apologies about playing by her own rules.

Vicki had driven herself tonight, too. Because of that, Jake and Anna had ridden together.

The bar was buzzing with people. Jake and Anna managed to grab the last two open seats. Anna ordered a glass of merlot and Jake had a beer.

As they waited for their drinks, Anna asked, "What do you need me to do to help you with the Fourth of July party? Because you're going to be out of town next week, aren't you?"

"I leave tomorrow."

"Oh, really? I didn't realize the conference was so soon."

Hospital CEO Stan Holbrook had personally asked Jake if he would attend a medical conference on research and development and bring back the information to share with the rest of the staff. It was proof positive that Jake was on Stan's radar and it seemed like another step toward securing the chief hospitalist position.

"Yes, I decided to fly in a couple of days early so I could spend some time with Bob Gibson, my mentor from med school. He's retired and living in New Orleans now. I haven't seen him in years."

"Sounds like fun. Are you boys going to tear up Bourbon Street?"

Jake laughed. "Hardly. That's a little too spring break for me. Besides, Bob hasn't been doing very well lately. He's been having some health problems. But he sounded good when I talked to him. He suggested we grab some dinner and then go listen to some jazz over on Frenchmen Street. It's quite a bit lower-key than Bourbon Street. After that, it will be all medical conference all the time and I won't have time for much sightseeing. But I'll bring back some Mardi Gras beads for you if you want."

"That's sweet of you, Jake. Only if you have time to get them. Please don't make a special trip into the drunken debauchery just for me."

"I would go to the ends of the earth for you."

There was something in his eyes that made her melt a little inside. It was an odd feeling because this was *Jake*. She wasn't quite sure what to say. They'd always kidded around, but somehow this didn't feel like a joke. A lot of things had felt different in the month since she'd been back in Celebration.

Or maybe she was reading too much into it after that kiss, which certainly hadn't felt like a joke—

"I see Burt," Jake said, staring at a point over Anna's shoulder. "That must be Vicki."

Anna turned around and saw her friend Vicki—actually, she was Emily's friend. Emily had suggested Jake and Vicki might hit it off since she was smart, pretty and a busy, professional woman who seemed to be more committed to her work as an attorney than hunting for a husband.

Vicki was standing in the restaurant's entryway, engaged in deep conversation with a bald man who was a little on the short and pudgy side. The two of them were already engaged in conversation, talking and laughing animatedly like old friends.

"Is that Burt in the brown jacket?" Anna said. "If so, the woman he's hugging is my friend, Vicki."

"Yep, that's Burt. Do they know each other?" Jake slid off of his bar stool and extended a hand to help Anna down.

"I hope so. If they didn't before they do now."

Come to find out, they did know each other. They'd dated in high school, but had lost touch. What a small world, they marveled. It was a wonder that they hadn't crossed paths before this since they both lived in the Dallas area and Vicki was an attorney who practiced family law; Burt was a psychologist specializing in family counseling. They may even have had clients in common.

Anna watched the years melt away for them right before her eyes. And she was happy for them, even if all branches of conversation seemed to lead back to *remember that time when...* or legal/family counseling shop talk. Even when Anna or Jake tried to steer the conversation toward something more inclusive, it managed to wind back around to a precious moment Vicki and Burt had shared.

Finally, after they had finished their entrées, Anna and Vicki excused themselves to the ladies' room.

"What a small world, isn't it?" Vicki said. "Burt was my big love back in the day. We lost touch after I found out that he'd gotten married. He's divorced now."

"*Whew*, what a relief," Anna joked. "Since he's here for a blind date. You know, the two of you should get together. Seems like that old spark is still there."

She was sincere and she certainly hadn't meant to sound snarky or jealous—God, no, she wasn't jealous. She was inspired by the sweet rekindling of long-lost love. But Vicki must have interpreted it as a dig because she turned and looked at Anna, her mouth forming a perfect, soundless O.

"We have been so rude tonight," she said. "Anna, I'm so sorry. The way Burt and I have monopolized the conversation tonight is just inexcusable."

Anna put a hand on Vicki's arm. "You have nothing to apologize for. I would love nothing more than to see you and Burt get to spend more time together. Really. I mean it. There's nothing like a second chance at love."

"Well, I feel just terrible. You went to all the trouble to fix me up with your friend, Jack—"

"Actually, it's *Jake*."

Vicki covered her face with her hands. "I'm sorry. I'm really batting a thousand tonight, aren't I?"

"The heart wants what the heart wants." Anna smiled

at her reassuringly. "You have absolutely no reason to be sorry."

As they made their way back to the dining room, Anna wasn't sure if the relief she felt was because she wouldn't have to make excuses at the end of the night about why she couldn't see Burt again or if it was because Vicki and Jake would not have a second date.

Chapter Seven

Jake had gotten back into town late the previous night after his trip to New Orleans for the weeklong medical conference. He hadn't slept well. Actually, he hadn't slept well the whole time he was gone. His mind kept wandering to places it had no business dwelling.

And then, *dammit*, once he'd gotten back into town, he was tempted to drive straight over to Anna's house, because all he could think about was how he'd missed her.

Thank God common sense reigned, because he'd gone home and crawled into his own bed instead of going to her.

The first thing this morning, he'd texted her and asked her to meet him for lunch in the hospital courtyard.

Our table on the patio? he'd asked.

The table that was shaded by a large oak tree. The day was mild and clear, the perfect opportunity to sit outside and get some fresh air.

I'm so there, she'd responded. I've missed you. But then she'd qualified it with, We need to firm up July 4 party plans.

Now, as he walked toward her, he couldn't get over how beautiful she looked, sitting at the table, soaking up the sunshine. Her auburn hair was pulled back off her face and when she looked at him and smiled, he saw that she wore hardly any makeup. She didn't need it. She looked fresh and gorgeous without it.

"Hey stranger," he said as he set his tray on the table. "Anyone sitting here?"

"I was saving that seat for someone very special," she said.

He leaned in and kissed her on the cheek. "How's it going? How's your wrist feeling?"

"No problem," she said, moving it in a circle. "It's pretty much back to normal now. What's in there?" Anna nodded toward the white plastic bag he carried.

"I brought you something." He pushed it toward her. "Open it."

She cast a questioning glance at him and he smiled at her.

"I think you're going to like it."

She opened the bag and peered inside. Then reached in and pulled out several strands of Mardi Gras beads and a CD.

"What's this? Wait a minute—is this what I think it is?"

"You won't believe this, but that reggae-jazz fusion group we saw at the jazz festival was playing at The Spotted Cat, a music club on Frenchmen Street. What are the chances? Here's the CD they were talking about at the jazz festival."

Anna held up the CD and examined it. "Are you kidding me? That's crazy. And I love it."

She was scanning the back cover of the CD. "'Love is in the Air' is on it." He noticed a flicker in her eyes.

"Yeah, there it is. I like that song." He noticed that she didn't meet his gaze. Suddenly, she was acting a little shy.

Keeping it light, he said, "I had to drag myself through the drunken debauchery to get those beads for you."

"Thank you for compromising yourself for me," she said, fingering the beads. She set the CD on the table and looked thoughtful as she traced the letters spelling out the name with her finger.

For a moment, the craziest thought crossed his mind—he would do anything in the world for her. What was happening between them? Because suddenly everything seemed different and the weirdest part was, it didn't scare him. Neither did the fact that, right or wrong, he wanted to explore it a little more. He'd realized that over the week that he was gone.

"Oh, my God, did you get a card from Vicki and Burt?" she asked, suddenly seeming more like herself.

It took a moment for the names to register. "Oh, right, Burt and Vicki. Hearing their names together threw me."

"Well, wait until you hear this. Did you get anything in the mail from them this week?"

"I had the post office hold my mail while I was at the conference. They're delivering it today. Why? What did you get from them?"

"You have to see this." She fished in her purse and then handed him a peach-colored envelope that was nearly the same hue as her scrubs. "I'm sure you got one, too, but I want to see your face when you read this."

He squinted at her, hoping for a hint about what was inside. She looked as if she could hardly contain herself.

"Open it," she said, gesturing toward the envelope.

Jake pulled out a white card and blinked at the picture on the front. It was Vicki Bright and Burt Jewell. Underneath the black-and-white photo, spelled out in bold, black letters, it said,

We're getting married!
Save the Date: December 24, 2015.

Jake's mouth fell open. Then he laughed. "Is this a joke? They just reconnected with each other *a week* ago. Can you even get printing done that fast, much less propose, address cards and mail them out? They obviously had a lot of catching up to do after we left them at the restaurant."

"Funny thing is, I thought Vicki didn't want to get married," said Anna. "Emily told me she was too immersed in her quest to make partner at her law firm. But it's not as if they just met. They were high school sweethearts. Maybe she was waiting for him?"

His stomach tightened in a weird way and as he looked into her beautiful blue eyes, there was that feeling again. The two of them had been separated for a decade and Anna had only been back in his life full-time for one month, but after all these years it seemed as if a lot had changed. Changed for the better. And he wasn't quite sure what to do with these feelings. One thing that remained constant was they wanted different things from life. She wanted marriage and a family. He...wasn't so sure.

"Well, we know we can set up the perfect couple," he said. "Apparently just not for each other."

"Don't count me out just yet. I have someone in mind to fix you up with for the July Fourth party. Cassie Davis, that nurse on the second floor."

"Cassie? Oh...she's nice. And pretty. She sort of reminds me of you in a way."

Anna threw him a look.

"Oh, well, poor Cassie. I guess that means you're not interested."

Why had he said that? Or at least, why had he said it that way? It wasn't a slam. Any guy would be lucky to have Anna. Unfortunately, the jackasses of the world, like her ex, always seemed to come in and mess things up for the good guys. Jake wondered if in her eyes he fell into that jackass category, dating beautiful women who weren't marriage material, so, a few months down the road, he could walk away with his bachelorhood intact.

"I didn't mean anything bad by it," he said.

Tell her. Tell her that a man would be lucky to have her love.

But the words stuck in his throat and then he convinced himself that he'd better quit while he was ahead, or at least before he dug himself in deeper.

"I don't know if it's a good idea to date someone I work with. Look how messy it got after people saw us together at the jazz festival."

Anna's right brow shot up the way it always did just before she made a smart-mouthed comment about something. But then, it was as if she stopped herself before she said what was on her mind. He realized what he'd said might've sounded as though he was calling their night at the jazz festival a date.

It wasn't.

Not technically.

God, he didn't want to pressure her.

No, if it had been a date…what would he have done differently? He might've asked her if she was available earlier, rather than just showing up at her house. But one of the things he loved about her—about *them*—was that they were spontaneous. They didn't have to schedule fun. Fun seemed to follow them wherever they went. It was as natural as—

"You're welcome to invite her, if you'd like," he said. "But how about we don't bring dates to the party? It's a lot of pressure."

He hoped that didn't sound wrong. Even though he didn't know how else it could sound.

"I mean, you can bring a date if you want. But I think I want to go solo to this one. Since we're cohosting. It might be easier."

"If I didn't know better, I might think you were asking me to be your date."

Her eyes sparkled as she sat there watching him. She was baiting him, but he wasn't going to bite.

"Even better, I was thinking Cassie could be your date for the wedding. Really, she's perfect, if you think about it. Stan Holbrook knows her. He thinks highly of her. Everyone does."

"If everyone loves her so much, why is she still available?"

She clucked her tongue at him and wrinkled her nose.

"Watch what you say there, buddy. You make it sound like she has some sort of defect. She's a good catch. Don't forget, you and I are *available*. Does that mean we're defective, too?"

"Of course not."

"Okay, then. Take Cassie to the wedding?"

"If it will get you off my back." He smiled at her to make sure she knew he was joking.

Sort of.

"Okay, good. That's one thing off my plate. You do realize I'm a step ahead of you here. Even though the dates with Vicki and Cheryl didn't work out, Cassie is a keeper. Or at least someone you don't need to toy with."

"I don't toy with women. Especially not women I work with."

She shrugged as if she were giving him that point. "You need to fix me up with someone decent. I mean, Joe and Burt are nice guys, decent guys, but they weren't for me. Obviously. So you'd better bring your A-game for this one. I don't want to be the third wheel on your wedding date."

He wouldn't mind her being the third wheel. No, actually it crossed his mind that maybe it would be a better idea if they went to the wedding together. But he knew what she would say to that. By the grace of God, things had not gotten weird after the kiss. He needed to rein it in a bit before his luck ran out.

Sitting here, looking at her, fresh-faced and lovely, his body was telling him exactly what he wanted—her, in her bed, with nothing between them but their feelings. But then reality crashed the party, reminding him that she wanted—she *deserved*—so much more than he could offer her.

For a moment, he let his mind go there. He was crazy about her in a way that he had never felt about any other woman in his life. Would it be so bad? Of course it wouldn't. But he had to stop pushing the envelope with her. If he kept on, he was bound to hurt her. Ruin everything between them.

And that was the last thing he wanted to do.

"Let me think about a date for you," he said.

Dylan Tyler came to mind. He had a good career and he and Anna had both found each other attractive—as they'd stated at the jazz festival. But he wasn't going to lie to himself. The fact that Dylan and Anna might be just a little too perfect for each other made him uncomfortable. Did he really want to tempt fate?

What the hell did it even mean, that he was thinking that way?

If he knew what was best for both of them, he would say goodbye now.

* * *

At least forty people had turned out for the party. Apparently, Jake's annual shindig had become something of an institution. One of the reasons his house was the perfect place for this party was that fireworks from at least three different local shows were visible over the water.

Since Anna had been in San Antonio until last month, and because Hal had been so funny about her friendship with Jake, this was the first year she'd been able to attend his infamous party, much less be involved in helping him host.

"Hey, Anna, you and Jake throw a great party," said her sister, Emily, who was sitting around a fire pit with Ty and Ben, two of Jake's three brothers, roasting marshmallows for s'mores. "I think they make a good team. Don't you, Ty?"

Emily could be such an instigator sometimes. She flashed a smile at Anna, then turned her charm on Jake's youngest brother, Ty. She could be a flirt *and* an instigator. Anna sat down on the arm of the Adirondack chair Emily was in. Her sister's long brown hair hung in soft waves around her tanned shoulders. The aqua halter top she wore accentuated her blue eyes. The glow of the fire made her cheeks look rosier than usual. Or maybe it was simply the fact that she was in her glory, enjoying the sight of the younger Lennox brothers engaging in a subtle tug-of-war for her attention.

"I'm glad you're having fun," Anna said.

"She's right, you know," said Ty. "Jake's Fourth of July parties are always good, but you've helped him kick it up another notch this year. I think there's something to this pairing."

Anna nudged her sister's leg, in a thanks-a-lot-for-getting-this-started gesture. "Well, what you see is what you get. You know Jake and I have always been good buddies."

"I think you two are good for each other," said Ben. "He seems so much happier lately—since you moved back."

The idea sent Anna's spirits soaring, despite the fact that she sensed a conspiracy.

Ty was a good-looking guy. He was an EMT, the kind who might be featured on the cover of a first-responders calendar. He'd always had a thing for Emily, but she'd always viewed him as a brother. Maybe that was the thing about knowing somebody since their paste-eating kindergarten years. Sometimes it was hard to see past the old and into the possibilities.

"Where is Luke tonight?" Anna asked. "I thought he'd be here."

She glanced at her sister. Emily had always had a thing for Luke Lennox. Wasn't it just the grand irony that Ty seemed to be attracted to Emily, but Emily was interested in Luke? And Luke… Who knew where Luke's head and heart were these days? He'd been pretty scarce since Anna had been back. He was nearly as bad as his older brother when it came to loathing commitment.

"Are they giving you a hard time?" As if on cue, Jake walked up beside Anna and rested a hand on her shoulder. Her skin prickled under his touch, and she held her breath, hoping Emily wouldn't start asking why she and Jake were trying to fix each other up...when the obvious answer was right there in front of them.

Well, that's what Emily would say.

And Anna couldn't believe she was even letting her mind go there. She and Jake were obviously wrong for each other. They wanted completely different things out of life, even if this attraction did seem to pull them both toward a middle ground where they could meet... but for how long? And to what end?

"Do you really think I'd let them get away with that?" Anna said.

She'd been working on the decorations and setting up for the party since midmorning. She'd strung stars-and-stripes bunting along the back of the house and festooned the tables with red, white and blue tablecloths, and napkins and centerpieces made of white hydrangeas and small flags arranged in vases that looked like mini-washtubs.

This was the first chance she'd had to slow down all day. She'd worked up until the guests had started arriving. Then she'd quickly changed from her shorts into her red sundress and she'd played hostess, greeting everyone, fetching drinks and doing her best to make them feel at home. Her stomach growled a stern reminder that she hadn't eaten much that day.

Now dusk was settling over the backyard. It was just about time to bring out the giant flag cake she'd made—a sheet cake with whipped cream icing, adorned with strawberries and blueberries to form the stars and stripes on the flag. She'd have just enough time to grab a bite and serve the cake before the fireworks started.

"I'm starving," she said to Jake. "I have got to get something to eat. Would you care to join me?"

"I'd love to," he said. "Let's grab some food and go down to the dock."

"The dock, hmm?" Emily muttered. "That sounds romantic."

Anna stepped on her sister's foot as she stood.

"Ouch!" Emily said. "That hurt."

"Mmm-hmm." Anna shot her sister a sweet smile. "I intended for it to. Mind your manners."

As they walked toward the food table, Jake asked, "What was that about?"

Anna shrugged and pretended to be much more focused on the barbecue than was really necessary. "Oh, you know how Emily can be. I was just keeping her in line."

"What's she getting you all riled up about now?"

Jake's voice was deep and ridiculously alluring. Anna slanted a glance at him.

"She's gotten it into her head that we shouldn't fix each other up."

Jake raised a questioning eyebrow, but something in his gaze seemed to say he knew what she was going to say next.

"She thinks you and I should date," Anna said. "She always has."

Jake shot her a lopsided smile that reminded her of the times when he used to triple-dog-dare her to do things she would've never tried on her own.

Or maybe she was simply imagining it.

Anna looked away, training her focus on the food, inhaling the delicious scent of barbecue and trying to ignore how her stomach had suddenly twisted itself into a knot. She helped herself to the barbecued ribs Jake had spent all day slow-cooking, a scoop of potato salad and some baked beans.

"Want a beer to go with that?" Jake asked.

He looked *good*, standing there in his blue jeans and bright blue polo shirt. Her stomach did a little flip, which she tried to convince herself was hunger.

But hunger for what, exactly?

The flames from the tiki torches cast shadows on his face, accentuating his strong jaw line and full lips. He was sporting that sexy-scruffy five-o'clock shadow that Anna had become inexplicably fond of. He fished a bottle of the micro-brew he'd picked up for the party out of the cooler and held it up for her to see.

"Yes, please. That sounds wonderful."

They'd been so busy facilitating that they hadn't had a chance to say much to each other, much less enjoy a beer together.

Jake grabbed another bottle out of the cooler and turned toward the dock.

She took her plate and followed him. It was one of the few unoccupied spaces, probably because it was set away from the food and festivities. Their friends were clustered in groups under the canopy of trees that stretched protectively over the large backyard. All the seats and places at the tables appeared to be occupied. In fact, people were sitting on the ground amidst the tiki torches and fire pit; everyone was talking and laughing and seemed to be having a great time. But right now, all Anna wanted was to find a quiet place away from the crowd where she could eat, and if that place happened to be on the dock, alone with Jake…all the better.

This was what she'd been missing all the years she'd been away. A lot of things had changed, but one thing that had become a tradition was that people loved to gather at Jake's house. She hadn't asked him, but she wondered if over the years his various girlfriends had played hostess. She made a note to rib him about it later.

But not now.

There wasn't time.

The sun was setting, and Anna knew if she didn't eat while she could, soon everyone would be shifting out from under the trees, toward the dock and the lakeshore to watch the fireworks. She didn't want to spend what little alone time they might have conjuring the ghosts of exes past.

For the first time that evening, as Anna sat there with Jake, she inhaled a full deep breath and relaxed.

On the dock, they sat side by side on the bench that overlooked the lake. The warm summer breeze must've blown out the tiki torch that Jake had lit earlier, because the only light came from the dusky twilight reflecting off the water.

He was sitting so close to her that his muscular biceps grazed her when he lifted his beer to take a sip.

All seemed right with the world as they sat next to each other listening to the symphony of cicadas, just as they had so often before. But this time, something felt different. There was a charge in the air. No matter how Anna tried to ignore it or explain it away or put herself on notice, she didn't care that it was a bad idea to allow herself to be drawn in by this strange, new magnetic pull that was so strong between them.

"It seems like everyone is having a great time," said Jake.

She was acutely aware that his knee had drifted over and was pressing against hers, and she was doing nothing to put some much-needed space between them. She didn't intend to do anything.

"Yeah, they are. We should do this more often."

"Do what? Have a July Fourth party?"

She was just about ready to swat his arm for the sarcastic remark, but he said, "Or should we do *this* more often?" He gestured between them. "I'd vote for this, myself."

She felt shy all of a sudden, as if he were testing her wit…and she couldn't come up with a good comeback. All her words felt clunky and strange and wrong.

Or maybe he was calling her bluff?

It sure seemed like it when he trailed his finger along the tender underside of her arm. The feel of his hand on her was her touchstone, her anchor, the one thing in this world that simultaneously frightened her and made perfect sense.

He set down his beer and turned his body to face her. He was looking at her with an intensity that had her gripping the edge of the bench to keep from reaching for him.

Despite the summer breeze blowing across the lake, the heat between them flared. He was playing with her hair, and she reached out and touched his hand. It was just meant to be a passing touch—something to anchor her, but it seemed to ignite that spark.

She wasn't sure who moved first, but suddenly they were kissing each other.

He kissed her exactly the way she hoped he would: deliberate and intense, as if he wanted to prove to her that they were *that* good together. That it really was electric. That it hadn't been a fluke that night when he'd first kissed her at the jazz festival. Right there in front of everyone. In front of their coworkers and their neighbors and God. In the moment, she hadn't worried about who saw them or questioned them or talked about them. She didn't think she would ever worry about it. This was Jake. The guy who had always looked out for her. Protected her.

She was sure he was still that guy who cared about her more than the man she'd married had ever done. But she wasn't the blindly foolish woman who'd convinced herself for years that her feelings for her best friend were purely platonic.

No. She definitely wasn't that woman anymore.

In this moment, she was just a woman who wanted a man. *This man*. And the sizzling hot, extraordinary kiss he was giving her. She would consider the consequences later.

Or maybe she wouldn't.

Maybe she'd pretend there were no consequences to worry about.

Maybe she worried too much.

Jake was kissing her and nothing else mattered. This

dock was their own world for two, their own universe. It was vast and amazing. This kiss wasn't about weddings and children and happily-ever-afters that she could never have with him.

Stop thinking so much, Anna.

This kiss wasn't about friendship and history and knowing each other inside and out.

The only thing that mattered was that this felt amazing. It worked. *They worked.* They were good together.

She wanted it, and he did, too.

She fisted her hands into his shirt and felt the warm, solid weight of his body against hers. He leaned into her, even closer, his hands moving across her back, down her to her hips, then sliding back up her sides and pushing against the weight of her breasts. He lingered there, liking it, she hoped. As if silently answering her, he shifted his body just enough to move his hands in so he could explore and caress.

He made a low, deep sound in his throat and she felt the vibration of it all the way through her own body, like fireworks on the Fourth of July or the rumble of a night train steaming its way through the heat of summer.

She wanted to live in that dark, rich sound; she wanted it to pick her up and carry her far away from every thought or intrusion of reality that might come between them.

But then, without warning the kiss ended. He pulled those delicious lips away. It was so abrupt it was disorienting, like soaring through the inky, starry sky one moment and then free-falling back down to earth the next.

"I'm so sorry." He moved back, raking his hand through his hair, putting some distance between them.

"Why are you sorry? Don't be sorry, Jake."

"This wasn't supposed to happen again," he said. "I promised myself I wouldn't kiss you again."

"So you've been thinking about kissing me again?"

He nodded. "I haven't been able to get those lips of yours out of my head." He seemed a little subdued. Maybe even a bit contrite.

"It's okay. It's fine, really. Would it make a difference if I confessed that I was hoping you'd kiss me again?"

She just blurted out the words. It was only the truth, and why shouldn't she tell him the truth?

Why? Well, she had a long list of why's for not confessing this particular truth, but they didn't matter right now.

"You deserve someone so much better than me, Anna." He leaned back and seemed to be trying to put even more distance between them.

"I've never met anyone who treats me better than you do."

He shook his head, looking so remorseful that it nearly broke her heart. "Believe me, you could do *so* much better. You *should* do better than me...than this. Especially after Hal."

No. She wasn't having any part of that.

"Don't be so hard on yourself, Jake. Remember, I've had two years to work through my failed marriage. I didn't rush right into dating the day after it happened. Not even the day I signed my divorce papers. It took you to get me back out into the world, albeit kicking and screaming, but I'm glad you nudged me out there."

"Even though the two dates I've fixed you up on have been complete and utter failures?"

"That's right. I sprained my wrist with the first guy and the other one married my sister's friend. If I didn't know you better, I'd think you were setting me up to fail. Is that what happened? Or was it leading me here?"

His right brow shot up. She loved the way he looked. It made her smile. *He* made her smile.

"I guess you have conquered your fear of getting back out there in the dating world."

If not for him, she'd still be hiding away.

"And you're the one who helped me do that," she said. "You've reminded me that romance isn't necessarily synonymous with pain. Thank you for that."

"But God, what are we doing, Anna?"

"Jake, why won't you let me in?"

There was a full moon tonight and the reflection of it rising over the water flickered in his eyes. He looked at her for a long moment and she could almost hear the jumbled thoughts churning in his head as he tried to put them in order.

"You're such a good person, Anna." He sounded preoccupied and she might've jumped to the conclusion that he was trying to let her down easy, but his expression and his body language told a completely different story. He was leaning in again. "You deserve someone equally as good."

"Shut up." She pressed her finger to his lips. "Don't ruin this moment."

His gaze, smoldering and intense and completely at odds with his protests, locked with hers.

"You just have to promise me one thing," he said.

Running the pad of her index finger over his tempting bottom lip, her wrist rubbed against the sexy stubble on his cheeks. Her body reacted with a warming shiver. He opened his mouth and gently caught her finger between his teeth. Nipped at it and sucked on it for a moment.

It felt like she'd been waiting her entire life for this moment. Despite his words, he certainly didn't seem to be in a hurry to get away. *Yeah*, he wasn't going anywhere.

Not right now, at least.

"Anything," she said.

She wasn't going to let him tell her he wasn't good enough for her.

She knew what she wanted, and he'd just slipped his arms around her again.

"No regrets," he said.

"No regrets," she answered. "But tell me something. How do you know that you're not good for me—that we're not good together—if we've never…tried it out?" She whispered the proposition inches from those lips of his, letting the promise tease his senses. "I'll bet we could be very good…together. The only thing I'd regret is if I never knew for sure."

He drew in a ragged breath and she scooted onto his lap, feeling the rock-solid proof of his interest underneath her.

"God, Anna, you're killing me," he murmured. His

breath was hot and he seemed more than a little *bothered* by the way he adjusted the angle of his hips so that their bodies aligned through their clothing.

He murmured something under his breath, but it was lost when he closed his mouth over hers and kissed her with a hunger that had him deftly turning her body so that she was straddling him.

It felt perfect, and dangerous, and maddeningly, temptingly delicious, awakening in her a hunger that she feared she might have to satisfy right here on the dock—with the guests behind the trees, only a few yards away. All someone had to do was walk down the path and around the corner and they would be discovered. But she didn't care. She wasn't thinking of problems or reasons why not, or second-guessing her actions or his reactions. It just felt so darn right, and that was all she cared about.

That thought cut the line that tethered her to reality and she let herself drift out on the tide of his kiss.

A few minutes later—or maybe it was hours, who knew?—Jake's phone rang. At first, he ignored it, but then it rang again.

"You'd better get that," Anna murmured. "It sounds like someone is trying to get you."

He wasn't on call, but if there was a big emergency at the hospital, Jake would've been among the first to be notified. Still tingling with awareness, Anna eased herself off of Jake's lap to give him some room. He fished his phone out of his pocket, but by the time he'd pulled it out, the phone signaled a voice mail.

"It's a 504 area code. That's New Orleans. Sorry, but I should pick up this message."

"Of course," she said.

As Jake listened to the voice mail, Anna watched his features contort into a mask of shock and disbelief. Then he stared at his phone for a moment before looking up at Anna.

"Is everything okay?" she asked.

He shook his head. "No. It's not. Bob Gibson passed away this morning."

Chapter Eight

Despite how strong Jake had tried to be, he'd ended up asking Anna, Emily and his brothers to tend to the guests while he stepped out for a few moments. Anna empathized with what he must've been feeling after receiving the news of Bob's death. Even though Jake was no stranger to personal loss after the death of both his parents, it never got easier.

After the fireworks ended, the guests began saying their goodbyes and calling it a night. It was a Saturday, but some of them, including Anna, had to work tomorrow. After all, the hospital was open 24/7. It didn't operate on bankers' hours.

Since she had to work, Emily, Ty and Ben had offered to tend to the basic cleanup—gathering trash and extinguishing tiki torches and the fire pit so that Anna could go home and get some sleep.

Her lips still tingled from his kiss. She didn't want to leave. She wanted to be there for Jake when he returned, but after thinking about it and weighing everything that had happened that night, she decided that maybe it was better to give him a little space. She'd call him tomorrow. Maybe ask him to go for a run after she got off work.

She was supposed to have Sunday dinner at her parents' house. Maybe she'd see if he wanted to come along. Lord knew he'd spent more than a few Sundays at her family's dinner table when they were growing up. Maybe going back to the comfort of the past would help him feel better.

The last thing she expected when she turned onto her street was to see his car in her driveway. But there he was, sitting in the car. It was almost eleven o'clock.

By the time she parked and let herself out of the car, he was standing there.

"How long have you been here?" she asked.

"Not too long," he said. "I'm sorry I bolted. I needed to clear my head."

She held up her hands. "No apologies needed. Come on in."

He nodded.

Once they got inside, he sat down on the couch and she went to the refrigerator and got two beers.

"Are you okay?" she asked as she handed one to him and settled herself on the couch next to him.

He rested his hand on the back of the couch and stared up at the ceiling, looking thoughtful.

"It's strange," he said, "to think that Bob is gone. He was so alive last week." Jake shook his head. "Being a doctor, you'd think I'd get used to the fact that people die and life goes on. But it never gets easier."

"I guess that's why it's important to live in the moment and appreciate the people in your life while they're there," she said.

"You're right. As I was driving around, I was thinking about what you said. About why I won't let you in." His voice was a hoarse rasp. "I don't know why, but I want to try. I mean, your strength humbles me, Anna. I've been running from my monsters for so many years. You don't run. You face your biggest terrors head-on. I don't know if I can be that strong—but..." His voice trailed off.

"Jake, listen to me. You need to hear what I'm saying to you." She cupped her hand under his chin and turned his face toward hers. Staring into his eyes, she said, "You're a good man, Jake Lennox. You need to accept that and believe it."

He caught her hand and brought it to his mouth, pressing a kiss into her palm. Then he slid an arm around her and closed the distance between them, brushing one light, hesitant kiss on her lips.

"This is different for me, Anna." His lips were mere inches from hers. "You are different for me."

"Are you saying that because you're trying to seduce me?"

He was familiar, yet different, for her. They were

picking up from where they'd left off on the dock, but at the same time, it felt brand-new. This was still Jake—the same big frame, the same dark hair setting off blue eyes as inviting as the Mediterranean. But he was changed. His body was tense; his face was flushed and way too serious. Desire laced with a little sadness colored his eyes a deeper shade of blue.

"I'm just picking up where we left off earlier. If that's okay...?"

She rested her hand on his shoulder, not saying it wasn't okay, but not giving him the green light either. Despite how she wanted to stop talking and just lose herself in him.

"Jake, I need to know... I know that this is different for us. But we can't seem to keep our hands off each other. And that's not a problem. It's definitely *not* a problem. I just need to know... Really, it's not. I just need to know...what are we doing?"

He looked her square in the eyes.

"I'm exactly where I want to be, Anna, and with the person I desire. Doesn't that tell you what we're doing... or what we're about to do?" His lips were mere inches from hers. "I want to make love to you, Anna Adams. Tell me that you want that, too."

"Oh, I want you, too, Jake. You have no idea."

She kissed him, wanting to make sure there was absolutely no doubt in his mind exactly how okay it was.

Then he leaned in and closed the rest of the distance between them. Then they fell into a kiss, arms wrapped around each other; his hands trailing down her back to cup her bottom, her hands in his hair, desperately pulling him closer, both of them impatient and ravenous as they devoured each other.

Anna had unleashed a want in him that rendered him desperate for something he never knew he needed. This was exactly how he imagined her body would feel. Now, he was greedy for her, needing to know every inch of her, eager to bury himself deep inside her.

She took his hand and led him to the one place in her house he had never been—her bed. Her bedroom was feminine and fashionable. A king-size bed sported a blue-and-yellow bedspread, turned down over soft white cotton sheets. There was a dresser and matching nightstand that held a table lamp, but he didn't turn it on after they stumbled into the room, clinging to each other as if their next breath depended on it.

How many nights since she'd been back in Celebration had he held her in his dreams, subconsciously breathing in her scent, taking possession of her body, loving her with her mind and his heart as he slept?

How was it that he was just admitting this to himself?

He unclipped her hair and dug his hands into the heavy auburn mass of it. Then he walked her backward until he could feel the bed behind her legs. As he eased her down onto the mattress, he buried his face in her hair, breathed in the scent of her—that delicious smell of flowers, vanilla and amber. A fragrance that was so intimate and familiar. Yet the newness of it hit him in a certain place that rendered him weak.

Smoothing a wisp of hair off her forehead, he kissed

the place where it had lain; then he searched her eyes, needing to make sure she was still okay with this.

"Make love to me, Jake," she answered before he could even say the words.

He inhaled a shuddering breath. As he pulled her into his arms, a fire ignited and he melted into the heat of her body. Relishing the warmth of her and the way she clung to him, he cradled her face in his palms and kissed her softly, hesitating, as he silently gave her one last chance to ask him to stop, to leave, to walk away from what was about to happen.

As if she sensed his hesitation, she pulled him into a long, slow kiss.

"Relax," she said. "I won't break. I promise. *No regrets*, Jake. Remember?"

For a moment, he looked at her in the dusk. The only light in the room was cast by a slim slice of light from the other part of the house and the glow of the full moon filtering in through the slanted blinds.

"Your lips drive me crazy," he muttered. "They have since that night I first kissed you. How is it that we've known each other for so many years and it took all this time for me to realize this addiction? Now, I look at that bottom lip of yours and it just makes me crazy."

He drew her lip into his mouth and she kissed him with urgency and demand as she tugged at his shirt, yanking it free from his pants. The move sent a rush spiraling through him. He felt the silk of her hands as they slipped under his shirt and up his back, turning his skin to gooseflesh. He couldn't stifle a groan.

He pressed his lips to her collarbone, exploring the

smooth, delicate ridge, and lingering over the hollow between her shoulder and throat. He stopped when he reached the top of her dress.

She made an impatient noise. So he found the hem of her skirt and began pulling it up, easing her body up and slightly off the mattress so that he could rid them of one of the barriers that stood between them.

"You're so beautiful," he whispered as he eased it over her head.

She lay there in just her panties, since she hadn't worn a bra beneath her sundress.

She tugged off his shirt. He sank back down beside her, tracing his fingertips down the slender column of her throat, splaying his hand to touch both beautiful breasts and then sliding it down to gently graze her stomach with his fingertips. When he reached the top edge of her panties, he slid his fingers beneath the silk to find her center. She gasped as his fingers opened her and slipped inside her. A rush of red-hot need spiraled through him and he nearly came undone with her as he watched her go over the edge.

As he slid her panties down, it was as if she sensed his own need. She made haste of unbuckling his belt and unbuttoning his jeans. Before he tossed his pants away, he pulled a condom from his wallet and sheathed himself. When they were finally free of the last barrier between them, his arms encircled her. He held her so close he could hear her heart beat. He shut out everything else but that sound and the need that was driving him to the brink of insanity.

All he wanted was *her*.

Right here. Right now.
Not the past.
Not the future.
The present.
Right here. Right now.

She pulled him even closer so that the tip of his hardness pressed into her. He urged her legs apart and buried himself inside her with a deep thrust.

As his own moan escaped his lips, his gaze was locked on hers. He slid his hands beneath her bottom, helping her match his moves in and out of her body until they both exploded together.

He held her close, both of them clinging to each other as the aftershocks of their lovemaking gradually faded. As they lay there together, sweaty and spent, Jake was still reveling in the smoothness of her skin, the passion in her eyes, the way they'd fit together so perfectly… She took his breath away. What they had right now was damn near perfect. And if it weren't for the fact that it scared him to death, he might've felt like he'd come home.

Had Hal been right? Had she been in love with Jake all along but just hadn't realized it?

Because Anna had never felt fireworks the likes of which she'd just experienced with Jake.

Her body still thrummed.

She lay with Jake in her bed for what seemed like hours, lost in the rhythm of his breathing. He was sleeping on his stomach with one arm thrown protectively over her middle, sacked out, sound asleep. Anna lay there frozen, the realization of what had just happened taking on gargantuan proportions in her brain.

Now what?

Looking back, she knew they'd been on a trajectory for what had happened tonight ever since Jake had come to San Antonio to rescue her. He'd packed her up, moved her back to Celebration. Now they'd crossed that line and she feared her worst nightmare might be waiting to jump out at her with dawn's first glimmer: that everything would be different now between Jake and her. That Hal had been right all along.

Had he somehow hit on something to which Anna had been so clueless? Or worse, had she simply been in denial all these years? She'd always prided herself on knowing herself—who she was, what she wanted and how to get it. She'd always known what was *real*.

How was it that she was here with Jake, feeling this dichotomy of emotions? She wanted to be here, there was no doubt about that. But *should* she be here? That was the question that turned everything on its axis.

She shifted her body so she could turn her head to the right and look at him as he slept. Jake's face was inches from hers. He was sleeping soundly, the sleep of the innocent, as if he didn't have a care in the world. Based on the pleasant look on his features, he might open his eyes and smile at her and tell her this thing that had happened between them was good. Hell, it wasn't just good; it was great. They were great together.

But one other thing Anna knew about herself was that she was a realist. She never kidded herself about important matters. She may have been the last to know about Hal's affair, but once she'd learned the truth—saw the proof in black-and-white in front of her eyes on that computer screen—not once had she tried to pretend it was anything else other than what it was: betrayal.

So, now, as she lay here watching this beautiful man—this man who was her best friend, this man who was *Jake*—sleep with his arm thrown over her middle, she knew she couldn't ignore the truth: life as they'd known it had just irreparably changed.

A swarm of butterflies unfurled in her stomach, but she wasn't sure what she was supposed to do about them.

It took Jake a couple of seconds to remember where he was when he opened his eyes. He rolled over onto his elbow and saw Anna. He was with her. In her bed. She was sleeping peacefully beside him.

And it all came back to him.

He'd fallen asleep, but he wasn't sure how long he'd been out.

He glanced around the room and located a digital alarm clock that glowed cobalt blue in the darkness.

Five minutes until four. In the morning.

Awareness of her sleep-warmed, naked body so close woke every one of his senses. He fought the urge to move closer, pull her to him and make love to her again. God, how he wanted to, but—

God, if he didn't know what was good for him—or maybe he should focus on how bad it would be for him…for *them*—he'd give in to this weakness and stay right here next to her.

But he couldn't.

He should leave now before the sun came up and he and Anna were forced into saying awkward good-mornings and goodbyes. He gently eased himself off the bed, moving slowly so as not to wake her. He gathered his clothes and went out to the hall bathroom where he dressed.

When he stepped back out into the hall, he saw Anna clad in a robe and framed in her bedroom doorway.

"Where are you going?" Her voice sounded small.

"I was going home."

"You don't have to leave." His arm settled around her middle again and he nuzzled his nose into her neck.

"Anna... I have to go."

Oh, hell. This was the awkward moment he'd dreaded.

"Are you okay?"

"Yes. Fine. Great, I mean."

Liar.

"Jake? Were you just going to leave without waking me?"

"Why would I wake you?" He knew she had to work in a few hours. She might have a hard time falling back asleep.

The look on her face was equal parts horror and disbelief. Obviously, he hadn't given the right answer. Crap.

"No regrets, right?"

That's what they'd promised each other. Now he wondered if in the heat of the moment she'd meant it, but now she was having second thoughts.

He cared about her.

He thought those protective feelings would edge out any possibility of regret. Kissing her had certainly erased the word *regret* from his vocabulary. Now, not only was the word back, but it seemed to be swimming in his blood. Yet he had no choice but to keep his word or risk ruining everything. In the moment, he'd had no idea that it would be so difficult to have *no regrets*.

She just stood there, blinking at him with sleepy eyes, clutching the lapels of her robe. She looked as if she wanted to shove the word *regret* up his left nostril.

"I didn't wake you because I know you're on the schedule tomorrow—er, later today—and think about how everyone will talk if you show up looking sleep-deprived."

She was still doing that frown-squint thing.

"I guess they wouldn't necessarily know I'd spent the night with you," he said.

He was trying to be funny. But somehow his words were making it worse. They sounded like excuses… that were full of regret. But for a fraction of a second, a traitorous part of him wanted to take her back to bed and show her the meaning of "no regrets."

Instead, he raked his hand through his hair as he stared toward the door.

Regret, the bastard, wasn't so easy for him to ignore either.

Standing there watching Jake walk toward the door, Anna felt very naked and exposed, and not just in the physical sense. But now was a heck of a time to worry about that, wasn't it?

Don't make this any weirder than it has to be.

Don't look back, only forward. Because if you're not going to let this one night of indiscretion ruin a perfectly good friendship, you're going to have to leave it in the past.

As she watched him walk away, she tried not to wonder if he'd ever spent the entire night with Miss Texas. How in the world could she have left without her underwear? And why did it feel as if she were the one doing the walk of shame?

"Will you at least let me make you some coffee?" she asked. "It will only take a few seconds."

He turned back to her, his hand on the front doorknob. "No. Thanks, though. You should go back to bed and get a little more sleep before work."

Sleep? Was he serious?

She glanced around her living room to keep from looking at him. Anywhere but him. Funny, how her own house could look both familiar and foreign at the same time. Would everything look different now that this had happened?

"I intend to," she said. But suddenly she was tired of tiptoeing around the crux of the matter. "Jake. We don't have to talk about this now, but we both know this shouldn't have happened. What were we thinking? No, just—"

She gave her head a little shake and held up her hand to indicate she didn't want him to answer that. Not right now.

She found the courage to hold his gaze, wanting to make sure he understood the gist of what she meant.

He nodded. "I need to go. Let's talk later. After we're both rested and thinking with clearer heads."

Her heart lurched madly, but then it settled into a still ache beneath her breastbone.

He already had the front door open, but he stopped in the threshold and turned around. She wasn't prepared for the pain she saw in his blue eyes.

"Anna, it's still me. We are still us. Let's not let anything change that, okay?"

That's exactly the point.

Jake was still Jake—the man who grew tired of lovers after a few months.

They were still them—chums who should've left well enough alone, keeping relations firmly in the friend zone.

When he stepped outside, he lingered on the porch and Anna moved to the door, unsure about whether she should give him a goodbye hug as she always used to do…or a kiss?

No, definitely not a kiss.

And apparently not a hug either, since he was already making his way down the stairs. The reality of this mess made her heart hurt.

Trying not to think about it, she gazed out the front door at her neighborhood bathed in the inky predawn. She didn't see it like this very often: still and peaceful, and, besides Jake, not a soul in sight.

Across the street, there was a basketball hoop on a stand. It stood like a sentry along the side of the driveway. In the manicured yard of the house to the right of that, kids' toys lay lifeless and untouched. In the distance, someone had left a porch light on. As Jake walked to his car, Anna inhaled a deep breath and smelled the scent of late-night laundry that lingered in the air. Fabric softener perfumed the muggy summertime air.

This was her life, not Jake's. Mr. Don't-Fence-Me-In would be an anomaly in this cozy, family-oriented neighborhood. He didn't want a wife to tie him down or kids who would complicate his bachelor lifestyle. He didn't even own his own house because he was still convinced that he would be leaving Celebration for bigger and better things in the future. Even if he got the chief hospitalist position, it didn't mean he would stay. In fact, he could parlay it into a better position elsewhere.

If Anna fell in love with him, she was doomed. He would never marry her and that meant—well, that meant he could break her heart. She'd been there, done that. She'd let Hal break her heart. She wasn't opening herself up to that kind of hurt again.

So that was that. End of story.

They'd made a mistake. Now it was time to salvage what was left.

They both just needed some space.

The car chirped and she could hear the locks disengage. The sound seemed to echo in the still of the night.

Before he got into the car, he repeated, "No regrets, right?"

"I know, Jake. Good night."

Chapter Nine

In less than twelve hours, Jake's life had gone to hell.

First, the news about Bob Gibson's death and then the ridiculous stunt with Anna. Word of Bob's death had come as such a shock—he'd looked fine last week. Sure, maybe he was moving a little slower than he had in the past, but everyone slowed down. How could it be that a person was on this earth and seemingly fine one minute and then the next minute…they were gone?

He'd turned to Anna for comfort. Because sometimes—most of the time—she felt like the only thing in his life that was real and solid and true. Now, he might have screwed that up, too.

He knew he'd been playing with fire when they'd kissed the first time. Then, not only had he kissed her again, but he'd ended up in her bed.

Three strikes and you're out.

But just as with the first time they'd kissed, attraction seemed to take over. When the magnet of her pulled at the steel in him, resisting seemed futile—for both of them.

Man up. When have you ever not been in control?

Maybe that's what scared him the most.

When had this change in the chemistry between them happened? Growing up, they'd edged close to that line once, but they'd decided right away that they made more sense as friends. Then they'd each gone away to separate colleges and it always seemed like one or the other of them was involved. Then Anna met Hal, married him and moved away. That had seemingly sealed their fate—even if they hadn't been consciously aware of it. After all, they'd been away from each other for the past ten years—four years of college and six years that encompassed Anna's marriage, separation and eventual divorce.

Now that she was free and back in Celebration, she was the same Anna he'd loved his whole life. Yet even thinking about the platonic *love* he'd had for her his whole life, everything had felt different in the weeks that she'd been back.

For a crazy split second, Jake wondered if he'd dodged long-lasting commitment with the women he'd dated because he'd been waiting for Anna. But the thought was ridiculous. How could he have been waiting for her when she was already married?

He shook off the absurd notion.

Thoughts like that were pinging around in his head,

keeping Jake awake long after he'd gotten home. He'd lain there in his cold, empty bed, tossing and turning, feeling the phantom touch of her on his skin, smelling her and alternating between mentally flogging himself for jeopardizing his relationship with the most important person in his life and trying to digest the reality of Bob's death.

His mentor was gone. Anna was upset.

And rightfully so. What the hell was wrong with him?

If anyone else had tried to take advantage of Anna that way, they would've had hell to pay. Jake would've made sure.

After tossing and turning for what seemed like hours, he'd showered, made a pot of coffee and dragged himself out to the dock for some fresh air. As the sun overtook the lifeless, gray sky, bringing it to life in a blaze of variegated splendor, the lake shone like pieces of a broken mirror reflecting his misery back at him.

So, what now? He still hadn't found the answers he was seeking. Everything was still as messed up and disjointed as it had been since he'd walked out the door of Anna's house this morning. She deserved more than he could offer, more than one night as friends with benefits. Because even if he wanted to try to give her more, he just couldn't trust himself for the long haul.

He'd been a product of a broken marriage. He'd been led through his parents' maze of lies—his mother leaving, but shouldering all the blame, his father turning out to not be the man Jake had thought he had been all those years. Hell, for his entire life.

Marriage had taken something good and drained all the life out of it. Even though it might've seemed as if he were copping out on Anna by taking this stance, she would thank him in the long run. She still believed in happily-ever-after and he'd damn sure see that she got nothing less.

He would make things right between them.

Somehow he would make things right.

Judging from where the sun was sitting in the eastern sky, it had to be well after eight o'clock. He needed to quit brooding and get up and do something constructive with his Sunday. Since Anna was working today, he'd see if she was free for dinner tonight. Then he'd check on flights back to New Orleans for Bob's funeral.

As he walked from the dock through the yard, he surveyed the evidence of last night's party: the canopy was still up, tables and chairs needed to be put away and there were still a few stray beer bottles. Not that he was complaining; he was grateful that someone had stepped in and done the majority of the cleanup...while he'd been with Anna.

And damn if she hadn't fit perfectly in his arms.

At that moment he hadn't given a rat's ass about anything else. She was the one person in the world who'd always been there for him—even across the miles and years, during the time they'd been apart. She'd never let him down.

Now, he had a sinking feeling he'd let her down in the worst way. He needed to talk to her and make sure she was okay. Because he wouldn't be okay until he knew she was.

Jake grabbed a couple of empty bottles that were in his path and threw them into the recycling bin that sat just outside the back door. He'd clean up the rest later, but now, he needed to talk to Anna.

He let himself in the back door of his house and found his phone on the kitchen counter. He started to text her, but he thought a voice mail might be better. Texts were so impersonal. Meaning and intention could get lost or misconstrued.

He clicked over to his phone's keypad and dialed Anna's number. He didn't expect her to pick up since she was working, and he was in the middle of composing a message when Anna answered.

"Jake?"

It took him a beat or two, but he pulled his thoughts together.

Keep it light. Keep it upbeat.

"Hey, stranger. I was calling to leave you a message, but I'm glad you picked up. What do you say to dinner tonight? I'll cook for us."

There was a pause on the line that stretched on a little longer than it should've.

"That sounds great, but I can't tonight. I'm busy. Besides, you don't owe me a consolation dinner, Jake. Really, you don't."

He leaned his hip against the kitchen counter, trying to decide if she was joking. He detected a hint of truth in her words.

Busy? As in a date?

Despite how badly he wanted to know, he wasn't about to ask her.

"What a coincidence, because I hadn't planned one single bite of consolation on tonight's menu. How about a rain check?"

She laughed and he was so relieved to hear that sound he closed his eyes for a moment to savor it.

"Yes, of course. That would be great. But, hey, I'm going for a run this afternoon after I get home from work." Her voice was soft and she sounded a little vulnerable. "You can join me if you want. Unless you're busy."

"You just turned down my invite to dinner. Of course I'm not busy.

"We can run and then I'll fix dinner for us. Consolation-free, you have my word," he said. "How can you say no?"

She was quiet for longer than she should've been and that made Jake uncomfortable.

"Oh, come on, Anna. Don't make me come to the hospital to do the Sadness Intervention Dance. Because I will. It will be humiliating as hell, but I will march right up there to the third floor and dance in front of the nurses' station. Then you'll get to explain it to Patty and Marissa."

"Look, I really do have plans later this evening, but come run with me. We need to talk. Meet me downtown in the park at four o'clock."

"By the gazebo?"

"Perfect. But I have to go now. I'll see you later."

He exhaled a breath he hadn't realized he'd been holding. This was definitely a step in the right direction. All he needed was the chance to make it right, and this boded well.

He'd taken some orange juice out of the refrigerator and was pouring it into a glass when his phone rang again.

Grabbing it with his free hand and still pouring with the other, he glanced at the caller ID, but it came up *number unknown*. Sometimes calls from the hospital registered like that. Since he wasn't on call this weekend, he wondered if it might not be Anna calling back from a landline to say she'd changed her mind about running this afternoon.

He pressed the talk button and held the receiver up to his ear. "You'd better not be calling to beg off."

Silence stretched over the line. After a moment, he almost hung up because it seemed as if no one was there.

"Yes, good morning. I'm trying to reach Jake Lennox." The voice was male, decidedly not Anna's.

"This is he," Jake said.

"Hello, Jake. It's Roger James. I hope I'm not calling too early."

Roger was Jake's landlord. The man and his wife lived in Florida. Since Jake paid his rent on time, he rarely heard from the home owner.

"Good morning, Roger. How are you?"

The two men made small talk for a few minutes—about Jake's career, about Roger and his wife June's plans to travel in the years ahead.

"Which brings me to my reason for calling," Roger said. "June and I are excited about our cruise and one of the things we're most excited about is streamlining our responsibilities. We wanted you to be the first to know that we're planning on putting the house you're living in on the market. Since you've been such a great tenant for so long, we wanted to offer you first right of refusal. Are you interested in buying the house? Since you've lived there for so long, seems like you might be ready to make that commitment now."

The park was crowded for a Sunday afternoon. Jake passed joggers and mothers pushing small children in strollers as he made his way across the grassy area to meet Anna. The weather was perfect, one of those cloudless robin's-egg-blue-sky days that should've had him feeling a lot better than he was when he finally spied Anna near the gazebo.

She was dressed in running shorts and a pink tank top that hugged those curves that were so fresh in his memory. Her hair was knotted up on top of her head and her long legs looked lean, strong and tanned as she did her prerun warm-ups.

He remembered how those legs felt wrapped around him and his body responded.

"Anna," he said, falling into sync with her as she performed lateral lunges to warm up her glutes. He did his best not to think about her glutes, and especially tried not to think about how his hands had been all over them as he pulled her body into his.

"Hey." She virtually pulsed with tension. Was that anxiety tightening her lips? He ached to touch her and had this mad vision of kissing her until she relaxed, but he knew that would only make things worse. So he kept a respectful distance. And tried his best not to think about her glutes.

"How was work?" he asked.

"Good," she said, going into the next sequence of stretches. Her movements were sharp and fast. Normally, she would've waited for him to start, maybe even stopped stretching to talk to him for a couple of minutes, but today she didn't.

And she was giving him one-word answers. Had he missed something here? Was she mad at him?

"Thanks for making time to get together," he said, immediately hating how he sounded so stiff and formal. For God's sake, this wasn't a business meeting. No, it was much more important. Thirty years of friendship was hanging in the balance here.

I mean, come on. We need to talk about this.

"Not a problem," she shrugged.

This was ridiculous.

"What's wrong?" he asked.

"Nothing," she said. "Just a long day…after a night rather short on sleep."

"If it makes you feel any better, I didn't get much sleep either."

"Why would that make me feel better?"

"Look, can we talk about this, please?"

"Jake, really, what is there to talk about?" she said.

He attempted a smile, but it didn't quite make it. As she brushed a strand of hair off her forehead, he saw her hand was trembling.

"Anna," he said. "Talk to me."

She took a deep breath. "Things got a little intense

last night." She shook her head. "You were vulnerable and I was so determined to help you feel better. I'm always trying to get you to open up." She lifted her shoulder, let it fall. "I guess I pushed it a little too far last night. Because you still won't let me in. I mean, there's the physical, and then there's letting me *in*."

She put her hand on her heart.

Jake shrugged, unsure what to say.

"Are you upset because I didn't spend the whole night with you?"

Apparently that was the wrong response, because she pinned him with a look that was almost a sneer, then turned away without answering.

"I wish letting you in were that simple. I mean, I'm not purposely keeping you at arm's length."

"Obviously not." She sat on the bench that was behind her and retied her shoe.

"Okay, so maybe we did get a little carried away last night. But when all is said and done, you don't want me, Anna. I'm not the man for you. You deserve so much more than I can give you."

"You already said that, Jake. I told you I disagree."

Wait. What was she saying? Did she think he was the man for her?

She turned and with a quick jerk of her head, she motioned for them to start their run.

Hell, he should've known this was going to happen. He was such an idiot.

"You said what we did, what happened between you and me, mattered to you, too. It does matter. I can't be *that girl*, Jake. The one who has casual sex with you and then goes out with someone else the next night."

"Anna, I know that—"

"Just, please let me talk," she said. Her voice was barely a whisper.

Jake went silent, waiting patiently, watching her.

Emotions seemed to be getting the best of her. Jake reached over and took her hand, but she pulled away, balled her hand into a fist and quickened her pace.

"Talk to me," he said softly. "It's me, Anna. It's still me."

"That's exactly what you said last night, and you're right—you are still *you*. I'd never expect you to change. You don't want to get married. Jake, I want a family someday. I know you don't. But I can't be your friend with benefits, hanging around and pretending we want the same thing."

"You may have noticed that I'm not the most experienced…woman in the world. I haven't been with a lot of men."

"Notice? Of course I didn't notice. You were great. Everything last night was great, except today you're upset and that kind of ruins everything."

She stopped running and stood there looking at him.

"You're only my second lover, Jake." She stared down at their hands. He was glad because he couldn't bear seeing the hurt in her eyes. He would never purposely hurt her for anything in the world. Not even for the best sex of his life— and what had happened between them last night was paramount.

If Hal had been her only other lover, she was a natural.

Or, Jake thought, maybe he and Anna were *that* good together.

God, he had to stop thinking like that. He'd caused her enough pain.

"You haven't had a lot of experience. It's not a big deal." He wanted to tell her that last night had taken him to places he'd never been, but he was afraid that would sound as if he wanted them to do it again. He wanted to. Damn, how he wanted to—he wanted to pull her into his arms right now and show her how much he wanted her and how good they were together—but then what?

All he had to do was look into her gorgeous blue eyes and he could see the hurt. He couldn't lead her down a dead-end path.

"You were married and faithful and that didn't give you a lot of opportunity for experience." *And some things simply came naturally.* "Plus, it's taken a while for you to get back on the dating path."

The dating path?

"Is that what this is?" she said dully. "The first step on the dating path?"

Her heart sank. She resumed jogging, hoping her inner anguish wasn't showing through in her eyes. Jake picked up the pace alongside her.

Of course this was the *dating path*. That's why Jake was fixing her up with his friends. If he was interested, he would've kept her for himself. He would've stayed the entire night rather than bolting like a stallion that had discovered a break in the fence.

After all, hadn't he told her before they'd crossed that line that he was still the same old Jake? He was who he was. She realized now what he probably meant was that making love wouldn't change him. It wasn't supposed to change anything. She'd promised him there would be no regrets and here she was on the verge of falling apart.

Get a hold of yourself, Anna.

Get a grip, girl.

Their relationship had been built on a solid foundation of friendship. She couldn't dig up that foundation now and replace it with a glass house. Because that's where a friends-with-benefits relationship would live, in a glass house that was likely to shatter as soon as one of them decided to slam the door.

In a split second that she saw the shattering glass in her mind's eye, she realized that even though she was sad, she needed to get a hold of herself and turn this around.

She had two choices: mope and lose, or cope and move on.

It wasn't hard to choose.

"You're right," she said. "It has taken me a while to get back on the dating path. I'm so glad you're okay with what happened between us and you won't let it change anything. No regrets, right? So, we're good, right?"

A look of relief washed over Jake's face and he reached out and squeezed her hand, holding it tighter than he should've. "That's exactly what I was hoping you would say."

Of course it was.

"Anna, you are amazing."

Of course she was. And if she told herself that, she might start to believe it. Because despite the cool-friend thing happening on the outside, on the inside the message that was echoing was, *He doesn't want you.* How had this gone so wrong? How had she not kept herself firmly planted in reality?

Somehow, she'd miscalculated. Somehow she'd misread the signs. She'd been turned on; he'd been vulnerable after the news about Bob. She'd been there, an easy refuge to temporarily unload his sorrows.

She imagined she could still feel the weight of his body on hers, feel the way he moved inside her.

"Okay, I'm glad we got that settled." Her voice was brisk. "I should get going, really."

"Anna? Are you okay?"

She was so pathetic that she thought for a moment she saw a flicker of worry flash in his eyes.

Well, Jake, you can't have it both ways.

But then it hit her; maybe it wasn't worry as much as it was pity.

Had it really come to this?

No. She wouldn't let it.

Jake Lennox might not be able to love her the way she wanted him to. But if it was the last thing she did, she'd make darn sure he didn't pity her.

"Of course. I told you. I'm fine. We're fine. No regrets."

She forced a smile, despite the fact that all she could think about was escaping to her house only a few blocks away. If she could get away from him and inside, she'd be okay.

"You don't look fine."

She conjured another smile. This one felt too big. "I told you I'm fine." *Liar, liar, pants on fire.* "I'm glad we're fine. But really, I need to go. I'm sure we both have things to do."

She knew she was smiling a little too widely and a very tiny part of her that she didn't want to acknowledge hoped Jake would see that she was so not okay, that she was drowning in it, actually. She'd fallen backward down a black hole that negated everything she wanted, and all that was left was this Cheshire cat smile and this need to run. God, she had to get out of there. Get somewhere she could think and make everything inside her feel right again. Because if she didn't, nothing in her world would be right.

Jake looked just as uncertain as she felt.

"Can I share something before we leave?"

Anna nodded.

"My landlord, Roger James, called me this morning. He's putting the house on the market. He gave me first right of refusal. What do you think about that?"

"What *I* think doesn't really matter," she said. "What do you think? Are you going to buy it? Plant roots?"

He shrugged and offered her a smile that wasn't really a smile.

"Who knows? Though I guess I need to figure it out pretty soon. Roger needs an answer soon. I've spent a lot of good years in that house. I've got my boat and a place to dock it. Where would everyone spend the Fourth of July?"

His smile was wistful.

"So what's the problem?" Anna asked. She hadn't meant to sound like such a witch.

"I haven't bought the place because I never intended to stay in Celebration. Not this long. But here I am. All these years have gone by...what am I doing?"

Anna felt her insides go soft. He was hurting and maybe she was being too hard on him. He'd lost a good friend, his home was being sold and last night they'd managed to jumble the only thing that made sense in either of their lives. She needed to cut him some slack, even if her own heart was breaking.

"Why are you always so hard on yourself? Look at all you've done. Not only do you have a good job, but you're in line for a promotion at the hospital. You're a valuable part of this community and you have friends who adore you."

She stopped short of saying, "And you have more women after you than you know what to do with." Clearly, he knew what to do with women.

"It's unexpected. I guess I just need some time to think about it. Buying a house is a big step."

"Maybe if you're eighteen."

Jake winced.

God, shut up, Anna. If you can't say something nice, don't say anything at all.

She bit her bottom lip to keep another snarky-sounding comment from slipping out.

"You're right. I'm thirty-four years old. I guess symbolically...buying this house feels like..." His voice trailed off and she gave him a couple of beats for him to finish the sentence, but he didn't.

So, she finished it for him. "Commitment?"

His eyes got large, like she'd just uttered the name "Bloody Mary" three times or spouted some other unmentionable.

"Touché," he finally answered.

Way to go, Anna. You made your point. Are you happy now?

She needed to leave so she could get herself together. Taking snipes at him, *especially* when he was clearly feeling bad about everything, wouldn't do anyone any good.

Besides, she'd been steering them toward her car, which was along the side of the park. Now they were there.

"Well, this is me," she said, pointing to her yellow VW Beetle. "I need to go. I have to be somewhere."

She clicked the key fob and heard the locks tumble. As if she didn't feel like enough of a heel for the way she was acting, Jake reached out and opened the car door for her. Why did he have to be nice when she was trying so hard to hate him right now?

Well, not *hate*. That wasn't the right word. She could never hate him.

In fact, what she was trying to feel was exactly the opposite…she was desperately trying not to fall in love with Jake Lennox.

"Thank you," she murmured as she slid behind the wheel.

He closed the door and she rolled down the window.

"I'm sure they don't need an answer tonight," she said. "Take some time to think about it. But, Jake, try not to overthink it. Just go with your gut."

He reached through the window and put his hand on her arm, snagging her gaze.

"You're right," he said. "I think we both need to stop overthinking things."

She watched him walk away. Damn him for being such a fine, fine man. And not just on the outside, but also inside.

She sat in the car for what felt like ages, long after Jake had disappeared from her line of sight, alternately feeling like an ogre and perfectly justified for pushing him away. This was exactly why friends didn't cross that line. It rendered things awkward and confusing. Despite how they'd promised each other that it would change nothing—that there would be no regrets—it had changed *everything*.

She needed to talk to someone who could help her put things into perspective.

She took her phone out of her glove box and texted her sister.

Need to talk to you.

Call me? Emily responded.

I'd rather talk in person.

Everything okay?

Anna didn't want to open the conversation over text. So, she answered with the only word that seemed to fit without going into detail.

Meh.

Is this about a guy?

Emily was so good at reading her.

Maybe.

I thought so. What are you waiting for? Get over here.

On my way.

Emily lived in an apartment just north of downtown. Anna arrived there in less than ten minutes and that was only because she hit every red light between the park and her sister's place.

When Emily answered the door she handed Anna a steaming mug of Earl Grey. Normally, Anna would've preferred iced water on a day like today, but hot tea was the sisters' ritual—just like she and Jake had the Sadness Intervention Dance.

Had was the operative word.

Anna's heart hurt at the thought of it. When they made each other sad, who was supposed to intervene with the dance now?

"Thanks, Em," she said as she accepted the mug and stepped inside. "What smells so good?"

"I'm baking cookies for tonight, but I think we need to do a taste test. There's oatmeal and chocolate chip."

"At least your apartment smells good. I'm sorry I don't. I just finished my run and wanted to come over before I went home to change to go to Mom and Dad's tonight."

"You don't smell bad, but just to be safe I'll hold my breath when I hug you."

Emily wrapped her arms around her sister. Anna was careful to not spill the tea. Then Emily took her sister's hand and pulled her toward her tiny kitchen. When Anna stepped inside, she could see a plate of deliciousness waiting for her atop her sister's glass-top café table.

"You're an angel, Em. This is exactly what I need."

Emily squinted at her sister, the concern obvious on her face. "What's going on?"

They sat down. Anna placed her cell phone on the table and took a sip of tea. It was supposed to fortify her, but instead it burned her tongue.

"I slept with Jake." As she blurted the confession, she set down the mug a little too hard. The table rattled and tea sloshed over the rim. Anna grabbed her phone to save it from the tea tidal wave and braced herself for her sister to call her a bull in a china closet or something equally as snarky. But when she looked up, Emily was staring at her wide-eyed and slack-jawed. She stumbled over her words for a moment, sputtering and spitting sounds that didn't form a coherent sentence.

"Oh! Uh. Well. Hmm. Ummm... Wow!"

Emily popped up and grabbed a paper towel and wiped up the spill with quick, efficient swipes. By the time she'd disposed of the soaked paper and returned to the table, she seemed to have collected herself. She smoothed her denim skirt and reclaimed her place at the table.

"I like that blouse on you," Anna said, suddenly feeling the need to backpedal. "You look good in magenta. I can't wear that color."

"Don't change the subject," Emily said. She gave her head a quick shake and a smile broke out over her pretty face. "This is the best thing I've heard in…maybe ever. Did I call it or what?"

"Stop gloating. It's not like that."

"Not like *what*?"

"It's not like however you're imagining it. Because if you knew how it really was, you wouldn't be smiling."

Emily's hand flew to her mouth. "No! Oh, no. Is Jake bad in bed?"

Anna squeezed her eyes shut for a moment, trying to block out the memory of exactly how far from the truth that was.

"No… Jake is actually quite good."

Emily's mouth formed a perfect O and her eyes sparkled. "*Ooh!* Do tell."

God, she couldn't believe she was talking about this. Even if it was Emily. She didn't kiss and tell…well, actually, with Hal there hadn't been much to talk about. So…

"Tell me everything," Emily insisted.

"I'm not going to give you a blow by blow—"

Emily snorted. She *actually* snorted.

Anna cringed when she realized her unfortunate choice of words. She couldn't help but think how gleeful Joe Gardner would've been if he'd heard that pun. He probably would've bowed down in reverence.

Anna frowned at her sister. "Are you thirteen years old? Get your mind out of the gutter."

"Well, this is a conversation about sex and according to you, it was mind-blowing. I'm not seeing the problem here."

Ah, the problem. Right.

Anna took a deep breath and, using very broad terms, she brought her sister up to date on the situation.

"I will not allow this to degenerate into a friends-with-benefits pseudo-relationship. But I'm so attracted to him, sometimes I can't seem to help myself. I knew exactly what I was doing last night, and I knew exactly how I would feel afterward, but I did it anyway. And I'm afraid I might do it again if I get the chance."

"Wow" was all that Emily could offer.

Anna plucked a chocolate chip cookie off the plate. It was still warm and gooey. Sort of like her resolve with Jake—unless she turned into the superwitch she'd been at the park.

"I'm mad at myself, but I'm taking it out on him. I mean, I know he feels bad because I'm acting like this and his good friend just died, and now *this*. What is wrong with me, Em? Was Hal right? Could he see all along that I was attracted to Jake? You saw something. Am I as much to blame for the breakup of my marriage as Hal was?"

And now she was babbling—because this wasn't about Hal. It was about Jake and her and how everything was now upside down.

"Don't be ridiculous," Emily said. "You weren't the one who cheated. I'm sorry to bring that up. But it's true. How can you be guilty of feelings you never knew you had. I mean…unless these feelings aren't new?"

"No! I promise you, this is as big a surprise to me as it is to you. Come on, this is *Jake*."

"Well, sis, I hate to break it to you, but Jake is pretty darn sexy."

"Tell me about it." Anna raked both hands through her hair and stared up at the ceiling.

"I am not going to play a game of 'Don't. Stop. Don't. Stop.' I just need to know how to get things back to where they were before. How do I do that, Em?"

The refrigerator motor hummed and, overhead, one of the fluorescent lightbulbs blinked a couple of times.

Emily sipped her tea, looking thoughtful. "First, if you're sure this relationship isn't good for you, you can't sleep with him again."

"I know that," Anna said. "I wish I could promise you I won't do it again."

"Hey, don't promise me. That's all on you. Personally, I think you two would make the perfect couple."

"Emily, stop. Jake and I want different things. He doesn't want to get married. He definitely doesn't want kids. I hate to admit this, but I'm not getting any younger. I do want kids. I never thought I'd be one of those women lamenting her biological clock. But here I am."

"God, you two would have gorgeous children."

"Emily. Have you heard a word I said?"

"Of course I have. But it's true."

Anna *tsk*ed. "*Really?* Are you going to torture me after I turned to you for help?"

Anna resumed her tea-gazing, and Emily reached out across the table and took her sister's hand.

"Even though it's my prerogative as your younger sister, I won't tease you. The next time you're alone with him, if you're afraid you're going to be tempted, text me an SOS and I'll come and rescue you."

"Actually, that's not a bad idea," Anna said. "The only thing is, unless I fix things with him, it's a moot point. I was so mean to him this afternoon, I'm ashamed of myself. I wouldn't blame him if he didn't want to talk to me. I don't even like me after the way I acted."

"Then that's all the more reason you need to talk to him," Emily said.

Anna grimaced.

"Don't be such a baby," Emily said. "Based on what you said, he was trying to meet you halfway this afternoon and you were a total B. You need to reach out and make this right. Tell him exactly what you told me. Except for the part about being in love with him."

Anna jerked ramrod straight in her chair. "I did *not* say that."

Emily tilted her head and smiled. "You didn't have to, sweetie. It's written all over you. You're oozing *Jake love* out of your pores."

Feeling her cheeks burn, Anna buried her face in her hands. "Am I that obvious?"

Emily nodded. "Sorry, hon, just calling it as I see it."

"Then I definitely can't…"

"You can't what?" Emily's voice sounded impatient in that way that only a sister could get away with.

"I can't call him. I certainly can't see him."

"So you're just going to let him walk away? You're essentially going to set a match to a thirty-year friendship and watch it burn? Is that what you want?"

"No." Even though the word came out as a whisper, Anna nearly choked on it.

"Then call him, for heaven's sake." With a manicured finger, Emily slid Anna's phone across the table. Anna recoiled and fisted her hands in her lap as if the cell would burn her if she touched it. "The longer you put it off, the more difficult it's going to be."

"I don't know what to say."

"Invite him to dinner tonight. You know Mom and Dad would love to see him. And Mom always cooks enough for fifteen. Think about it. A family dinner will take both of you back to your roots. How many times did he have Sunday dinner with us when we were kids? He was like a part of the family."

Hence the problem. Only he certainly didn't feel like a brother. Anna wondered if he ever had. She sighed. "Funny you mention it. I'd intended to invite him before everything got so weird."

"Then do it." Emily stood, pushing back her chair with the bend of her knees. The wrought iron scraped a mournful plea on the tiled kitchen floor. She picked up Anna's phone and handed it to her. "I'm going to go put in a load of laundry."

In other words, her sister was going to give her some privacy.

Once Emily cleared the room and before Anna could overthink it, she opened her phone address book to the contacts that were saved as favorites—all six of them—and pressed the button to call Jake's phone.

He picked up on the third ring.

"Hey, Jake, how about dinner tonight with the Adams family?"

Chapter Ten

"Jake, honey, it's so good to see you," said Judy Adams. "It's been far too long."

"Thanks for letting me come to dinner tonight," he said, offering Anna's mom a smile.

"You have a standing invitation. Please don't wait for that daughter of mine to invite you."

Judy gave Anna a pointed look and Jake smiled at the way she blushed.

"Thank you," he said. "I appreciate that."

"Would you care for more lasagna?" Judy offered. "Hand your plate to Norm and he can dish it up for you."

"It's delicious, but I'm stuffed. In fact, everything was fabulous."

"I'm sorry we couldn't make it to the party yesterday," Norm said. "We'd promised my folks that we would take them to see the fireworks over in Plano. Now that they are in the retirement community, we have to get over there every chance we get."

Jake nodded. That was the thing about the Adams family; they seem to have longevity in their genes... and in relationships. Both sets of Anna's grandparents were still alive and together. This move to the retirement community for Norm's folks was a new turn of events. Earlier, Judy had mentioned that her parents were on a cruise around the world.

The Adamses' world was different from—in fact, it was polar opposite to—the one he'd grown up in. While the Adamses had always been generous to include him, more often than not he'd felt like an outsider looking in. That was all on him, though. It was nothing they'd done. They'd always been as warm and welcoming as they were this evening.

Jake glanced at Anna, who had been quiet for most of the dinner, allowing her sister to entertain with tales of crazy customers at the restaurant and a few sidebars about customer woes at the bank. As he listened to her talk, he wondered why his brother Luke had never shown an interest in Emily. The woman made no secret about her affinity for him. No doubt Luke had his reasons, and far be it from Jake to interfere.

Anna caught him staring at her. She gave him a shy smile and turned her attention back to the lasagna that she'd been pushing around on her plate. He'd been so glad to get her call. After the way they'd left things earlier in the park, he wasn't sure what to do next. He would've figured it out, because there was no way he was going to let this indiscretion come between them. He was simply going to give Anna some room until she was able to realize that, yeah, they may have feelings for each other—and there was nothing more that he wanted than to have her in his bed every night—but he wasn't the man for her.

The only conclusion he'd come to was he would make the ultimate sacrifice by putting a lid on his feelings for her to make sure that, eventually, she ended up with a man who deserved her.

They'd arrived at Judy and Norman Adams's place in separate cars. So they hadn't had a chance to talk. Yet here they sat in the same dining room, at the same table, in the same places that they'd occupied on all those Sundays all those years ago.

Judy and Norman each sat at each end of the table; Jake and Anna sat to Judy's right, Emily across the table from them. The dining room still had the same traditional feel and furniture set—a large table in the center of the room, a sideboard and china cabinet on opposite walls, blue-and-white wallpaper depicting old-fashioned scenes of men and women courting on benches and under trees. What did they call it? Tool or toile—something like that. It didn't matter.

What was important was that despite how everything had changed between him and Anna, there was still that connection, that lifeline that kept them from drowning. Sharing a meal with the Adamses felt as if they'd stepped back in time nearly a decade and a half. Suddenly, what he needed to do was as clear as the crystal goblet on the table.

He was going to let bygones be bygones and fix her up with Dylan Tyler. The guy had asked about Anna several times since he'd seen her at the jazz festival. Jake had had his trepidations about fixing up the two of them—if he was honest with himself, the feelings probably stemmed from his being afraid that Anna and Dylan might actually be a good fit. Not that he thought the dates he'd arranged for her wouldn't work, but it just took a few go-rounds to realize who would work—who would be the best person for her.

Jake mulled it over as he helped clear the table. That was one thing about the Adamses; they all pitched in and it made him feel even more like family when Judy and Norm didn't excuse him from doing his part—even after all these years.

During cleanup, he and Anna made small talk and, to the untrained eye, nobody probably realized anything was different. God, he hoped not. All he had to do to set himself straight was think of looking Norman Adams in the eye and telling him that he'd had a one-night stand with his daughter.

Yeah, that put everything into perspective.

When they finished washing the dishes, he said to Anna, "Want to take a walk around the old neighborhood?"

The unspoken message was "It's time we talked about this." He could tell by the look on her face she understood and that she was ready to talk.

Outside, twilight was settling over the old neighborhood. Fingers of golden light poked through the branches of the laurel oaks and the sun had painted the western sky with broad strokes of pink, orange and dusky blue.

It was always bittersweet coming and going from the Adams house. Because the house he'd grown up in was right next door. After leaving for college, Jake had only been back for Christmas and to visit his dad occasionally when he wasn't taking classes over the summer. When his dad had married Peggy—two years after Jake's mom had died—the house had gone from feeling discombobulated to cold and unwelcoming. Peggy, who was only twelve years older than Jake, had no interest in being a mother to Karen Lennox's children. The moment she moved in, it was apparent that the countdown clock had begun for when she could get the four boys out of *her* house and out from under the obligation of caring for them. At the time, Jake didn't realize what she was doing—even worse, he didn't realize that his father was allowing this woman to push his sons out of their own home. But that was because his father had always played the victim, making his wife out to be the villain who had walked out on her own family.

As Jake and Anna stepped out onto the sidewalk, Jake tried not to look too hard at the house next door to the Adams family. It looked cold and haunted and only dredged up the worst memories. As far as Jake knew, Peggy still lived there. He and his brothers hadn't had contact with her since the day of his father's funeral, when somehow Peggy had managed to let all four Lennox brothers know that she and their father had been together a lot longer than they had realized. They'd started seeing each other the year *before* his mother had left the family.

That was when everything had clicked into place. His mom hadn't just randomly left the family as his dad had led them to believe. She'd left because her husband was involved with another woman, and just a few days later she died in that accident, unable to defend herself or let her voice be heard—that she fully intended to come back for them once she was able to get herself established. Even though Jake had no hard evidence of this, he felt it down to his bones. It was so out of character for his mother to abandon her home and the children she adored. She had probably been flummoxed by the realization that the man she'd trusted with her heart was in love—or under the spell of—another woman.

The only good thing Peggy had ever done for Jake and his brothers was to tell them the truth, which had vindicated their mother. Of course, it had also revealed their father for the weak, henpecked, poor excuse of a man that he really was—letting Peggy dictate the fate of his family, turning a blind eye and simply going along for the ride because it was the path of least resistance.

If Jake had had trepidation about marriage and family before his father's death, Peggy's revelation was the wax that sealed the deal. Jake would never let himself be that influenced by a woman. After living with Peggy for years and seeing what she'd done to their father and family, Jake vowed never to let a woman render him weak like that.

As he turned his back on his childhood home and walked with Anna in the other direction, a warm evening breeze tempered the fierce July heat, making it almost pleasant to be outside. Still, Jake felt the heat of apprehension prickle the back of his neck because of what he was about to do. He just needed to figure out how to say it. He could go all corny and sentimental opening with the old saying, "If you love something, set it free." But that was a little dramatic. So he opted for taking the more direct route. But before he could find the words, Anna spoke.

"You might have wondered why I asked you here tonight."

He smiled because that was a line from some corny black-and-white television show that they'd been obsessed with one summer a long time ago.

"Actually, I think I have a pretty good idea. Anna—"

"No, let me go first. Please?"

He nodded. "Okay."

"I owe you an apology for how I acted this afternoon... and this morning."

"You don't have to apologize."

"Yes, I do. Because you don't deserve to be treated that way. No wonder you're afraid of commitment if women turn into needy, beastly creatures. Or am I the only one who acts like that? I'm so bad at this."

"Stop," Jake said. "You aren't being unreasonable. Don't ever compromise what's important to you. Okay?"

She nodded.

"Funny, how you and I had a better time with each other than any of the blind dates we've been on," Jake said after they'd cleared the Adamses' white colonial-style home. "But I've thought a lot about what you said, and you're right. You're not the kind of woman who sleeps with one guy and dates others."

Realizing that this preamble might sound as if he was going in a completely different direction than what he meant, he quickly added, "I would love to be with you, Anna. In fact, if I could create the perfect woman for me she would be someone just like you—"

"Only someone who didn't want the ultimate commitment, right?"

"I know that sounds ridiculous. Anyone of your caliber deserves everything she wants. I'm sorry, but I don't see myself ever getting married. That means no kids, which is probably a good thing, because if I got married and had a family, I'd probably screw up worse than my parents did."

Anna shook her head. "Are you really going to let your parents' mistakes steal the happiness of family from you? Isn't that just adding to tragedy on top of tragedy?"

"This is where you and I differ. We have completely different takes on what constitutes happiness. Family and happiness are not synonymous in my book."

"What about your brothers? You guys are pretty close. How can you say they don't bring you happiness?"

He thought about it for a moment. "My relationship with my brothers is so different it's hard to explain. Of course, I wouldn't trade them for anything in the world, but that relationship doesn't do anything to convince me that marriage is the right path for me. It's completely different. Anna, you have to remember that growing up I was more of a caregiver to my brothers, a parent rather than a sibling."

He was starting to feel hemmed in, cornered, having to defend himself. And that feeling made him want to run. But he couldn't. He and Anna needed to work through this. He had things to say to her, and he wasn't going to leave until those things were said and they were okay.

As he tried to cool his jets and regroup his thoughts, the question of what he might be capable of that would be worse than cheating and vilifying a dead spouse—the way his father had—niggled at the back of his brain. Of course, he didn't make a habit of lying and cheating. That's why he broke up with women when the relationship had run its course.

He glanced at Anna as they turned the corner off their childhood street. He did have a modicum of self-control. Except when it came to Anna, apparently. But Anna wanted both marriage and kids. As much as he wanted her—needed her—it wouldn't be fair to lead her down a dead-end path.

"There's still the bet," she said, sounding more like her old self. "Now that we've had a couple of warm-up rounds and we know the kinds of people who aren't right for us, maybe we should regroup and get going on that again. I'm going to win, you know."

Yes, thank you, that was his Anna. Her spirit had returned. Or at least she was trying. If he was completely truthful with himself, he wasn't convinced that Anna's too-broad smile was completely sincere. It called to mind those people who believed projecting the emotion that they wanted to feel would make it a reality—or something like that. But this was a start in the right direction.

"No, you're not. Because there's someone I want to fix you up with."

She groaned. "Who?"

"What do you think of Dylan Tyler?"

"The new doctor who works at Celebration Memorial?"

"The one and only."

"Dylan Tyler... Since the first time I heard his name, I wanted to ask, is he a good Southern boy with a double first name, or is that his first and last?"

"Very funny," Jake said.

Anna gave a one-shoulder shrug. "I don't know. He's handsome. I guess. I've not had the chance to get to know him."

"Now's your chance. I have it on very good authority that he would love to ask you out."

There was that too-wide smile again. It didn't match the dullness in her eyes.

"Oh. Goody."

"Wow. Your enthusiasm is overwhelming. Could you tone it down a bit?"

Anna shrugged again. "I don't know. You know how I feel about dating doctors. Do you think it's a good idea, since we work together? I mean, you saw how rumors flew when people thought you and I were..."

The same pink that had colored her cheeks earlier in the dining room was back. He knew exactly what she was thinking, and damned if his body didn't respond.

The primal, completely base part of his brain kicked in. God, if he didn't have good sense, he'd pull her into his arms right now and remind himself how much he wanted her.

But sparks faded and then you were left with real life.

What had happened between them was a cautionary tale, and if he really cared about her, he wouldn't lead her on.

Dylan Tyler called Anna the following day and asked her to be his date to the Holbrook wedding.

And she'd said yes.

Really, it wasn't as daunting as it seemed at face value. Given the circumstance, there would automatically be a barrier between them. The daughter of Celebration Memorial Hospital's CEO was getting married. Everyone would be on their best behavior.

Not that she expected Dylan to bring anything less.

This date felt safe. Like going to prom with the friend of a friend...even though her prom had happened more years ago than she cared to admit.

Tick...tick...tick...

Darn that biological clock.

Jake would be there.

Now she just needed to remind him that he'd agreed to ask Cassie Davis to be his date, and make sure he didn't revert to his old ways and ask someone like Miss Texas.

She hadn't given it much thought since they'd been otherwise occupied...with him being away at the conference...and them planning the Fourth of July party…and, well, everything else. But they needed to get back to their original plan. It was the only way to get their friendship back on track.

She jabbed the up button and tried to ignore the cold, hollow emptiness in the place where her heart should be. As she stood there, she tried not to think about how Jake had said his perfect woman would be someone like her. If she didn't know that he meant well and didn't believe that he would never purposely hurt her, she might think he was playing her.

Someone just like her, but not her.

Was that supposed to be a consolation prize? Because it sort of felt like a slap in the face.

She gave herself a mental shake.

Come on, Anna. You know the rules. It would be fruitless to try and change them.

Anna adjusted her grip on her insulated lunch bag, which contained a turkey sandwich on whole wheat with lettuce and tomato, an apple and some carrots. She had to go light since she had no idea whether or not she could fit into the cocktail dress she was going to wear to the wedding. It had been so long since she'd had a fancy occasion to wear it, she wasn't sure how it would fit. When she and Hal were married, it seemed as if there was something or another every other night, but the dates Jake had arranged had been informal and the dresses she'd purchased for them had been casual and not suitable for a wedding.

Funny, she hadn't missed the stuffy occasions at all. She didn't mind getting dressed up, but the so-called friends who really weren't friends at all… She didn't even want to give them a second thought. She hoped Hal's girlfriend was better suited to inane cocktail chitchat than she was.

You know what? On second thought, no. She didn't hope she was better at it. She hoped the woman was twice as miserable as she had been and that the so-called friends made it even harder on the girlfriend than they had on her.

Wow. That sounded really bitter.

She didn't want to be that way. Really, she didn't. But after all she'd been through, couldn't she simply get a break?

A little voice inside of her told her that maybe Dylan was her break. Or at least a step in the right direction. He was a good-looking guy. Light brown hair with sun-streaks that looked natural. They'd better be. She refused to date a man who spent more money on his hair than she did. And if they were natural, at least that meant that he liked to spend time outside. That was one thing they'd have in common, besides working for Celebration Memorial.

Anna wasn't prepared to list the fact that they were coworkers in the pros column just yet. In fact, she was very nervous about it. At least he worked on the second floor and rarely, if ever, got up to the third floor, which was why she hadn't had a chance to get to know him.

But Jake had handpicked Dylan for her. That had to mean something, didn't it? Especially given the delicate nature of their own relationship right now.

She decided she owed it to herself to approach it with an open mind. She'd given Jake the advice that "if you keep doing what you do, you'll keep getting what you get." Maybe she needed to borrow a page from her own book.

The elevator chimed and Anna waited for the people who'd ridden down to step out. Then she got in and pushed the button for the third floor. As the doors were closing, she heard a woman call, "Hold the elevator, please?"

With a quick jab of her finger, Anna managed to reopen the doors before the car lifted off.

As if fate had conjured her, Cassie Davis rushed inside, uttering a breathless "thank you so much. You know how slow these elevators are. If you hadn't waited for me, I'd be late. As it is I'm cutting it close."

"No problem," Anna said. "I'm glad I could help."

She was glad they weren't clock watchers up on three. Then again, she was usually early or right on time like she was today, but she understood how missing the elevator could cost you a solid five minutes, and it always happened at the most inopportune times.

"I guess I could've taken the stairs," Cassie said. "But given how my morning has started, I probably would've fallen on my face. I just hate being late."

"Me, too," Anna said, studying the woman with her pretty peaches-and-cream complexion, blue eyes and auburn hair. Yes, she would remind Jake that he'd agreed to take Cassie to the wedding. Cassie was perfect for him. Maybe even a little too perfect, but she couldn't think about that right now.

The elevator dinged to signal its arrival at the second floor.

"Cassie, I don't mean to be nosy, but are you dating anyone?"

The woman did a double take as she started to exit the elevator. Anna jabbed the door open button again to give Cassie time to answer.

"No. I'm not. Why do you ask?"

If it was possible to be simultaneously happy and disappointed, that was how Anna felt hearing the news. But of course she wasn't involved with anyone. She'd been practically drooling over Jake that day Anna had filled in on the second floor.

"Because I have someone I want to fix you up with."

Cassie smiled. "Oh? Do I know this person?"

"You do. It's Dr. Lennox. Are you interested?"

Cassie's jaw dropped for a moment. "Absolutely."

"Good. He's going to call you soon. Today probably. Can he find your number in the hospital personnel directory?"

"Yes."

"Good." She looked so happy and Anna tried to convince herself it was a good thing. It *was* a good thing. Jake would have an appropriate date for the wedding and Anna would…just have to be okay with that. At least she got to pick his date.

When the door started to close, Cassie reached out and stopped it. "I need to ask you a question, though." Her brows were knit. "I thought you and Dr. Lennox were involved."

Anna mustered her best smile. "Jake and I are good friends. He's like a brother to me."

Cassie looked even more confused. "Oh. Okay…?"

"I need to run. Neither of us wants to be late."

Anna waved and Cassie pulled her hand away. As the doors closed, she looked as if she were trying to decide whether Anna was playing a practical joke on her. Anna knew that because that was what she would've been wondering if the tables were turned.

Poor Cassie.

Actually, no. Not poor Cassie. Lucky Cassie.

Just don't fall in love, she wanted to warn Cassie.

The elevator chugged slowly up to the third floor and when the doors finally opened on the maternity ward, Anna's heart skipped a beat when she saw Jake standing at the nurses' station. His back was to her. But she'd recognize those shoulders anywhere.

She drew in a deep breath to steady herself.

"I didn't know you were pregnant," she said as she approached, trying to use humor to cover her own nerves. He turned around at the sound of her voice.

He ran a hand over his flat stomach. "Oh, am I showing?"

Anna laughed as she reached over the counter that defined the nurses' station and set her lunch bag, keys and phone on the desk.

"What are you doing up here in baby-land, Dr. Lennox? Are you lost?"

She spied the personnel directory, looked up Cassie Davis and wrote her name and phone number on a piece of note paper that was next to the computer.

"I just happened to be in the neighborhood."

"Is that so? Well, then, you are lost. Walk with me and I'll help you find your way."

Good grief, if there were a ship called *The Mixed Messenger*, Jake would've been the captain, because one minute he was making love to her, and the next he was fixing her up on a blind date. Before the fireworks on the Fourth of July, she wouldn't have thought twice about him dropping by like this...for no reason. Now she just needed to put what had happened out of her mind and remember how things used to be.

"Will you cover for me for a few minutes?" Anna asked Patty and Marissa.

"Sure thing," Patty said, looking up from the patient charts she'd been pretending to be engrossed in.

Anna could feel her coworkers watching her and Jake as they walked toward the elevator bank where they would have the most privacy, at least for the five minutes that it took the elevator to chug its way up to the third floor.

"Did Dylan call you?" he asked once they were out of earshot.

"He did."

"Good. And you two have a date?"

"We do. And so do you."

"No I don't."

"I'm fixing you up with Cassie Davis."

"I'm going out of town tomorrow. I'm going back to New Orleans for Bob's funeral."

"I'm sorry. I'm glad you're able to go, though."

The stress showed around his eyes. There was a tightness in his lips and in the way he held himself that had Anna wanting to give him a shoulder massage... and offer other means of stress relief—that she couldn't even believe she was thinking about, given where crossing that line had gotten them.

She blinked away the thought and held out the piece of paper with Cassie's number.

"Here, take this. She can be your date to the wedding this weekend. You will be back in time for the wedding, right?"

Jake nodded, but he looked as if he were about ready to balk at her suggestion to call Cassie. Anna preempted his protest.

"Look, you're the one who agreed to let me find you a date for the occasion. Cassie is nice. And appropriate. The chief knows her and will instantly realize that you have good taste in women. Besides, it's not like you have a lot of suitable options."

He took the paper and shoved it in his lab coat pocket.

"I know you have a lot of your mind, but will you call her before you leave for New Orleans?"

Jake shrugged, obviously not very enthusiastic about the date.

"I don't know that I really even need a date. I can just go to the ceremony and give my congratulations. It's not as if a date is mandatory."

"Yes, it is mandatory. You and I have a bet going on. If I'm going with Dylan, then you have to go with Cassie."

Technically, she knew he didn't have to do anything he didn't want to do. For that matter, he didn't have to go to the wedding either. But it was in his best interest to do so. And so was bringing a date like Cassie.

"You told me that you'd do anything to get things

back to normal between us. Taking Cassie to the Holbrook wedding will go a long way toward that end."

He shot her an incredulous look and she knew that he knew that she was making this up as she went along. But there was some substance to it. Because maybe if she saw him with another woman—a woman who was good for him, who might possess whatever it was that she lacked to change his mind about commitment—maybe they could get back to being just friends.

But what if he really fell for Cassie?

Didn't it always happen that way? A man swore he'd never get married, until the right woman came along and turned his entire belief system on its head. Whether or not Cassie was that woman, Anna hoped that seeing him with someone else would shock her own system enough to stop her from falling in love with Jake.

Because it seemed no matter how she tried to put on the brakes, her heart just kept careening toward disaster.

Chapter Eleven

Jake hated funerals.

Not that anyone loved them, but he'd developed a particular aversion since attending his mother's all those years ago.

Funerals weren't for the dead; they were for the living, a means to say goodbye, or maybe it was more apt to say that they were a reality check to make you aware that everyone's clock was ticking, that every day that you were fortunate enough to wake up and see the sun rise, you were also one day closer to death.

Funerals were a stark reminder to stop putting off the things you wanted to do and to handle everyone you loved with care, because death spared no one—it was the one thing that all humans had in common, Jake mused as he stood in sober contemplation and looked around.

The turnout at Bob Gibson's service was overwhelming. Standing room only.

Jake's plane had been delayed. By the time he'd arrived in the church and squeezed in among the latecomers standing along the back wall, one of Bob's sons, who looked to be about Jake's age, was already giving the eulogy.

"There are so many things in life that are uncertain, but love—unconditional love—is one of the few things you can invest in and get a return that far exceeds the outlay. My parents' marriage—the example they set—always had a profound effect on my life."

Lucky guy.

"Love isn't easy. In fact, by nature, it's complicated and messy, but without it, what do we have? A career? A fancy car? A big house? But what does it all mean without someone to share it?"

Jake's shirt collar was beginning to feel a little tight. He reached up and loosened his tie. The sun was streaming in through the stained-glass windows and the effect gave the sanctuary an otherworldly feel. A large portrait of Bob sat on an easel in front of the podium from which his son spoke. The way one shard of light hit the frame, it seemed to cast a halo over Bob's image.

Jake shifted his weight from one foot to the other, alternately looking at Bob's son, who looked a lot like him, and his friend's photo.

"I'm sure Mom won't mind me sharing that there were times in their marriage when the obstacles seemed nearly insurmountable, when both of them, in turn, had to sacrifice what each wanted for the other. But they always put each other's wants and needs ahead of their own. My parents rode out the storm when it got tough. My dad always told me you don't give up on the people who matter."

During Jake's internship, Bob had been more of a father figure to him than his own dad. Jake recalled a couple of times when Bob had to exercise some tough love, calling him on his own BS and giving him a reality check when he got too full of himself. Even though Jake didn't believe it at the time, it was now clear that his mentor's high expectations were one of the driving forces that saw him through the challenging years of becoming a doctor.

You don't give up on the people who matter.

How many times had Bob said that to him? More important, how many times had he demonstrated it?

The last time he saw Bob, they'd talked about marriage and family. Bob had seemed perplexed when Jake had told him he had no plans to get married. In fact, he'd urged him not to close his mind. And much like what his son was saying today, he'd warned Jake of the shallow trappings of succees. And also, he'd advised him to not let his career consume him because the body aged and success was a fickle mistress who didn't offer a whole lot of warmth in your golden years.

What does it all mean without someone to share it?

As the choir began singing "Amazing Grace," Bob's son returned to the church pew. He sat between his mother and a younger woman, who Jake guessed was his wife. He put an arm around each of them. Something in that protective gesture—or maybe it was the picture of his mentor bathed in that holy light—evoked a feeling that was strange and foreign.

Just last week Bob had been so alive. And now he was gone.

Something shifted inside Jake.

Feeling a little light-headed, he tugged at his collar again. It was just the heat—and possibly the prospect of ending up alone...or even worse, dying without allowing himself to love.

The rest of the week went by in a blur. Even though he'd only taken off one day, Thursday, flying to New Orleans and back on the same day, he just couldn't seem to get everything back in sync when he got to work on Friday.

To compound matters, he also realized on Friday morning he hadn't called Cassie to ask her to the wedding. He only remembered when she said hello to him as he passed the second-floor nurses' station.

He was surprised that Anna hadn't been on his case about it. But what was almost more disconcerting was when he realized how little he'd seen of her this week.

He paused in front of Cassie, not quite sure what to say, uncertain if it would be insulting to ask her to a big event the day before it happened or—"Hi, Cassie."

It was one of those rare moments when they were the only two at what was usually a hub of activity.

He figured he might as well ask. She could always say no and call him a cad for waiting until the last minute. If he ended up going to the wedding stag, at least he could tell Anna that he'd tried.

Cassie was cute, he supposed. Auburn hair—similar to Anna's—with large, sparkling blue eyes that seemed to light up when he stopped in front of her. He hated to admit it, but even though they worked on the same floor, he'd never really noticed her unless she spoke first. Not that he meant to be rude or disrespectful, but he was usually so focused on patients and their charts that sometimes he navigated the hospital on autopilot.

"Hey, so," he said, stumbling over his words, "I'm sorry this is such late notice. I meant to ask you earlier. Actually, I meant to call you, but I— Anna gave me your number. You know Anna Adams, right?"

Cassie smiled at him enthusiastically as she bobbed her head. "Right, she mentioned that she would like to give you my number."

Wait. Should he be doing this here? The hospital didn't have a no-fraternizing policy. So officially, he wasn't breaking a rule. But something just didn't feel right.

"I'd love to get together sometime," Cassie offered, seeming to sense his hesitation.

"Good. Are you free tomorrow night? Stan Holbrook's daughter is getting married and I, uh, RSVP'd for a plus-one."

Wow, that sounded enticing.

But it didn't seem to dull Cassie's shine. "That sounds lovely."

She jotted something on a piece of paper and handed it to him. "This is my address. I wrote my phone number down in case you need it. What time should I be ready?"

* * *

The next day, Jake had picked Cassie up at five-thirty for the six-thirty wedding. Even though she looked lovely, he couldn't seem to take his eyes off Anna, whom he'd picked out in the crowd in the hotel ballroom. She was with Dylan, of course. They were sitting two rows ahead of where he and Cassie were seated. Upon seeing them together, Jake instantly regretted setting them up.

What was wrong with him? He couldn't stand the thought of being tied down, but he hated the thought of her with someone else. The thought of Dylan possibly putting his hands on her the way he had the night they were together had him fisting his hands in his lap as they waited for the bridesmaids to finish parading down the aisle.

Cassie reached out and touched his hand. "You okay?"

Jake relaxed his hands. "Yeah," he whispered. "Fine."

Of course, that was the moment Anna made eye contact with him and smiled.

"She looks beautiful, doesn't she?" Cassie said.

Was he that obvious? Apparently so, since most of the guests were turned in their seats watching the bridal party parade, but Jake was facing forward, staring at Anna.

He was relieved when Stan Holbrook and his daughter finally appeared and everyone stood up and gave the bride their attention. Even Cassie stopped asking him questions and stood silently as the bride floated by.

What had happened to him over this past month since Anna had been back? She was Anna, through and through, but she was different, too. Or at least he was different.

In the good old days, the one thing Jake disliked almost as much as a funeral was a wedding, but tonight as he listened to this man and woman that he didn't even know exchange their vows and promise to love and honor and cherish each other until death did them part, something similar to what he'd experienced at Bob's funeral stirred inside him again.

What does it all mean without someone to share it?

Jake wished he knew the answer to the question, because it seemed as if it held the key to eternal happiness... or a life sentence without it.

After the ceremony was over, he lost sight of Anna as the guests filed out of the ballroom into another lavishly decorated room that was twice the size of the first.

A server with a tray of champagne stopped in front of them.

"Would you like something to drink?" Jake asked.

"Yes, thank you."

When he only took one flute off the tray, Cassie asked, "Don't you like champagne?"

"Oh, I forgot to mention I'm on call tonight. So I can't drink. It's your lucky night. I'm your designated driver."

Cassie lifted her glass to Jake and sipped the golden liquid.

It was in that moment of brief silence that Jake spied Anna and Dylan across the room. They were just entering the ballroom. Dylan had his hand on the small of Anna's back, causing the same possessive force that had driven Jake to fist his hands to consume him again.

"When did Anna start dating Dr. Tyler?" Cassie asked.

"They're not dating." Jake realized his tone might have been a little brusque.

"Well, that's good for you. Isn't it?"

"Why would you say that?"

Cassie cocked her head to the side and smiled up at him. "It's pretty obvious that you have a thing for her."

Oh, hell.

"So, is it that obvious?"

"Pretty much," she said with a sweet smile.

Out of respect, Jake did his best to avoid looking at Anna—since he was that obvious. One of the great things about Cassie Davis was that she was exceedingly easy to talk to. She was great at making conversation. As the various courses of the dinner were served, they not only made lively conversation with the other guests at their table—some of whom they knew from the hospital—but they also talked to each other about neutral subjects, like recent happenings at the hospital and the food they were served for dinner, such as the merits of the steak versus the salmon. She was funny and quick-witted and quite enjoyable, but there was absolutely zero chemistry between them.

Cassie was the kind of woman who would be fun to hang out with, but she was definitely 100 percent in the friend zone, and he had a feeling the feeling was mutual. She shared a lot of the same qualities that he found so attractive in Anna—they were both nurses, they both had a similarly unpretentious way about them that cut through the nonsense and went straight to the heart of the matter. Cassie was also fun to dance with when the music started and an all-around nice person, but that was as far as it went.

As the night went on, it became clear that Anna was either otherwise occupied or avoiding him, too. Because other than the smile that they exchanged before the ceremony, they hadn't had any contact.

And then the unthinkable happened. The wedding band decided to change things up. The singer said, "This one is by special request." The band broke into the first strains of "Don't Worry, Be Happy."

Immediately, his gaze snagged Anna's across the ballroom. He wasn't so sure it was an appropriate request to make at a wedding, but he was glad Anna had done it. Of all the icebreakers—well, aside from taking Cassie to the wedding at Anna's insistence—Jake hadn't been able to think of any that would get them back to the other side of the line that they had crossed. It had actually started to feel like a futile battle—a one-man war with himself.

What does it all mean without someone to share it? Don't worry. Be happy.

Cassie must've noticed, because she said, "Go ask her to dance. You can't ignore her all night. Good grief, I think I need to be your romance coach. And I mean that in the most platonic way possible, just in case there was any question. But somehow I don't think so. Go dance with her and then I need to think about leaving. I have to be at work early tomorrow."

* * *

"I can't believe you requested this song," Anna said once she was on the dance floor with Jake.

"Don't Worry, Be Happy" was one of those songs that was too slow to fast-dance to, but too fast to slow-dance to. So they did a modified version of the swing dance where Jake alternately sent her spinning out in turns and pulling her back in close.

"I didn't request it," he said as he reeled her back in and held her for a moment. "I thought you did."

Anna pulled back and looked at him. "Are you kidding? The guy in the band said someone requested it."

"I wish I had," Jake said. "Looks like fate intervened and requested for us."

"I guess so. How was New Orleans? I haven't had a chance to talk to you since you got back."

He looked so handsome in his suit and tie. The deep charcoal of the merino wool fabric echoed his dark hair and offset his blue eyes in a way that made her a little breathless. Good thing she could blame it on the dancing.

"It was a quick trip, and you know how I feel about funerals—"

"Yeah, the same way you feel about weddings."

He arched a brow and nodded solemnly. He really was taking Bob's death harder than she'd realized. She had the urge to pull him in close and hug him until all the anguish melted away.

But she knew better than that.

"Looks like you and Cassie are getting along well," Anna said.

This time when he reeled her in, he pulled her in close, slipped his right arm around her waist and held her left hand, guiding her to a slow sway. Her curves molded to the contours of his lean body, making her recall what had happened a week ago tonight.

"Cassie's a lot of fun," he said.

If Anna didn't know better, she might've thought the muddy feeling that washed over her was her heart sinking. But she was happy for her friend; really, she was. She wanted Jake to meet someone who could take his mind off all the ick that had happened lately. Someone who was just in it for the fun. He really was due for an upswing, and Cassie sounded perfect.

"Does that mean there's going to be a second date?"

He stared down into her eyes and she felt the connection all the way down to her soul.

"No, I don't think Cassie and I are suited to date. But we should definitely put her on the list to invite her to the Fourth of July party next year."

Oh. She knew she shouldn't read too much into that comment. He was just making conversation, not future plans. A lot could change in a year. He could meet the woman of his dreams. She could meet...someone.

"I'll make a point of adding her to the guest list."

She could feel the warmth of his hand on the small of her back, and for a moment she lost herself in the feel of it. Even though other people had joined them on the dance floor, for a moment it was just them. And it was so nice.

"So, how about you and Dr. Tyler? You are looking pretty cozy over there."

"Cozy? I wouldn't call it that. He's nice."

Jake's eyes widened. "You're perfect for each other. He's a great guy, Anna. Really, he is. I'm happy for you. I'm sensing that I'm getting closer to winning the bet?"

"You're getting a little ahead of yourself there, bucko. It's kind of hard to get to know a person at a function like this. It almost feels more like going through the motions with a rent-a-date—or maybe *arrange-a-date* is a better way to put it. In fact, maybe you should consider that before you write off Cassie. Keep an open mind."

Jake had a funny look on his face. Maybe he was considering Cassie in a different light.

"What are you thinking about?" she asked.

He was gazing at her so intensely, it was obvious that he wanted to say something—

"What, Jake?"

Their song ended and the band started a set of Southern rock 'n' roll, but Jake didn't move his hands and Anna stayed in his semi-embrace.

"Bob's funeral had a stronger impact on me than I realized. Life is short and there's no time to waste. It hit me like a train."

Wow. This was news. Where was he going with it?

She had to lean in closer because the music was so loud. She could smell his aftershave and that heady mix of sexy that was uniquely Jake. For a fleeting moment, she thought she could stay right here, breathing him in the rest of her life. But then there was a cold hand on her shoulder—a hand that wasn't Jake's—and it made her jump.

"Hey, guys," said Dylan. "Mind if I cut in and dance with my date, buddy?"

No. She wanted to hear what Jake had to say. But the moment was over, ruined. It was probably way too noisy to have that conversation now anyway.

"Sure thing, buddy," Jake said, stepping away from Anna and extending his hand for Dylan to shake. Dylan gave Jake's hand a hearty pump.

Ahh, the international man-sign for *I hear you, I see you; no harm, no foul.*

"Cassie and I need to leave anyhow. She has to work early in the morning and I'm on call. You know what it's like to be the only sober man at a rollicking party."

He winked at Anna.

"Hey," she said before he turned to walk away.

"But they haven't even cut the cake yet," she said.

"Have a piece for me, okay?"

Dylan put his hand on her shoulder, and she had to fight the urge to take a step away from him to reclaim her personal space.

"Call me later so you can finish telling me what you were saying about Bob's funeral. It sounds important."

There was that intense look again. It had her stomach flipping all over again.

"Okay," he said. "Don't you kids stay out too late. Anna, we will talk later."

Chapter Twelve

Anna was surprised when Jake's text came through. She didn't think he'd contact her since it was after ten o'clock, much less ask if he could come over.

Dylan had dropped her off about fifteen minutes ago and she was glad she hadn't immediately changed out of her cocktail dress and scrubbed her face free of makeup. All that she'd had time to do was kick off her shoes, take down her hair and brew herself a cup of tea.

After she'd texted Jake back, she remembered he was on call. So she added some water to the kettle so she could offer him a mug of something nonalcoholic when he arrived.

As she bobbed her own tea bag up and down, more for something to do with her nervous energy rather than to hurry up the tea, she couldn't help but wonder what was so urgent that he needed to talk to her tonight.

Unless he'd been worried about Dylan putting the heavy pressure on her and was dropping by to make sure she was in for the night, safe and sound. Dr. Tyler had tried to make a campaign for a nightcap, but Anna had nipped that in the bud right away. And to Dylan's credit, he hadn't pushed. Although he had told her he'd like to see her again. That was the part of dating that never got any easier—how did you let someone down easy and tell them you just weren't feeling it?

He was a great guy. Any woman in her right mind would be thrilled to spend an evening with him. He was good-looking—even if he wasn't her type. But why wasn't he? He was handsome, successful and funny. He didn't chew with his mouth open. Yet that indefinable je ne sais quoi was missing, and no matter how Anna tried to concentrate on the good, all she could think about was that she just wasn't that into him.

He wasn't Jake.

Damn you, Jake Lennox. Have you ruined me for all men?

If Anna could've slapped herself, she would've. She was sitting here pouting like a petulant child who was moping because she didn't get exactly what she wanted.

Buck up, buttercup. You don't always get what you want.

Sadly, she couldn't even convince herself that Dr. Tyler might be what she needed if she just gave it time.

No, what she needed was to be on her own for a while. This dating bet with Jake had started out as fun, but suddenly it had turned so serious. And that wasn't fun.

Or maybe what wasn't fun was the possibility of Jake changing his mind about Cassie. It had dawned on her that maybe he could tell how down she was at the wedding and didn't want to completely ruin her night with the confession that he actually was feeling it with Cassie.

Okay, now she was just assessing.

But just to be safe, maybe she should fix Cassie up with Dylan. They'd make a good couple.

Anna had gathered the flowers from the Fourth of July centerpieces and put them in a large vase, which sat in the middle of her kitchen table. The flowers caught her eye and took her back to that night one week ago. It hadn't been too much later than it was right now when things began to heat up with Jake.

Anna's heartbeat kicked up as she remembered the way he'd leaned in and kissed her on the dock, pulling her onto his lap and then coming back to her house to finish what he'd started.

Her breath hitched in her chest. What if that was why he was coming here tonight? He might not even realize that was what he was doing.

And that was exactly how things *just happened* between two people who knew better, who swore that they wouldn't fall into that friends-with-benefits trap. They started dropping in for late-night visits and—*Oh! Oops! Gosh, I didn't mean for that to happen…* And pretty soon they'd established a pattern of *Oh! Oops!*

Gosh! I promise it'll never happen again...after this one last time.

And damn her all to hell. She wasn't going to call him and tell him not to come over.

For a split second—actually, it was more like a good several minutes, a fantastic several minutes—she played out her own *Oh! Oops! Gosh!* production in her head.

What was she doing? The only thing that might be worse than having slept with Jake was to continue sleeping with Jake, knowing full good and well how he felt. He was her drug, and she needed to go cold turkey if she had any self-respect at all. Good grief, this wasn't only about that; it was about self-preservation.

She grabbed her phone and pulled up Emily's number. Before she could change her mind, she texted, SOS! It's urgent! Need you to come over now and save me.

She'd just pushed the send button when Jake knocked at the door.

So, he was still choosing to knock and wait, rather than doing their special knock and walking in the way he always had in the past. Then again, it was pretty late. She had locked her door behind Dylan, not that he would come walking in uninvited, but it just felt like an extra barrier between her and her date and the night.

And now Jake was here.

She padded to the door in her bare feet and looked out the peephole. There he was—all six foot four of him, with his perfect hair and perfect face and those perfect arms that had held her so close she didn't know where her body ended and his began.

Oh, dear God, Emily, please get here as soon as you can.

As she unlocked the dead bolt and pulled open the door, it dawned on her that she and Emily had never seriously talked about the SOS call. In fact, they'd sort of joked about it. Emily was probably working tonight. Of course she was on Saturday night.

Oh, crap.

Oh, well... Maybe she should ask for a sign from fate. Toss it up to the heavens. If she should sleep with Jake just one more time, Emily would *not* show up. If it was a bad idea, her sister would come to her rescue.

In the kitchen, the teakettle whistled, as if calling her on her BS.

I know, I'm a weak, weak woman. So shoot me.

Well, she would probably want to be put out of her misery if she let it happen again... But others had died for much less.

"Good evening, Dr. Lennox. Won't you come in?"

That was corny, she thought as she stepped back to allow him inside. Oh, well, that was what they did sometimes. That was why they were so darn good together—

But Jake wasn't moving. His feet were planted firmly on the front porch, and Anna was sobered by his stiff demeanor. He didn't look like a man who'd come to seduce a woman who would be oh-so-easy to take.

Oh, God! He's going to marry Cassie.

Anna actually took a step forward and looked out on the porch to see if maybe Cassie was waiting there to deliver the happy news with him. But no, he was alone.

"Are you going to come in? Or are you going to stand there and let the mosquitoes in?"

Jake flinched. "Sorry."

He moved inside like a man on autopilot—or maybe someone who wasn't feeling well.

She shut the door behind him and turned the lock. "Are you okay?"

"No, not really—" He made a face. "What's that noise?"

"Oh! It's the teakettle. I put on some water to make you a cup of tea since you're on call tonight."

Anna hurried back to the kitchen to stop the racket.

"What kind of tea would you like? I have English Breakfast, Earl Grey and peppermint. The peppermint is caffeine-free, but the bergamot in the Earl Grey supposedly has properties that will lift your spirits."

"I don't care," he called from the other room. "Whatever you have handy."

She glanced at her phone, which was lying on the kitchen counter, to see if Emily had responded. Nothing. Not a single word in response to her SOS.

Hmm. Okay, then.

They'd have a cup of tea—she opened a package of Earl Grey, just in case Jake needed the caffeine—and see where fate led them.

Anna carried the two mugs of tea into the family room, set them on the trunk that she used as her coffee table, and took a seat on the couch next to Jake, leaving just enough room to be respectable, but not enough room to send the keep-your-hands-off-me signal.

Careful, Anna...

Oh, shut up. Loosen up. Maybe Jake was right; maybe she needed to stop overthinking things.

"Is this about the house?" *Of course it wasn't. Although she was curious and it was a neutral subject.* "Have you made a decision about whether or not you're going to buy it? I love that house. I can't imagine you living anywhere else."

"Good, because Roger accepted my offer today."

"Jake, that's fabulous news. I'm so happy for you." She threw her arms around him and it felt so right. "And selfishly, I'm glad because that means you're staying put. Because I can't imagine being that far away from you again."

He pulled back slightly and looked at her. For a heart-rending moment, she couldn't read him.

God, had she said the wrong thing?

"I mean…since I just moved back. And all."

He was just frozen. Looking at her. She'd always known what he was thinking. Sometimes better than she'd known her own mind. But now…? Not so much.

"What's going on, Jake? I'm worried about you."

"Don't be," he said. "Or maybe you should be. Because I don't know what's happening to me. One minute, I was so sure where my life was going and what I wanted and what I didn't want. The next, everything was different. I just started seeing my life from a whole new perspective."

Uh-oh. Maybe this is about Cassie.

They had looked awfully cozy at the wedding, talking and laughing.

Oh, my God. He is here to break the news to me

gently. Of course, it wasn't as if Cassie was a complete stranger. Not even really a blind date. They worked together. He'd said it himself, he wanted someone like Anna, but not Anna… Jake was getting ready to settle back into another stretch of monogamy. Only it was with Cassie, and if anybody had the potential to move mountains and change his mind, she was the woman. And Anna had insisted they go out.

Oh, what have I done?

Jake scrubbed his face with his hands and gave his head a quick shake. "I'm sorry I came barging in here so late, and I start right in with what's on my mind and I didn't even ask you how things turned out with Dylan."

"That doesn't matter. I need to know what's going on with you."

Her heart was hammering so fast and loud that she was afraid he could hear it.

"Well, I can't say anything else until I know how everything went with Dylan. I need to know—are you going to see him again? It's important, Anna. Because whether or not you are could have a direct bearing on what I'm about to say."

Why? "What difference does it make?"

The look on Jake's face was so serious, she decided to quit playing games.

"He's fine. He's nice. I guess. A little possessive for my taste. Ha! I feel like I'm channeling you."

Then, the strangest thing happened. Jake was smiling at her in a way that made her lose her breath and she knew, she just knew that he was going to lean in and—

But at the sound of the front door opening, he flinched and diverted his lean toward his tea.

What?

Emily bounded into the room. "I got here as soon as I could."

Maybe it was because of Emily's abrupt entrance or maybe it was because she was giving him the look of death as she all but escorted him out, saying that she and Anna were having a girls' night and no guys were invited.

For the second time that night, Anna did not get to hear what Jake needed to tell her and seemed to be having so much trouble saying.

Damn her sister.

Damn that SOS text. Why had she been such a chicken, when in the end all she wanted to do was make love to Jake?

She'd followed him out to the porch, trying to ignore the fact that Emily was lurking in the living room. Anna had reached out and shut the door, putting a barrier between them and Emily.

"Jake? What were you going to say?"

Jake glanced back at the door and then at Anna. "Not now. Go back inside with Emily and I'll talk to you tomorrow."

Then his phone rang.

"It's the hospital. I need to take this. I'll talk to you later."

Rather than leaning in to kiss her, as she was so sure

he was going to do before Emily arrived, he picked up the call, saying good-night with a distracted wave.

She'd asked for a sign from fate and if this wasn't as clear as crystal, she didn't know what was. Still, all day Sunday, she waited for Jake to call as he'd said he would. She didn't want to call him since she wasn't sure how late he had been at the hospital dealing with the emergency.

Finally, at a quarter past two, she got a text. From Jake.

I know this is short notice, but are you busy tonight?

Defying common sense and her better judgment, Anna's heart leaped.

She didn't even wait a respectable amount of time to text him back. She grabbed her phone and typed, No plans, why?

Good. I've made arrangements for you to have one last date. I'm sure this guy is the one.

What? Was he kidding? He had nearly kissed her last night and now he was fixing her up on another blind date?

She typed, Sorry, I don't think so. I'm just not up for it.

How humiliating. Obviously, he was trying to pawn her off on someone to get her off his case.

She started typing again, Look, Jake, you don't need

to pair me up with someone to get me off your case. I get it. I understand.

As she hit Send on the second message, a message from Jake came through.

Please, just do this for me? This is the last date. I promise. I will never try to fix you up with anyone else again after tonight.

Oh, for the love of God. Was he really doing this?

She was about to type No and then turn off her phone. Instead, she opted for the path of least resistance.

I will meet him for a cup of coffee and that's it. And I'm driving myself. Then I'm off the hook. And just so you know, in case he doesn't want to waste his time, I'm giving him fifteen minutes max. And the clock will start the minute I walk in the door.

She probably sounded like a major B about it, but this hurt. And Jake was clueless. Or maybe he wasn't. Maybe he knew exactly what he was doing. If he'd come over last night to disengage, this date from out of the blue had completed the job for him.

A couple of moments later, Jake texted back, Actually, he has a seven o'clock reservation at Bistro St. Germaine. I guess you could have coffee in the bar. So, maybe get there a little early so they can give away the reservation if you really don't want to have dinner with him.

Really? Bistro St. Germaine?

She texted Emily, Are you working tonight?

But Emily didn't respond. She was probably tired of coming to her sister's rescue. Especially since, after Emily had scared Jake away last night, Anna hadn't been very gracious.

Anna had been in such a snit that Emily had opted for going home about half an hour later, once she knew that Jake was at the hospital and there was no risk of him coming back.

In fact, since he was going to such great lengths to pair her up with somebody—anybody, it seemed—it was pretty darn clear that there was no risk of him coming back at all.

It was just as well. She would give him space and maybe in a little while they could figure out how to be *them* again.

Even so, in that half hour last night, Anna had endured her sister's lecture of why she should avoid guys who didn't want to commit.

Hello? Wasn't that why she'd called in the first place? But she just let Emily say her piece.

It was just as well that her sister didn't return her text now.

To clear her head, Anna decided to go for a run. With each step, with each pounding of the pavement, she took out her frustrations and let off steam. Until she'd worn herself out, until she was so numb she felt nothing.

As she dragged herself back home, exhausted and emotionally spent, she vowed to take care of herself for a change. She'd spent so many years contorting and configuring her life to appease Hal, and in the time she'd been home, she'd let herself fall for another man who didn't want the same things she did—

She stopped herself.

Really, Jake hadn't done anything wrong. He hadn't lied or cheated. He may have led her on a bit, but she'd gone willingly, knowing what he wanted didn't align with what she wanted. So really, if anyone should shoulder the blame in that regard, it was Anna.

But that was where she was going to take care of herself.

She wasn't going to beat herself up.

Facts were facts: she and Jake were magnetically attracted to each other, but it simply wouldn't work.

End of story.

Around five-thirty, Anna freshened up, and prepared to make herself presentable. She washed her hair and blew it dry.

She kept her makeup very light, because she didn't wear much anyway.

Then she surveyed her closet and decided on a cute little shift with a bold blue and white print. It seemed brighter and happier than she felt.

The run had helped her let go of some of the sting of Jake's rejection-disguised-as-a-fix-up. It still hurt, but it had subsided to a dull ache. By that time, she'd decided she couldn't take it out on the guy who was meeting her tonight. Sure, she was only going to give him fifteen minutes, but she wasn't going to be rude or mean or vent her frustrations to him. After all, his only sin was that he wanted to meet her.

She would let him know that while she appreciated

his interest, this meeting had been a mistake. It wasn't a good time. She simply wasn't available right now. Not when her heart belonged to another.

A man who couldn't return her feelings.

When she got to Bistro St. Germaine, there was a space open on Main Street in front of the restaurant. It must have been her lucky day.

She glanced at her clock on her dashboard. Right on time. The sooner she went in, the sooner the meter would start ticking and the sooner she could leave. As she let herself out of the car and approached the restaurant, she rehearsed her preamble about bad timing and leaving early and being sorry to waste his time.

Wait. What was his name?

Oh, great. In the haze of her hurt and fury, she hadn't even asked Jake for the guy's name. He should've told her that up front. She thought about texting Jake to ask, but she really didn't want contact with him right now.

The way she felt right now was proof-positive that she needed distance. She didn't want to hate him. The only way she could stop that or any more damage from happening was to let her wounds heal. Right now, contact with Jake only tore them deeper.

She took a deep breath and squared her shoulders. She centered herself by reminding herself that the hapless, nameless man who should be waiting for her in the bar would not bear the brunt of her sorrow.

The floor-to-ceiling doors that opened onto the sidewalk in front of the bar were open. A few of the outside bistro tables were occupied, but nobody looked as if he might be waiting for a blind date. Anna circumvented the hostess stand, where Emily would be if she was indeed working tonight, and entered the bar via the open sidewalk doors.

The bar was virtually empty, save for a man and a woman making eyes at each other at a cozy corner table and four middle-aged women who occupied a four-top. Okay, so he wasn't an early bird. She pushed the button on her phone: six forty-six. Their reservation wasn't until seven. So technically she was early...as Jake had suggested.

What if her mystery date didn't show until seven?

So not only was it an inconvenience, it was awkward. *Now what?*

Anna turned in a circle for one more look to make sure she hadn't inadvertently missed him. She hadn't. Great.

She decided to sit at the bar and order a cup of tea—chamomile tea. She couldn't drink coffee because that was too much caffeine too late in the day, and she was already wound up as it was. She certainly didn't want to order a glass of wine because that would send the wrong message. When the guy arrived, she would simply tell him there had been a miscommunication and she had to leave at seven o'clock.

If she were thinking about Jake, she would want to strangle him. But she wasn't thinking about him. Nope, not at all. He was the furthest person from her mind.

The bartender had just brought her tea—she felt a little silly sitting at a bar drinking chamomile tea...but who cared? The bartender had just placed it in front of her when she heard Emily say, "Oh, my gosh, there you are. How did I not see you when you passed the hostess stand?"

That was an odd choice of words.

"How did you know I'd be here to even walk past the hostess stand?"

Emily opened her mouth to say something but then closed it quickly and glanced up at the ceiling, before she said, "I don't know what you're talking about. But I have something to show you, so come with me."

"What? No, Emily. I'm meeting somebody and, well, it's a long story, but this is not a good time. I just got my tea, and you know if I step away for even a second, my date will arrive."

"Hey, Porter," Emily said to the bartender, "watch my sister's tea for her, okay? If someone shows up looking for her, tell him she'll be right back."

Emily winked at him. She actually winked. But that wasn't the only thing that was odd. First of all, she hadn't said anything about Anna being on a date tonight after she'd had to come rescue her last night, and completely let slide the fact that Anna was drinking *chamomile tea* at a bar. God, the mileage she could've gotten out of that one.

Instead, she was all but pulling Anna off the bar stool and herding her toward the dining room.

Then the cherry on top of all the prior weirdness happened when Emily stopped suddenly and turned to her. "Look, don't be difficult tonight." She looked deadly serious. "Just go with this. Trust me, you'll thank me later."

"What?"

Emily gave an exasperated shake of her head and continued leading Anna out of the bar, across the entry and into the dining room.

What the heck was Anna supposed to say to a warning like that? When Emily got serious, which wasn't very often, she always meant business.

So what was going on?

Whatever it was, Anna decided to heed her sister's advice and just go with it.

Emily paused in front of the door to the private dining room. It was closed, but the room was partitioned by a wall with dark wood wainscoting on the bottom and leaded, beveled glass on top. The glass was fogged to give the diners privacy. Anna could see a flickering light coming from the other side, but she couldn't see who was inside.

The sudden frightening thought that the mystery man was somehow in cahoots with Jake—and had gotten her sister involved to trick her into having dinner—nearly had her hyperventilating.

Well, she wouldn't stay. He couldn't make her. And neither could Jake.

Fifteen-minute rules still applied, and she pulled out her phone, clicked the button and saw that the guy had exactly five minutes.

He can always take home a doggie bag. Give her meal to Jake, the louse. She'd made it perfectly clear she would only stay for fifteen minutes and then they'd agreed that Jake would never fix her up on a blind date again.

Would he really go to these lengths to win this absurd bet between them?

Anna didn't have time to ponder it because all of a sudden Emily threw her arms around her and said, "I am so happy for you."

Then she opened the door to the private dining room, grabbed her hand and tugged her inside.

It took a moment for Anna to register what was happening because the room was filled with red roses and candlelight and Jake was there and he was thanking her sister...for her help?

Then, after Emily left the room and shut the door behind her, he said, "God, you can be so difficult sometimes. I thought you weren't going to come."

"What are you doing? Jake, what's going on?"

They were the only two in the room. There was no mystery man and now Jake was reaching for her hand.

"I've tried twice now to tell you something important, but we keep getting interrupted. So, I figured I needed to go to drastic measures to get you alone.

"Anna, I'm your date. I'm the one. You're the one. That has become so clear to me since you've been back in Celebration. I guess sometimes it takes a lifetime to see that the love of your life has been right in front of you all along."

A peculiar humming began sounding in Anna's ears and her knees threatened to buckle beneath her. Was this really happening?

"I lost you once to a man who didn't deserve you, and I'd be an idiot to let you get away again."

Was he saying he wanted a *commitment*? *But Jake didn't, not the kind she needed.*

But maybe she needed to stop overthinking it. Stop making everything so blasted heavy and just go with it.

She loved him. She'd been in love with him her entire life. So what was the problem? Marriage hadn't given her the happily-ever-after she'd expected. So, just—

But then Jake was down on one knee and he had a small black box in his hand.

"I love you, Anna. I don't want another day to go by that I don't wake up and see your face first thing when I open my eyes. Will you do me the honor of being my wife and building a family with me? If you say yes, I promise I will make sure you have no regrets."

With tears streaming down her face, Anna was so choked up that all she could do was nod, but that was enough of a go-ahead for Jake—her mystery man, the last man she'd ever date, the one man she'd spend the rest of her life with—to take the ring from the box and slip it on her finger.

The gorgeous, classic round diamond sparkled in the candlelight as if it were celebrating with them. The sight of it on her finger and her hand in Jake's was instantly sobering.

"I love you so much," she said.

He pulled her into a deep kiss, the magic of which was only interrupted by Emily's voice. "So, I gather she said yes?"

Tears glinted in her sister's eyes.

"I did. I don't think I've ever been this happy."

Emily put her hands on her hips. "Sorry, but I have

to ask. If you two are marrying each other, who won the crazy bet?"

"We both did," Anna and Jake answered together.

* * * * *

MR (NOT QUITE) PERFECT

JESSICA HART

For John, perfect for me, with love.

CHAPTER ONE

MAKING MR PERFECT by Allegra Fielding
You've met a new guy. You're hot, hot, hot for each other. He's everything you ever wanted. But have you noticed that the infatuation phase never lasts? 'Fess up, ladies. How long before you're out with the girls and you find yourself saying, 'He'd be perfect if only he talked about his feelings/cooked occasionally/arranged a surprise mini-break/unfriended his ex on Facebook/insert peeve of your choice? He's still hot, you still love him to bits, but he's not quite *as perfect as he seemed at first.*

Are we asking too much of men nowadays? In a fairy tale, Prince Charming's task is clear. He has to hack his way through a thicket, slay a dragon and rescue the princess. Easy. In real life, we want our men to do a whole lot more to deserve us. Here at Glitz *we've been conducting our own super-scientific survey over a few cocktails (pomegranate martinis, anyone?) and it seems that we want it all. The perfect boyfriend, it turns out, can fix our cars and dance without looking like a total dork. He looks good and he'll get rid of that spider in the shower. He'll sit through a romcom without complaining and be strong enough to literally sweep us off our feet when required.*

But does such a man exist? And if he doesn't, is it possible to create him? Glitz *gives one lucky guy the chance of the ultimate makeover. Read on and see how one unreconstructed male rose to the challenge of becoming the perfect man. Meet—*

ALLEGRA LIFTED HER fingers from the keyboard and flexed them. Meet who?

Good question. Funny how the world was full of unreconstructed males until you actually needed one. But as soon as she had started asking around, it turned out that nobody wanted to admit that their boyfriends were anywhere near imperfect enough to take part in her experiment.

With a sigh, Allegra closed the document and shut down her computer. Had she been too ambitious? But Stella had liked the idea. The editor in chief had inclined her head by an infinitesimal degree, which signified enthusiasm. Now Allegra had a big break at last—and it would all fall apart if she couldn't find a man in need of a major makeover. One measly man, that was all she needed. He had to be out there somewhere…but where?

'Ouf!' Allegra threw herself extravagantly into the armchair and toed off her mock-croc stilettos with a grimace of pain. The needle-thin metal heels were to die for, but she had been on them for over twelve hours and while they might be long on style, they were extremely short on comfort.

Max didn't even look away from the television. He was stretched out on the sofa, flicking through channels, looking oddly at home in her sitting room. He had been tidying again, Allegra registered with a roll of her eyes. You would never catch the magazines being neatly lined up on the coffee table when it was just her and Libby. The radiators would be festooned with bras and thongs and the surfaces comfortingly cluttered with useful stuff like nail polish remover, empty shoe boxes, expired vouchers, cosmetic samples and screwed up receipts. She and Libby knew to check down the back of the sofa for chargers. They knew where they were with the mess.

There was no point in trying to tell Max that, though. Libby's brother was an engineer. They said cosy sitting room, he said tip.

She massaged her sore toes. 'My feet are *killing* me!'

'Why do you wear those ridiculous shoes?' Max demanded. 'It's like you put yourself through torture every day. Why don't you wear trainers or something more comfortable?'

'Because, Max, I work for *Glitz*,' said Allegra with exaggerated patience. 'That's a *fashion* magazine and, while I realise that as Mr Hasn't-got-a-clue you don't know what fashion is, I can assure you that my editor would send me home if I turned up in trainers!'

'They can't sack you for what you wear,' said Max, unimpressed.

'Stella can do whatever she likes.' Such was her editor's power and personality that Allegra found herself glancing over her shoulder and speaking in hushed tones whenever her name was mentioned.

'That woman's a monster. You should tell her where to get off.'

'And lose my job? Do you have any *idea* how hard it was to get a job at *Glitz*?' Cautiously Allegra wiggled the blood back into her poor toes. 'People kill for the chance to work with Stella. She's like the high priestess of fashion. She's totally awesome.'

'You're terrified of her.'

'I'm not terrified,' said Allegra, not quite honestly. 'I *respect* her. *Everyone* respects her.'

Everyone except her mother, of course, but then it took a lot to impress Flick Fielding, as Allegra knew to her cost. She suppressed a little sigh at the thought. She had been so hoping that Flick would approve of the fact that Stella had given her a job in the face of such competition, but her mother had only raised perfectly groomed brows.

'*Glitz?*' she'd echoed as if Allegra had boasted of a first journalist job with *Waste Collectors Weekly* instead of a top-selling glossy magazine. 'Well, if you're pleased, then of course…well done, darling.'

Allegra would never have applied to *Glitz* in the first place if she had known that Stella had once mocked Flick's choice of outfit for an awards ceremony. Flick, a formidably high-powered journalist, had not been amused.

Still, Allegra wouldn't allow herself to be downcast. She just needed to make her mark at *Glitz* and a good reference from Stella would make her CV stand out anywhere, whatever her mother might say. And *then* she would get a job that would really make Flick proud of her. Sadly, that would probably mean boning up on politics and economics rather than shoes and handbags, but she would worry about that when the time came. For now the important thing was to impress Stella.

'Well, I think you're mad,' said Max. 'It's bad enough having to wear a suit to work every day.'

Allegra eyed the striped polo shirt that Max changed into the moment he got home with disfavour. 'Thank God they *do* make you wear a suit,' she said. 'Even you can't go too far wrong with a suit and tie. The rest of the time, it's like you've got an unerring sense of what will be *least* stylish.'

'What do you mean?'

'Well, take that…*that*,' she said, pointing at his top and Max looked down at his chest.

'What's wrong with it?'

'It's hideous!'

'It's comfortable,' he said, unbothered. 'I don't care about style.'

'You don't say,' said Allegra sarcastically.

It was quite incredible how lively Libby had ended up with such a stuffy brother! Max didn't have a clue about music, or clothes, or anything other than engineering, as far as Allegra could tell. He didn't look *too* bad in a conventional suit, but his taste in casual wear made her wince every time.

'I wouldn't even use that thing you're wearing as a duster,' she said.

'You wouldn't use anything as a duster,' Max countered. 'You never do any housework.'

'I do!'

'Where does the dustpan and brush live?'

There was a pause. 'Under the sink?'

He made a bleeping noise. 'In the cupboard under the stairs.'

'There's a cupboard under the stairs?'

'I rest my case.' Max shook his head and returned his attention to the television.

Gingerly, Allegra tested her feet and decided that she could manage a hobble to the kitchen to find something to eat. She was starving. Like the sitting room, the kitchen was so tidy nowadays she hardly recognized it.

Max had moved in a couple of weeks earlier. Libby's three-month placement in Paris had coincided with the break-up of her brother's engagement, and she had offered him her room while she was away.

'Would you mind?' she had asked Allegra. 'It's only for a couple of months before he'll get a chance to go out to Shofrar, so it's hard for him to find somewhere temporary. And I'm worried about him. You know what Max is like; he's not exactly big on talking about feelings, but I think he must be really gutted about Emma.'

'Why did she break it off, do you know?' Allegra had been shocked when she heard. She'd only met Emma a couple of times, but she'd seemed perfect for Max. An engineer like him, Emma had been pretty, nice...the word *boring* shimmered in Allegra's head but it was too unkind so she pushed it away...practical, she decided instead. Exactly the kind of sensible girl Max would choose and the last person Allegra would have expected to have broken it all off six months before the wedding.

'He hasn't told me.' Libby shook her head. 'Just says it's all for the best. But I know he was planning for them to go out to Shofrar together and now that's all off...well, I'd feel better if you were around to cheer him up. As long as you really don't mind.'

'Of course I don't mind,' said Allegra. She'd been at school with Libby and had spent many holidays with her friend's family while Flick was working. Max was the brother she had never had, and over the years she had bickered with him and relied on him almost as much as Libby did.

'At least I know he's not a serial killer or anything,' she'd said cheerfully. 'I'll stop him missing Emma too much.'

In fact, she didn't see much of him. Max left for work early in the morning, and she was out most evenings. When they did coincide, like now, Max grumbled about her untidiness and Allegra criticised his clothes. They fought over the remote and shared the occasional takeaway. It was all perfectly comfortable.

And why wouldn't it be? Allegra asked herself as she opened the fridge and studied its contents without enthusiasm. This was Max, after all. Libby's brother. Allegra was fond of him, when she wasn't being irritated by his wardrobe and that way he had of making her feel like an idiot a lot of the time. Max wasn't ugly, but he wasn't exactly a hunk either. Certainly not a man to set your heart pattering.

Apart from that one night, of course. Don't forget that.

Allegra sighed as she picked out a low-fat yoghurt. Did everyone have an irritating voice in their head that would pop up at the least convenient times to remind them of precisely the things they most wanted to forget?

And it wasn't a night, she felt compelled to argue with herself, rummaging for a teaspoon. It had been an odd little incident, that was all. Not even an incident, really. *A moment.* And so long ago, really she had almost forgotten it.

Or she would have done if that pesky voice would let her.

No, it was all very comfortable. It was *fine*. Allegra was glad Max wasn't gorgeous or sexy. It made it easy to be relaxed with him. Which wasn't to say he couldn't make more of an effort on the clothes front. He didn't seem to care what he looked like, Allegra thought critically. That shirt was appalling and he *would* fasten it almost to the neck, no matter how often she told him to undo another button. He had no idea at all. If he smartened himself up a bit...

And that was when it hit her. Allegra froze with the teaspoon in her mouth.

Max. He was *perfect!* Why on earth hadn't she thought of him before?

She'd pitched the 'create a perfect boyfriend' idea to Stella at an editorial meeting the previous week. It was the first of her ideas that she'd been given the go-ahead to follow up, and Allegra had been fired with enthusiasm at first. But she had begun to wonder if she could make it work without the right man.

And now she had found him, lying in her own sitting room!

Already Allegra's mind was leaping forward, all her excitement about the project refuelled. She would write the best article *ever*. It would be fun, it would be interesting, it would tap into every woman's fantasy of making her man perfect. It would win awards, be syndicated worldwide. Stella would gasp with admiration.

At this point Allegra's imagination, vivid as it was, faltered. Stella, gasping? But a little strategic tweaking and the fantasy still worked. All right, Stella would look as enigmatic as ever but her words would be sweet. *Allegra*, she would say, *you're our new star writer. Have a massive salary.*

I'd love to, Stella, Allegra imagined herself saying in reply, super casual. *But the* Financial Times *has made me an offer I can't refuse.*

Surely her mother would be impressed by the *FT*?

Sucking yoghurt thoughtfully from her spoon, Allegra went to the kitchen doorway from where she could study Max without being observed.

He was still on the sofa, still flicking through channels in search of the news or sport, which was all he ever watched. Definitely not the kind of guy you would check out in a bar. Brown hair, ordinary features, steady blue-grey eyes: there was nothing wrong with him, but nothing special either.

Yep, he was perfect.

Max played rugby so he was pretty fit, but he didn't make anything of himself. Allegra mentally trimmed his hair and got rid of the polo shirt only to stop, unnerved, when she realised that the image of him lying on the sofa bare-chested was quite…startling.

Hastily, she put the shirt back on in her imagination. Whatever, the man was ripe for a makeover.

All she had to do was get Max to agree. Scraping out the yoghurt pot, Allegra tossed it in the bin with a clatter and squared her shoulders. Only last week she'd written an article on the benefits of thinking positive and getting what you wanted. It was time to put all that useful research into practice.

Back in the sitting room, she batted at Max's knees until he shifted his legs and she could plonk herself down on the sofa next to him. 'Max,' she began carefully.

'No.' Max settled his legs back across her lap and crossed his ankles on the arm of the sofa, all without taking his eyes off the television.

'What do you mean, *no*?' Forgetting her determination to stay cool and focused, as per her own advice in the article, Allegra scowled at him. 'You don't know what I'm going to say yet!'

'I know that wheedling tone of old,' said Max. 'You only use it when you want me to do something I'm not going to want to do.'

'Like what?' she said, affronted.

'Like waste an entire hot bank holiday Monday sitting in traffic because you and Libby wanted to go to the sea.'

'That was Libby's idea, not mine.'

'Same wheedle,' said Max, still flicking channels. 'And it was definitely your idea to have a New Year's Eve party that time.'

'It was a great party.'

'And who had to help you clear up afterwards before my parents came home?'

'You did, because you're a really, really kind brother who likes to help his sister and his sister's best mate out when they get into trouble.'

Max lowered the remote and looked at Allegra in alarm.

'Uh-oh. You're being nice. That's a bad sign.'

'How can you say that? I'm often nice to you. Didn't I make you a delicious curry last weekend?'

'Only because you wanted some and didn't want to admit that you'd broken your diet.'

Sadly, too true.

'*And* I said I'd go to that dinner and pretend to be your fiancée,' she said. 'How much nicer can I get?'

Max pulled himself up to look at Allegra with suddenly narrowed eyes. 'You're not going to back out, are you? Is that what this is about? Now that Emma's not around, I really need you.'

'Aw, Max, that's sweet!'

'I'm serious, Legs. My career depends on this.'

'I do think the whole thing is mad.' Allegra wriggled into a more comfortable position, not entirely sorry to let the conversation drift while she worked out exactly how to persuade Max to agree to take part. 'I mean, who cares nowadays if you're married or not?'

'Bob Laskovski does,' said Max gloomily.

At first he had welcomed the news that the specialist firm of consulting engineers he worked for was to be taken over by a large American company. An injection of capital, jobs secured, a new CEO with fantastic contacts with the Sultan of Shofrar and some major projects being developed there and elsewhere in the Middle East: it was all good news.

The bad news was that the new CEO in question was

a nut. Bob Laskovski allegedly had a bee in his bonnet about the steadying influence of women, of all things. If ever there was going to be unsettling going on, there was bound to be a female involved, in Max's opinion. But Bob liked his project managers to be in settled relationships and, given the strict laws of Shofrar, that effectively meant that, male or female, they had to be married.

'God knows what he thinks we'll do if we don't have a wife to come home to every night,' Max had grumbled to Allegra. 'Run amok and seduce local girls and offend the local customs, I suppose.'

Allegra had just laughed. 'I'd love to see you running amok,' she'd said.

Max had ignored that and ploughed on with his explanation. 'If I don't turn up with a likely-looking fiancée, Bob's going to start humming and hawing about whether I'm suitable for the job or not.'

It was ridiculous, he grumbled whenever given the opportunity. He had the skills, he had the experience, and he was unencumbered by ties. He should be the perfect candidate.

There hadn't been a problem when Bob had first said that he was coming over to London and wanted to meet the prospective project managers. That was another of Bob's 'things', apparently: he liked to vet them personally over individual dinners. God knew how the man had had the time to build up a vast construction company.

Max hadn't thought about it too much when the invitation to dinner had arrived. He and Emma had been going to get married anyway, and she was bound to go down well with Bob. Max was all set for his big break.

And then Emma had changed her mind.

Max still couldn't quite believe it. He might have lost his fiancée, but he was damned if he was going to lose the

Shofrar job too. Still, at least Allegra had been quite willing to help when he broached the idea of her standing in for Emma. For all her silliness, she could be counted on when it mattered.

'But just for an evening,' she had warned. 'I'm not going to marry you and go out to Shofrar just so you can be a project manager!'

'Don't worry, it won't come to that,' said Max, shuddering at the very thought of it.

'There are plenty of examples of relationships busting up before and after engineers get out there, and once you're actually doing the job and behaving yourself it's not a problem. All I need to do is get Bob's seal of approval. Everyone says it's worth humouring him.

'It'll just be a dinner,' he assured her. 'All you need to do is smile and look pretty and pretend that you're going to be the perfect engineer's wife.'

Of course, *that* was going to be the problem. He'd eyed Allegra critically. She'd been dressed in a short stretchy skirt that showed off her long legs, made even longer by precarious heels. 'Maybe you'd better wear something a bit more…practical,' he'd said. 'You don't really look like an engineer's wife.'

Allegra, of course, had taken that as a compliment.

'I don't mind going along to the dinner with you,' she said now. 'I may not be much of an actress, but I expect I can pretend to love you for an evening.'

'Thanks, Legs,' said Max. 'It means a lot to me.'

'But…' she said, drawing out the word, and his eyes narrowed suspiciously; he never liked the sound of 'but'. '…there *is* just one tiny thing you could do for me in return.'

She smiled innocently at him and his wary look deepened. 'What?'

'No, your line is, *Of course, Allegra, I'll do whatever you want*. Would you like to try it again?'

'What?' he repeated.

Allegra sighed and squirmed round until she was facing him. She tucked her hair behind her ears, the way she did when she was trying to look serious, and fixed him with her big green eyes.

'You know how hard it's been for me to make my mark at *Glitz*?'

Max did. He knew more than he wanted, in fact, about Allegra's precarious foothold on the very lowest rung of the glossy magazine, where as far as he could make out, emotions ran at fever-pitch every day and huge dramas erupted over shoes or handbags or misplaced emery boards. Or something equally pointless.

Allegra seemed to love it. She raced into the flat, all long legs and cheekbones and swingy, shiny hair, discarding scarves and shoes and earrings as she went, and whirled out again in an outfit that looked exactly the same, to Max's untutored eye.

She was always complaining, though, that no one at the magazine noticed her. Max thought that was extremely unlikely. Allegra might not be classically beautiful but she had a vivid face with dark hair, striking green eyes and a mobile expression. She wasn't the kind of girl people didn't notice.

He'd known her since Libby had first brought her home for the holidays. Max, callous like most boys his age, had dismissed her at first as neurotic, clumsy and overweight. For a long time she'd just been Libby's gawky friend, but she'd shed the weight one summer and, while it was too much to say that she'd emerged a butterfly from her chrysalis, she had certainly gained confidence. Now she was really quite attractive, Max thought, his gaze resting on her face and drifting, quite without him realising, to her mouth.

He jerked his eyes away. The last time he'd found himself looking at her mouth, it had nearly ended in disaster. It had been before he'd met Emma, a moment of madness one night when all at once things seemed to have changed. Max still didn't know what had happened. One moment he and Allegra had been talking, and the next he'd been staring into her eyes, feeling as if he were teetering on the edge of a chasm. Scrabbling back, he'd dropped his gaze to her mouth instead, and that had been even worse.

He'd nearly kissed Allegra.

How weird would *that* have been? Luckily they'd both managed to look away at last, and they'd never referred to what had happened—or not happened—ever again. Max put it out of his mind. It was just one of those inexplicable moments that were best not analysed, and it was only occasionally, like now, when the memory hurtled back and caught him unawares, a sly punch under his ribs that interfered oddly with his breathing.

Max forced his mind back to Allegra's question. 'So what's changed?' he asked her, and she drew a deep breath.

'I've got my big break! I've got my own assignment.'

'Well, great…good for you, Legs. What's it going to be? A hard-hitting exposé of corruption in the world of shoes? Earth-shattering revelations on where the hemline is going to be next year?'

'Like I'd need your help if it was either of those!' said Allegra tartly. 'The man who wouldn't know fashion if it tied him up and slapped him around the face with a wet fish.'

'So what do you need me for?'

'Promise you'll hear me out before you say anything?'

Max swung his legs down and sat up as he eyed Allegra

with foreboding. 'Uh-oh, I'm starting to get a bad feeling about this!'

'*Please*, Max! Just listen!'

'Oh, all right,' he grumbled, sitting back and folding his arms. 'But this had better be good.'

'Well...' Allegra moistened her lips. 'You know we have an editorial conference to plan features for the coming months?'

Max didn't, but he nodded anyway. The less he had to hear about the workings of *Glitz*, the better.

'So the other day we were talking about one of the girls whose relationship has just fallen apart.'

'This is *work*? Gossiping about relationships?' It didn't sound like any conference Max had ever been in.

'Our readers are *interested* in relationships.' Allegra's straight, shiny hair had swung forward again. She flicked it back over her shoulder and fixed him with a stern eye. 'You're supposed to be just listening,' she reminded him.

'So, yes, we were talking about that and how her problem was that she had totally unrealistic expectations,' she went on when Max subsided with a sigh. 'She wanted some kind of fairy tale prince.'

Princes. Fairy tales. Max shook his head. He thought about his own discussions at work: about environmental impact assessments and deliverables and bedrock depths. Sometimes it seemed to him that Allegra lived in a completely different world.

'We had a long discussion about what women really want,' she went on, ignoring him. 'And we came to the conclusion that actually we want everything. We want a man who can fix a washing machine and plan the perfect date. Who'll fight his way through a thicket if required but who can also dress well and talk intelligently at the theatre. Who can plan the perfect romantic date and sort out your tax and dance and communicate...'

Max had been listening with growing incredulity. 'Good luck finding a bloke who can do all that!'

'Exactly!' Allegra leant forward eagerly. '*Exactly*! That was what we all said. There isn't anyone like that out there. So I started thinking: what if we could *make* a man like that? What if we could create a boyfriend who was everything women wanted?'

'How on earth would you go about that?' asked Max, not sure whether to laugh or groan in disbelief.

'By teaching him what to do,' said Allegra. 'That's what I pitched to Stella: a piece on whether it's possible to take an ordinary bloke and transform him into the perfect man.'

There was a silence. Max's sense of foreboding was screaming a warning now.

'Please tell me this isn't the point where you say, *And this is where you come in*,' he said in a hollow voice.

'And this is where you come in, Max,' said Allegra.

He stared at her incredulously. She was smiling, and he hoped to God it was because she was winding him up. 'You're not serious?'

'Think about it: you're the ideal candidate. You haven't got a girlfriend at the moment...and frankly,' she added, unable to resist, 'unless you get rid of that polo shirt, you won't get another one.'

Max scowled. 'Stop going on about my shirt. Emma never minded it.'

'Maybe she never *said* she minded it, but I bet she did.' On a roll, Allegra pointed a finger at Max. 'The thing is, Max, that shirt is symptomatic of a man who can't be bothered to make an effort. I'm guessing Emma was just too nice to point that out.'

Max ground his teeth. 'For God's sake, Allegra! It's

comfortable. Since when has comfort been an indictable offence?'

'There are plenty of other new comfortable shirts out there that aren't striped or buttoned too high at the collar, but you won't buy them because that would mean changing, and changing is hard work,' said Allegra. 'And it's not just a question of clothes. You need to change how you communicate, how you *are*. How much effort you put into thinking about your girlfriend and what will make her happy.'

Closing his eyes briefly, Max drew a breath and let it out with exaggerated patience. 'Allegra, I have no idea what you're talking about,' he said.

'Why did Emma call off your engagement? I'll bet it was because you weren't prepared to make an effort, wasn't it?'

'No, it wasn't,' said Max, goaded at last. 'If you must know, she met someone else. It's not as if it's a big secret,' he went on, seeing Allegra's awkward expression. It was obviously just as much a surprise to her as it had been to him. 'I just don't particularly feel like talking about it all the time.'

'Emma seemed so nice,' said Allegra hesitantly after a moment. 'She didn't seem like someone who'd cheat on you.'

'She didn't.' Max blew out a breath, remembering how unprepared he had been for Emma's revelation. 'She was very honest. She said she'd met someone who works for one of our clients, and she didn't want to sleep with him until she'd told me how he made her feel. He made her realise that we didn't have any passion in our relationship any more.'

'Eeuww.'

That was exactly what Max had thought. 'I mean,

passion!' He practically spat out the word. 'What in God's name does *passion* mean?'

'Well, I suppose…sexual chemistry,' Allegra offered. She hesitated. 'So were things in the bedroom department…?' She trailed off delicately.

'They were fine! Or I thought they were fine,' Max amended bitterly. 'I loved Emma, and I thought she loved me. She was always talking about how compatible we were. We had the same interests. We were *friends*. It was her idea to get married in the first place, and I couldn't see any reason not to. We'd been together three years and it was the obvious next step.

'Then Emma meets this guy and suddenly it's all about magic and chemistry and getting swept off her feet!' Max's mouth twisted. 'I said to her, magic doesn't last. Having things in common is more important than sparks, but she wouldn't listen to reason.' He sighed, remembering. 'It was so unlike her. Emma used to be so sensible. It was one of the things I loved about her. She wasn't silly like—'

Like you.

Max managed to bite the words back in time, but he might as well not have bothered because they hung in the air anyway.

Allegra told herself she didn't mind. She had more important things to worry about, like getting her assignment off the ground.

'I don't think you should give up on Emma, Max,' she said persuasively. 'You two were good together. It sounds to me as if she was feeling taken for granted.'

'You being the great relationship expert,' said Max dourly.

'I know what I'm talking about when it comes to failed relationships,' Allegra pointed out, unfazed. 'It wouldn't surprise me at all if Emma is just looking for more attention from you. And that's where I can help you,' she added cunningly, gaining confidence from the fact that Max hadn't scoffed yet. 'If you really want her back, put yourself in my hands. It's a win for all of us, Max. I get my article written, you get Emma back, and Emma gets the perfect man!'

CHAPTER TWO

THERE WAS A long silence. Max's eyes were narrowed. He was definitely thinking about it, Allegra realised jubilantly, and she forced herself not to say any more. If he felt she was pressurising him, he would back away. Softly, softly, catchee monkey.

'What *exactly* would be involved?' he asked cautiously at last, and Allegra kept her eyes downcast so that he wouldn't see the triumph in them. She didn't want to spook him now.

'The idea is for you to complete a series of tasks,' she began. 'Sort of like a knightly quest…' She stopped as his face changed. Oops, looked like she'd lost him already with the knightly quest. Hurriedly, Allegra switched tactics. Practical details, that would appeal to Max.

'So your first task would be to have cocktails—'

'I can't stand those poncy drinks,' he started grumbling immediately. 'I don't know how you women can sit there sucking through straws and fighting your way through umbrellas and cherries.'

'—with Darcy King,' Allegra finished talking over the top of him.

A pause. Max sat up straight. 'What, not…?'

'Yes, *the* Darcy King.'

Idiot. She should have mentioned Darcy right at the

start. Darcy was every red-blooded male's fantasy, a lingerie model with a sweet face and a sinful body. Allegra could practically see Max drooling already. If Darcy wouldn't win him round to the assignment, nothing would.

'You, Max Warriner, have the chance to go on a series of dates with Darcy King herself. Think about what your mates will say when they hear about *that!*'

'Darcy King wouldn't want to go out with me!'

'Not if you were wearing that shirt, she wouldn't, but that's the whole point,' said Allegra at her most persuasive. 'Can we take you—an engineer with no dress sense and rudimentary social skills but with some useful abilities like how to put a flat pack from Ikea together—and turn you into the sophisticated, well-dressed kind of man that Darcy would like to go out with?'

Max looked as if he wasn't sure how to take that. 'She must have a boyfriend already, looking like that.'

'Apparently she finds it hard to find men who can get past what she looks like and be interested in *her*,' said Allegra. 'Ianthe interviewed her a couple of months ago and it turns out she's just like the rest of us, kissing a lot of toads and still hoping to find her prince.'

On the other side of the sofa, Max didn't bother to disguise his incredulity. 'And you think *I* could be Darcy King's prince?'

'Actually, no.' Hmm, this was tricky. She didn't want to discourage him, but it wouldn't be fair to get his hopes up either. 'I mean, even if you were to fall madly in love, it's hard to imagine you having a future together. I don't see Darcy wanting to go off to Shofrar.'

'True. There's not a lot of work for lingerie models out there,' Max agreed. 'But if we were madly in love, would that matter?'

For one awful moment Allegra thought that he was

taking the whole matter seriously, but when she shot him a worried look he didn't quite have time to conceal the mocking gleam in his blue-grey eyes, and she grinned and shoved him.

'You know what I mean,' she said. 'It's just a fun assignment, but Darcy gets to have a good time, and you might learn something about dealing with women. If you want to get Emma back, Max, this could be just the chance you need. Are you really going to turn it down because you don't want to be seen sucking a cocktail through a straw?'

Max considered her. 'That would be it? Drinking a cocktail with Darcy King?'

'Well, obviously we'd need to make a few changes,' said Allegra airily. 'Get you a new wardrobe, a new haircut, that kind of thing, but the stylist would help you with that.'

'*Stylist?*'

'You're really lucky.' Allegra lowered her voice reverentially. 'Dickie said he'd style the shoot personally.'

'Shoot? What shoot? And who the hell is Dickie?'

He really didn't have a clue, did he? 'Dickie Roland is only the most famous stylist in London at the moment,' she said. 'He's a superstar! I think his name is actually Georges, but in the fashion world he's just known as Dickie after his trademark bow tie. He's worn it ever since he came to London from Paris, and it's hard to imagine him without one now.'

'I hope you're not planning to ask me to wear a bow tie!'

'No, no, that's Dickie's "thing". He'll just make you look fabulous.' Allegra sighed. Max clearly had no idea what an honour it was to be styled by Dickie. 'But you have to promise to be nice to him. Dickie's brilliant, but he can be a bit…temperamental.'

Max pinched the bridge of his nose. 'I can't believe I'm actually discussing being styled!' he muttered.

'You'd want to look nice for Darcy, wouldn't you?'

'I haven't said yes yet,' he warned quickly. 'What else is involved in this assignment of yours? It's got to be more than putting on a shirt and slurping a cocktail.'

'Once you've got through the cocktails, the next task is to cook Darcy dinner—and no ordering in a pizza. You have to cook it yourself.' Darcy was a vegetarian and the meal had to be a romantic one, but Allegra would break that to Max later. For now she just had to get him to agree in principle. There would be time enough to talk him through the pesky details once he'd agreed.

Max grunted. 'I could probably manage a meal, as long as she's not expecting anything fancy.'

'The whole point is to make an effort to cook something *Darcy* would like,' said Allegra, smoothing impatience from her voice. It wouldn't do to put his back up now, just when she had him nibbling at her hook! 'When you're having a drink, you'll have to talk to her and find out what sort of food she prefers, and if she likes fancy, then you're going to have to cook fancy. But I wouldn't be surprised if she likes things simple,' she added hastily as Max's brows drew together.

'Okay. So cocktail, cooking...what else?'

Best to take the next bit in a rush. 'You'd need to do something cultural without looking bored—we're thinking the theatre, perhaps, or the opening of an art exhibition—and that's it, really. Then it's just the ball,' Allegra finished breezily and put on a bright smile, hoping that Max might have missed the last task.

No such luck. 'Please tell me you're thinking about a round thing that you kick around a field!'

'Not *exactly*...'

'Come on, Legs, there's something you're not telling me, isn't there?'

'All right, it's a costume ball being held for charity. You'll have to dress up—and learn to waltz.'

There, it was out, but, as expected, Max had started shaking his head at 'costume'. 'No way,' he said firmly. 'I don't mind having a go at the other stuff, but dressing up? And *dancing?* I'd rather stick pins in my eyes!'

'Oh, Max, *please!* We have to have the ball. Darcy's really looking forward to it, and learning how to dance would be such a great gesture. It would be so...*romantic.*'

'What's romantic about making a tit of yourself on the dance floor?'

'I've always wanted to go to a ball like that. Not just a dinner dance bash but a real ball, with proper ball gowns and waltzing...' Allegra's eyes were dreamy at the mere thought of it, and she pressed a hand to the base of her throat as she sighed.

She had grown up in a house full of books, but Flick's shelves were lined with heavyweight biographies and award-winning literary novels. Flick was dismissive of commercial fiction, and as a child Allegra's books had been uniformly worthy. It had been a revelation to go and stay with Libby's family, where the house was full of dog-eared paperbacks with broken spines and yellowing pages.

Best of all, Max's mother had a collection of Regency romances and Allegra had devoured them every time she went. She loved the ordered world they portrayed with those rakish dukes and spirited governesses. She loved the dashing way the heroes drove their curricles, their curling lips, their codes of honour.

And their tight breeches, of course.

Best of all were the ball scenes, which were charged with sexual tension as the hero and heroine clasped hands and danced, oblivious to anyone but each other.

A wistful sigh leaked out of her. 'I'd love to waltz,' she

told Max, who was predictably unimpressed. 'It's my fantasy to be swept masterfully around a ballroom by a dashing hero, who knows just how to dance me unobtrusively out onto a terrace where it's dark and warm and the air is sweet with the scent of summer flowers and he's dancing with me along the terrace but he's overcome by passion and he presses me up against the balustrade and tells me he loves me madly and can't live without me and he's begging me to marry him—'

Running out of breath, she broke off to find Max watching her quizzically.

'I'm glad you stopped,' he said. 'I was wondering if I should throw a glass of water at you to stop you hyperventilating.'

'You've got to admit it would be romantic,' Allegra insisted.

Max showed no sign of admitting any such thing. He got back to the business in hand.

'Why not get that boyfriend of yours to take you if you want to go so much? What's his name? Jerry?'

'Jeremy.'

'That's right. Of course he's a Jeremy,' said Max dismissively. 'I bet he knows how to dance. I only met him once but he struck me as a guy who knows how to do everything.'

Jeremy had been very accomplished, that was for sure, but he was much too serious to go dancing. He was interested in politics and the economy. He could talk about the arts and international relations. He had been well-dressed and charming. Not the most practical guy in the world perhaps, but Allegra couldn't imagine him ever needing to assemble any flat packs in any case.

'In fact, why not get him to do your whole assignment?'

Max said and Allegra sighed and tucked her legs more comfortably beneath her.

'It wouldn't be much of a transformation story,' she said. 'Besides, I haven't seen him for a while. He wasn't really my boyfriend.'

She had tried to be upset when Jeremy stopped calling, but honestly, it had been a relief not to have to try quite so hard for a while. Jeremy's conversation might be impressive but it was light on humour and, in spite of growing up with Flick Fielding as a mother, the sad truth was that Allegra's interests veered more towards celebrity gossip and shoes than political intrigue. Flick would be appalled if she had guessed, and Allegra did her best not to disappoint her mother, but sometimes it was hard to keep up.

'We only went out a couple of times,' she said. 'Jeremy was just…someone Flick introduced me to.'

That would be right, thought Max. Allegra's mother liked to keep her daughter toeing the line and would soon veto any unsuitable boyfriends. Tricky Flicky, as she was known by those unfortunate enough to have been subjected to one of her gruelling interviews, was a media heavyweight, famous as much for her style as for her incisive questioning. Much as they might squirm under the lash of her tongue and steely-eyed gaze, politicians lobbied to be interviewed by Flick Fielding. Flick had gravitas, they all agreed that.

Whereas Allegra…Allegra was warm and funny and creative and kind, but gravitas? No.

Max had never understood why Flick, with all her brains, didn't just accept that rather than trying to force Allegra into her own mould.

'So, you're not heartbroken?' he asked Allegra cautiously. Because he had learnt that with women you never could tell.

'No.' Allegra blew out a long sigh and pushed her hair away from her face. 'Jeremy was just the latest in a long line of men who turned out not to be The One after all. I had such high hopes when I first met him too.'

'You know, you might get on better if you stopped letting your mother choose your boyfriends.' Max kept his voice carefully neutral but Allegra bridled anyway.

'She doesn't *choose* them!'

'Come on, when have you ever gone out with someone your mother wouldn't approve of?'

'I happen to like men who are attractive and intelligent and witty and successful,' Allegra said defensively. 'Of course she approves of them.'

'Maybe I should have said that you should try going out with someone because you like him, not because you think your mother will.'

'I *did* like Jeremy.' Clearly ruffled, Allegra wriggled her shoulders. 'Anyway, that's all beside the point. Jeremy's not around and you are, and Max, you're *perfect* for my assignment! There's so much scope for you to improve.'

'Thanks a lot!'

'You know what I mean. You could get so much out of it too. You should be leaping at the chance to learn how to give a woman what she really wants! You're going to Shofrar in a couple of months and the piece won't be out until after you leave, but if you play your cards right you could win Emma back and take her with you. That's what you want, isn't it?'

Was it? Max thought about Emma. She'd been so easy to be with. They'd been comfortable together, and it would be good to have that back again. Of course he wanted her back…but he wanted her the way she had been before she lost her head and started wanting more of everything: more excitement, more passion, more attention, more effort. Max thought the whole idea was to find someone you didn't *have* to make an effort for, but apparently he was wrong about that.

He missed Emma, though, and he missed the warm feeling of knowing that you'd found the woman you wanted to settle down with. He would never find anyone better than Emma. She was perfect for him.

'Yes,' he said. 'Of course I do.'

'Well, then,' said Allegra, satisfied. 'I bet if Emma gets wind of the fact that you're going out with Darcy she'll be jealous.'

'I wouldn't really be going out with her,' Max pointed out.

'Emma won't know that, will she? She'll be back in no time, you'll see.'

'I don't know.' Max pulled down his mouth. 'I wouldn't bet on it, and in the meantime I really don't want to dress up and learn to dance just on the off chance that she does. I can't imagine Emma caring about whether I can waltz or not.'

'You couldn't imagine her being carried away by passion either,' Allegra pointed out.

'No, but—'

It was at that point that Allegra gave up on arguments and threw pride to the winds. Grabbing his hand, she held it between her own.

'Oh, please, Max! Please, please, please, please, *please!* Please say you'll do it! This is my big chance to impress Stella. If I don't find someone to take part in this assignment, I won't get another one. I'll be a failure!' she said extravagantly. 'My career will be over before it's begun and how will I tell Flick?'

She leant beseechingly towards him and Max found himself snared in the big eyes. Funny how he had never noticed before how beautiful they were, or how green, the lovely dark mossy green of a secret wood...

Secret wood? Max gave himself a mental slap. God, he'd be spouting poetry next!

'I know you don't think much of *Glitz*,' Allegra was babbling on, 'but this is my career! What else am I going to do if I'm a failure as a journalist?'

'You could illustrate those children's books the way you always said you were going to.' He and his family shouldn't have been surprised when Allegra announced that she was going to follow Flick into journalism, but none of them had ever had her down as a writer. Max always thought of her drawing—quick, vivid sketches that brought a face or an animal to life in a few simple lines.

She drew back, thrown by his suggestion. 'I can't make a living as an illustrator.'

What she meant was: Flick wouldn't be pleased. Flick wanted a daughter who would follow in her footsteps, a daughter who would be a journalist on television or for some respected newspaper. Flick had no time for Allegra's 'little drawings'. Max thought it was a shame.

'It's just a few hours of your time, Max.' Allegra reverted to the problem in hand.

Would it cost him that much to help her? Max found himself thinking. She was so longing to be a success, and she deserved a break. She'd been a good friend to Libby— and to him, he acknowledged. Allegra tried so hard to be ruthless and driven like her formidable mother, but she just couldn't quite manage it. She liked to pretend that she was tough, but she was a sucker for every sob story that came along. Allegra would never admit it, but she was hampered by warmth and kindness and humour from ever pleasing Flick.

'And if I say no, I suppose you'll refuse to pretend to be my fiancée when I meet Bob Laskovski?'

Allegra looked momentarily disconcerted and Max had to stop himself rolling his eyes. It had obviously never crossed her mind that she could do more than beg him to help her. She had such a transparent expression. He could read the agonizing in her green eyes, practically hear her wondering how she could possibly threaten to go back on her promise when she'd given her word.

If he had any decency, he'd put her out of her misery and tell her that he'd do her stupid assignment, but it was fun to see how far she would go for a success she could lay at Flick Fielding's feet—and frankly, Max considered, if he was going to make an idiot of himself, he deserved some amusement in return.

'Er, yes…yes, that's right,' said Allegra after a moment and put up her chin in a futile attempt to look ruthless. 'A favour for a favour. If you don't help me with this, you can forget about me pretending to be your fiancée!'

'But you promised,' Max protested, scowling to disguise his amusement as Allegra squirmed. She was big on keeping her promises. 'If you don't come with me to that dinner, I won't get the job in Shofrar and you know how much that means to me.'

'This assignment means a lot to *me*,' Allegra pointed out, but she didn't look very comfortable about it. 'That's the deal: take it or leave it.'

'That's blackmail!' said Max.

'And your point is…?' she countered bravely.

It was all Max could do not to grin. He heaved a disgruntled sigh instead. 'Oh, all *right*. If you're going to be like that, I don't have much choice, do I? I'll take part in your precious assignment—but you'd better not have been joking about Darcy King!'

One moment he was pretending to glower at Allegra, the next his arms were full of her. Beaming, she launched herself at him, pushing him back down onto the sofa cushions as she hugged him. 'Oh, I love you, Max! Thank you, thank you, thank you!' she babbled, blizzarding kisses over his face. 'You won't regret it, I promise you. I'm going to change your life, and it's going to be perfect!'

Allegra ran from the lift as fast as she could on her polka dot slingbacks. The shoes were a fun twist to the rest of her look, a demure tweed two-piece with a short skirt and three-quarter length sleeves that channelled her inner executive-cum-fashion diva, and Allegra had been pleased when she left home. She projected confidence and style, as befitted a girl on the verge of her big break.

Until her tights laddered, that was.

If only she hadn't stopped to say hello to Mrs Gosling, but how could she run past when her elderly neighbour's face lit up at the prospect of someone to talk to? Mrs Gosling spent most of her days walking her dog, an excitable mutt called, for reasons Allegra had never understood, Derek, and that morning she had been all tangled up in the lead while Derek literally ran rings round her.

Late as she was, Allegra had had to stop and disentangle Mrs Gosling and hear about Derek's latest antics. Allegra had a friend whose small daughter Molly loved to be told how naughty Derek was, and Allegra had taken to writing out each story, exaggerating for effect, and illustrating them with little sketches of Derek's mischievous face. Molly adored them.

'You should put them into a book,' Libby had said. 'The Glorious Adventures of Derek the Dog. Mrs G would love it.'

But Allegra had shrugged the idea aside. 'They're just for Molly really.'

But that morning she had only listened with half an ear as she sorted out the lead and bent to greet Derek, who jumped at her in ecstasy.

That was the end of the tights.

Oh, God, she was so late! Red-faced and panting, Allegra practically fell through the doors into *Glitz*'s super hip offices. The editorial department sprawled over the top floor of a converted warehouse. Most days the buzz hit Allegra the moment she got out of the lift. She loved the gloss of the office, the smell of new clothes and expensive perfumes, the stark décor contrasting with the colourful scatter of accessories and shoes displayed like works of art. She loved the frantic thrum in the air, the way it was punctuated with dramatic cries and screams of excitement.

Except when Stella was present, of course, in which case everyone was very quiet unless asked to speak.

It was ominously silent when Allegra collapsed against the reception desk, a funkily curved piece of steel, and held her hand against her side.

'The editorial meeting's just started,' Lulu, the receptionist, lowered her voice and eyed Allegra with sympathy. 'You know Stella hates it when anyone is late. You'd better pretend you fell under a bus or something.'

'I might as well if I don't get in there and get my assignment,' groaned Allegra, forcing herself upright.

Smoothing down her hair, she took a deep breath and headed towards the conference room, only to be called back by Lulu's frantic whisper.

'You can't go in like that!' She pointed at Allegra's legs. 'Tights!'

Allegra clutched her head. She'd forgotten her tights

for a moment. She'd soon learnt to keep a spare pair in her bag, but changing them would take precious seconds.

'What's worse?' she asked Lulu desperately. 'Being late or laddered tights?' Lulu's astounded expression was answer enough. Clearly, Allegra shouldn't have needed to ask. 'You're right, I'd better change...'

It was Allegra's second mistake of the day. Dashing into the loos, she found Hermione, one of the marketing interns, sobbing her heart out in a cubicle, and by the time Allegra had coaxed her out and listened to her tale of woe, she was not only horribly late but had acquired two mascara smudges on the pale cashmere jumper tucked so stylishly into her skirt.

That was what you got for dispensing comforting hugs, thought Allegra bitterly as she stripped off her tights, but she was in such a hurry to get the new ones on that she managed to stick a finger through them.

'Oh, sod it!' At least this time the ladder was hidden under her skirt. Bundling the first pair into the bin, Allegra swiped at her hair. She looked completely manic, but there was nothing she could do about it now. If she didn't get into that editorial meeting, she'd lose out on the assignment. Ianthe Burrows was probably already putting forward an alternative.

'Sorry,' she mouthed generally, sliding into the conference room at last and every head swivelled to stare at her, with her flushed cheeks and tousled hair. There was a resounding silence. Stella didn't say anything but her gaze rested for a crushing few seconds on the smudges before dropping to Allegra's knees as she stood frozen just inside the room.

Against her will, Allegra found herself following her editor's gaze to where the ladder had snaked out from under her skirt. Horrified, she watched it unravel over her knee and head down her leg. She could practically hear the unzipping sound.

Why was there never a black hole around when you needed to jump into one?

'Editorial meetings start at ten,' said Stella, and Allegra cringed at the lack of inflexion in her voice.

'Yes, I know…I—' She broke off. She couldn't explain about Derek and Mrs Gosling and Hermione. Stella wouldn't care and Allegra would sound like an idiot. Even more of an idiot. 'I'm sorry,' she said instead.

A fractional incline of Stella's head served as her dismissal. The conversation returned to the latest couture debut, and Allegra slunk into a chair at the back. Pulling out notebook, pen, iPad and PDA, she willed the burning colour in her face to fade.

Fortunately, she didn't appear to have missed too much and as the discussion warmed up into articles about how to give a rock'n'roll twist to the latest looks, and the pros and cons of being friends-with-benefits, she kept her head down and let her racing pulse slow. Mindlessly doodling Derek winding Mrs Gosling up in his lead, she listened to the arguments for and against sleeping with a friend. It wasn't something she would do herself. She'd be afraid that it would spoil the friendship. Because how could it possibly be the same afterwards?

What would it have been like if Max had kissed her all those years ago? Allegra was aware of an odd jolt of heat at the thought. It had to be the thrill of the forbidden, because Max was practically her brother.

Eeuww, the very idea was disturbing at a whole load of levels! But there had been something hot and dangerous in the air that night, something that risked changing everything, and they'd both known it. Perhaps that was why they had pulled back before they did something they would both have regretted.

Because if they'd kissed, they wouldn't have stopped at a kiss, and then it really *would* have been awkward. It wasn't even as if Max was her type, Allegra thought, even as she began an absent sketch of how he had looked lying on the sofa the night before. And she certainly wasn't his. Emma was neat and dainty and blonde, a sweet little pixie, while Allegra was leggy and chaotic.

No, it was much better that they'd stayed just friends, without any jiggery-pokery, as Ianthe liked to refer to sex. They would never have been able to share the house, like now, if they'd slept together, and she wouldn't have felt comfortable asking him to take part in the assignment.

Thank God they hadn't actually kissed.

Or done anything else.

Pursing her lips, Allegra studied her drawing. It looked like Max, but the mouth wasn't *quite* right... She made a slight adjustment to his upper lip and his face sprang to life so abruptly that her heart jumped a little: steady eyes, stubborn jaw, a quiet, cool mouth. She hadn't realised how well she had memorised the angles of his cheek, the way his hair grew. She had made him look...quite attractive.

Her mouth dried and all at once she was remembering how she had hugged him in her excitement the night before. She hadn't thought about it. He was Max, and he'd just agreed to take part in something Allegra knew he was going to hate. Hugging him was the obvious thing to do.

But when her arms were around his neck and her lips pressed to his cheek, she had suddenly become aware of how solid he was, how *male*. How familiar and yet how abruptly strange. The prickle of stubble on his jaw had pressed into her cheek and she'd breathed in the clean masculine smell of him and something had twisted hard and hot in her belly.

Something that had felt alarmingly like lust. Which of course it couldn't have been because, hey, this was *Max*.

Beside her, Georgie, one of the few journalists who was as junior as Allegra, leant over and raised her eyebrows appreciatively. 'Your guy?' she mouthed.

Allegra shook her head, unaccountably flustered. 'Just a friend.'

'Right.' Georgie's smile was eloquent with disbelief.

Quickly Allegra sketched in Max's shirt, including every stripe, and the collar that was buttoned too high, and Georgie's smile faded.

'Oh.'

Quite, thought Allegra. She should do less thinking about Max's mouth and more remembering his absolutely appalling taste in shirts.

'Allegra!'

The deputy editor's voice made Allegra jerk her eyes to the front, where Stella was looking sphinx-like and Marisa, her deputy, harried. 'Could we have a moment of your attention?'

Allegra fought the impulse to say, *Yes, miss*. 'Yes, of course.'

'*Making Mr Perfect*...did you get anywhere with that?'

Clearly expecting the answer to be no, their eyes were already moving down the list, on to the next idea. This was her moment.

'Actually, yes, I did,' Allegra said and a ripple of surprise ran round the room.

'You found someone to take part?' Stella's expression was as inscrutable as ever but Allegra told herself that the very slight life of her editor's immaculate brows was a good sign.

'Yes,' she said.

'Who is he?' That was Marisa.

'The brother of a friend of mine. Max.' Why did just saying his name suddenly make her feel warm?

'What does he look like?' asked Marisa practically. 'I suppose it's too much to hope that he's a hunk?'

Allegra glanced down at her sketch of Max on the sofa: solid, steady-eyed. Ordinary. Nothing special. Her eyes rested on his mouth for a moment and there it came again without warning, a quick, disturbing spike of her pulse. She looked away.

'I wouldn't say that he was a *hunk*, exactly,' she said cautiously, 'but I think he'll brush up well.'

'Sounds promising. What's he like?'

'He's a civil engineer,' said Allegra, as if that explained everything. 'He's pretty conventional, plays rugby and doesn't have a clue about style.' She lifted her shoulders, wondering how else to describe him. 'He's just a bloke, really.'

'No girlfriend in the wings? We don't want anyone making a fuss about him spending time with Darcy.'

Allegra shook her head. 'He's just been dumped by his fiancée and he's going to work abroad soon so he's not interested in meeting anyone else at the moment. He's perfect,' she said.

'And he knows exactly what's involved?' Marisa insisted. 'He's happy to go ahead?'

Happy might be stretching it, thought Allegra, remembering uneasily how she had had to blackmail Max, but this was no time for quibbling. Her big chance was *this* close, and she was ready to seize it.

'Absolutely,' she said.

Marisa glanced at Stella, who nodded. 'In that case, you'd better get on to Darcy King and set up the first date straight away.'

CHAPTER THREE

'So THIS IS where you work.' Max looked around him uneasily. The office was aflutter with gorgeous glossy women, all eyeing him as if they had never seen a man in a suit before and weren't sure whether to laugh or pity him.

It ought to have been gratifying to be the focus of so much undivided female attention, but Max was unnerved. He felt like a warthog who had blundered into a glasshouse full of butterflies.

Why the hell had he agreed to this stupid idea? He'd been lying there minding his own business and then Allegra had slid onto the sofa next to him and before he knew what was happening he'd been tangled up in her idea and lost in those mossy eyes and suddenly all he cared about was making her happy.

He'd even suggested his own blackmail. He must have been mad.

But the smile on Allegra's face had lit up the room and left him scrabbling for breath, and when she'd thrown herself into his arms the feel of her had left Max oddly light-headed. Her hair had trailed silkily over his face as she threw her arms round him and pressed her lips to his cheek, and the smell of her perfume had sent his mind spinning.

To Max's horror, his body had taken on a mind of its

own. Without him even being aware of what he was doing, his arms had clamped round her and for a moment he had held her against him and fought the crazy urge to slide his hands under that skimpy top and roll her beneath him.

Which would have been a very, very, very bad idea.

The next instant Allegra had pulled back, babbling excitedly about the assignment. As far as she was concerned, it had just been a sisterly hug.

That was all it *had* been, Max reminded himself sternly.

And now it seemed he was committed to the charade. 'The first thing is to smarten you up.' Allegra had gone all bossy and produced a clipboard and a list. 'Can you take an afternoon off? You're going to need a complete makeover.'

Max didn't like the sound of that. He didn't like the sound of *any* of it, come to that, but he'd given his word.

'I could take some flex leave,' he said grudgingly. He didn't want anyone at work to get wind of what was happening. That morning he'd told them that he was going to the dentist and, looking around *Glitz*'s glossy offices, he couldn't help thinking that root canal surgery might be preferable to what lay ahead.

He was going to be styled by the great Dickie himself. Allegra had impressed on Max what an honour this was. 'If he's bored or irritated, Dickie's likely to storm off, so please just be nice!' she said again as she led him between glass-walled offices and down to a studio, her sky-high heels clicking on the polished floor that she had told him was known as the runway. Apparently this was because everybody could see and comment on the outfits passing, something Max would rather not have known. He could feel all the eyes assessing his hair, his suit, his tie, his figure as he followed Allegra.

She was in businesslike mode today in skinny trousers, an animal-print top and those fearsome-looking boots, but he had to confess he preferred it when she wore a dress. She looked less...intimidating.

Plus, it showed off her legs, which were pretty spectacular.

'I'm always nice,' said Max.

Allegra cast him a look over her shoulder. 'You weren't nice about the outfit I wore last night.'

Max had been heating up a curry when she had appeared in the kitchen doorway, wearing the most extraordinary outfit. A riot of clashing colours and patterns, Max hadn't known how to describe what she was wearing, but when she'd twirled and asked what he thought, he'd made the big mistake of telling her. Words like fruit salad and dog's dinner had passed his lips.

He wouldn't be offering any more sartorial advice.

'Here we are.' Fretfully, Allegra pushed him into the studio. 'Just...nod and smile. And follow my lead,' she muttered under her breath, fixing a bright smile to her face and dragging Max towards a tiny, imperious figure with close-cropped grey hair, huge red spectacles and a red and white dotted bow tie.

'You didn't tell me I'd have to be careful not to step on him,' Max murmured and Allegra hissed at him to be quiet.

'Dickie, I'm so thrilled to be working with you,' she said, practically curtseying.

Dickie nodded regally, and they exchanged the obligatory air kiss before he turned his gaze to Max. 'And oo iz thees?' he said, his French accent so thick that Max thought he had to be putting it on.

'Max Warriner,' he said, stepping forward and shaking Dickie's hand firmly before Allegra could pretend that he was a deaf mute. He sure as hell wasn't going to kiss Dickie. 'Good to meet you,' he said briskly.

Dickie looked at his hand as if he had never had it wrung before, and then at Allegra, who smiled apologetically.

'Max is here for the *Making Mr Perfect* feature,' she said, lowering her voice. 'You know, the one with the complete makeover.'

'Ah, *oui*...' Dickie eyed Max's outfit, a perfectly serviceable suit and tie, and shuddered extravagantly. 'I see 'e needs one!'

'It's the first date tonight,' Allegra said. 'He's meeting Darcy King for cocktails at Xubu.'

Xubu, as Max had heard at length, was the latest hot ticket, the place to see and be seen, and Allegra had been desperate to go. Fortunately—for her, if not for Max—Darcy King's celebrity had opened the doors and Allegra was delighted.

'I don't see why you're so happy,' Max had said. 'You're not going.'

'Of course I have to be there,' Allegra said. 'I'm writing the article. And the photographer will be there too.'

'It doesn't sound like much of a date to me,' Max grumbled, but Allegra had brushed that aside.

'It'll be fun!'

Fun. Max shook his head, thinking about it.

'You can see how much work he needs,' Allegra was saying to Dickie, who was circling Max with much rolling of eyes and shrugging of shoulders. 'He'll need a whole new look if he's going to impress Darcy.'

'I will do what I can,' he said, plucking at Max's jacket with distaste. 'But zis, zis must go! And ze shirt—if you can call zat zing a shirt—and ze trousers...ze shoes too... Burn it all!'

'Now hold on—!' Max began, only to yelp as Allegra placed her heel firmly on his foot.

'Don't worry, Dickie. I'll take care of it. Take off your jacket,' she ordered Max out of the corner of her mouth.

'This is my work suit!' he muttered back as he took it off reluctantly. 'Don't you dare burn it.'

'Don't panic. I'll just take it home where it doesn't upset Dickie.'

'What about upsetting *me*?'

Allegra ignored him. 'What sort of look do you think for cocktails?' she asked Dickie. 'Funky? Or suave and sophisticated?'

Dickie stood back and studied Max critically, mentally stripping him of the offending clothes, and Max shifted self-consciously.

'I zink sophisticated, but with an edge,' Dickie proclaimed at last.

'Perfect,' said Allegra, the traitor. 'Not too obvious, but interesting. A look that shows Darcy he's confident enough to make his own fashion statement? A little quirky, perhaps?'

Fashion statement? Jeez…Max pinched the bridge of his nose as Allegra and Dickie talked over him. He should be checking the material testing results, or writing up the geological survey for the motorway-widening bid, not standing here like a dumb ox while they wittered on about fashion statements!

'Quirky?' Dickie considered. 'Per'aps you 'ave somezing zere…'

Max was convinced now that the French accent was put on. No one could really speak that ridiculously.

Although, for a man prepared to wear that bow tie, being ridiculous obviously wasn't a problem.

'What do you think?' Allegra asked anxiously. 'Can you do something with Max?'

For answer, Dickie spun on his heel and clapped his

hands at his minions, who had been waiting subserviently, talking to each other in hushed voices as they waited for the great man to pronounce.

'Bring out ze shirts,' he ordered.

'Behave,' Allegra whispered in Max's ear.

'I am behaving!'

'You're not. You're glaring at Dickie. Do you want me glaring at Bob Laskovski over that dinner?'

'No,' he admitted.

'Well, then.'

Allegra could see Max balking as racks of clothes surrounded him like wagons and Dickie started snapping his fingers at his assistants, who leapt forward and held up shirts side by side. Max's eyes were rolling nervously like a spooked horse and he practically had his ears flattened to his head, but Allegra stood behind Dickie and mouthed 'remember the dinner' at him until he sulkily complied and agreed to try on some shirts.

Unbuttoning his cuffs, he hooked his fingers into the back of his shirt and dragged it over his head and Allegra and Dickie both drew a sharp breath. Who would have guessed that Max had such a broad, smooth, *sexy* back beneath that dull shirt? Allegra felt quite…unsettled.

Dragging her eyes away, she made a big deal of making notes of Dickie's choices in her notebook, but her gaze kept snagging on the flex of Max's muscles as he shrugged in and out of shirts. Dickie kept turning him round—deliberately, Allegra was sure—so sometimes she saw his shoulders, sometimes his chest. And then they brought on the trousers, and there were his bare legs. Why had she never noticed before what great legs Max had?

'Allegra!' Dickie snapped his fingers in front of her face, startling her. 'What do you think?'

Allegra looked at Max. He wore a darkly flowered

button-down shirt with a striped tie that clashed and yet complemented the colours perfectly. Trousers and jacket were beautifully cut, shoes discreet. If it hadn't been for the mutinous expression, he would have looked super-cool.

'I love it,' she said. 'He's really rocking that flowered shirt.'

Max hunched a shoulder. 'I feel like a prat.'

'Well, you don't look like one for once,' she said.

'He needs an 'aircut of course,' said Dickie, eyeing Max critically.

Allegra checked her list. 'That's booked in next.'

'And a manicure.'

'Oh, no,' said Max, backing away. 'No, no, no, no, no!'

'Yes, indeed.' Allegra smiled blandly at him. 'Now don't make a fuss. It won't hurt at all.' She pretended to consult her list again. 'Although I'm not sure I can say the same for the back, sack and crack wax we've got you booked in for after the manicure…'

'Back, sack…?' Aghast, Max opened and closed his mouth before obviously spotting the dent in her cheek where she was desperately trying not to laugh. 'Why, you…' Grinning with relief, he playfully shoved at her arm.

Allegra was giggling, but tailed off when she realised everyone was standing around staring at them. How uncool of her.

She cleared her throat. 'Yes, well, take that outfit off for now. Let's do something about that hair.'

Max ran his finger around his collar. His *flowery* collar. He felt ridiculous. His hair had been washed and conditioned and cut and it was just as well it hadn't been any longer or that fool of a barber—excuse him, hairstylist—would have had it flopping all over his face. He had been shaved too, swathed in hot towels. Actually that hadn't been too bad—until they had slapped on some cologne without his say-so. His eyes were still watering.

If any of his mates saw him now, or caught him stinking like a tart's boudoir, he would never hear the end of it. Thank God this was the last place he would meet anyone he knew. The dimly lit bar was crowded, but if anyone else in there was an engineer, they weren't like any civil engineers Max had ever met. Everyone seemed to be at least ten years younger than him and half of them were outrageously dressed. Unbelievably, his own absurd shirt didn't stand out at all compared to what everyone else was wearing. He might have to forgive Allegra for it after all. He'd been so certain that she'd deliberately manoeuvred Dickie into choosing the flowery shirt as a joke.

'Isn't this place fab?' Across the table, Allegra was bright-eyed as she surveyed the crowd. Dom, the photographer, was sitting next to her and together they were keeping up a running commentary on celebrities they had spotted and what everyone was wearing. Max had tuned out after a while. He hoped Darcy King would turn up soon and make this purgatory worthwhile.

'Don't look now...' Allegra leant forward with a little squeal of excitement '...but that's Chris O'Donnell sitting behind you!'

'No! Not Chris! Squeeeee!'

She looked at him. 'You don't know who Chris O'Donnell is, do you?' Without waiting for his reply, she turned to Dom. 'He doesn't know who Chris O'Donnell is.'

Dom stared at Max. 'You just jetted in from Mars or something, man?'

'Chris O'Donnell is the ultimate bad boy rocker,' said Allegra, apparently shocked to her core by the depths of Max's ignorance. 'He just got voted sexiest man in the country, and he'd certainly have had my vote…' She sighed wistfully.

Max raised his brows. 'I didn't know you had a taste for bad boy rockers, Legs. Not your usual type, surely? I don't see your mother approving.'

Allegra flushed. 'I wouldn't want him as a boyfriend or anything, but you've got to admit he's smokin' hot…'

'So have you told Flick about your major new assignment?' Max said, not wanting to get into a discussion about which men Allegra thought were hot. He was fairly sure the list wouldn't include a civil engineer, flowery shirt or not.

Not that he cared about that. It was just uncomfortable to talk about that kind of stuff with someone he'd known for so long. It would be like discussing sex with his sister.

'I rang her last night.' Allegra's brightness dimmed slightly.

'Was she pleased to hear about your big break?'

'Well, you know Flick.' Her smile was painful to watch and Max cursed himself for asking. He should have known Flick would disappoint her. 'She did say "Well done" when I explained that it might mean a promotion if the article was a success. But she's writing about the political implications of the economic crisis; you can't blame her for not being impressed by my piece on whether it's possible to create the perfect boyfriend. I suspect she thinks it's a bit silly.'

Max had thought precisely the same thing but now, perversely, he was outraged at Flick's dismissal of Allegra's assignment. 'Did you tell her all that stuff you told me, about how these were the kind of issues that really matter to a lot of young women?'

Allegra sighed. 'I don't think boyfriend trouble quite ranks with the global downturn in the economy in my mother's scheme of things.' She squared her shoulders, sat up straighter. 'And she's right, of course. I should take more interest in political issues.'

She was nothing if not loyal to her mother, Max thought, still irrationally annoyed by Flick's response. Would it have killed her to have encouraged her daughter for once? Poor Allegra tried so hard to get her mother's approval. She had to want it bad to feign an interest in politics, given that he'd never heard her or Libby utter a word on the subject.

And she was going to find it hard, as demonstrated by the fact that barely had her resolve to be more politically aware fallen from her lips than her attention was caught by a girl teetering past in ludicrously high shoes. 'Omigod, I am totally stealing that vampire chic look!'

Max was obscurely pleased to see her revert to her frivolous self. 'Vampire chic?' he echoed, knowing the disbelief in his voice would annoy her, and sure enough, she gave him the flat-eyed look she and Libby had perfected when they were twelve.

Back to normal. Good.

'You just don't get it, do you?' she said. 'Look at you! We bring you to the hottest place in town, and you sit there like you were wishing you were in some grotty pub!'

'There's no "like" about it. I *am* wishing I was in a pub.'

'Here, have a drink.' Allegra passed him the drinks list. 'Maybe that'll cheer you up—and no, you can't have a pint.'

Morosely, Max scanned the list and choked when he saw the prices. 'They want *how* much for a cocktail?'

'Don't panic, you're not paying for the drinks,' she said. 'But, in all other respects, this is a real date, so start looking as if you're looking forward to meeting Darcy, not as if you're waiting to have your eyes poked out with a sharp stick.'

She shook her head as Max tried to ease the tightness around his neck. Dickie had a throttling way with a tie. 'Relax!' she said, leaning across the table to slap his hand away from his throat, and the scent of her perfume momentarily clouded Max's brain.

'You're so repressed,' she told him as he blinked the disturbing awareness away. 'Now listen, you're going to meet Darcy any minute and you're going to have to make an effort. This is your first task. You need to make sure she likes you enough to accept your invitation to dinner cooked by you, which is your second task.'

'You've explained all this,' said Max grouchily.

'And, just in case you were thinking of falling at the first hurdle so that you don't have to carry on, I'll just remind you that we haven't had that dinner with your boss yet.'

Why had he ever put the idea of blackmail into her head? She had taken to it like a natural. He'd created a monster.

'Remember, you're interested in Darcy, not in a lingerie model,' Allegra carried on bossily. 'Ask her questions but don't interrogate her—and don't expect her to take all the burden of the conversation either.'

'I've been on dates before, you know.'

Allegra ignored that. 'She'll be hoping to meet someone interesting and interest*ed*, someone charming and witty who can make her laugh, but who's got some old-fashioned manners—don't forget to stand up when she arrives—and who can make her feel safe but sexy and desirable at the same time.'

'And I'm going to be doing all of this with you listening in and Dom here taking pictures?'

'You'll hardly notice us after a while,' she assured him, then straightened as Dom nudged her. 'And here she comes! Good luck,' she mouthed to Max as he adjusted his tie and slid out of the banquette to greet Darcy.

He couldn't help staring. Spectacular was the only word. Of course he'd seen photos before, blown up across billboards or plastered across magazines, but in the flesh Darcy was breathtaking. She glowed with sex appeal, from her artfully tumbled blonde hair to the bee-stung mouth and the voluptuous body.

'Your tongue's hanging out,' Allegra said in his ear, and Max shut his mouth with a snap.

'You must be Max,' said Darcy in the famously husky voice and Max unscrambled his mind.

'I am. It's good to meet you, Darcy,' he said and stuck out his hand, but she only laughed and brushed it aside as she moved forward to kiss him on the cheek, enveloping him in a haze of perfume and allure.

'Let's not be formal,' she said while every man in the room watched him enviously. 'I hear we're going to be great friends!'

Dry-mouthed, Max stood back to usher her into the banquette. 'It sounds like you know more than I do,' he said with an accusing glance at Allegra, who was greeting Darcy cheerfully. What else hadn't she told him?

'Don't worry, darling,' said Darcy, patting his hand. 'It's going to be fun.'

Darcy and Max were getting on like the proverbial fire in a match factory. Allegra told herself she should be pleased that it was going so well. She took a gulp of the sparkling water she'd ordered as she was supposed to be working.

Darcy was obviously enjoying herself. She threw her head back and laughed her glorious laugh. She propped her chin on her hands and leant forwards, as if the famous cleavage needed attention drawn to it. She flirted with those impossibly long lashes and ran her fingers up and down Max's arm. Max, unsurprisingly, wasn't complaining.

He was doing much better than she had expected, Allegra had to admit. After that stunned moment—and she couldn't honestly blame him for that—he had recovered quickly and, while he wasn't exactly *charming,* he had a certain assurance that came from not caring what anybody else thought of him, and a kind of dry humour that seemed to be going down well with Darcy anyway.

Which Allegra was delighted about, naturally.

No, really, she was. Personally, she didn't think it was necessary for Darcy to touch him *quite* so often, but Darcy was obviously the tactile type. Not her fault that Allegra's fingers were twitching with the longing to reach across the table and slap her hand from Max's arm.

Who would have thought Max would brush up so well too? She'd thought he would dig in his heels at the flowery shirt but, apart from a few fulminating glances sent her way he'd clearly decided to honour his part of the agreement. Unlikely as it was, the shirt suited him beautifully. Something about the fabrics and the exquisite cut of the garments gave him a style he had certainly never possessed before.

It would take more than a shirt to turn him into an über hunk, of course, but Allegra had to allow that he didn't look as ordinary as he usually did.

It was amazing what a difference a good haircut made, too. She found herself noticing all sorts of things about him that she had never noticed before: the line of his jaw, the crease in his cheek, the uncompromising brows.

Vaguely disturbed, Allegra bent her head over her notebook. She was listening to the conversation between Max and Darcy as unobtrusively as possible and scribbling notes for the article she would write up when the final task was completed.

The article that could change her career and put her in a position to apply for jobs on magazines with a little more gravitas. If she got it right.

So why was she letting herself be distracted by the way Max's smile had suddenly started catching at the corner of her eye, the way it had suddenly started making her pulse kick as if it had startled her?

He was only smiling, for God's sake. She *wanted* him to be smiling at Darcy. She was supposed to be pleased with the way it was going, not feeling cross.

Darcy was telling Max a long story about the house she was having built, and he was offering advice about foundations and geological surveys. He'd obviously forgotten her advice about being witty and charming, but Darcy was hanging on his every word.

Disgruntled, Allegra gave up listening after a while. She wasn't going to fill her article with engineering talk, however fascinating Darcy might find it. Dom had taken his pictures and left some time before, and she let her pen drift: Derek the Dog dancing on his hind legs, Mrs G tipsy on cocktails, Flick smiling proudly—Allegra had to imagine that one.

Then she sketched Darcy leaning forward, lips parted breathlessly, and Max himself. But somehow she found herself drawing the Max she knew, the Max who wore a crummy polo shirt buttoned too high at the neck and lay on the absurdly feminine sofa, king of the remote, and she felt a pang of something she chose not to identify.

'Hey, those are great!' Darcy leant across the table and plucked the notebook away before Allegra had a chance to react.

She studied the drawings, chuckling. 'Who's the cute

dog? Look, Max, that's you...' Her smile faltered as she took in the polo shirt. 'At least...?'

Max peered at the sketch. 'Yep, looks like me.'

Allegra was blushing furiously. 'They're just doodles...'

'No, really, they're very good,' said Darcy. 'You clever thing.' She tapped a finger on the picture of her. 'You've caught me exactly, hasn't she, Max?'

'It's unmistakably you, but a drawing can't really capture your charm,' he said and Darcy laughed her trademark husky laugh, delighted, while Allegra concentrated on not throwing up.

If she wasn't much mistaken, Max was *flirting*. He must really like Darcy. Perhaps it was time to leave them alone. Ignoring the sinking feeling in her stomach, she took her notebook back from Darcy. 'I should go.'

'Don't go yet.' To her surprise, rather than wanting to get rid of her, Max handed her the drinks list. 'If you've finished working, you might as well have a proper drink.'

'Absolutely,' said Darcy with a sunny smile. 'You deserve it for setting up this article. I just know we're going to have a good time.' Her fingers teased Max's shoulder and Allegra's fingers tightened around the menu. 'I can't believe Max here hasn't been snapped up already, can you?'

'It's beyond comprehension,' Allegra agreed, but then made the mistake of glancing at Max. A smile hovered around his mouth and, for no reason she could name, her mouth dried.

'Try something with a ridiculous name,' he said, deadpan, and nodded at the drinks list. 'I'm longing to make a fool of myself ordering for you.'

Allegra swallowed and wrenched her gaze away to concentrate fiercely on the drinks list. Could she be coming down with something? She felt feverish and twitchy, and a nerve was jumping under her eye.

The list kept swimming in front of her eyes and she frowned in an effort to focus, but whenever she did the only cocktails that jumped out at her were called things like Screaming Orgasm or Wet Kiss. This was supposed to be fun. She should take Max up on his challenge and make him order something silly.

Why couldn't she grin and say: *I'd like a Sloe Screw Against the Wall, please, Max? Could I have Sex on the Beach?*

But all at once her throat was thick and she was having trouble swallowing. She handed the list back without meeting his eyes. 'I'll...er...have a martini, please.'

'Chicken,' said Max, beckoning over a waitress.

Darcy started to tell Allegra about a shoot she'd been on the day before. She knew Dickie and Stella and a host of other people at *Glitz*, and she was so friendly that it was impossible to dislike her, in spite of the way she kept flirting with Max, little touches on his arm, his shoulder, his hair. Every now and then her hand would disappear under the table and Allegra didn't want to think about what she was touching down there.

Allegra kept her attention firmly focused on Darcy's face, which was easier than being stupidly conscious of Max sitting next to Darcy and not looking nearly as out of place as he should have done. More and more, Allegra was convinced that she was sickening for something. She didn't feel herself at all. She was glad when the drinks arrived, but she drank hers a little too quickly and, before she knew what had happened, Darcy was beckoning for another one.

'You're one behind us,' she said gaily.

CHAPTER FOUR

So Allegra had another and then she and Darcy agreed to have another. Why had she been so uptight earlier? She was having a great time now, exchanging disastrous date stories with Darcy while Max sat back, folded his arms and watched them indulgently.

'Like you've never had a disastrous date,' Allegra accused him, enunciating carefully so as not to slur her words.

'What about this one?' said Max.

'We're talking about *real* dates,' she said indignantly.

Darcy nodded along. 'When your heart sinks five minutes in and you spend the rest of the evening trying to think of an excuse to leave early.'

'Or, worse, when you really like someone and you realise they're just not that into *you*,' said Allegra glumly.

A funny look swept across Max's face. 'I've got no idea what you're talking about,' he said.

Darcy had already moved on. 'I blame my father,' she said. 'He's spoilt me for other men. None of my boyfriends has ever been able to live up to him.'

'You're lucky to have a father,' Allegra said wistfully.

Her birth certificate just showed her mother's name. Flick refused to talk about Allegra's father. 'He was a mistake,' was all she would ever say and turn the subject.

When she was a little girl, Allegra had dreamed that her father would turn up one day and claim his daughter. She could never decide if she'd rather he was a movie star or the prince of some obscure European principality. Usually she opted for the latter; she thought she would make a good princess.

But no father ever came for her.

Thinking about fathers always made Allegra feel unloved and unwanted. If she wasn't careful, she'd start blubbing, so she smiled instead and lifted her glass. 'Oh,' she said, peering owlishly into it when she discovered it was empty, 'let's have another round.'

'I think you've had enough,' said Max, signalling for the bill instead. 'It's time to go home.'

'I don't want to go home. I want another martini.'

Max ignored her and put a surprisingly strong hand under her elbow to lift her, still protesting, to her feet. 'Can I get you a taxi, Darcy?'

'You're sweet,' Darcy said, 'but I might stay for a while.' She waved at someone behind them, and Allegra turned to follow her gaze. 'I'm just going to say hello to Chris.'

'Omigod, you know *Chris O'Donnell?* Allegra squeaked, but Max had already said a brisk goodbye and was propelling her towards the exit while she gawked over her shoulder in a really uncool way.

'What are you *doing*?' she complained. 'I was *this* close to meeting Chris O'Donnell.'

'You're completely sozzled,' said Max, pushing her through the doors. 'You wouldn't even remember him tomorrow.'

'I so would,' she said sulkily, and then reeled when the cold hit her. It was September still but there was an unmistakable snap of autumn in the air. If it hadn't been for his firm grip on her arm, she might have keeled right over.

Max looked down at her shoes—they were adorable peep-toes in a dusty pink suede with vertiginous heels—but he didn't look impressed. 'We'd better get a taxi,' he sighed.

Allegra's head was spinning alarmingly and she blinked in a vain attempt to focus. 'You'll never get a taxi round here,' she said but Max just propped her against a wall while he put his fingers in his mouth and whistled for a taxi. Annoyingly, one screeched to a halt straight away.

Having taken up position by the wall, it was harder than Allegra had anticipated to get over to the taxi. In the end Max had to manoeuvre her inside, where she collapsed over the seat in an undignified sprawl. She managed to struggle upright in a brave attempt to recover her dignity, but then she couldn't find her seat belt.

Her fumbling was interrupted by Max, muttering under his breath, who reached across her to locate the belt and clip it into place. His head was bent as he fiddled with the clip, and Allegra's spinning head jarred to a halt with the horrifyingly clear urge to touch his hair.

Clenching her fists into her skirt to stop her hands lifting of their own accord, she sucked in a breath and pressed her spine away from him into the seat, desperate to put as much space between them as she could.

'I think it all went well tonight,' she said. The idea was to sound cool and formal, to show Max that she wasn't nearly as sloshed as he seemed to think, but perfectly capable of carrying on a rational conversation. Unfortunately her voice came out wheezy, as if she had missed out on her share of oxygen.

Allegra cleared her throat and tried again. 'Darcy's lovely, isn't she?'

Yes, she was. Max had to agree. Darcy was a fantasy come to life, in fact. She was gorgeous and sexy and friendly and sweet-natured. So why hadn't he been able to relax and enjoy himself?

Max scowled at the back of the taxi driver's head as he fastened his own seat belt. Beside him, Allegra was still burbling on about what a great evening it had been, and how nice Darcy was. She obviously hadn't spent the entire evening being distracted.

Darcy was very touchy-feely, that was for sure. Max had been aware of her fingers trailing up and down his arm and over his thigh, but how could he enjoy it when Allegra was sitting opposite, scribbling notes in her book as if he were some kind of experiment she was observing?

It was mad. He, Max Warriner, had Darcy King *right beside him*, Darcy King *flirting with him*, and he couldn't concentrate. He was too aware of Allegra, eyeing him critically, her mouth pursed consideringly while she watched Darcy paw him. It obviously didn't bother her in the least.

It wasn't even as if there was any comparison between the two women. Darcy was lush, flirty, sex personified, while Allegra was slender, too thin really. So why did he keep remembering how it had felt when she hugged him? She'd been so soft and so warm, and her fragrance had enveloped him, and every bit of blood had drained from his head.

'And you were brilliant too,' said Allegra indistinctly. Her head kept lolling forward and Max had a sudden and very weird compulsion to unclip her seat belt again and ease her down so that she could lie with her head in his lap and sleep all the way home.

The taxi turned a corner and Allegra leant right over towards him before the car straightened and he caught the tantalising scent of her hair before she was thrown upright again. 'I feel a bit strange,' she said in a small voice.

'You'll be fine when you've had something to eat,' said Max bracingly, and she made a face.

'Ugh...I couldn't face eating anything.'

'Of course you could. We'll pick up a pizza on the way home.'

'Pizza? Are you mad?' Allegra demanded, roused out of her dopey state. 'Do you know how many calories there are in every slice?'

'You've just been guzzling cocktails,' he pointed out. 'A bit of pizza isn't going to make much difference after that. Besides, you're skinny enough. You could do with putting on a bit of weight, if you ask me.'

Allegra just looked at him pityingly. 'You've never worked in women's fashion, have you?'

'And I dare say I never will,' said Max without the slightest regret.

'Oh, I don't know. Now you've worn a flowery shirt, who knows what will happen?'

'That's what I'm afraid of,' he said glumly.

There was a silence, not uncomfortable. Lost in thought, Allegra was looking out of the window at the imposing façades along Piccadilly. It was long past the rush hour, but the traffic was still inching through the lights. They could do with a decent traffic pattern analysis, Max thought, doing his best to keep his mind off the tempting line of Allegra's throat or the coltishly sprawled legs revealed by the short flirty skirt he had been trying not to notice all evening. It was a pale mint-green, made of some kind of floaty, gauzy stuff, and she wore it with a camisole and a pale cardigan that just begged to be stroked. Darcy had cooed over its softness when she reached over and ran her hand down Allegra's sleeve, exclaiming the way women did over each other's clothes. Max had watched, his throat dry, and he'd fought the weird compulsion to push Darcy aside and stroke Allegra himself.

It was all very unsettling. He'd never given any thought to what she was wearing before—other than to boggle at the shoes she wore sometimes—so why was he suddenly acutely aware of the way her skirt shifted over her thighs when she sat down, or how some silky fabric lay against her skin?

Her face was partly turned away, and what he could see of her cheek and jaw was soft in the muted orange glow from the street. It was just this stupid assignment of hers, throwing them together in a way they'd never been before, Max decided. The sooner they got back to normal the better.

Ignoring Allegra's protests, Max ordered a large pizza the moment they got in. Allegra collapsed onto the sofa, rubbing her poor toes and moaning about the calorie count, but her mouth watered when the pizza arrived.

'I suppose I could have a tiny slice,' she said.

They sat on the floor, leaning back against the sofa with the pizza box between them. Allegra lifted a slice and took a bite, pulling at the stringy cheese with her fingers as she chewed. She would regret it in the morning, but God, it tasted good! And Max was right; she was already feeling better.

Closing her eyes, she pushed the calorie count from her mind and savoured the taste and the contrasting textures: the smoothness of the tomato paste, the chunky onions, the rubbery cheese, the bite of chorizo.

'Mmm...' She pushed a stray piece of cheese into her mouth and opened her eyes only to find Max watching her with an odd expression. 'What?' she asked.

'Nothing,' he said, looking away. 'You ought to eat more often if you enjoy it that much.'

'Are you kidding? I'd be the size of a house!'

But in that brief moment when their eyes had met, something had shifted in the air between them. Something that reminded Allegra uneasily of the night when Max had *not* kissed her.

The last thing she ought to be remembering right now.

She really shouldn't have had so many martinis. No wonder she was feeling so odd. Why did she suddenly feel as if she had to search around for something to say to break the silence? This was Max. She'd never needed to make conversation with him. Apart from that night, the one she wasn't thinking about. But now the silence between them thrummed with an unease that left her heart thumping inexplicably.

To distract herself, she picked up another piece of pizza. 'You'll have to do better than pizza when you invite Darcy over to supper.' There went her voice again, wobbling ridiculously up and down the register.

'I'm inviting Darcy to supper?'

'It's your second task,' she reminded him through a mouthful of pizza. 'The perfect boyfriend is not only sophisticated enough to enjoy cocktails, he's also a home-loving guy who can cook a delicious meal.'

'Well, I hope Darcy likes a roast, because that's all I can do.'

'Better make it a nut roast. She's a vegetarian.'

Max stared at her in consternation. 'A *vegetarian?* You didn't tell me that!'

'I didn't want to bamboozle you with too much information at once.'

'You mean you knew I'd back out,' he grumbled.

'Come on, Max, you make it sound like she eats babies!

They're only vegetables. I'm sure you can manage something. It doesn't have to be complicated, but you do need to cook it yourself. Libby's got a cookbook with some good recipes in it.'

Glad of an excuse to get away from the oddly strained atmosphere in the sitting room, Allegra pushed the last piece of pizza into her mouth and jumped up. Licking her fingers, she went into the kitchen and came back bearing the recipe book.

'Goat's cheese ravioli…that sounds nice,' she said as she flicked through the pages. 'Roasted vegetable tart… leek risotto…there's loads in here you could try.'

She handed the recipe book to Max, who looked through it without enthusiasm. 'Emma used to do all the cooking,' he said.

'Maybe she would have liked it if you'd done more,' said Allegra.

'Emma loves cooking,' he said defensively.

'I'm sure she does, but that doesn't mean that she wouldn't have appreciated it if you took a turn occasionally. You know, this is exactly the kind of thing you should get out of this exercise,' Allegra went on, warming to her theme. She was feeling more herself again, thank goodness. 'You've got a real chance here to learn how to please her. To show her that you've changed, that you're prepared to make an effort for her. I don't think you should give up.'

Max eyed her suspiciously. 'You seem very keen for me to get back together with Emma.'

'I'm keen for you to be happy,' she corrected him. 'And you seemed happy when you were with her.' It was true. Not to mention that *she* had been happier when he had been with Emma. There had been none of this uneasy awareness then. Max had just been someone to come across at the occasional family party—his family, not hers, naturally; Flick wasn't big on jolly get-togethers—to share a quick, spiky exchange for old times' sake and forget about until the next time.

It wasn't that Max had been dull, but his life was so far removed from Allegra's that she had never really *looked* at him until that awkward evening when something had clicked in the air, as surely as a bolt sliding into place. She'd been able to convince herself that that had been an aberration, especially when he'd met Emma, but now… it was making her nervous. She shouldn't be feeling jittery around Max. She shouldn't be noticing his mouth or his hands or the fact that beneath that shirt he wore was a lean, muscled body. It was all *wrong*.

The sooner he got back together with Emma the better. Then everything could go back to normal.

And clearly Max thought the same.

'I *was* happy with her,' he remembered. 'We had so much in common. We were friends! I still can't believe she'd give up everything she had for some guy she'd only known a few weeks.'

'It won't last,' Allegra said confidently.

'I didn't realise you were a great expert on passion!'

She forgave him the snide comment. Emma was still a very sore point, that much was clear.

'I've done my share of falling passionately in love, only to wake up one day and think: what am I doing?' she told him. 'Trust me, Emma will do the same, and you need to be there when she does. You need to show her that you've listened to what she said and that you're prepared to do whatever it takes to get her back.'

'Don't tell me: you're writing the *Glitz* agony column this month?'

'You may mock,' said Allegra with dignity, 'but it's good advice. If you really want Emma back, you should start paying attention and, in the meantime, get in touch with her. Send a text or something, no pressure.'

'And say what?' asked Max, who was at least listening, if unwillingly.

'Just say you're thinking of her,' said Allegra. 'That'll be enough for now.'

'I can't believe you're making me do this.' Max was in a grouchy mood and Allegra had to practically push him along the street towards the dance studio.

She had booked a private lesson so that Max could learn how to waltz before the costume ball. Darcy was thrilled by the idea, a fact that Allegra had yet to pass on to Max. 'I can't wait,' she'd confided to Allegra. 'I've never been out with anyone who knew how to dance properly.'

It would be Max's hardest test, but Allegra was determined that he would succeed. It wouldn't be much of an article if she had to report that he could manage some chit-chat over a drink but that when it came to really making an effort he had flunked out.

Besides, she was longing to learn how to waltz herself. Not that she had anyone to waltz with, but maybe her prince would be waiting at the ball. He'd be tall, dark and handsome, and unaccountably stood up by his date, and he would twirl her around the ballroom in his arms while Max was impressing Darcy with some nifty footwork.

Allegra's fantasy ground to a halt as Max balked at the sign on the door, an unfortunate pink decorated with fairies.

'We're not going in here?'

She could practically see him digging his heels into the concrete and she took his arm in a firm grip. 'There are no fairies inside, I promise. You just have to be brave and get past the door!'

Grumbling, Max let her manoeuvre him inside and up some stairs to the dance studio. Afraid that he would conveniently forget the arrangement, Allegra had gone to waylay him outside his office after work. She'd hung around on the pavement, feeling conspicuous in her pencil skirt, cropped jacket and funky boots, and deeply unimpressed by the style standards in civil engineering. Male or female, everyone who came out seemed to be safely dressed in sensible dark suits.

Allegra had twisted her ankle out to admire her studded suede boots. She would hate to work anywhere that dull. She hadn't seen a single outfit with any colour or flair. If this was the environment where Max spent his days, it was no wonder he had such appalling dress sense.

Hugging her arms together against the cool autumn breeze, she'd shifted from foot to foot as she kept an eye on the door. If Max didn't come out soon, she would have to go in and get him.

And suddenly there he was.

He'd pushed through the doors with two other men. They were identically dressed in suits and ties. Max wasn't the tallest or the best-looking, but for some reason Allegra's heart kicked when she caught sight of him. He was laughing at something one of the others said as he turned away, lifting a hand in farewell, and he ran lightly down the steps, scanning the street as he went.

He was looking for her. The realisation made her heart give another odd little jump and she was smiling foolishly when his gaze crossed hers, only to stop and swing back and meet her gaze. Their eyes locked with what Allegra could have sworn was an audible click and for a moment it was as if a question trembled in the air between them.

Then Max rolled his eyes and came towards her and

the moment was broken. He was just Max—staid, conventional Max. Libby's brother. Nothing more.

'I see you didn't trust me to make my own way to the dance studio,' he said as he came up.

Allegra felt as if she ought to kiss him on the cheek or something, but all at once she felt ridiculously shy. She wouldn't have hesitated at work, but she was on Max's ground now and it seemed too intimate to give him a casual hug.

So she kept her arms wrapped around herself and turned to walk beside him instead. 'You've got to admit that you didn't seem very keen when I reminded you about the dance lesson this morning,' she said. 'You'd rather stick pins in your eyes, you said.'

'I'm here, aren't I?'

'Only because I just happened to mention at the same time that I could still pull out of the dinner with your boss.'

'Yes, who would have guessed you'd turn into such a proficient blackmailer?'

Allegra spread her hands. 'We all have to use the talents we have,' she said modestly. 'I'm helping you with the dinner for Darcy too, don't forget. I believe in the carrot and stick approach.'

'I'm still waiting for some carrot,' said Max.

Now she put the flat of her hand against Max's back and pushed him into the studio. It was a large room with two mirrored walls and the faintly sweaty smell of packed exercise classes.

At least today they had the place to themselves. Allegra introduced Max to Cathy, the dance instructor she had hired at huge expense. A TV veteran, Cathy was famous for bringing unlikely celebrities up to scratch on the dancing front, but it was soon obvious that Max was going to be her biggest challenge.

'It's like trying to move a block of wood around the floor,' she complained. 'Allegra, you come and dance with him and see if he's more relaxed with you.'

It was exactly what Allegra had been hoping for. She leapt up and took her place in the middle of the empty floor with Max, but the moment she put one hand on his shoulder and the other in his palm, awkwardness gripped her. She hadn't anticipated how close Max would feel, how intimate it would seem to be standing together, holding each other.

'Right, Max, remember what I told you: you're stepping to the top of the box, and Allegra, you go back,' said Cathy, prowling around them. 'Off we go. One, two, three…top of the box, slide across, back…one, two, three…'

Allegra's mouth was dry, but she took a deep breath and tried to remember the instructions. She kept her eyes fixed on a spot behind Max's shoulder, which made it easier not to think about how warm and firm his fingers were, or the way his hand at her waist seemed to be sizzling through her top. Out of the corner of her eye, she could still see the edge of his jaw, rigid with concentration. It was very distracting and she kept forgetting where her feet were supposed to go.

'Stop! I can't stand it!' Cathy shrieked eventually, and Max and Allegra sprang apart with a mixture of relief and embarrassment.

Cathy heaved a dramatic sigh. 'I thought you told me you and Max were friends?' she said to Allegra.

Allegra and Max looked at each other. 'We are…sort of.'

'Sort of?'

'We've known each other a long time,' Max said after a moment.

Cathy arched an eyebrow. 'You surprise me. You were holding each other as if you'd never met before.' She sighed and regarded them both severely. 'Hug each other,' she ordered.

'What?'

'Hug each other,' Cathy repeated with exaggerated patience as Allegra and Max both did double takes.

'You mean…?' Allegra gestured vaguely, prompting another big sigh from Cathy.

'I mean put your arms around each other and squeeze. You know how to hug, don't you?'

'What's the object of the exercise?' asked Max, who clearly didn't want to get any closer than Allegra did.

'I want you to relax and feel comfortable with each other. A hug will help you get over any awkwardness. Well, go on,' she said when neither of them moved.

Clearing her throat, Allegra turned reluctantly to face Max. 'Sorry,' she mouthed at him and Max rolled his eyes in reply.

They had a couple of false starts where they stepped towards each other only to bang their heads together, or find their arms so awkwardly positioned that they had to pull apart and start again, but they were laughing by that stage and on the third try they got it right.

Allegra ended up with her arms around Max's waist, while he held her pressed against him. It felt as if they had slotted into place. Max was just the right height. Allegra fitted comfortably against him, her eyes level with his jaw, and if she turned her head, she could rest her face into his throat.

He had discarded his jacket but was still wearing a shirt and tie. The shirt was a very dull pale blue and the tie totally uninteresting, but Allegra had to admit that he smelt nice, of clean cotton and clean male. It was surprisingly reassuring being able to lean into his solid strength and feel that he wouldn't shift or topple over.

It had been another frenetic day at *Glitz* and Allegra had spent most of it galloping up and down the corridors and being screamed at. They were putting the next issue to bed and tension was running higher than usual, which made it stratospheric. It was as if the whole office was suffering from PMT.

But now she was being forced to rest against Max for a minute or two. In spite of herself, Allegra let out a little sigh and relaxed. It was weird, but being held by him like this felt…safe.

'Good,' said Cathy. 'Now squeeze each other tighter.'

Obediently, Allegra tightened her arms around Max's back as he pulled her closer, and suddenly it didn't feel safe at all.

Suddenly it felt dangerous, as if the floor had dropped away beneath her feet and left her teetering on the edge of a dizzying drop. The urge to turn into Max and cling to him was so strong that Allegra couldn't breathe with it. Her chest was tight, her pulse booming with an alarmed awareness of him. He held her rigidly and his body was hard—and when Allegra shifted uneasily against him she realised that—*oh?*—it wasn't just his chest that was hard.

Oh.

Before she had a chance to work out what she felt about that, Cathy was clapping her hands.

'Right, let's try again,' she said briskly and Max practically shoved Allegra away from him. His body might have been enjoying being pressed up against her, but his mind obviously hadn't. He scowled as Cathy ordered them back into position.

'Remember what I told you about the box step?' she said as Max and Allegra took hold of each other awkwardly, careful to keep a gap between them. 'Step to the top of the box, slide your feet together, step back, slide together… Off you go!'

It was easier without the distraction of being pressed right against him, Allegra told herself. That flood of heat had just been a physical reaction, exactly as Max's had been. It was what happened when you squashed a man and a woman together. It didn't *mean* anything.

'No, no!' Cathy threw up her hands. 'Max, you go *forward*, Allegra you're stepping *back*! Now, try again, and this time try and concentrate on what you're doing.'

Right, concentrate. Allegra stifled a nervous giggle as she fluffed it again, and Max muttered under his breath.

Cathy sighed.

They set off again, and managed two sides of the box before Max trod heavily on Allegra's foot, making her yelp, at which point they both started laughing. It was partly embarrassment, partly relief that the awful awareness had dissipated.

Cathy was less amused. 'You're both hopeless,' she said when their time was up. 'If you want Max to impress Darcy at the ball, you're going to have to practice. At least master the basic steps and we can try and add some turns next week.'

CHAPTER FIVE

'Turns?' Max grumbled as they slunk out. 'You mean we have to go round and round as well as backwards and forwards?'

'It's a lot harder than it looks,' Allegra agreed, winding her scarf around her throat. 'I've waltzed so often in my fantasies that I thought I'd be quite good at it. I can't believe I was so crap,' she said despondently.

'In your fantasy you don't dance with me, that's why,' said Max, feeling obscurely guilty about spoiling the waltz for her.

'True.' She perked up a little as they headed down the street. 'I'd be much better with my Regency duke.'

'Your what?'

'The duke who waltzes me out on the terrace, begs me to become his duchess and ravishes me,' said Allegra as if it was the most normal thing in the world. 'I told you about my fantasy.'

'You didn't mention any dukes.'

'I think he probably *is* a duke,' she said, having considered the matter. 'He's got a dreadful reputation as a rake, of course, but underneath he's deeply honourable.'

'He's not very honourable if he ravishes you right outside a crowded ballroom,' Max pointed out.

'You're such a nitpicker,' she said without heat.

Max shook his head. 'I can't figure you out, Legs. One minute you're obsessed with fashion or celebrity gossip, the next you're fantasising about dancing with dead aristocrats.'

And that was before you took into account the sweet and funny Allegra who drew cute cartoon animals, or the one who tried so hard and so unsuccessfully to be cool and high-minded so that she could please her demanding mother. The one who fretted constantly about her weight or the one who sat on the floor and ate pizza with relish.

It was only since moving into the house that Max had come to realise that there was more to Allegra than he had thought. If he'd been asked to describe her before then he would have said sweet, a bit scatty, a bit screwed up by her mother.

And now...now he was learning new things about her every day. Like the way she left the bathroom a tip, the way her face lit up when she smiled. Like the smell of her perfume. The way she tilted her chin.

The way she felt. Max's mouth dried at the memory of that ridiculous hug Cathy had insisted on. After a couple of false starts, Allegra had fitted into him as if she belonged there, and his senses had reeled alarmingly at the feel of her slenderness pressed against him.

And it wasn't just his senses that had reacted. Max shifted his shoulders uncomfortably in his jacket, remembering how aroused he had been. Hold her tighter, that fool Cathy had said. What was he supposed to do when a soft, warm woman was melting into him and her perfume filled his head and it was all he could do to stop his hands sliding under that silky top, rucking up that sexy skirt so that he could run them hungrily over her long thighs?

This was all Emma's fault. If they'd still been together, he wouldn't have been sex-starved, and he certainly wouldn't have been thinking about Allegra like some kind of pervert.

She was lucky that treading on her toes was all he had done.

At least it had been easier once they'd started laughing. It was a relief to know that Allegra couldn't dance for toffee either. When he wasn't wanting to rip her clothes off, he and Allegra got on much better than he had expected.

She'd been teaching him how to cook so that he could impress Darcy, and kept coming back from *Glitz* laden with ingredients and advice from the food editor. Max wasn't learning much, but he enjoyed leaning against the worktop and watching her face as she chopped enthusiastically, throwing weird ingredients together in ridiculously complicated meals. Emma was a great cook, Max remembered loyally. Meat and two veg, exactly what you wanted to eat, perfectly cooked. None of Allegra's nonsense.

Although there was something oddly endearing about the nonsense all the same. Even if it did taste rubbish.

'You say you want to be a serious journalist, but I've only ever seen you talk seriously about cosmetics or the latest soap,' he said, still puzzling over her.

A brisk wind was swirling dead leaves along the gutter and Allegra pulled her coat closer around her. 'People are more than one thing,' she said loftily. 'Talking of which, what did you do to Dickie?'

'I didn't do anything,' said Max in surprise.

'He was so fragile this morning that the entire office had to whisper! Stella's assistant told the intern who told me that when Stella asked him what was wrong, he said it was all your fault!'

'I just took him to the pub.'

Allegra had sent him off for another styling session with Dickie the night before. Max had grumbled, but he'd gone along and without Allegra there had been able to come to an understanding with Dickie. Make the whole process as quick and painless as possible, he had suggested, and they could go and have a decent drink.

'Can you believe it?' he went on. 'The guy's been in London for ten years and he's never had a decent pint.'

'You took *Dickie* to a *pub?*' Allegra had stopped dead and was looking at him in horror.

'You told me to be nice to him,' Max reminded her.

'Making him go to a pub and getting him drunk on beer isn't being nice!'

'He had a great time. I'm taking him to a rugby game next.'

Allegra opened and closed her mouth, unable to get out a coherent sentence. 'Dickie…rugby…?'

'I don't know why you're all so terrified of him. He's a perfectly nice guy once you get past all the affectation.'

'That's it. My career is over.'

'Don't be silly,' said Max, taking her arm and steering her across the road at the lights. 'Dickie likes me. Although if I'd thought about it, ending your career might have been a good move. I'd never have to waltz again.'

'Darcy's going to be here any minute. Are you almost ready?'

Allegra put her head around the door to the kitchen, where Max was putting the final garnish to the romantic vegetarian meal for two that they had planned together.

At least, she had planned it and Max had reluctantly agreed to cook it. 'I don't see why I can't just give her pasta with a tomato sauce,' he'd grumbled.

'Because this is a special occasion. You want Darcy to know that you've made a real effort to cook something that she'll really like.'

Eventually they had settled on a pear, walnut and gorgonzola salad to start, followed by mushroom strudels with a tarragon cream sauce, and then margarita ice cream with chocolate-dipped strawberries. Allegra had been pleased with it, but after several practice runs, she had strudel coming out of her ears and she couldn't face another chocolate-dipped strawberry, which wasn't something she ever thought she would say.

'I'm all set,' said Max. 'I just need to change.'

'I'll make the living room look nice,' Allegra volunteered. Max was supposed to be thinking about that as well, but when she had suggested it he had just looked blank.

At least everything was tidy, the way it always was when Max was around. Allegra set out candles and plumped up the cushions before putting on the playlist of romantic music she had compiled specially. Max didn't have a clue about music or romance, so she'd known better than to suggest that he did it.

She was lighting candles when he came back. 'It's a bit gloomy in here, isn't it?' he said, looking around. 'Darcy won't be able to see what she's eating.'

'It's not gloomy. It's *romantic*.'

Allegra straightened from the candles and studied Max, who had replaced his checked shirt with one in a dark mulberry colour that shrieked expensive and stylish. He was wearing new black jeans too, and all in all he was looking mighty fine. So fine, in fact, that she forgot about the match burning in her hand.

'Ouch!' Allegra shook the match from her hand and sucked her finger. 'Is that the shirt Dickie picked out for you?' she asked, covering her sudden confusion by bending to pick up the match.

'Of course.' Max plucked at it in distaste. 'You wouldn't catch me buying a red shirt, but Dickie insisted.'

'He was right. You look good,' said Allegra honestly. She tossed the blackened match into the bin and turned back to face him. She had herself back under control. 'If I could just make one teeny change…?'

Without waiting for Max to agree, she walked over and undid another button at his throat. Ignoring his protests, she turned her attention to his cuffs, unfastening them and rolling them up above his wrists.

But standing so close to him was making her feel a bit light-headed, and she was excruciatingly conscious of her fingertips grazing his forearms with their fine, flat hairs. The air had shortened, making her heart pound ridiculously. She wanted to say something light, something casual to break the atmosphere, but her mind was a blank and she didn't dare meet Max's eyes in case…

In case *what?*

In case he kissed her. In case *she* kissed *him*.

Allegra swallowed hard. This was silly. She'd just got over that mad period when she'd been so inexplicably conscious of him. The last few days had been fine, cooking, talking easily, sniping at each other, laughing with each other. They'd dutifully practised the basic waltz step and even seemed to be getting the hang of it. It had been just like the old days.

And now he'd put on a new shirt and that awful thump was back in her belly. Allegra didn't like it one little bit.

Clearing her throat, she patted the second sleeve into place and stepped back. 'There, that's better,' she said.

Max immediately started fidgeting with his cuffs. 'It looks so messy like this,' he complained until Allegra had to slap his hands away.

'Leave them! Those cuffs are the difference between looking like a nerd and looking like a hunk.'

'A *hunk?*' Max echoed, revolted.

'Okay, not a hunk,' she amended, 'but more normal, anyway. Like you might possibly have some social skills. And, talking of which,' she said as she struck another match to light the rest of the candles, 'remember this evening's about making Darcy feel really special. Ask her lots of questions about what she does and how she feels about things.'

'Yeah, yeah, we've been through this,' said Max, straightening the knives and forks on the table.

Allegra blew out the match and admired the way the flames danced above the candles. 'Are you sure it's all under control in the kitchen?'

'Positive. I wrote out a time plan, and I don't need to do anything until seventeen minutes after she arrives.'

'Right. Seventeen minutes. Because you wouldn't want to eat a minute later than scheduled, would you?' Allegra rolled her eyes, but Max was unfazed.

'You're the one who wants the meal to be a success,' he pointed out. He looked at his watch yet again. 'Shouldn't she be here by now?'

'I sent a car. I hope she's not going to be late. We can't really have a drink until she gets here, and I'm gasping for one.'

'We could practice our waltz steps,' Max suggested without any enthusiasm, but Allegra jumped up.

'That's a great idea. We need to be able to wow Cathy with our progress next week.'

They had practised several times now and it no longer felt uncomfortable to rest one hand on his shoulder, or to feel his arm around her waist. They set off briskly, moving their feet around an invisible box, the way Cathy had taught them, while Allegra hummed an approximation of a waltz.

'Hey, we're getting good at this,' Max said after a while. 'Shall we try a turn?'

Allegra was up for it but, the moment they tried to do something different, their feet got muddled up and they stumbled. Disentangling themselves, they tried again. This time they managed so well that Max got fancy. They were both elated at their success and, laughing, he spun her round and dipped her over his arm with a flourish.

And there it would have ended if they hadn't made the mistake of looking into each other's eyes. They could have straightened, still laughing, and it would have been fine.

But no! Their eyes had to lock so that the laughter evaporated without warning, leaving their smiles to fade. Allegra was still bent ridiculously over Max's arm but she couldn't tear her gaze from his. The air felt as if it was tightening around them, squeezing out all the oxygen, and her pulse was booming and thudding. She couldn't have moved if she had tried.

Later, she wondered if she had imagined the fact that Max's head had started to move down to hers. Certainly at the time she didn't know whether to be relieved or disappointed when the shrill of the doorbell jerked them both out of their daze.

'Darcy!' Flustered, Allegra pulled out of Max's hold and smoothed down her hair. What was she *doing*? She had forgotten all about the article for a few moments there.

Allegra had forgotten quite how beautiful Darcy was. Max greeted her at the door and when he showed her in she seemed to light up the room. Her blonde hair fell over one shoulder in a fishtail braid that looked casual but must have taken her hours to achieve, and her skin glowed. She was wearing an electric-blue dress that showed off her stupendous figure. If Allegra wasn't much mistaken, the dress was from a high street chain rather than a designer but Darcy made it look stunning. From her bee-stung lips to the tips of her Christian Louboutin shoes—no whiff of the high street *there*—she was perfect.

By rights, Allegra ought to hate her, but Darcy was so warm and friendly that it was impossible.

'This all looks wonderful,' she said, looking around the room. 'You've gone to so much trouble, Max!'

Max took it without a blink. 'Nothing's too much trouble for you, Darcy,' he said, but he avoided Allegra's eyes. 'Now, let's have some champagne…'

Everything was going swimmingly, Allegra thought later. Dom turned up a few minutes later and took a few pictures of Max in the kitchen, and then of Max and Darcy sitting at the table with the starter, but once he had gone they were able to enjoy the meal. The three of them chatted so easily that Allegra kept forgetting that she was supposed to be just an observer, and after a while she put her notebook aside.

She had imagined that taut moment of awareness just before Darcy rang the doorbell, she told herself. Look at them now, talking like old friends. There was no crackling in the air between them, no zing every time their eyes met. She had made the whole thing up.

The food wasn't too bad either. What it lacked in presentational flair, it made up for in efficiency, with Max putting each course on the table with military precision.

All in all, the second task was a huge success, Allegra congratulated herself.

'Coffee?' Max asked at last.

'Actually, I'd love a herbal tea if you've got one,' said Darcy, and Max rolled an agonized look at Allegra.

'In the cupboard above the kettle,' she said.

The moment Max went out to put the kettle on, Darcy leant towards Allegra. 'Can I ask you something?'

'Sure,' said Allegra in surprise.

'Are you guys...?'

'What?'

'You and Max,' said Darcy delicately. 'I asked Max if you were an item, but he said you were just friends.' She looked at Allegra. 'Is that right?'

Allegra felt unaccountably miffed at the way Max had disclaimed any interest in her, but she could hardly deny it. 'Of course,' she said, taking a casual sip of wine. 'Max is practically my brother.'

'Oh, that's good. So you won't mind if I asked Max to dinner at my place?'

Allegra choked on her wine. 'Dinner?' she spluttered.

'Yes. Not as part of the *Glitz* deal, but like a proper date.'

'You want to date *Max*?'

Darcy laughed a little self-consciously. 'I think he's cute.'

Max? *Cute*?

'He's not like the usual guys I date,' Darcy went on.

Allegra thought of the actors and rock stars who had been linked to Darcy, über hunks every one of them, and she blinked. 'You can say that again.'

'I kinda like him,' Darcy confessed. 'Do you think he'd say yes?'

A famous lingerie model inviting him to spend the evening alone with her at her house. Like Max would turn *that* invitation down.

'You should ask Max, not me,' said Allegra stiffly.

'You don't sound very keen on the idea,' said Darcy, who was a lot more perceptive than she looked. 'Are you sure you don't mind?'

'It's not that. It's just…well, Max puts on a good show, but his fiancée broke off their engagement not very long ago. I wouldn't want him to get hurt again. I mean…'

Allegra was floundering, wishing she had never started on this. '…It's just that you're so gorgeous and you must have so many men after you. I…I'd hate it if you were just amusing yourself with Max and he ended up taking you too seriously. And I can see why he would,' she said with honest envy. 'I can't imagine any guy not falling heavily for you.'

'You'd be surprised,' said Darcy with a touch of bitterness. 'I don't understand why I've got such a reputation as a man-eater. Nobody ever worries that I might be the one to get hurt, do they?'

'Max isn't your usual type,' Allegra pointed out and Darcy nodded.

'That's why I'd like to get to know him better. I'm sick of guys who are all moody and dramatic, or who just want to be with me so they can get their name in the papers.'

'Well, you certainly wouldn't need to worry about that with Max.'

'Great. Well, if you're sure you're okay with it, I'll ask him.'

Allegra wasn't at all sure that she *was* okay with it, but she couldn't think of a single reason why not. Max was a grown man. He didn't need her to look after him, and she could hardly veto his chance to fulfil every man's fantasy of going out with Darcy, could she? He deserved some fun after Emma's rejection.

So why did she have this leaden feeling in her stomach?

When Max came back with the coffee and the herbal tea, Allegra took her mug and excused herself. 'I'll leave you two together,' she said with a brilliant smile. 'I need to go and write up my notes. Have fun.'

* * *

'What do you mean, you're not coming?' Max stared at Allegra in consternation.

'I'm going to dinner at Flick's,' she pointed out. 'Plus, I'm not invited.'

'I thought you'd be going too. And Dom.'

'Max, Darcy's invited you to supper. It's nothing to do with the article.'

'Why?' he asked, puzzled.

'Crazy thought, but maybe she likes you.'

Thrown by this new information, Max dragged a hand through his hair. The truth was that he hadn't really listened when Darcy had invited him the evening he'd cooked her dinner. It was after Allegra had gone to her room, and he'd just assumed that another task was involved.

Darcy *liked* him?

'You mean, like on a date?' he asked cautiously and Allegra rolled her eyes. She was doing something complicated with her hair in front of the mirror over the mantelpiece.

'I'd have thought you'd have been over the moon,' she said, through a mouthful of hairclips.

'Darcy King wants to go out with *me*?'

'I know, I thought it was unlikely too,' said Allegra, fixing another clip into place.

Max sat on the sofa and tossed the remote from hand to hand. Darcy King. She was gorgeous, sexy, warm, *nice*. Why wasn't he ecstatic?

'I thought I was just signing up for this article of yours,' he said grouchily. 'I didn't realise I'd be getting involved in other stuff as well.'

'It's just dinner, Max. I don't suppose she's planning on a bout of eye-popping sex straight away.'

Apparently satisfied with her hair, Allegra turned from

the mirror. It never failed to amaze Max how she could spend so long achieving a range of hairstyles, each messier than the last. That evening she had twisted it up and fixed it into place with a clip, but bits stuck out wildly from the clip, and other strands fell around her face. Max's fingers itched to smooth them behind her ears, but the idea of sliding his fingers through that silky hair was so tantalising that for a moment he lost track of the conversation.

'You ought to be flattered,' she said.

'I am,' said Max, wrenching his mind back from a disturbingly vivid image of pulling that clip from her hair and letting it fall, soft and shiny, to her shoulders. 'It's just…I don't want to complicate things.'

'What's complicated about dinner? You had dinner with Darcy the other night and this time you won't even have to worry about the cooking.'

'It's not that.' How could he tell Allegra that, much as he liked Darcy, he found her a bit overwhelming? 'It's not long since I was engaged to Emma,' he said, grasping at the excuse. 'It feels too soon to be getting involved with anyone else.'

Allegra's face softened instantly and then she snarled every one of his senses by coming to sit on the sofa beside him and placing her hand on his knee.

'I'm sorry, I keep forgetting that you must still be gutted about Emma.'

Max didn't think gutted was quite the right word, in fact, but with Allegra sitting so close, her green eyes huge and warm with sympathy, it was all he could do to nod.

'Darcy knows you were engaged,' Allegra went on, with a comforting rub on his thigh. At least, Max assumed it was meant to be comforting, although in practice it was excruciatingly arousing. If she moved her hand any higher, he couldn't be responsible for his actions... As unobtrusively as he could, he shifted along the sofa.

Allegra was still talking, still looking at him with those big, earnest eyes, completely unaware of the effect she was having on him. 'She won't expect you to fall madly in love with her, Max. It'll just be dinner. Darcy's nice, and it'll be a boost for your ego, if nothing else. You should go and forget about Emma for an evening.'

It wasn't Emma he needed to forget, it was the feel of Allegra's hand on his leg, but Max heard himself agreeing just so that he could get up before he grabbed her and rolled her beneath him on the sofa. He had to give himself a few mental slaps before he had himself under control enough to change and go back down to the sitting room, where Allegra was perched on the armchair and bending over to ease on a pair of precipitously-heeled shoes. She was in a dark floral sleeveless dress with black lace over the shoulders and a skirt that showed off miles of leg in black stockings, and Max's throat promptly dried all over again.

Those loose strands of hair had slithered forward when she bent her head and she tucked them behind her ears as she glanced up to see Max standing in the doorway. There was an odd little jump in the air as their eyes met, and then both looked away.

'You look nice,' Max said gruffly.

'Thank you.' Her gaze skimmed his then skittered away. 'Is that one of the shirts Dickie picked out for you?'

'Yes.' Self-consciously, he held his arms out from his side. 'Why, is it too casual?'

'It's perfect—or it would be if you rolled up your cuffs, and...' Allegra pointed at her throat to indicate that his collar was too tightly buttoned.

She had a thing about his collar, but Max knew from experience that it wasn't worth the argument. With a long-suffering sigh, he unfastened another button before starting on his cuffs. She had a thing about those too. He could do them up again as soon as she'd gone.

'So, you're seeing your mother,' he said after a moment. 'What's it going to be? A cosy night in with just the two of you?'

Max knew as well as she did that Flick didn't do cosy, but Allegra couldn't help smiling a little wistfully. She adored her mother, and it made her feel disloyal to wish sometimes that Flick could be a little—just a little!—more like Libby and Max's mum, who was easygoing and gave wonderful hugs and would happily watch *I'm a Celebrity Get Me Out of Here!* instead of the news. The first time Allegra had been to stay with Libby they had had supper on their laps in front of the television, and it had felt deliciously subversive.

'I think there'll be a few people there,' she told Max as she wiggled her feet into a more comfortable position in her shoes. 'She says she's got someone she wants me to meet.'

Max started on his second cuff, his expression sardonic. 'Flick's setting you up with a new boyfriend?'

'Maybe.'

'You don't sound very keen.'

She hadn't, had she? She'd sounded like someone who would really rather be staying at home. That would never do.

Allegra stood up and tested her shoes. 'Of course I'm keen,' she said. 'The men my mother introduces me to are always intelligent, cultured, amusing, interesting... Why wouldn't I be keen?'

'No reason when you put it like that,' said Max. He had dealt with his cuffs and now he stood in the centre of the room with his hands in his pockets, looking sulky and surly and disconcertingly attractive. Allegra almost told him to button up his shirt again so he could go back to looking stuffy and repressed.

'I'm feeling positive,' she said airily. 'This guy could be The One. I could be on my way to meet true love!'

Max snorted. 'Well, don't make a date for Wednesday, that's all.'

He had finally heard from Bob Laskovski's office. Bob and his wife would be in London the following week and the dinner to meet Max and his 'fiancée' was arranged for the Wednesday night. Max was nervous about the whole business, Allegra knew. He wasn't comfortable with deception, but he was desperate for the Shofrar job. Perhaps that was why he was so grouchy at the moment?

Darcy was welcome to him, Allegra told herself as she flipped open her phone to call a cab. She couldn't care less that Max was having supper with a lingerie model. *She* was going out to have a great time and meet a fabulous new guy. And, who knew, maybe she'd find true love at last as well.

Flick still lived in the four-storey Georgian house in a much sought after part of Islington where Allegra had grown up but it never felt like going home. The house was immaculately decorated and most visitors gasped in envy when they stepped inside, but Allegra much preferred the Warriners' house with its scuffed skirting boards and faded chair covers.

Flick's dinner parties were famous, less for the food, which was always catered, than for the company. Politicians, media stars, business leaders, diplomats, writers, artists, musicians, journalists…anyone who was anyone in London jostled for a coveted invitation to sit at Flick's dining table. No celebrities, pop stars or soap opera actors need apply, though. Flick insisted on a certain intellectual rigour.

Thus Allegra found herself sitting between Dan, a fast-track civil servant, obviously destined for greatness, while William, on her right, was a political aide. They both worked in government circles and were both high-flyers, full of gossip and opinion.

Toying with her marinated scallops, Allegra felt boring and uninformed in comparison. She couldn't think of a single clever or witty thing to say.

Not that it mattered much. The conversation around the table was fast and furious as usual, but no one was interested in her opinion anyway, and it was enough for Allegra to keep a smile fixed to her face.

Beside her, Dan had launched into a scurrilous story about a politician everybody else seemed to know but who Allegra had never heard of. She laughed when everybody else laughed, but she was wondering how Max was getting on with Darcy. Would he sleep with her? Allegra realised that she had stopped smiling and hurriedly put her smile back in place.

Why did she care? Max would be leaving soon anyway, and it wasn't as if he was interested in her. True, there had been that moment when their eyes had met earlier, when she was putting on her shoes and had glanced up to find him watching her and something had leapt in the air between them.

It was just because they were spending so much time together for the article, Allegra told herself. It wasn't that she would really rather be sharing pizza with Max in front of the television than sitting here at this glamorous, glittering party. Of course she wouldn't.

Oh, God, she had missed Dan's punchline. At the other

end of the table, she caught Flick's eye and the tiny admonishing frown and sat up straighter.

Beside her, William was filling her glass, teasing her out of her abstraction. His eyes were warm, and she was picking up definite vibes. Allegra gazed at him, determined to find him attractive. She'd already established that he'd split up with his long-term girlfriend a year ago. A mutual thing, he'd said. They were still friends.

So no obvious emotional baggage. Unlike Max, who was still sore about Emma.

William was very good-looking. Charming. Assured. Also unlike Max.

He would be staying in London. Unlike Max.

He seemed to be finding her attractive. Unlike Max.

He was perfect boyfriend material. Unlike Max.

If William asked her out, she would say yes.

Definitely. She might even fall in love with him.

CHAPTER SIX

'I HAVEN'T HAD a chance to talk to you yet, Allegra,' Flick said, coming back into the dining room, having said goodbye to the last of her guests, a cabinet minister who was tipped for a promotion in the next reshuffle. She frowned at Allegra, who was helping the caterers to clear the table. 'The caterers are paid to tidy up. Leave that and let's have a chat.'

No one looking at them together would guess that they were mother and daughter. Where Allegra was tall and dark and a little quirky-looking, Flick was petite and blonde with perfect features, steely blue eyes and a ferocious intelligence. Allegra was super-proud of her famous mother, but sometimes she did wonder what it would be like to have a mother who would rush out to hug you when you arrived, like Libby and Max's mother did, or fuss over you if you were unhappy.

A chat with Flick didn't mean sitting over cocoa in the kitchen. It meant being interrogated in the study about your career and achievements. Which in Allegra's case were not very many.

Sure enough, Flick led the way to her book-lined study and sat behind her desk, gesturing Allegra to a chair as if for an interview.

'Another successful evening, I think,' she said complacently.

'The food was lovely,' Allegra said dutifully, stealing a surreptitious glance at her watch. One in the morning... Was Max still with Darcy? He'd seemed surprisingly reluctant to go, but surely, once faced with Darcy's glowing beauty, he wouldn't be able to resist?

'You seem very abstracted, Allegra.' Flick had her razor-sharp interviewing voice on. 'I noticed it during dinner too. Not very good manners. Would you rather go?'

'No, no, of course not...' Nobody could make her stammer like her mother and, because she knew it irritated Flick, Allegra pulled herself together. 'I'm sorry. I'm just a bit preoccupied with an assignment I've got for *Glitz*.'

Flick sat back in her chair and raised her brows. 'I hardly think an article on the latest fashion trend compares to the kind of issues that everyone else here has to deal with every day.' She unbent a little. 'But I read your little piece on shoes last week. It was very entertaining. The ending was a little weak but, otherwise, your writing has improved considerably. What's the latest assignment?'

Allegra started to explain about the idea behind the article, but it sounded stupid when her mother was listening with her impeccably groomed head on one side. 'I'm hoping that if I can make a success of it, Stella will give me more opportunities to write something different.' She stumbled to a halt at last.

Flick nodded her approval. She liked it when Allegra thought strategically. 'I suppose it's experience of a sort, but you'd be so much better off at a serious magazine. You remember Louise's son, Joe? He's at *The Economist* now.'

Allegra set her teeth. 'I'm not sure I'm ready to write about quantitative easing yet, Flick. *The Economist* would be a bit of a leap from *Glitz*.'

'Not for someone who's got what it takes—but you've never been ambitious,' said Flick regretfully. 'But you do look very nice tonight,' she conceded. 'Those dark florals are good for you. The earrings aren't quite right, but otherwise, yes, very nice. William seemed rather taken,' she added. 'Are you going to see him again?'

'Perhaps.' The truth was that when William had asked her out, Allegra had opened her mouth to say yes and then somehow heard herself say that she was rather busy at the moment.

'He's got a great future ahead of him. I'd like to see you spend more time with people like that instead of these silly little assignments for that magazine. I mean, who are you working with at the moment?'

'Max.' Funny how his name felt awkward in her mouth now. 'You remember, Libby's brother,' she said when Flick looked blank.

'Oh, yes...rather dull.'

'He isn't dull!' Allegra flushed angrily.

'I don't remember him striking me as very interesting,' said Flick, dismissive as only she could be.

Allegra had a clear memory of thinking much the same thing once. So why was she wishing that she could have spent the evening with him instead of flirting with William, who was everything Max would never be?

'I didn't realise he was a particular friend of yours.' Her mother's eyes had narrowed suspiciously at the colour burning in Allegra's cheeks.

'He wasn't. I mean, he isn't. He's just living in the house for a couple of months while Libby's in Paris.'

'I hope you're not getting involved with him?'

'Anyone would think he was some kind of troublemaker,' Allegra grumbled. 'He's a civil engineer. It doesn't get more respectable than that.'

'I'm sure he's very good at what he does,' said Flick gently. 'But he's not exactly a mover and shaker, is he? I've always worried about the way you seem happy to settle for the mediocre, rather than fulfilling your potential.' She shook her head. 'I blame myself for letting you spend so much time with that family—what are they called? Warren?'

'Warriner,' said Allegra, 'and they're wonderful.'

'Oh, I'm sure they're very kind but I've brought you up to aim for the exceptional.'

'They *are* exceptional!' Normally the thinning of Flick's lips would have been a warning to Allegra, but she was too angry to stop there. 'They're exceptionally generous and exceptionally fun. Max's mother might not win any style awards, but she's lovely, and his dad is one of the nicest, most decent, most honourable men I've ever met,' she swept on. 'I only wish I'd had a father like him!'

There was a moment of appalled silence, while her last words rang around the room. Flick had whitened. Allegra's lack of a father was a taboo subject and Allegra knew it.

'I'm sorry,' she said, letting out a long breath. 'But why won't you tell me about my father?'

'I don't wish to discuss it,' said Flick tightly. 'In your case, father is a biological term and nothing more. I'm sorry if I haven't been enough of a parent for you.'

'I didn't mean that,' Allegra tried to break in wretchedly, but Flick moved smoothly on.

'I can only assure you that all I've ever wanted is the best for you. You have so much potential if only you would realise it. I really think it would be a mistake for you to tie yourself down to somebody ordinary who'll just drag you down to his level.'

She should have known better than to try and press Flick about her father. 'You don't need to worry,' said

Allegra dully. 'There's no question of anything between Max and me and, even if there were, he's going abroad to work soon.'

'Just as well,' said Flick.

It *was* just as well, Allegra told herself in the taxi home. Flick had suggested that she stay the night in her old room, but she wanted to go back to the flat. She didn't want to admit to herself that she needed to know if Max had stayed with Darcy or not and it was like a sword being drawn out of her entrails when she opened the door and saw Max stretched out on the sofa.

'You're back early.' Funny, her voice sounded light and normal when her heart was behaving so oddly, racing and lurching, bouncing off her chest wall like a drunk.

'It's half past one. It's not that early.'

'I suppose not.' Allegra went to sit in the armchair. She picked at the piping. 'So, how was your evening?'

'Fine. Yours?'

'Oh, you know. Lots of clever, glamorous guests. Witty conversation. Delicious food. The usual.'

'Your average social nightmare.'

Allegra laughed and toed off her shoes so that she could curl her feet up beneath her. She was feeling better already.

'So, did you find your true love over the canapés?' Max asked.

'I don't know about that,' she said. 'I sat between two handsome, ambitious single men specially picked out for me by my mother.'

Max's gaze flickered to her face and then away. 'So who's the lucky guy?'

'Neither.' Reaching up, she pulled the clips from her hair and shook it loose, oblivious to the way Max's eyes darkened. 'I've decided I need a relationship detox. I might abstain from all men for a while.'

'That would be a shame.'

'I'm sick of feeling that they only ask me out because I'm Flick Fielding's daughter.' It was the first time Allegra had said it out loud and she winced as she heard the resentment reverberating around the room.

'That's not why they ask you out,' said Max roughly.

'Isn't it? Why else would they? I'm not clever the way they are. I can't contribute to the conversation. I've got nothing to offer.'

'You're beautiful,' said Max. 'Come on, Legs, you must know you are,' he said when she gaped at him. 'You're gorgeous. Any man would be glad to be seen with you. I don't know who you sat next to tonight, but if you think he was more interested in Flick's influence than in the way you looked, you're not thinking straight!'

He would have been the one not thinking straight if he'd been sitting next to Allegra while she was wearing that dress. He would have been mesmerised by her arms, bare and slender, by those expressive hands, by the glow of her skin and the way the straight shiny hair threatened to slip out of its clips. He would have spent his whole time imagining how it would look falling to her shoulders, the way it was now.

He wouldn't have been able to eat, Max knew. His mouth would have been too dry and he'd have been too busy watching the sweep of her lashes, the brightness of her eyes, the tempting hollow of her cleavage, the curve of her breasts… And thinking about her bare knees under the table, the long, sexy legs in those ridiculous shoes.

His head felt light and he realised it was because he'd stopped breathing. Max sucked in a steadying breath. Where had all that come from?

'I didn't know you thought I was beautiful,' said Allegra, sounding thrown.

'I thought so many other people would tell you there was no need for me to do the same. You're still deeply irritating, mind,' he said in an effort to drag the conversation back onto safe ground, 'but of course you're beautiful. I thought you knew.'

'No.' Allegra bent her head, pushing back the hair that slithered forward, but he still couldn't see her face properly.

It was probably just as well. Max was uneasily aware that something tenuous had insinuated itself into the air, like a memory hovering just out of reach, or a forgotten word trembling on the tip of a tongue. Something that seemed to be drawing the air tighter, squeezing out the oxygen so that his chest felt tight and his breathing oddly sticky.

Could Allegra feel it?

Apparently not. Even as he struggled to heave in another breath, she was lifting her head and focusing on him with those eyes that seemed to get more beautiful every time he looked into them.

'Tell me how you got on with Darcy,' she said, sounding so completely normal that Max squirmed inwardly with humiliation. *She* wasn't finding it hard to breathe. She wasn't aware of the tension in the air, or snarled in a knot of inconvenient and inappropriate lust.

'I wondered if you'd end up staying the night,' she went on, but not as if she cared one way or the other.

So he obviously couldn't admit that she was the reason he wasn't tucked up next to the world's favourite lingerie model right now.

Because Darcy had made it very clear that she was up for a lot more than just dinner, but it hadn't felt right, not when he'd spent most of the evening wondering what Allegra was doing and who her bloody mother had lined up to sit next to her. Flick might be keen on big brains, but

Max was prepared to bet that they were men too, and that they wouldn't be above a flirtatious touch every now and then: Allegra's shoulder, her hand, her knee...

It was only when Darcy had looked at him strangely that he'd realised he was grinding his teeth.

What was wrong with him? Max had wanted to tear out his hair. There he was, sitting across the table from *Darcy King*, with a clear invitation to get his hands on that luscious body. It was the opportunity of a lifetime, a fantasy come true for a million men like him, and all he could think about was his sister's scrawny friend! He had to be sickening for something. Or certifiable.

Or both.

He liked Darcy, he really did, but it had been awkward. He told Allegra what he'd told Darcy, which was the best excuse he could come up with at the time.

'I don't really want to get involved with Darcy,' he said. 'She's nice but...well, I don't see her fitting into my life, do you? I can't imagine someone like Darcy out in Shofrar, and I don't feel like being just a novelty plaything for her. I know most other men would give their eye teeth to be toyed with by her, but I'm not sure it would be worth it.'

It wasn't really an excuse. It was *true*. Not that Allegra seemed to be convinced.

She looked at him strangely. 'I doubt that Darcy's thinking about anything serious,' she said. 'It would only be a bit of fun. Where does Shofrar come into it?'

'That's where my life is going to be,' said Max stiffly, even as he winced inwardly at what a pompous jerk he sounded. But the words kept coming out of his mouth without taking the trouble of detouring through his brain. 'There's no point in getting involved with someone who can't hack it away from a city.'

Meaning *what* exactly? He wasn't surprised at the way Allegra's face clouded with disbelief.

'So, let me get this right. You're saying that you're not going to have sex unless you can get married to someone who won't mind being dragged out to some desert hellhole so that she can play second fiddle to your career?'

'Yes…no!' What *was* he saying?

'Isn't that going to be a bit limiting?'

Max was beginning to sweat. He hadn't felt this out of control since Emma had blithely broken off their engagement.

Emma! He grabbed onto the thought of his fiancée. *Ex*-fiancée. 'Look, I'm not the sort of guy who goes out with models,' he said with a tinge of desperation. 'In a fantasy, maybe, but I really just want to be with someone like Emma. I think being with Darcy made me realise that I wasn't really over Emma yet.'

Which might even be true. Not the realisation, which in reality hadn't crossed his mind at the time, but that he was still missing Emma at some level.

Now that he thought about it, Max thought it probably was true. It would explain the muddle inside him, wouldn't it? Max *hated* feeling like this, as if he were churning around in some massive washing machine, not knowing which way was up. Not knowing what he thought or what he felt. He hadn't felt himself since Emma had wafted off in search of passion.

'I sent Emma a text, just like you suggested,' he told Allegra almost accusingly, and she sat up straighter.

'Did she reply?'

'While I was on my way to Darcy's. So I was thinking about her before I got there.'

That *was* true, although he hadn't really been thinking about Emma in a yearning way, more in a how-odd-I-don't-really-feel-anything-when-I-see-your-name-now kind of way. Until a week or so ago, Max would have said that all he wanted was to hear from Emma and try to get back to normal again, but when he'd read her text he hadn't felt the rush of relief and hope that he'd expected.

At least Allegra was looking sympathetic now. 'I can see that would throw you a bit,' she said fairly. 'What did Emma say?'

'Nothing really. Just that she was fine and how was I?'

'Oh, that's very encouraging!' Allegra beamed at him and he looked back suspiciously.

'It is?'

'Definitely. If Emma didn't want to stay in contact, she wouldn't have replied at all. As it is, she not only responded, she asked you a question back.'

'So?'

'So she's opening a dialogue,' Allegra said with heavy patience. 'She's asked how you are, which means you reply and tell her, and say something else, then she gets the chance to react to that... Before you know where you are, you're having a conversation, and then it's only a matter of time before you decide you should meet.'

She sat back, satisfied with her scenario. 'It's a really good sign, Max,' she assured him. 'I bet Emma's bored with her passionate guy already and was thrilled to hear from you.'

Max couldn't see it. *Thrilled*. There was an Allegra word for you. Emma wasn't the kind of woman who was *thrilled* about things. It was one of the things he had always liked about her. Emma didn't make a big fuss about anything. She was moderation, balance, calm—unlike some people he could mention.

He looked at Allegra, who was curled up in the armchair, bright-eyed and a little tousled at the end of the evening, apparently unaware that her dress was rucked up, exposing a mouth-watering length of leg. When he thought about Allegra, he didn't think moderation. He thought extravagance. Allegra dealt in extremes. She *adored* things or she *loathed* them. She was wildly excited at the prospect of something or dreading it. She was madly in love or broken-hearted. It was exhausting trying to keep up with the way her emotions swung around. Emma had never left his head reeling.

Of course, Emma was the one who had thrown up her nice, safe life for a passionate affair, so what did he know?

Max hunched his shoulders morosely. Women. Just when you thought you understood them, they turned around and kicked your legs out from beneath you, leaving you floundering.

Look at Allegra, who had just been Libby's mildly annoying friend. He'd known exactly where he was with her. True, there had been that odd little moment a few years ago but, apart from that, it had been an easy relationship. Nothing about her seemed easy now. He couldn't look at her without noticing her skin or the silkiness of her hair. Without thinking about her legs or her mouth or the tantalising hollow of her throat.

Without blurting out that she looked beautiful.

Max didn't know exactly what Allegra had done to change, but she had done *something*.

Now she was fiddling with her hair, smoothing it behind her ear, grooming herself like a cat. 'So have you replied to her?' she asked.

'What?' Mesmerised by her fingers, Max had forgotten what she was talking about.

Allegra looked at him. 'Have you replied to Emma?' she repeated slowly, and Max felt a dull colour burning along his cheekbones.

'Oh. No, not yet.'

'You're playing it cool?'

Max was damned if he knew.

What if Allegra was right? What if Emma really was waiting to hear from him? If they could miraculously make everything right, get married as planned, and go out to Shofrar? He ought to feel happy at the idea…oughtn't he? But all he really felt was confused.

He met Allegra's expectant gaze. Playing it cool sounded a lot better than not having a clue what was going on.

'Something like that,' he said.

'Allegra!' Max banged his fist on the bathroom door. 'What in God's name are you doing in there?'

'Nearly ready,' Allegra called back. Carefully, she smoothed her lipstick into place and blotted her mouth. She wouldn't for the world admit it to Max, but she was nervous about the evening ahead. This dinner with Bob Laskovski and his wife was so important to him. She didn't want to let him down.

Max had been in a funny mood for the last few days. Allegra had decided that hearing from Emma had thrown him more than he understood. He was in denial, but it was obvious that he really wanted Emma back. Why else would he resist Darcy?

It had been easier to go out and leave him to be morose on his own, and when William got in touch after dinner at Flick's she had agreed to meet him for a drink after all. The whole relationship detox thing would never have worked anyway, Allegra decided. She should at least give him a chance.

William was good company, good-looking, and she enjoyed herself, and she wouldn't let herself think that looking at William's patrician mouth didn't make her stomach hurt the way it did when she looked at Max's.

Because there was no point in thinking about Max that way.

Allegra couldn't even explain what kind of way that was, but it was something to do with a trembly sensation just below her skin, with a thudding in her veins that started whenever Max came into the room. It was something to do with the way every sense seemed on full alert when he was near.

Being so aware of him the whole time made her uncomfortable. It was crazy. It was inappropriate. It didn't make sense.

It was just the assignment, she tried to reassure herself. It was just spending so much time with him. It wasn't *real*. A temporary madness, that was all. Max would go to Shofrar and she would go back to normal.

She couldn't wait.

Max had been very clear. He wasn't interested in a quick fling. He was looking for someone who could be part of his life, someone who would share his interests and not mind being dragged around the world. It wasn't Darcy, and it sure as hell wasn't her either, Allegra knew. She was the last kind of girl Max would ever want to get involved with…and the feeling was mutual, she hurried to remind herself whenever that thought seemed too depressing. It wasn't as if she wanted to leave London. She had a career here.

She might not be changing the world or writing groundbreaking articles, but she was doing what she wanted to do…wasn't she? Allegra's mind flickered to illustration then away. Drawing cartoon animals wasn't a serious job. She could do better for herself, as Flick was constantly telling her.

Besides, the article about Max was going to be her big break. She had already written the first half and it was pretty good, even if she did say so herself. Perhaps she was spending rather too much time sketching Max while she thought, but it was inevitable that she should be thinking about him. Right now, that was her job, that was all.

'*Allegra*! We're going to be late!' Max had just raised his fist to rap the bathroom door again when Allegra pulled it open. She smiled brightly at him, gratified by the way his jaw slackened.

'What do you think?' She pirouetted in the doorway. She was in the most demure outfit she could find, a killer LBD with a sheer décolletage and sleeves. Even Max couldn't object to a black dress, Allegra had reasoned, but she'd been unable to resist pimping up the plainness with glittery earrings and bling-studded stilettos. There was only so much plain dressing a girl could do, and she was counting on the fact that Max and his boss were men and therefore unlikely to even look at her shoes.

'Do I look sufficiently sensible?' she asked, and Max, who had evidently forgotten that his fist was still raised, lowered it slowly.

'Sensible isn't quite the word I was thinking of,' he said, sounding strained.

Allegra was disappointed. 'I've put my hair up and everything,' she protested. Her hair was so slippery it had taken ages to do, too.

'You look very nice,' Max said gruffly. 'Now, come on. The taxi's waiting. We need to get a move on.' His gaze travelled down her legs and ended at her shoes. 'Can you make it to the taxi?'

'Of course I can,' said Allegra, unsure whether to be pleased or miffed that he had noticed her shoes after all.

Her hair was precariously fixed, to say the least, so

Allegra settled back into the seat and pulled her seat belt on with care. She loved London taxis, loved their bulbous shape and the yellow light on top. She loved the smell of the seats, the clicking of the engine, the straps that stopped you sliding around on your seat when they turned a corner. Sitting in a taxi as it drove past the iconic London sights made Allegra feel as if she was at the centre of things, part of a great vibrant city. It gave her a thrill every time.

Every time except that night.

That night, the streets were a blur. Allegra couldn't concentrate on London. She was too aware of Max sitting beside her. He was sensibly strapped in too, and he wasn't touching her. He wasn't even close, but that didn't stop her whole side tingling as if the seat belt had vanished and she had slid across the seat to land against him.

She swallowed hard. This was so *silly*. She shouldn't have to make an effort to sound normal with Max.

'So,' she said brightly, 'what's the plan?'

'Plan?'

'We ought to get our stories straight about how we met at least.'

Max frowned. 'Bob's not going to be interested in that kind of thing.'

'His wife might be.'

It was obvious Max hadn't thought of that. 'Better stick to the truth,' he decided, and Allegra's brows rose.

'Won't that rather defeat the object of the exercise?'

'I don't mean about the pretence,' he said irritably. 'Just that I know you through my sister, that kind of thing.'

It all sounded a bit thin to Allegra, but Max clearly didn't think his boss was going to interrogate them in any detail. She just hoped that he was right.

'I don't think you'll have to do much but smile and

look as if we might conceivably be planning to get married,' Max said.

'How besotted do you want me to be?' she asked provocatively. It was easier needling him than noticing how the street lights threw the planes of his face into relief, how the passing headlights kept catching the corner of his mouth. 'I could be madly in love or just sweetly adoring.'

'Just be normal,' he said repressively. 'If you can.'

They were to meet Bob and his wife at Arturo's, a quiet and classic restaurant no longer at the forefront of fashion but still famous for its food. When they got there, Max paid off the taxi and ran a finger under his collar. He'd wanted to wear a plain white shirt but Allegra had bullied him into putting on the mulberry-coloured shirt Dickie had picked out for him, with a plain tie in a darker hue.

'Bob's going to wonder what the hell I'm doing in a red shirt,' he grumbled as he eased the collar away from his throat.

'Stop fiddling, you look great,' said Allegra. She stepped up and made his senses reel by straightening his tie and patting it into place. 'Really,' she told him, 'you look good. You just need to relax.'

'Relax, right,' said Max, taking refuge in sarcasm. 'I'm just going for the most important interview of my career so far, which means lying through my teeth to my new boss. What's there to feel tense about?'

'We don't have to lie if you don't want to. Why not just tell Bob the truth about Emma?'

For a moment Max was tempted. Wouldn't chucking in the towel be easier than spending the evening trying to convince Bob Laskovski that it was remotely credible that a girl like Allegra would choose to be with him? She was so clearly out of his league.

When she had opened the bathroom door and smiled at

him, it had been like a punch to his heart. 'Do I look sufficiently sensible?' she had asked while he was still struggling for breath, while he was trying to wrench his eyes off the way her dress clung enticingly to her slender body.

True, her arms and shoulders were covered but that sheer black stuff was somehow even more tantalising than bare skin would have been. It seemed to beckon him forward to peer closer, hinting at the creamy skin half hidden beneath the gauzy film of black. Between the sheer arms and shoulders and the tight-fitting dress, Max felt as if there were great neon arrows angled at her throat, at her breasts, at the curve of her hips: *Look here! Look here!*

The dress stopped above her knees—*Look here!*—revealing those killer legs of hers—*And here!*—ending in absurd shoes that were studded with mock jewels. Her earrings swung and glittered in the light and her hair, twisted up and back more neatly than usual, gleamed.

Once the oxygen had rushed back to his head, Max had been able to think of lots of words to describe Allegra right then: sexy, erotic, dazzling, gorgeous... Had he already mentioned sexy? But *sensible? Suitable?* Max didn't think so.

Now she was adjusting his tie and standing so close her perfume was coiling into his mind, and lust fisted in his belly. For a wild moment the need to touch her was so strong all Max could think about was grabbing her, pushing her up against a wall and putting his hands on her, touching her, feeling her, taking her.

Horrified by the urge, he took a step back. What was happening to him? He didn't do wild. He was sensible, steady, an engineer, not some macho type acting out his caveman fantasies.

Max shook his head slightly to clear it. This whole article business was getting to him, that was all. The sooner he got to Shofrar, the better. *That* was what he wanted, not to rip his little sister's friend's clothes off. And for Shofrar he needed Bob Laskovski's approval. Was he really going to risk blowing the project manager role he'd coveted for so long just because he was distracted by Allegra's perfume?

'No,' he said. His voice was a little hoarse, but firm. 'I want to stick with what we agreed.'

'Okay.' Allegra smiled at him and tucked her hand through his arm. 'In that case, let's go and get you that job, tiger.'

CHAPTER SEVEN

AT WORK, BOB LASKOVSKI was always referred to in hushed tones, and Max was expecting his boss to be an imposing figure. Headshots on the website showed a serious man with a shiny pate and a horseshoe of white hair but, in person, Bob was short and rotund with an easy smile and eyes that crinkled engagingly at the corners.

Max was relieved when Allegra let go of him so that he could shake hands with Bob, who turned to introduce his wife. No trophy wife for Bob: Karen Laskovski was silver-haired and very elegant. No doubt Allegra could have described what she was wearing in exhaustive detail, but Max just got an impression of warmth and charm and a light blue outfit.

And now it was his turn. Allegra smiled encouragingly when he glanced at her, and Max cleared his throat.

'This is my fiancée, Allegra.'

There, the lie was out. Max was sure he could hear it clanging around the restaurant and waited for the other diners to look up and shout *Liar! Liar!* but nobody seemed to notice anything unusual, least of all the Laskovskis. Couldn't they *see* what an ill-assorted couple he and Allegra were?

But no, apparently not.

'What a pretty name!' Karen exclaimed as Allegra beamed and shook hands.

'It means cheerful,' said Allegra.

'And you look like it's a good name for you,' said Bob, who had blinked a couple of times at Allegra's shoes.

Allegra smiled and, to Max's horror, she took hold of his arm once more and leant winsomely against his shoulder. 'I've got a lot to be cheerful about,' she said, fluttering her lashes at him. 'I'm just so excited to be marrying Max and going out to Shofrar with him. Hopefully,' she added, beaming a smile at Bob, who nodded approvingly.

'It's a great thing when you're both looking forward to a posting,' he said as he gestured for everyone to sit down. 'Especially a place like Shofrar, where there isn't much to occupy you if you're not working. Too often we see young engineers coming home early because their wife or partner isn't happy. But you're obviously going to be an ideal engineer's wife,' he said to Allegra.

Max covered his choke of disbelief with a cough. Hadn't Bob noticed Allegra's shoes? Couldn't he *see* that she was the last person who would be happy in the desert?

As for Allegra, she was well into her role. 'I don't mind where I am, as long as I'm with Max,' she said.

Forget journalism, she should have been an actress, thought Max, unaccountably ruffled. But Bob and Karen seemed to be lapping it up.

'It reminds me of when we were first married,' Karen said with a reminiscent smile at her husband. 'I didn't care as long as I could be with you.'

'Mind you, we were never really apart,' said Bob, covering her hand with his. 'We were high school sweethearts. I fell in love with Karen the moment I saw her, didn't I, honey?'

Max couldn't understand it. Bob was supposed to be

talking about contracts and deliverables, or quizzing Max on his project experience, not wittering on about love. Naturally, Allegra was encouraging him.

'Oh, that's so wonderful!' she cried, clapping her hands together. 'So you two believe in love at first sight?'

Max wanted to drop his head onto the table.

'We sure do,' said Bob with a fond glance at his wife, who gazed adoringly back at him. 'How about you two? You known each other a long time?'

'Years,' said Allegra, launching into an explanation of her friendship with Libby. 'For most of that time, Max and I ignored each other completely.'

'Aha!' Karen leaned forward. 'So what changed?'

For the first time, Allegra's cheery confidence faltered. 'I…well, I'm not sure…it just crept up on us, I guess.' And then she had the nerve to turn to *him*. 'What do you think, Max? When did you first realise that you were in love with me?'

It was as if the restaurant had jarred to a halt. The world went still and Max was frozen with it, pinned into place as Allegra's words rang in his head.

When did you first realise that you were in love with me?

He couldn't be in love with Allegra, Max thought in panic. There was some mistake. He'd put his hand up to momentary lust perhaps, but *love*? No, no, no, no. She was pretending, Max reminded himself with a touch of desperation. She didn't really believe he was in love with her.

So why had her words settled into place in his head as if they belonged there?

Allegra turned in her seat so that Bob and Karen couldn't see her give him a warning dead-eye look. 'Was it when I let you paint my toenails?' she asked.

Paint…? What? Max's brows snapped together until he

realised belatedly that she was trying to prod him into responding. God knew what his expression had looked like as he'd sat there, stunned at the realisation that he had, in fact, fallen in love with Allegra.

Fool that he was.

But not so foolish he would humiliate himself by letting anyone guess, Allegra least of all.

Max recovered himself with an effort. 'I think it was more when I realised how distraught you were at the idea of me going to Shofrar,' he said, pretending to consider the matter. He looked at Bob and Karen. 'It was only then I understood just what I meant to her.'

There was a whack on his arm. 'I was not distraught!' Allegra said indignantly.

'You were weeping and wailing and begging me not to go, remember?'

'You are such a big fibber!' she protested, but she was laughing too.

'*I'm* a fibber? What was that about me painting your toenails?'

'I never cry,' she insisted to Karen, who looked from one to the other in amusement.

'Well, however you fell in love, I can just tell that you two are perfect together!'

'We think so, don't we, sweetheart?' That was Allegra again, playing it for all it was worth. She leant confidingly towards Karen. 'Of course, Max can be a bit grumpy at times, but I know he adores me.'

The little minx.

Fortunately Bob chose that moment to ask Max about the project he was working on and Max seized on the chance to drag the conversation back to safe territory.

But Karen was asking about the wedding, and Max found it harder than he'd thought to concentrate on engineering while beside him Allegra had launched into a vivid description of an imaginary wedding ceremony, her dress, what the bridesmaids would be wearing, how the tables would be decorated, and a host of other details that Max had never even considered in connection with a wedding.

He listened incredulously with one ear. Where did Allegra *get* all this stuff from? Oh, God, now she was sketching outfits on the back of an envelope she'd dug out of her jewelled bag and Karen was oohing and aahing.

'Oh, that's darling!' she exclaimed, and in spite of himself Max craned his neck to see what Allegra had drawn. There she stood in a slender dress with a low wide neckline and that was unmistakably him next to her, dressed in a morning suit and a *flowery waistcoat*.

'Over my dead body,' he muttered in Allegra's ear, and she pressed her lips together but he could see her body shaking with suppressed giggles.

'Women and weddings, huh?' said Bob as Max caught his eye. 'Take my advice, just go along with whatever they want.'

'I guess your mom will want to be involved in the wedding plans too?' Karen said to Allegra, ignoring the men.

'Er, yes.' Max could see Allegra trying to imagine poring over table decorations with Flick. 'Yes, she will, of course, but really it's just between Max and me, isn't it?'

'Quite right,' said Bob, 'and the sooner you get on with it the better, am I right, Max? But I'm not sure you're going to have time to get married before you go out to Shofrar. You'll have to come back for the wedding.'

Max looked at Bob and then at Allegra, whose face lit with excitement. 'Does that mean...?' she asked Bob, and he nodded and smiled.

'Sure. Of course Max gets the job.'

Allegra squealed with excitement and flung her

arms around Max. 'Oh, Max, you got it! You're going to Shofrar!'

Her cheek was pressed against his, and unthinkingly his arms closed around her, pulling her tight. Bob and Karen were watching indulgently and when Allegra turned her head and smiled, it seemed the most natural thing in the world to kiss her.

Her mouth was soft and lusciously curved and so close it would have been rude not to, in fact. And it would look good, Max thought hazily, unable to wrench his gaze from her lips. The Laskovskis were expecting him to kiss Allegra. That was what engaged couples did when they got good news. It would seem odd if he *didn't* kiss her.

One hand slid up her spine to the nape of her neck. For one still moment he looked straight into the deep, mossy green of Allegra's eyes and all rational thought evaporated. There was nothing but her warmth, her scent, her mouth.

Her *mouth*.

He couldn't resist any longer. He'd forgotten why he needed to, forgotten everything but the need to seal the gap between them. He drew her head towards him—or perhaps she leant closer; Max never knew—and angled his lips against hers, and the taste and the touch of her blew his senses apart so that he could almost have sworn that the restaurant swung wildly around them.

She was warm and responsive, pliant against him, and their mouths fitted together as if they were meant for each other. The astonishing rightness of it rose in his chest and surged through him like a tide, blocking out doubts, blocking out reason, blocking out everything that wasn't Allegra: the scent of her, the feel of her, the sweetness of her.

Afterwards, Max calculated that the kiss couldn't have lasted more than a few seconds, but at the time it seemed to stretch to infinity and beyond. He never knew where he found the strength to pull away, but somehow he had drawn back and was staring into her eyes once more. The lovely green was dark and dazed, and her expression was as stunned as his must have been.

'Yep,' said Bob to Karen, 'the sooner those two get married the better, I'd say.'

Desperately, Max tried to pull himself together. His blood was pounding, which was crazy. It had just been a kiss, hardly more than a peck on the lips. There was no reason for his heart to be throbbing still like that, for his lungs to have forgotten how to function.

He had to get a grip, focus on the job. He had what he wanted. He was going to Shofrar to be a project manager, just like he had planned. He ought to be elated, not thinking about the way Allegra's words were ringing in his ears: *You're going to Shofrar,* she had exclaimed in delight.

You're going, not *we're going.*

They were all picking up their glasses and Bob was toasting Max's promotion. Max stretched his mouth into a smile.

You, not *we.*

That was how it should be, Max told himself. In a few weeks, he would get on a plane and fly out to the desert and Allegra wouldn't be there. He would get on with his life and she would get on with hers. Their lives were on separate tracks, heading in different directions.

If Libby ever got married, they might meet at her wedding or the occasional christening but that was far in the future. They might have forgotten this evening by then, forgotten that kiss, or perhaps they would share a wry smile at the memory. It wouldn't matter then.

Max couldn't imagine it.

He stole a glance at Allegra. She looked as if she had forgotten it already, he thought with resentment. *She* wasn't flailing off balance. There was a faint flush along her cheekbones, but otherwise she seemed perfectly composed as she chatted to Karen.

'What are you going to do with yourself in Shofrar, Allegra?' Karen asked. 'If Max is anything like Bob, he'll be at work all day. You really need a career that can travel with you.'

Allegra opened her mouth but Max got in first. 'Allegra's an illustrator,' he said. 'She's going to write and illustrate children's books.'

'Really?' Karen was fascinated but Allegra was already shaking her head.

'Oh, well, I'm not sure I'm good enough,' she began.

'She's brilliant,' Max told Karen, ignoring Allegra's kick under the table. 'She just doesn't know it.'

It was true, he thought. She would be so much happier illustrating rather than running around meeting the crazy deadlines at *Glitz*, but she wouldn't change because for some reason Flick had a bee in her bonnet about Allegra's drawing. She was always putting it down, so of course Allegra thought it wasn't good enough, but Max was convinced her illustrations had something special about them.

Karen made Allegra tell her all about the book she was going to write and, in spite of the vengeful looks Allegra was sending his way, Max noticed that she had plenty of ideas. She might say that she was dedicated to journalism but she had obviously thought about the stories starring the infamous Derek the Dog. Max wished she would write the book and forget about Flick's opinion for once. Perhaps she never would in real life, but at least she could pretend to have the perfect career for this evening.

Because this evening was all they had. After tonight, the pretence was over. He had better not forget that.

Beside Max, Allegra was wishing Karen wouldn't ask quite so many interested questions about a book she had no intention of writing. They were just silly little stories she had made up, not even a real book, but Karen certainly seemed thrilled by the idea and claimed her grandchildren would love Derek the Dog. If she wasn't careful she would find herself writing the pesky thing, Allegra thought with an inner sigh. She could just imagine what Flick would think of *that*!

Perhaps she could use a pseudonym?

Aware of a flicker of excitement at the thought, Allegra pushed it firmly out of sight. She had enough going on in her head right now, what with thinking about a non-existent book and trying *not* to think about the way Max had kissed her.

And especially not about the way she had kissed him back.

There was a disquieting prickle still at the nape of her neck where his hand had rested. Her lips felt tender, as if his had seared hers, and she kept running the tip of her tongue over them, as surreptitiously as she could, checking that they hadn't swollen.

The jolt of sensation when their mouths met had shaken her. Kissing Max wasn't supposed to feel like that. It was supposed to be a meaningless peck of the lips, the kind of kiss she gave out every day to her colleagues at *Glitz*.

It was hard to tell what Max thought about it. For one breathless moment afterwards they had stared at each other, but then his eyes had shuttered and now he was immersed in a technical discussion with Bob. He was talking about *concrete*. It wasn't fair. He shouldn't be able to kiss her and then calmly carry on discussing road building!

Karen and Bob were entertaining company and the meal was delicious, but Allegra couldn't enjoy it. She was too aware of Max, who was his usual taciturn self, and who, having kissed her and dropped her in it with Karen, had proceeded to ignore her for the rest of the evening.

It wasn't good enough, Allegra thought crossly, tapping her Jimmy Choos under the table. She had done everything he'd asked of her. She'd been charming, but Max hadn't even *tried*. If it wasn't for her, he wouldn't even *have* his rotten job, Allegra decided, but now he'd got what he wanted he had obviously decided he didn't need to bother with her any more.

Her smile was brittle by the time they said goodbye to Bob and Karen outside the restaurant. The Laskovskis were walking back to their hotel and, after one glance at Allegra's shoes, Max didn't even bother to suggest the Tube. Instead he put his fingers in his mouth and whistled at a passing taxi. If it had been Allegra, the taxi would have sailed on past in the other direction and she didn't know whether to be relieved or put-out that it responded instantly to Max's whistle, turning across the traffic and drawing up exactly in front of them.

Her feet were definitely relieved.

Haughtily, she got in and made a big performance of putting on her seat belt. Max told the taxi driver the address and settled beside her, apparently unperturbed by the taut silence. Allegra folded her lips together. *She* wasn't going to break it. She had made enough small talk for one night, thank you very much! She turned her head away and looked pointedly out of the window, but she was so aware of him sitting just a matter of inches away across the seat that she might as well have turned and stared right at him.

It wasn't even as if he was doing anything. He was just sitting still, his face in shadow, his eyes fixed on the ticking taxi meter. He could at least jiggle his leg or do something annoying so that she had an excuse to snap at him.

As it was, she was just getting crosser and crosser, and more and more frustrated.

Why, why, why had he had to kiss her like that? It had been all right up to then. The pretence had been fun and she had been able to dismiss her bizarre awareness of him as a temporary aberration, a passing symptom of sexual frustration. Nothing that meant anything, anyway. She'd been able to think of him as just Max.

He'd spoiled everything by kissing her. It had been so perfect, as if her whole life had just been about getting her to that place, that moment, where everything else had fallen away and there had just been her and Max and a longing for it never to end gusting through her.

How could she think of him as just Max now?

She wished he'd never kissed her.

She wished he'd kiss her again.

The realisation of just how much she wanted it made Allegra suck in her breath. This was mad. She was furious with Max. She couldn't want to kiss him at the same time. She couldn't want him to reach across and pull her towards him, couldn't want his hands on her, his mouth on her, not when he'd ignored her all night and clearly had no interest in kissing *her* again.

But she did.

The silence lengthened, stretched agonizingly. Just when Allegra opened her mouth to break it, unable to bear it any longer, Max let out a sigh.

'I'm sorry,' he said simply.

At least it gave her the excuse to turn and look at him. 'Sorry?' she echoed, unable to stop the pent-up frustration from tumbling out. 'I should think so! Do you have any idea how hard I worked all evening to suck up to the Laskovskis? I got you your bloody job all by myself!'

'I know,' Max began, but Allegra wasn't stopping now that she had started.

'You hardly said a word all evening—oh, except to embarrass me by telling Karen I was going to write a book! What did you do that for?'

'I think you should write one. I think it would be brilliant.'

Allegra wasn't going to be mollified. 'It would not be! It would be stupid! I had to sit there and pretend that I was all excited about it and now Karen's expecting me to send her a copy when it's published! It's not funny,' she added furiously, spotting the ghost of a smile hovering around Max's mouth. 'I felt an absolute fool. As if it wasn't bad enough pretending to be in love with you!'

'You did it really well,' said Max. 'You were brilliant at that too, and you're right, you got me the job. Thank you,' he said quietly. 'Really, Allegra: thank you.'

Perversely, his gratitude just made her feel worse. She hunched a shoulder. 'I only did it so that you'd do the article.' She sounded petulant, but that was how she felt.

'I know.'

'But you could have helped,' she grumbled. 'You were useless! I can't believe the Laskovskis were taken in. A real fiancé would have looked at me, maybe smiled occasionally, taken every opportunity to get close to me, but not you! It was like you couldn't bear to touch me.'

'That's not true,' said Max tautly. 'I kissed you.'

As if she could have forgotten!

'Only when I threw myself into your arms! *Pretending* to be a loving fiancée, thrilled for her future husband's promotion,' Allegra added quickly, just in case he had misinterpreted her instinctive reaction. She had been so pleased for him too, she remembered bitterly. 'Although I don't know why I bothered. You gave the impression you'd rather have been picking up slugs!'

'What?' Max sounded so staggered that Allegra wondered if she might have exaggerated a little, but she had gone too far to back down now. Besides, she had been bottling it up all evening and it was good to get it off her chest.

'I might as well have been a pillar of your precious concrete for all the notice you took of me all evening!'

Max uttered a strangled laugh and dragged a hand through his hair. 'It wasn't like that,' he began.

'Then why did you ignore me?'

'Because I didn't trust myself, all right?' he shouted, goaded at last. 'Because if I hadn't ignored you, I wouldn't have been able to keep my hands off you! I'd have kissed you again and again and I wouldn't have been able to stop. I'd have dragged you down under the table and ripped that bloody dress off you so I could kiss you all over your body and to hell with my boss sitting there with his wife and the rest of the restaurant...'

He broke off. His chest was heaving and he looked wild-eyed as he glared at Allegra. 'So now you know. There, are you satisfied now?'

'But...but...' It was Allegra's turn to gape.

'Of course I wanted to touch you!' Max said furiously. 'I've wanted it ever since you opened the bathroom door. I haven't been able to think about anything else all evening. I had to sit there, trying to talk to my boss, when all I could think about was how easy it would be to slide my hand under your dress, about how it would feel to unzip it, all the time knowing it would never happen! And you wanted me to do chit-chat as well?'

He was glowering at her as if he hated her, but a treacherous warmth was stealing along Allegra's veins, dissolving her own anger into something far more dangerous, while the spikiness in the atmosphere evaporated into quite a different kind of tension.

He wanted her.

Desire twisted sharp and sure in her belly. His hair was standing on end where he had raked his hand through it and he looked cross, rumpled, *gorgeous*. When had he become so…so…so *hot*? Why hadn't she noticed?

Allegra's heart thudded in her throat and her mouth dried with a mixture of anticipation and apprehension. She had been sent once to try bungee jumping for an article and she had felt just like this when she'd stood on the edge of the bridge: terrified, thrilled, longing to be brave enough to jump but afraid that she would never have the courage.

She had done it, though. She could do this too, if she really wanted to. Allegra moistened her lips.

Max wanted her.

She wanted him.

Allegra's mind was still busy calculating the risk when her mouth opened and she heard herself say, 'How do you know?'

Thrown, Max stared at her. 'How do I know what?'

'That it would never happen.' Allegra watched, appalled, as her body took over, shifting towards him, reaching out for his hand, setting it on her knee, all without a single instruction from her brain.

What was she *doing*? she thought in panic, but her hands seemed to have acquired a will of their own. *Stop it*, she told herself frantically, but the message wasn't getting through, and now her legs were getting in on the act, quaking with pleasure at the warm weight of his hand.

Max swallowed. 'I'm not sure this is a good idea, Legs,' he said in a constricted voice, but he didn't seem to have any better control over his hands than she did. His fingers were curling over her knee, pressing through her sheer tights into the soft skin of her inner thigh, and she couldn't prevent the shudder of response clenching at the base of her spine.

'I'm not sure either,' she admitted with difficulty. She willed her knees to press together and squeeze out his hand but they wouldn't cooperate.

'It could be that we're just getting carried away by the pretence,' Max said but he didn't lift his hand. Instead his knuckles nudged aside the hem of her dress so that he could stroke higher inside her thigh.

Allegra felt lust crawling deeper, digging in. It would take over completely if she didn't regain control, but his skimming fingers were searing such delicious patterns on her skin she couldn't think clearly.

'Bound to be that,' she agreed breathlessly. 'And the whole article thing. It's getting a bit out of hand. We're spending too much time together.'

'Yep,' said Max, as his fingers played on the inside of her thigh, higher, higher, higher, until Allegra squirmed in her seat. 'We should stop right now.'

'We should,' she managed.

'Unless...'

'Yes?' Her breathing was too choppy to get anything else out.

'Unless we get it out of our system,' Max suggested. Had his voice always been that deep, that darkly delicious? 'Just one night, and then we can forget all about it. What do you think?'

Think? How could she be expected to think when his fingers were stroking so exquisitely that she couldn't breathe properly and she was giddy with the dark pleasure of it? Oh, God, if his hand went any higher, she would come apart.

If it didn't, she would explode. Either way, they would end up with a horrible mess all over the taxi seat.

Struggling to stop herself pressing down into his hand, she scrabbled for some words to put together. 'I think… that's…a good idea…' she gasped and Max smiled, a wicked smile she hadn't known he possessed.

When he withdrew his hand, Allegra almost moaned in protest before she realised that the taxi had stopped in front of the house. Max paid the driver while she made it waveringly to the front door on legs that felt boneless.

She was still fumbling with the keys as Max came up behind her. Wordlessly, he took them from her and opened the door.

'After you,' he said, but there was a telltale hitch in his voice that made Allegra feel obscurely better. So it wasn't just her having trouble breathing.

She didn't want to put on the hall light, so she waited, trembling with anticipation, in the dark until Max had closed the door behind them. A muted orange glow from the street lights outside filtered through the glass pane above the door. It was enough to see him turn, see the gleam of his smile as he moved towards her, and then his hands were on her and at last—at last!—his mouth came down on hers, angling desperate and demanding.

This time there was none of the piercing sweetness she had felt in the restaurant. Instead his kiss was hot and fierce, and Allegra felt need explode inside her, vaporising the last lingering remnants of rational thought. Her mind went dark and she kissed him back, wild with hunger, wanting his hands on her harder, hotter, *harder*.

No, there was no sweetness now. It felt like more of a struggle as to who needed most, who could give most, who could take most. Allegra scrabbled for his tie, at the buttons on his shirt, while his hands pushed up her dress urgently and his mouth blazed a trail to her breast. The hunger rocketed through her, so powerful it thrilled and terrified her in equal measure, and when they broke apart the narrow hallway echoed with the rasp of their ragged breaths.

Chest heaving, Max pressed their palms together and lifted their arms slowly above her head so that he could pin her against the wall.

'We're going to regret this,' he said, even as he bent his head to kiss her throat, making every cell in her body jolt, turning her insides molten.

'I know.'

'It's crazy.' His lips drifted downward in a searing trail over her skin that left her breathing in tatters.

'You're right,' she managed, sucking in a gasp as he explored the sensitive curve of her neck and shoulder and arching into the wicked pleasure of his mouth.

When he released her wrists to jerk her closer, she whimpered with relief. Now she could tug his shirt free so that she could slide her palms over his firm, smooth back, letting herself notice how his muscles flexed beneath her touch. He was gloriously solid, wonderfully warm. She wanted to burrow into him, lose herself in him.

'It'll just spoil things,' she said unevenly, holding onto the track of the conversation with difficulty.

'It will. It'll never be the same again,' said Max, his voice low and ragged. 'I'm never going to be able to forget how you taste,' he warned her. 'I'll never forget how you feel, how soft you are.'

'So…we should stop,' she tried, even as she pressed him closer, revelling in the feel of how hard he was, how strong, how male. Her blood was thumping and thudding and throbbing with urgency and she wanted him so much that she couldn't think about anything else.

'We probably should,' said Max, his hands sliding

under her dress, his mouth hot on her skin. 'But there's a problem.'

Allegra shuddered under his touch. 'A…a problem?'

'Yes.' He lifted his head and brought his hands up to frame her face. 'The problem is, I don't want to stop, do you?'

She ought to say yes. She ought to put a stop to this right now. Max was right. They would regret this in the morning. But how could she say stop when her body was arching towards his and her skin yearned for his touch and her blood was running wild and wanting him blotted out everything else?

Her arms wrapped round his neck and she pulled him closer for a deep, wet kiss. 'No,' she murmured against his lips, 'I don't want to stop.'

CHAPTER EIGHT

ALLEGRA SURFACED SLOWLY to an awareness of an unfamiliar weight lying across her waist. She blinked at a bedside table. Not hers. The arm thrown over her wasn't hers either. A warm male body was pressed against her back, a face buried in her hair. Steady breath stirred the air against her shoulder and she quivered as memory came whooshing back.

Max. Omigod, she had slept with Max!

Now what was she going to do?

Allegra lay very still. Max was sound asleep and she didn't want to wake him until she had worked out how she was going to react.

Could she pretend that she'd had too much to drink? But she had known exactly what she was doing, and Max knew it.

Okay, so she'd be casual. *Thank goodness we've got that out of our system, now we can move on*: that kind of thing.

Only being casual wasn't going to be easy when she'd just had the best sex of her life. Her body was still buzzing pleasantly in the aftermath, and she flushed at the memory of the careening excitement, the heart-shaking pleasure that had left her languid and replete at last.

It would be so much easier if the sex had been disappointing, or even average. If Max had been a pedestrian lover, as conventional and dull as his suits. Instead...Allegra's blood tingled, remembering the shattering sureness of his hands, of his mouth...oh, God, *his mouth*... In spite of herself, her lips curved. Who would have thought that the crisp and efficient engineer was capable of *that*?

How much more passion had Emma wanted?

Allegra wished she hadn't thought about Emma. She'd been on the verge of turning over and waking Max, but now she'd remembered reality. Last night hadn't changed anything. Max would be going to Shofrar soon, and if he took anyone with him it wouldn't be his sister's frivolous, fashionable friend.

And Libby! That was another complication. How would she feel if she knew Allegra had slept with her brother? But Allegra couldn't keep a secret from her best friend. Allegra gnawed her bottom lip. She wished she could rewind the hours and go back to the night, to the darkness where nothing had mattered but touch and feel and taste, the glorious slide of flesh against flesh, the spiralling excitement, the splintering joy.

What time was it anyway? Very cautiously, Allegra reached towards the phone on the bedside table. Sensing her movement in his sleep, Max mumbled a protest and tightened his arm about her, pulling her back against his hard body. It felt so good that Allegra's heart contracted, but she made herself wriggle free and grope once more for the phone.

Her fingers closed round it and she peered at the screen: 08:45. Holy smoke!

'Max!' She sat bolt upright in bed. 'Max, wake up! It's nearly nine o'clock!'

'Wha...?' Max struggled up, scowling at the abrupt awakening. His eyes were screwed up, his hair ruffled. Allegra wanted to take his face between her hands and kiss the grouchiness away. She wanted to push him down into the pillows and lose herself in his touch.

Instead she leapt out of bed, out of temptation. 'I'm going to be late!' she said, scrabbling frantically for her clothes. She found a bra, a pair of tights… What the hell had happened to her dress?

'Wait…' The sleep was clearing from Max's face and his expression changed as he watched Allegra pounce on the dress that lay in a puddle on the floor, where it had fallen last night. He had a vivid memory of unzipping it slowly, of listening to the enticing rustle as it slithered down over Allegra's hips, of catching his breath at the sight of her in a black push-up bra and lacy thong.

'Allegra, wait,' he said again as memory after memory of the night before flashed through his mind like an erotic slide show.

She turned, tousle-haired, wide-eyed, clutching her pile of clothes to her chest, forgetting that it was a little late for modesty. 'Didn't you hear what I said? It's nearly nine!'

'Nearly *nine*?' This time it got through. He scrambled out of bed, stark naked. 'Shit! I was supposed to be at work half an hour ago!'

'You can have the shower first,' she said. 'You're quicker than me.'

Max hesitated, dragged a hand through his hair. He was *never* late for work, but he couldn't leave it like that. He might not have thought ahead last night, but he knew the morning wasn't supposed to be like this, and he found himself saying the words he never thought he would hear coming out of his mouth: 'We need to talk.'

'I know,' said Allegra, not quite meeting his eyes, 'but later.'

Perhaps later was better, Max told himself as he showered and shaved as quickly as he could, which was pretty damn quickly. By the evening he might have had a chance to get a grip of himself. It would have been too hard to talk with Allegra's scent still clogging his brain, with his heart still thundering with the memory of her sweetness, her warmth, her wicked, irresistible smile. She had turned him upside down, inside out.

She had turned him wild.

Max shrugged on his shirt, knotted his tie, dressed himself in his civilised suit, but underneath he still felt stripped bare. He'd been unprepared for the wildness of his need for her, for the way the feel of her set something free inside him.

So free that he'd lost his mind, lost himself. Max set his jaw, remembering the foolishness he'd spouted, the incoherent words that had tumbled out of him as they'd moved together, up and up through swirling darkness towards the shattering light. He hadn't known what he was saying, but now the words were out, how the hell was he going to put them back?

He was at the round table, filling out a visa form for Shofrar, when Allegra got home that night. The moment he heard the key in the door, every cell in his body seemed to leap in anticipation, but he had his expression well under control by the time she appeared in the doorway.

There was a pause, then Allegra said, 'Hi.'

'You're back late.' Max hated the accusing note in his own voice. Anyone would think that he was keeping track of her, that he'd been sitting here, just waiting for her to come home.

'I've been to the launch of a new jewellery collection.' Allegra hesitated, then came into the room. She was wearing skinny leopard-print jeans, a tight T-shirt and a leather jacket, with chunky earrings and shiny boots. Her hair was pulled back in one of those messy twists that Max disliked. She looked funky, hip, a million miles from the elegant woman who'd taken his arm last night.

From the woman who'd short-circuited every single one of his fuses last night.

She unzipped her jacket and dropped her bag on the sofa. 'What are you doing?' she asked, perching on the arm so that she could take off her boots.

'A visa application for Shofrar,' said Max.

Allegra glanced up from her right boot. 'Already?'

'I saw Bob Laskovski again today. One of the project managers out there has been in a car accident. He's okay, I think, but they're bringing him back to hospital here. Bob wanted to know if I could go out earlier.'

She stilled. 'How much earlier?'

'The end of next week.'

'Oh.'

'Bob was asking about wedding dates,' said Max, relieved to hear that he sounded so normal. 'He was anxious to reassure me that I could come back in a month or so to sort stuff out, and that you could join me whenever you're ready.'

'I see,' said Allegra. She bent her head and went back to fiddling with her boot. 'Well...that's good. You must be pleased.'

'Yes,' said Max. He should be delighted. This was exactly what he had wanted, after all. So why didn't he *feel* pleased?

He wished Allegra would look up. He wished she didn't look so trendy. He wished they hadn't started on this awful stilted conversation when they should be talking about the night before. 'What about your article? Can we fit in the last tests by next week?'

She pursed her lips, considering, apparently unbothered

by the fact that he would be leaving so soon. 'I've arranged with Darcy that you'll go with her to the opening of the new Digby Fox exhibition on Tuesday evening,' she said.

'Who's Digby Fox?' he said, disgruntled.

'Only the hottest ticket in the art world at the moment. He's a really controversial artist but anyone who's anyone will be there to look at his new installations.'

'And Darcy wants to go to this?' Max couldn't hide his scepticism.

'She wants to change her image and be taken more seriously. And Digby Fox is really interesting,' she told him. 'But that would be your last challenge. The costume ball isn't for another month, you'll be gutted to hear, so you'll miss that.'

'What, no waltzing after all?'

'No.' Allegra's smile was a little painful.

'I'm sorry,' said Max.

'No you're not,' she said, sounding much more herself. 'You told me you'd rather stick pins in your eyes than waltz.'

'I'm sorry to let you down,' he clarified. 'I promised I'd do it.'

'It can't be helped. If you can make it to the Digby Fox preview I'll have enough material,' she said. 'It's a shame about the ball, but maybe I'll ask William if he'd go with Darcy. I'm sure he knows how to waltz.'

William? Max bristled at her careless assumption that he could be so easily replaced. The last thing he'd wanted to do was make a fool of himself at some stupid ball, but still…

Allegra was being exasperatingly reasonable. Why couldn't she go all dramatic and start weeping and wailing about the tragedy of her unfinished article? Max would feel so much better if she did. All this politeness was getting to him. They needed to stop this and talk about the night before.

'Look, Legs,' he began but, before he could finish, his phone started to ring. Max cursed.

'Aren't you going to get that?'

'It can go to voicemail.'

'It might be important.'

Muttering under his breath, he snatched up the phone and looked at the screen in disbelief.

'Who is it?' asked Allegra.

'It's Emma,' he said slowly.

Allegra got up, dropping her left boot on the floor. 'You should talk to her,' she said. 'I'm going to get changed anyway.'

She left her boots lying as they were, and Max watched, churning with frustration, as she walked out barefoot. The boots looked as abandoned and forlorn as he felt, and Max bent to put them neatly side by side as he pressed the answer button on his phone.

'Hello?' he said.

In her room, Allegra leant back against the door and drew a deep breath. That had gone better than she'd feared. She'd been calm, cool. She hadn't cried. She hadn't thrown herself into his arms and begged him not to go, although it had been a close run thing when he'd told her that he was going to Shofrar next week.

Next week.

It was all for the best, Allegra told herself. Let's face it, last night had been a one-off. It had been incredible, amazingly so, but they were still the same people as they'd been before, who had different lives and wanted different things. Of course it was tempting to imagine that they could recreate the previous night, but really, what would be the point? It would just make it harder to say goodbye in a week's time.

Emma had rung at just the right time. She was what Max really needed. Allegra hoped that she was telling Max that she had made a terrible mistake and wanted to go back to him. She really did.

A nasty headache was jabbing right behind her eyes and her throat felt tight. Allegra pulled the clip from her hair and changed her tight jeans for a pair of pyjama bottoms patterned with faded puppies, sighing at the comfort. Wrapping a soft grey cardigan around her, she padded back down to the kitchen and poured herself a bowl of cereal. She was tempted to eat it there but it felt like avoiding Max, and that would make it seem as if last night was a big deal, which it wasn't at all. Besides, she hadn't heard his voice when she passed the sitting room door, so presumably he'd finished talking to Emma.

Sure enough, when she carried her bowl back to the living room Max was sitting at the table once more, but he wasn't filling in his form. He was staring ahead, turning his pen abstractedly between his fingers. He looked tired, and a dangerous rush of emotion gusted through Allegra.

What would it be like if she could go over and massage his shoulders? Would he jerk away in horror, or would he let his head drop back against her breasts? Would he let her slide her arms down to his chest so that she could press her lips to his jaw and kiss his throat the way she had done the night before?

Allegra's chest was so tight that for a moment she couldn't move. She could just stand in the doorway in her old pyjama bottoms and the sleeves of her cardigan falling over her hands, and when Max glanced up and their eyes met the jolt in the air was so unexpected that she jerked, slopping the milk in the bowl of cereal she held.

'Allegra...' After that one frozen moment, Max pushed back his chair abruptly and got to his feet, only to stop as if he had forgotten what he was going to say.

'How was Emma?' Allegra rushed to fill the silence. She slouched over to the sofa and stretched out on it to eat her cereal, deliberately casual.

Max hesitated. 'She wants to meet.'

'Hey, that's great news!'

'Is it?'

'Of course it is.' Allegra kept beaming, which was quite hard when you were trying to eat cereal at the same time. 'Come on, Max, you want her back. You know you do.'

'If I wanted her that much, I wouldn't have slept with you last night,' he said.

'That didn't mean anything. We both agreed that.' Deliberately she finished her cereal, scraping around the bowl, not looking at Max. Just another slobby evening, nothing on her mind.

'We knew what were doing,' she persevered when Max said nothing. 'It was meant to be a bit of fun, wasn't it?—and it *was*, but it's not as if either of us want a relationship. We know each other too well for that. We'd drive each other mad!'

Allegra had been practising this speech all day, but Max didn't seem impressed. He came over to the sofa, took the bowl from her unresisting hand and set it on the table. Then he nudged her legs so that she lifted them for him to sit down.

Just the way she had nudged his that night she had looked at him and decided that he was perfect for her article. Allegra almost winced at the jab of memory as she settled her legs across his lap. She had thought she had known Max then, but she hadn't had a clue. She'd known nothing about the clean male scent of his skin or the enticing scrape of his jaw. Nothing about the lean, lovely strength of his body or the dark, delicious pleasure of his hands. Nothing about how it felt when his mouth curved against her flesh.

Max studied the puppies on her pyjama bottoms a moment then lifted his eyes to hers. 'What if I *did* want a relationship, Legs?' he said, and the last of Allegra's breath leaked out of her lungs.

'You're...not serious?' she managed.

'Why not?'

'Because it's crazy. You said it yourself last night. Madness, you said. We'll regret it in the morning, you said.'

'I know I did,' he said evenly. 'But the thing is, I didn't regret it. I still don't.'

'Max...'

'Do you regret it?' he asked her and Allegra couldn't look away, couldn't lie.

'No. No, I don't.'

He stroked one of her bare feet thoughtfully, making her suck in a sharp breath. 'Then why don't we try it again? We might not regret that either.'

His hand was warm and firm and she could have sworn she felt his touch in every molecule. Unable to prevent a quiver of response, she made herself pull the foot away and draw up her legs.

'It was just sex,' she said, keeping her voice steady with an effort. 'It was great, don't get me wrong, but I don't think we should read more into it than that.'

'Okay,' said Max. 'So why don't we have great sex until I leave?'

'Because...' Couldn't he *see*? 'Because it's too hard to stop great sex becoming something else, and then where would we be?'

'In a relationship?'

'And what would be the point of that? You're going to Shofrar next week?'

'No, you're right,' Max said. 'What was I thinking?'

'I know what you were thinking *with*,' said Allegra in an effort to lighten the conversation, and a smile tugged at the corner of his mouth.

'Maybe,' he said.

'It *was* lovely,' she said, unable to keep the wistful note from creeping into her voice, 'but I can't see me in the desert, can you?'

'No,' he said slowly. 'No, I can't.'

'You need someone like Emma,' Allegra ploughed on, struggling to remember the script she had prepared. 'Someone who can really be part of your life.' Someone not like me, she added bleakly to herself. 'I'm sure that when you meet her again you'll remember just how important she was to you before. It's only a couple of months since you wanted to marry her,' she reminded him. 'You need to think about what really matters to you and let's go back to being friends.'

'And last night?'

No wonder she hadn't spent any time being sensible before. Being sensible hurt. But it didn't hurt as much as falling in love with him would hurt, or the inevitable moment when Max would realise that sex wasn't enough, that *she* wasn't enough.

Just like she hadn't been enough to keep her unknown father around.

Like she was never quite enough to please her mother.

Allegra drew a breath and summoned a smile. 'Last night wasn't real,' she said. 'It was lovely, but I think it would be easier if we pretended that it never happened.'

Pretend it never happened. Easy for *her* to say! Max yanked his tie savagely into place. Bloody Dickie had picked out another humdinger for him to wear to the preview of Digby Fox's exhibition: a fluorescent green shirt with a red tie, and a tweed jacket in hunter green.

'It's bold, it's assertive, it's *you*,' Dickie had assured him when Max had refused absolutely to consider any of it. 'Just try it,' he had coaxed and in the end, Max had given in for a quiet life. It was the last time he'd have to make a fool of himself, after all.

Dickie had been on the verge of tears when he'd heard that Max wouldn't be going to the costume ball after all.

'I had *such* a marvellous outfit in mind for you too,' he'd mourned.

Another reason to be grateful that he was going to Shofrar early, Max decided as he dressed grimly.

Allegra had cancelled their dancing lessons, which meant that he never needed to waltz again. And what a relief *that* was! He wasn't missing those lessons at all. If he had found himself remembering the times he and Allegra had practised twirling around the room, it was only because he felt bad at letting her down. He knew how much she had been looking forward to the ball.

Now she would be going with William.

Not that he cared that Allegra had been able to replace him so easily, Max reassured himself hastily. He was well out of it.

He regarded his reflection glumly. He looked a total prat. The neon-green shirt made him look as if he should be directing traffic. At least Dickie had had to accept his refusal to grow a designer stubble. Max rubbed a hand over his freshly shaven jaw. The truth was, he'd nearly given way on that too when he'd realised how disappointed Dickie was that Max wouldn't be able to take him to a rugby match the way he'd promised.

He seemed to be letting everyone down at the moment.

With a sigh, he picked up the jacket Dickie had assured him was the last word in style and headed for the door. He was to meet Allegra and Darcy at the gallery. Max couldn't say that he was looking forward to the evening ahead, but he'd done his homework. Allegra had pressed a book on modern art into his hands so that he would impress Darcy with his knowledge but, having ploughed through it, he was none the wiser. He would just have to wing it, he decided. He could look thoughtful and mumble something about challenging perceptions and that would have to do.

And, after tonight, his obligations would be over. He could concentrate on handing over his projects at work and pack up the few belongings he'd brought with him when he'd moved out of Emma's. Everything was already stored in the attic in his parents' house. Max had been home to say goodbye to his parents that weekend so that he didn't get in Allegra's way, but it hadn't been as restful as he'd hoped. His mother had an uncanny ability to home in on the things Max least wanted to talk about and she kept asking how Allegra was and how they were getting on sharing the house. Max tried an austere 'fine' in reply, but oh, no, that wasn't enough.

'What aren't you telling me?' she'd demanded.

She didn't seem to understand that there were some things you couldn't tell your mother.

He couldn't tell her about the way his breath clogged every time he looked at Allegra. He couldn't tell her about the memories that circled obsessively in his head, memories of the hot, sweet darkness, of the pleasure that had leapt like wildfire, consuming everything in its path. He couldn't tell her how the feel of Allegra had blotted everything else from his mind.

'Allegra is fine,' he'd insisted to his mother.

Allegra certainly seemed fine. She was doing a lot better than he was, anyway.

She'd been bright and brittle ever since she'd sat on the sofa looking soft and oh-so-touchable in those silly pyjamas. Max's hands had itched to slide beneath the faded material, to peel that baggy cardigan from her shoulders and lay her down beneath him once more, but the moment he'd succumbed to temptation and stroked her foot, she had pulled away.

Last night wasn't real, she'd said. *Let's pretend it never happened.*

Max hadn't tried to change her mind. Allegra had made it clear that she didn't want him to touch her again, and he wasn't about to start forcing himself on a woman. She might have dressed it all up as wanting him to be happy, but Max wasn't a fool. What she meant was that she wouldn't be happy with him.

And, anyway, she was right. It was all for the best. He *couldn't* imagine Allegra in Shofrar. She wanted to stay in London, in the gossipy, glamorous world that was *Glitz*. What could he offer compared to that? A prefabricated house on a compound in the desert. Big deal.

So Max was doing his best to behave normally. He wasn't going to follow her around making puppy dog eyes. A man had his pride, after all. He met Emma for lunch and thought about what Allegra had said about Emma being what he needed. It seemed hard to remember now, but Max was prepared to try and Emma herself was dropping hints about the possibility of getting back together. Max told

Allegra that he and Emma were 'talking' and she seemed delighted, he remembered sourly.

At least he'd made someone happy.

His mood was not improved when he made it to the gallery and found Allegra already there with Darcy and a smarmy-looking man who Allegra introduced as William.

Max disliked him on sight. William had the lean, well-bred air of a greyhound. He had floppy hair and tortoise-shell glasses, which Max privately decided were fake and designed purely to make him look intelligent. And God, the man could talk! Darcy hung on his every word as William pontificated. He had an opinion on everything, as far as Max could make out. Max would have liked him a lot better if he'd taken one look at the pile of pooh on display and admitted that he didn't have a clue what it was all about.

Every surface in the gallery was painted white which was disorientating. Max was glad he didn't suffer from seasickness or he'd have been desperate for a horizon. Not that anyone else seemed to notice how weird the décor was. The gallery was jam-packed with trendy types clutching glasses of champagne. They were all talking at the tops of their voices and vying for the accolade of most pretentious comment of the evening. Clearly it was going to be a stiff competition.

Max himself was profoundly unimpressed by the so-called 'art' on display. As far as he could see, the 'artist' had run around gathering together as much junk as he could find, thrown it into piles and called it an installation. There was more art in a beautifully designed bridge than this claptrap, in Max's humble opinion.

William disagreed. He appointed himself guide and insisted on explaining every exhibit. Phrases like 'implicit sexual innuendo', 'aesthetic encounter' and 'anthropomorphic narratives' fell from his lips, while Darcy hung on every word. Allegra seemed distracted, though, and Max couldn't help wondering if she was jealous of the way William was so obviously basking in Darcy's attention.

That evening she was wearing a floaty skirt, clumpy boots and short tweedy jacket. Max wanted to think that she looked a mess, but somehow she looked as if she belonged there in a way he never would, neon shirt or no neon shirt. She had plenty of her old pizazz about her, but there was a tight look around her eyes and her smile wasn't as bright as usual.

'You okay?' he asked her as William steered Darcy on to the next exhibit.

'Yes. Why?'

'I don't know. You look a bit…tired.'

Great. Everyone knew that looking 'tired' meant you looked a wreck. The chatter bouncing off the white walls was making Allegra's head ache. She felt like a wreck too.

Usually she loved these gossipy, trendy affairs, but there were too many people crammed into the gallery and it felt claustrophobic in spite of the attempts to make the design feel airy and spacious. She had to squeeze her way through the throng. Digby Fox could pull in some A-list names. So far she had muttered 'sorry…excuse me…' to minor royalty, a prize-winning author and a celebrity chef. Ordinarily, Allegra would have been thrilled, but the only person she had eyes for was Max, who was looking resolutely out of place.

How on earth had Dickie persuaded him into that shirt? It was so loud it wasn't doing anything for her headache.

Allegra had had a tiring day listening to Dickie moaning about how much he was going to miss Max. Max had shown him how to order a pint in the pub; Max had introduced him to takeaway curry; Max had promised to take him to a rugby match. He seemed to hold her personally responsible for Max's promotion.

Max made love to me! Allegra had wanted to shout. *I'm going to miss him much, much more than you.*

She didn't, of course. Dickie was still Dickie and her career was all she had to hold onto at the moment.

'You should have said *non*,' Dickie had grumbled in the accent Max swore was put on. 'Non, ze article isn't finished, you cannot go yet.'

If only it had been that easy.

She had tried to convince him that she had enough for an article, but Dickie had been counting on dressing Max for the costume ball. ''e would 'ave looked *magnifique*,' he said forlornly.

Allegra secretly thought that was unlikely. Max would never be handsome. He would never be magnificent. He was quietly austere and understated and ordinary and she wanted him more than anything she had ever wanted in her life.

And, oh, she would have loved to have waltzed with him at the ball!

The last few days had been awful. It was exhausting trying to pretend that everything was fine, reminding herself again and again that she'd done the right thing in turning down the chance to spend this last week with him. She had told Max that she wanted him to be happy, and she *did*. She'd just been unprepared for how much it would hurt when he took her advice and contacted Emma. Max was being a bit cagey about things and Allegra supposed it was none of her business, but she knew that he and Emma had met and that they were 'talking'. If she were Emma she would be moving heaven and earth to get back together with Max.

If she were Emma, she would never have left him in the first place.

Allegra had tried hard. She had thrown herself into work and been to every party she could blag herself into. She'd called William and invited him tonight, hoping that Max would somehow be less appealing in contrast, but instead the contrast had worked in Max's favour, and William was dazzled by Darcy. For all his intellect and ambition, he was clearly just as susceptible to Darcy's gorgeous face and even more gorgeous body as the next man, and Allegra herself might just as well have been invisible for all the notice he took of her.

It was lucky that she wasn't in love with William, Allegra reflected glumly. Nobody wanted her at the moment.

Max had wanted her. For a moment Allegra let herself remember the heat that had burned like wildfire along her veins, the taste of his skin and the wicked, wonderful torment of his mouth. The way the world had swung giddily around, the shattering pleasure. She could have had that again, but she had said no, and now it seemed that he was getting back together with Emma.

Allegra sighed. It made it so much worse when the only person you could blame for your misery was yourself.

CHAPTER NINE

THINK ABOUT YOUR career, Allegra told herself fiercely. *Think about this amazing article you're going to write that's going to impress the notoriously unimpressable Stella and open doors for a career in serious journalism. Think about how pleased Flick is going to be with you when your analysis of the latest political crisis hits the headlines.*

But before she could tackle politics and the global economy she had to make a success of *Making Mr Perfect*.

Rousing herself, Allegra poked Max in the ribs as William headed into the next room of the gallery, Darcy breathlessly in tow. Caught up in the crowd, Allegra and Max were trailing behind them.

'You're supposed to be impressing Darcy with your knowledge of modern art,' she muttered.

'I would if there was any art here,' said Max. 'How does this guy get away with it?' He studied a plate, encrusted with dried baked beans, that was set carefully on a table next to a rusty oil can. Craning his neck, he read the price on the label and shook his head. 'He's having a laugh!'

'Digby Fox likes to challenge conventional expectations about art,' Allegra said dutifully, but her heart wasn't in it.

'You can't tell me you actually like this stuff?'

'Not really,' she admitted, lowering her voice as if confessing to something shameful. 'I prefer paintings.'

Ahead of them, William had stopped in front of a collection of torn bin bags that were piled up against the stark gallery wall. 'A searing commentary on modern consumption,' he was saying as Max and Allegra came up.

Allegra was sure she heard Max mutter, 'Tosser.'

'One can't fail to be struck by the nihilistic quality of Digby's representation of quotidian urban life,' William went on while Darcy looked at him with stars in her eyes.

'It's powerful stuff,' she said, her expression solemn. 'It makes you feel *small*, doesn't it?'

William nodded thoughtfully, as if she had said something profound, and turned to Max, evidently deciding it was time to include him in the conversation. 'What do you think, Max?'

Max pretended to contemplate the installation. 'I think it's a load of old rubbish,' he pronounced at last.

William looked disapproving and Darcy disappointed, but a giggle escaped Allegra. Oh dear, sniggering at childish jokes didn't bode well for her future as a journalist with gravitas.

'Yes, well, shall we move on?' said William, taking Darcy's arm to steer her on to the next exhibit.

Max caught Allegra's eye. 'Let's get out of here,' he said. 'This is all such bollocks and we can't even get a decent drink.'

She opened her mouth to insist that they stayed, to point out that she had a job to do, but somehow the words wouldn't come. 'I don't suppose it would matter if we slipped out,' she said instead, looking longingly at the exit. Max was right. What was the point of staying? 'I'd better go and tell Darcy and William, though.'

'You really think they're going to notice that we've gone?'

'Probably not—' she sighed '—but allegedly Darcy's here for the article, and I invited William. I can't just abandon them without a word. I'll go and tell them I've got a headache and see you outside.'

It was amazing how her spirits lightened at the prospect of escaping with Max. By the time Allegra had pushed her way through the crush to William and Darcy, who were at the very back of the gallery by then, and then to the front again, she was hot and bothered and practically fell out of the door to find Max waiting for her.

Outside, a fine London mizzle was falling and Max's hair was already damp, but it was blessedly cool and Allegra fanned herself with the exhibition catalogue. 'That's better,' she said in relief, heading away from the noise of the gallery.

'I was beginning to think you'd changed your mind,' said Max, falling into step beside her.

'No way. I had to fight my way out, though. I can't believe how many people there were in there.'

Max snorted. 'Talk about the emperor's new clothes!'

'It was a bit rubbish,' Allegra allowed.

'Literally,' he said sardonically. 'So, do I gather Darcy wasn't devastated about me leaving her with William?'

'I'm afraid she was delighted. She might have thought you were pretty cute once, but she's forgotten all about you now that she's met William.'

'She wasn't really interested in me anyway,' said Max. 'She was just bored and looking for someone different.'

'Well, William's certainly that. Political aide and lingerie model…it's not an obvious combination, is it? But Darcy thinks William's really clever, and she loves the way he talks to her as if she'll understand what he says.'

A grunt. 'He was showing off, if you ask me.'

'Yes, but can you blame him? Darcy's so beautiful.'

'I can blame him for ignoring *you*,' said Max, scowling. 'I thought you two were going out?'

'Not really. We'd just had a drink a couple of times. It's not as if we'd ever—' Allegra stopped.

Slept together. Like she and Max had done.

There was a tiny pause while her unspoken words jangled in the silence. Allegra developed a sudden fascination with the shop window they were passing.

Max cleared his throat. 'Do you mind?' he asked. 'About William?'

'No, not really,' she said with a sigh. 'He's nice, but I don't think he's my kind of guy.'

'Who is?'

You are. The words rang so loudly in Allegra's head that for one horrified moment she thought that she had spoken them aloud.

'Oh, you know, the usual: tall, dark, handsome, filthy-rich…' She hoped he realised that she was joking. 'The truth is, I'm still trying to find a man who can match up to my Regency duke.'

'The terrace ravisher?'

'That's the one. I don't know anyone with a fraction of his romance,' she told Max.

'You don't think holding out for an aristocrat who's been dead for a couple of hundred years is going to limit your options a bit?'

'I'm hoping they'll invent a time travel machine soon,' said Allegra. 'In the meantime, I've got my fantasy to keep me warm.'

Max raised his brows. 'Whatever turns you on,' he said and they promptly plunged into another pool of silence.

He had turned her on. Allegra's pulse kicked as she remembered that night: the way they had grabbed each other, the frenzy of lust and heat and throbbing need. It hadn't been tender and beautiful. It had been wild and frantic and deliciously dirty. A flush warmed her cheeks, thinking about the things Max had done, the things she had done to him. She had turned him on too.

They had turned each other on.

Desperately trying to shove the memories away, Allegra was glad of Max's silence as they walked. At that time of the evening the back streets of Knightsbridge were quiet, apart from an occasional taxi passing, engine ticking and tyres shushing on the wet tarmac. Allegra was glad she had worn her boots rather than the more glamorous stilettos she'd dithered over. At least her boots were comfortable—well, relatively. She had to be careful not to twist her ankle falling off their substantial platform soles but otherwise they were almost as good as the trainers Max had once suggested she wear to work.

Max. Why did everything come back to him now?

She was agonizingly conscious of him walking beside her. His shoulders were slightly hunched and he had jammed his hands into his trouser pockets. Damp spangled his hair whenever he passed under a street lamp. He seemed distracted and she wondered if he was thinking about Shofrar. This time next week he'd be gone.

Something like panic skittered through Allegra at the thought, and she shivered involuntarily.

'You cold?' Max glanced at her.

'No, not really.'

His brows drew together as he studied her skimpy jacket. 'That's not enough to keep you warm. Didn't you bring a coat?'

'No, I—' But Max was already pulling off his jacket

and dropping it over her shoulders. It was warm from his body and the weight was incredibly reassuring.

'I'm not cold,' he said, 'and, besides, it doesn't matter if this shirt gets ruined. I am never, ever going to wear it again!'

'To be honest, I wouldn't have said it was really you,' said Allegra as she settled the jacket more comfortably around her, and Max smiled faintly.

'Don't tell Dickie that. It'll break his heart.'

She longed to take his arm and lean into his side, but she couldn't do that. Allegra kept her eyes on the pavement instead and clutched the two sides of the jacket together. She needed to show Max that she was fine about him leaving, that she had put that night they had shared behind her, just as she had said she would.

He had been in touch with Emma and it was too late now to tell him that she had changed her mind. It would make things even more awkward if he knew that she thought about him constantly, and that a dull ache throbbed in her chest whenever she thought about saying goodbye.

So she lifted her chin and summoned a bright smile. 'I don't suppose you'll have much need of a fancy wardrobe in Shofrar,' she said, determinedly cheerful.

'Nope. White short-sleeved shirt, shorts, long trousers for business meetings, and that's about it,' said Max. 'I won't ever need to dither over my wardrobe again.'

Allegra's smile twisted painfully. 'A life away from fashion. That'll make you happy.'

'Yes,' said Max, but he didn't sound as sure as he should have done. Of course he would be happy when he was there, he reassured himself. He couldn't wait. No styling sessions. No dancing lessons. No being told to roll up his cuffs, no need to consider what to wear. No messy house.

No Allegra.

The thought was a cold poker, jabbing into his lungs and stopping his breath. It was all for the best, of course it was, Max reminded himself with a shade of desperation. Going out to Shofrar was the next step in his career. It was what he had worked for, what he wanted. He would love it when he was there.

But he was going to miss her, there was no use denying it.

They were making their way slowly towards Sloane Street, along a side street clustered with antique shops and art galleries. Many were open still to cater for the after work crowd, and they had passed more than one gallery having a preview party much like the one they had just come from.

Allegra was absorbed in thought, her gaze on the window displays, which meant Max could watch her profile. Knowing that he could only look at her when she wasn't looking at him now made his chest tighten. When had she become so beautiful to him? Max's eyes rested hungrily on the curve of her cheek, on the clean line of her jaw and the lovely sweep of her throat. With her face averted he couldn't see her mouth, but he knew exactly how luscious it was, how her lips tipped upright at the corners and curved into a smile that lit her entire face.

God, he was going to miss her.

'Oh…' Unaware of his gaze, Allegra had stopped short, her attention caught by a single painting displayed in a gallery window.

The painting was quite small and very simple. It showed a woman holding a bowl, that was all, but something about the colours and the shapes made the picture leap into life. Compared to this, Digby Fox's installations seemed even more tawdry. This quiet painting was clearly special even though Max didn't have the words to explain how or why that should be so.

Holding the jacket together, Allegra was leaning forward to read the label. 'I thought so,' she said. 'It's a Jago Forrest. I've always loved his paintings.'

Max came closer to read the label over her shoulder. At least, he meant to read it, but he was too distracted by Allegra's perfume to focus. 'I've never heard of Jago Forrest,' he said.

'I don't think many people have. My art teacher at school was a fan, or I wouldn't have known about him either. He's famously reclusive, apparently… Oh, it looks like he died last year,' she went on, reading the label. Cupping her hands around her face, she peered through the window into the gallery. 'It says this is a retrospective exhibition of his works.'

'Why don't we go in and have a look?' said Max on an impulse. If you'd asked him a day earlier if he'd voluntarily go into an art gallery, he'd have scoffed, but the little picture in the window seemed to be beckoning him inside. 'At least we can look at some real art this evening as opposed to piles of rubbish.'

Inside, it was quiet and calm with none of the aggressive trendiness of the earlier gallery. A strikingly beautiful woman with cascading red curls welcomed them in and told them they were welcome to wander around, but she looked at Allegra so intently that Allegra clearly began to feel uncomfortable.

'If you're about to close…'

'No, it's all right. I'm sorry, I was staring at you,' said the woman. She had a faint accent that Max couldn't place. Eastern European, perhaps. 'We haven't met before, have we?'

'I'm sure I'd remember,' said Allegra. 'You've got such gorgeous hair.'

'Thank you.' The woman touched it a little self-consciously. 'I think perhaps I'm too old for such long hair now but Jago would never let me cut it.'

Her name, it turned out, was Bronya, and she had been Jago Forrest's muse for nearly twenty years, living with him in secluded splendour in an isolated part of Spain. She told Allegra that Jago had refused to see anyone, but that after he'd died she had decided to make his work accessible once more.

'But his portraits are so tender,' said Allegra. 'It's hard to believe that he disliked people that much.'

Bronya smiled faintly. 'He was a complicated man,' she said. 'Not always easy to live with, but a genius.' She looked sad for a moment. 'But I mustn't hold you up. Take your time looking round,' she said, gesturing them into the gallery. 'This is his most recent work down here, but some of his earlier paintings are upstairs if you'd be interested to see those too. Are you *sure* we've never met?' she said again to Allegra. 'You seem so familiar…'

Max found Jago Forrest's paintings oddly moving. Many were of Bronya, but he'd also painted countrywomen with seamed faces and gnarled fingers, and there were several young models he'd painted in the nude, portraying their bodies with such sensuousness that Max shifted uneasily.

'Let's go and look upstairs,' said Allegra eventually, and Max followed her up the spiral staircase. At the top she stopped so abruptly that he ran into her.

'Careful—' he began, but then he saw what had brought her up short. A huge portrait dominated the wall facing the staircase. It showed a young woman in a languorous pose, her arm thrown above her head and a satiated smile on her face. But it wasn't the overtly sexual feel to the painting that made Max's face burn. It was the woman's face, and the expression that was carnal and tender at the same time.

'She's beautiful, isn't she?' Bronya had followed them upstairs and stood beside them, misinterpreting their silence. She glanced at Max and Allegra. 'She and Jago had a passionate affair, oh, it must be twenty-five years ago now.'

She laughed lightly. 'I was jealous of her for a long time. I was so afraid that Jago would go back to her, but their affair must have ended very bitterly, I think. She was his passion, and I was his love, that's what he always told me. It's sad it didn't work out. You can see how much she loved him in her face, can't you?'

'Yes,' said Allegra in a strange wooden voice. She was very white about the mouth, and Max moved closer to put a steadying hand on her shoulder.

'Perhaps you recognise her?' Bronya paused delicately, looking curiously at Allegra.

'Oh, yes,' Allegra said, and turned to look straight at her. 'That's my mother.'

'Oh my God...' Bronya's hand crept to her mouth. 'Your eyes! That's why you seemed familiar...you've got Jago's eyes!' She stared at Allegra. 'You're his daughter!'

Max was worried about Allegra. She looked cold and lost as she stood on the pavement outside the gallery. He'd tried to put his arms round her, but she side-stepped his hug, holding herself together with an effort that left her rigid.

'I'll take you home,' he said, but she shook her head.

'I need to talk to my mother,' she said, and Max flagged down a taxi without arguing.

She hadn't said anything in the taxi, and now the taxi was pulling up outside Flick's house. 'Would you like me to come in with you?' he asked, not liking the frozen expression on her face.

'I'll be fine,' she said. 'I think this is a conversation Flick and I have to have on our own.'

'I'll wait then,' said Max.

'Don't be silly.' At least he'd brought a flicker of animation to her face and she even managed a smile of sorts. 'I could be hours. You go on home.'

Max didn't like it, but he could hardly insist on barging in with her so he waited until Allegra was inside before giving the taxi driver directions back to the house.

He couldn't settle. He threw himself on the sofa, then got up to go to the kitchen. He switched on the television, turned it off. He kept thinking of Allegra, and how she must have felt learning who her father was after all those years of not knowing. Why hadn't Flick told her? Max knew how much Allegra had yearned for a father. He'd seen how wistfully she had watched his father with Libby and, although his father treated her as an honorary daughter, it wasn't the same as having a father of her own.

The sound of her key in the lock had him leaping to his feet and he made it into the narrow hallway in time to see Allegra closing the front door. She was still wearing his jacket and when she turned her face wore an expression that made Max's heart turn over.

He didn't think. He just opened his arms and she walked right into them without a word.

Max folded her against him and rested his cheek on her hair as she clung to him, trembling. She was cold and tired and distressed, but holding her gave him the first peace he'd had in days.

'Come on,' he said gently at last. 'I'll get you a drink. You look like you need it.'

He made her sit on the sofa while he poured her a shot of whisky. Allegra eyed the glass he handed her dubiously. 'I don't really like whisky,' she said.

'Drink it anyway,' said Max.

Reluctantly she took a sip and choked but, after patting her chest and grimacing hugely, the colour started to come back to her cheeks and she tried again.

Max sat on the sofa beside her, but not too close. 'Better?'

'Funnily enough, yes.' She swirled the whisky around in the glass and her smile faded. 'I just made my mother cry,' she told Max. 'I don't feel very good about it.'

The indomitable Flick Fielding had *cried*? Max couldn't imagine it at all.

'What did she say when you told her about the portrait?'

'She was furious at first,' said Allegra. 'The portrait was supposed to have been destroyed, Bronya had no right to bring it to London, she would slap an injunction on her to make her remove it… She was pacing around her study, absolutely wild, but when I said it was a beautiful picture she just stopped and covered her face with her hands. It was like she just collapsed.' Allegra took another slug of whisky. 'I've never seen Flick cry before. It was awful.'

'Is it true? Was Jago Forrest your father?'

She nodded. 'Everything Bronya told us was true. They did have this incredibly passionate affair. Flick said that she was too young to know better but it's obvious even now that she loved him. Maybe she still does. She said that it almost destroyed her when he left her.'

Absently, Allegra sipped her whisky. 'It's funny to think of her being young and desperately in love, but it also makes a kind of sense now. She's hidden behind a mask of cool intelligence so that no one guesses that she was ever that vulnerable. I suppose keeping everyone at arm's length means that nobody has a chance to hurt you.' Allegra's expression was sad. 'Poor Flick.'

'Poor you,' said Max, unable to resist reaching over to tuck a stray hair back behind her ear. 'What happened?'

'Flick got pregnant but Jago didn't want a child.' Max could tell Allegra was struggling to keep her voice level, and he moved closer to put a comforting arm around her shoulders. She leaned into him gratefully, still cradling the glass between her hands.

'He gave her the money for a termination, but at the last moment, Flick decided she didn't want to go through with it and Jago was furious. He told her it was him or the baby, and she chose to have the baby.' Allegra swallowed. 'She was convinced that he loved her too much to really let her go, and she thought if she could just show him his child he'd change his mind.'

'And he didn't?'

Allegra shook her head. 'Flick said she took me round to his studio after I was born. She said she couldn't believe he would be able to resist me. She said I was perfect.' Her voice wobbled a little and she took another slug of whisky to steady it.

'She said, "You were absolutely perfect, and he looked at you as if you were a slug", and then he told her she would have to choose once and for all. He wanted her to get rid of me, apparently, and when she refused, that was it. He said that as far as he was concerned he'd washed his hands of the problem when he gave her money for the abortion, so she could forget asking him for any support.'

Max tightened his arm around Allegra. She was doing pretty well telling the story, but he'd seen her face when she repeated what Flick had told her about Jago's reaction. Doubtless it had been hard for Flick, but couldn't she have spared Allegra knowing that her father had looked at her as if she were a slug?

'And was that it?' he asked.

'She never saw him again and she was too angry and bitter to pursue him for support. She wouldn't discuss him at all.'

'I can see it was hard for her,' said Max, 'but why didn't she tell you? You had a right to know who your father was.'

Allegra let out a long sigh. 'She said she knew that if she told me I'd want to get in touch with Jago, and she was afraid that he'd reject me the way he'd rejected her. And I think, from what Bronya told us, he probably would have done. He was a genius, but he doesn't sound a very kind person. Flick said she couldn't bear the thought of him hurting me.' She swallowed hard. 'She said she was sorry—I don't think she's ever said that to me before. I hated seeing her so upset. It was like the world turning upside down.'

'You're upset too,' Max pointed out. 'It's been just as hard for you.'

'Well, at least I know who my father was now,' said Allegra bravely. 'And I understand Flick better. I used to think that she didn't really want me,' she confided, 'but she gave up her great passion for me, and she tried to protect me, so that feels good to know.'

'It was a lot for you to learn in one day,' said Max, a faint frown in his eyes. Allegra's composure was brittle and he could feel the tension in her body. 'How do you feel?'

'I'm fine,' she said brightly. 'I just...well, it's not every day you find out your father is a famous artist.'

'Would you rather not have known?' Max asked gently.

'No, it's better to know,' said Allegra. 'At least I can stop dreaming.' She smiled as if it hurt. 'I used to think that the only reason I didn't have a father was because Flick hadn't told him about me. I dreamt that he'd find out about me somehow and come and find me, and I'd be so precious to him. He'd look at me the way your dad looks at Libby.'

Her mouth started to wobble and she took her bottom lip between her teeth to keep it steady. 'So I suppose...I always, always wanted a father, but now it turns out that I had a father but he didn't want me.'

Her face crumpled and Max, who was normally terrified of tears, gathered her on to his lap as she let go of the storm of emotion at last. His throat tight, he held her softly and let her cry it all out until the wrenching sobs subsided to juddering sighs.

'Jago might have been a genius, but he was a fool,' he murmured, touching his lips to her hair without thinking. 'He missed out on knowing just what an amazing daughter he had.'

'I'm not amazing,' she said, muffled in his collar. 'My father was a genius, and Flick's got drive and intelligence, and I'm just...me. I'm not particularly good at anything.' Her voice clogged with tears again. 'And now I know what Flick gave up for me, I can understand just what a disappointment I am to her. I can't be what she wants me to be.'

'Then be what *you* want to be,' said Max. He put her away from him and held her at arm's length so that he could smooth her tangled hair back from her face and look straight into her eyes. 'You've spent your whole life trying to please your mother, Legs, and now it's time to please yourself. Decide what you want to do, and do it.'

Decide what you want. What Allegra really wanted was for Max not to go to Shofrar, but how could she beg him to stay when she knew how much the job meant to him? He'd let her cry over him, and she knew how much he must have hated that. Telling him how much she dreaded him going would have been little more than emotional blackmail.

So she'd knuckled the mascara from under her eyes and put on a smile and pretended that she was fine.

And now he was leaving. His bags were packed and sitting neatly in the hallway. The taxi to take him to Heathrow was due any minute.

The last few days had been a blur. Max's colleagues had thrown a leaving party for him. Allegra hadn't asked, but she was sure that Emma would have been there. The following night Dickie had insisted on farewell drinks in the pub Max had introduced him to. Darcy had come with William. She'd hugged Max and wished him well but it was obvious that she only had eyes for William now. Libby rang from Paris, Max's parents from Northumberland.

But now everybody had gone, the phone was silent and it was just the two of them waiting for the taxi in the sitting room. Allegra's heart was knocking painfully against her ribs. She didn't know whether she was dreading the moment of saying goodbye or longed for it to come so that at least this awful waiting would be over. It was early, not yet seven, and Allegra would normally have been in bed, but she couldn't let him leave without saying goodbye.

Without saying thank you.

She had come downstairs in her old pyjama bottoms and a camisole top, pulling on a cardigan against the crispness of the autumn morning. Her face was bare, her hair tousled.

There was too much to say, and not enough. Allegra's throat ached with the longing to tell Max that she loved him, but what would be the point? She didn't want to embarrass him, and besides, Emma would be waiting for him at the airport.

'Can you let me have Max's flight details?' Emma had rung the night before. Allegra had forgotten how friendly and downright *nice* Emma was. It was obvious that Max hadn't told her about the night he and Allegra had spent together, and it had certainly never crossed Emma's mind that Allegra might be any kind of rival.

Because she wasn't. She was the one who had told Max that they should pretend that night had never happened, Allegra reminded herself. She could hardly blame him when that was exactly what he did. It wasn't his fault that she had fallen in love with him.

Allegra was doing her best to convince herself that her feelings for him were just a temporary infatuation. Falling properly in love with him would be such a totally stupid thing to do. Again and again, Allegra ticked her way through a mental list of reasons why loving Max was a bad idea, and Emma was right there at the top.

Emma would be waiting for him when he got to the airport, and Allegra was fairly certain that she was going to tell Max that she loved him. If Allegra told him the same thing, it would put Max in an impossible situation.

Or maybe not. If you were Max, going out to work in the desert, and you had to choose between a ditzy fashionista and a genuinely nice, attractive fellow engineer who would be able to share your life completely, how hard a choice would it be?

Not very hard at all.

So Allegra stuck with agonising small talk when all she wanted to say was *I love you, I love you, I love you*.

Max was no more at ease and their conversation kept coming out in sticky dollops, only to dry up just when they thought they'd got going.

He hadn't learnt a thing about style. He was wearing one of his old suits, and if he hadn't deliberately chosen his dreariest shirt and tie it had been a lucky accident that he'd succeeded in putting on both. He looked dull and conventional.

He looked wonderful.

Allegra had to hug her arms together to stop herself reaching for him.

For the umpteenth time, Max pulled up his cuff to check his watch, but when his phone rang they both jumped.

'Taxi's here,' he said unnecessarily.

'Yes.' Allegra's throat had closed so tight it was all she could force out.

'So...it looks like this is it.'

'Yes.'

'I'd better go.'

Allegra was gripped by panic. She hadn't said anything that she wanted to! Why had she wasted these last precious minutes? Now all she could do was follow him out to the narrow hallway. She opened the door while Max picked up his briefcase and suitcase. He stepped out and looked at the taxi which was double-parked in the street before turning back to Allegra. He put down his cases again.

'Come out to the airport with me,' he said impulsively, and Allegra's heart contracted. She would have given anything to have an extra half hour with him in the taxi but she thought about Emma, waiting there to surprise him. It would spoil everything if she turned up too.

Emma was perfect for Max. He would realise that when he was in Shofrar, and he so deserved to be happy.

'I can't.' Allegra swallowed painfully. 'I need to get to work, but have a good flight,' she said with a wobbly smile, and stepped forward to give him what was meant to be a quick hug. 'I'll miss you,' she whispered.

Max's arms closed around her and he held her to him, so tightly that Allegra could hardly breathe, but she didn't care. She wanted to stay like that for ever, pressed against him, smelling him, loving him.

'I'll miss you too,' he whispered back.

They stood there, holding each other, neither wanting to be the first to let go, but eventually the taxi driver wound down his window. 'You planning on catching that plane, mate?' he called.

Reluctantly, Max released Allegra. 'I need to go.'

She nodded, tears shimmering in her eyes, and wrapped her arms around herself as she stood on the doorstep, careless of the cold on her bare feet, and watched as Max threw his cases into the back of the taxi. With his hand on the open door, he hesitated and looked back at Allegra as if he would say something else. For one glorious moment she thought that he was going to change his mind and stay after all, but in the end he just lifted his hand, got into the back of the taxi and shut the door.

The driver said something over his shoulder and put the taxi into gear. He put the indicator on and waited for a car that was coming up the street to pass. The car paused and flashed its lights politely to let him out. *No!* Allegra wanted to scream at it. *No, don't let him go!*

But it was too late. One last glimpse of Max through the window, and then the taxi was drawing away. Her heart tore, a slow, cruel rip as she watched it down the street, watched it turn left and out of sight.

And then he was gone.

CHAPTER TEN

'WHAT'S THE LATEST on the *Making Mr Perfect* piece?' Stella's steely gaze swept round the editorial conference before homing in on Allegra, who was doing her best to hide in the corner.

'Er, it's almost done,' said Allegra. The truth was that she couldn't bring herself to reread what she'd written about Max. It was all too raw.

She missed him terribly. In the past, when a relationship had ended, she'd been miserable for a day or two, but all it had taken was a new pair of shoes or a funny tweet to perk her up again. Now, it felt as if there was a jagged rip right through her heart, a bloody wound clawed open afresh every time she thought about Max. Missing him wasn't the vague sense of disappointment she'd felt before. It was the leadenness that had settled like a boulder in the pit of her stomach. It was the ache in her bones and the awful emptiness inside her.

Allegra was wretched. She hated going back to the house, hated going into the sitting room and seeing the empty sofa. She ached for the sight of him stretched out on it, rolling his eyes at her shoes. She missed the way he tsked at her untidy ways, the way that smile lurked at the corner of his mouth.

Without realising it, she had memorised every angle of

his face, every crease at the edges of his eyes. She could sketch him perfectly, but you couldn't hold a drawing, you couldn't touch it and feel it. You couldn't lean into it and make the world go away.

She hadn't been able to face finishing the article and had spent her time reading obsessively instead, escaping into the ordered world of her favourite Regency romances. A world where there were no exasperated civil engineers, no stupid jobs that took the hero overseas, no heartbreak that couldn't be resolved and sealed with a waltz around a glittering ballroom.

Now, with Stella's beady eye on her, Allegra struggled to remember that she had a job to do. 'I just need to tidy it up.'

'Done?' Stella snapped. 'How can it be done? You haven't been to the costume ball yet.'

Allegra cleared her throat. 'Unfortunately, we're going to have to miss out the ball. Max can't take part any longer. He's gone overseas.'

'What do you mean, *he's gone*?' Stella demanded. 'What about the article?'

'I thought I could end it at the Digby Fox preview.'

That didn't go down well. Stella's eyes bored into her. 'The whole point was to end with the ball,' she said icily. 'The fairy tale/knightly quest angle only makes sense if you follow it through to the ball. Get whatever-his-name-is to come back.'

Her immaculately polished fingernails drummed on the table while the rest of the editorial staff studiously avoided looking at either her or Allegra. Stella's displeasure could be a terrible thing to behold and nobody wanted to be associated with Allegra if she was in the firing line.

'I can't do that,' Allegra protested. 'He's got a job to do.'

Around the table there was a collective sucking in of breath. When Stella told you to do something, you did it. You didn't tell her that you couldn't. Not if you wanted to keep your job, anyway.

Incredibly, Stella didn't erupt. Her nails continued to click on the table, but her eyes narrowed thoughtfully. 'Then I suggest you find some way of including the ball anyway. Get Darcy to go with this new man of hers. She's always tweeting about how perfect he is. You could compare and contrast,' said Stella, warming to the idea. 'Show how what's-his-name was a failure and the new guy isn't.'

'His name's Max,' said Allegra clearly, ignoring the winces around her. 'And he isn't a failure!'

'He is as far as *Glitz* is concerned,' said Stella. 'Set up the ball and take a photographer. At least this way you can salvage something from the mess this article seems to have become.' Her eyes rested on Allegra's outfit. 'And sharpen yourself up if you want to stay at *Glitz*,' she added. 'You've let yourself go lately, Allegra. Those accessories are all wrong with that dress, and your shoes are so last season. It gives a bad impression.'

Allegra didn't like it, but she knew Stella was right. She *had* let herself go. She'd been too miserable to care about what she wore, but misery wasn't getting her anywhere. Every day when she checked her email she let the mouse hover over the 'new message' icon and thought about sending Max a message. She could keep it light, just ask how he was getting on. Just to hear from him.

But what would be the point? She didn't want to hear that he was enjoying Shofrar or that he was perfectly happy without her. She didn't want to hear that he had taken her advice and made it up with Emma. And what else could he tell her? That he loved her and missed her as much as she loved and missed him? Allegra couldn't see Max sitting at his computer and writing anything like that, even if he felt it. It just wasn't his style.

Once or twice, she poured out her feelings in an email, but she always came to her senses before she clicked 'send' and deleted it all instead. Max would be appalled, and it wasn't fair to embarrass him like that.

No, it was time to accept that Max had gone and that he wasn't coming back, time to stop reading and start deciding what to do with her life.

Be what you *want to be.* Max's words ran round and round in her head. Somewhere between finding out who her father was and Max leaving, Allegra had lost her certainty. What if Max had been right all along and she didn't really want to be a journalist at all?

The assignments Stella gave her now seemed increasingly silly. Allegra wrote a piece comparing the staying power of various lipglosses, and another on whether your hairdresser knew more about you than your beauty therapist. One day she did nothing but follow celebrity tweets and write a round up of all the banal things they'd said.

When Stella told her to invent some reader 'confessions' about their kinkiest sex exploits, Allegra couldn't even enjoy herself. She even got to work at home so that she didn't have to worry about anyone looking over her shoulder and raising their eyebrows. Once she would have found it fun, and let her imagination run wild, but now all she could think of was that night with Max, when they hadn't needed handcuffs or beads or uniforms. They hadn't needed a chandelier to swing from. They'd just needed each other.

Her blood thumped and her bones melted at the mere memory of it.

Allegra dropped her head into her hand and rubbed her forehead. Max was right about this too. She couldn't persuade herself any longer that working for *Glitz* was a stepping-stone to a glittering career in serious journalism. The *Financial Times* seemed further off than ever.

And who was she trying to fool? She didn't have what it took to be a serious journalist. She didn't even *want* to be a serious journalist.

Now all she had to do was decide what she *did* want to be. Allegra pushed her laptop away and picked up a pencil. She always thought better when she drew.

Except when she drew Max, when she just missed him.

With an effort, Allegra pushed him from her mind and sketched a quick picture of Derek the Dog instead. She drew him with his head cocked, his expression alert. He looked ready and eager to go. Allegra wished she felt like that.

Smiling, she let her pen take Derek on an adventure involving a double-decker bus, a steam engine, a jumbo jet and an old tugboat, and so absorbed was she that she missed the couture debut of the funkiest new designer in town. Everyone at *Glitz* had been buzzing about it, and Allegra too had one of the hottest tickets in fashion history.

She looked at her watch. If she rushed, she might still be able to squeeze in at the back, but then she'd have to get changed out of her vegging wear and she just couldn't be bothered.

Allegra sat back, startled by what she had just thought. Couldn't be bothered for *the* collection of the year? She examined herself curiously. Could it be true? Had she really changed that much?

Yep, she decided, she really had. Now all she had to do was think up a convincing excuse for her absence when everyone asked the next day. It would need to be a *really* good reason. Being struck down by a deadly virus wouldn't cut it. Any fashionista worth her salt would drag herself out of hospital if she had a ticket.

Allegra scratched her head with her pencil. She would just have to tell them she had been abducted by aliens— Struck by a thought, she ripped off a clean sheet from her drawing pad. Maybe it was time Derek went into space…

'You look amazing, like a fairy tale princess,' Allegra told Darcy. It was the night of the ball and they were squeezed in at the mirror in the Ladies', along with all the other women who were checking their lipstick and adjusting the necklines of their ball gowns. None of them looked as stunning as Darcy, though.

'I *feel* like a princess!' Pleased, Darcy swung her full skirt. The eighteenth-century-style dress was silver, with a embroidered bodice and sleeves that ended in a froth of lace at her elbows, and the skirt was decorated with bows and ruffles. On anyone else it would have seemed ridiculous, but Darcy looked magical. 'I always wanted to wear a dress like this when I was a kid,' she confided.

What little girl hadn't? Allegra had to admit to some dress envy, even though she knew she would never have been able to wear anything that fussy. She herself was in a slinky off-the-shoulder number that Dickie had found in one of the closets at *Glitz* that morning. It was a gorgeous red and it flattered her slender figure, but Allegra was feeling too dismal to carry it off.

'Ah, bah!' Dickie had said when she tried to tell him that. 'Eez *parfaite* for you.'

Allegra protested that she was only there as an observer to watch Darcy and William so she didn't need a ball gown, but Dickie had thrown such a hissy fit about her ingratitude that in the end she had just taken it.

Not that it mattered *what* she was wearing. Next to

Darcy, nobody was going to notice her. At least she wouldn't have to watch Max dancing with her. Remembering how they had learnt to waltz together brought such a stab of longing that Allegra had to bite her lip until it passed. She had left her hair loose, the way Max liked it. Oh, God, she *had* to stop thinking about him…

'Hey, I hear you wrote a book, you clever thing,' said Darcy, leaning into the mirror and touching the tip of her ring finger to her flawless cheekbones, just to check that her make up was perfect. It was.

Allegra was startled out of her wretchedness. 'Who told you that?'

'William.' Darcy practically licked her lips every time she said his name. The two of them had been inseparable ever since the preview. It was an unlikely combination, the political aide and the lingerie model, but they were clearly mad about each other. 'Your mum told him. He says she's boasting about you to everyone.'

'*Really?*' Allegra was surprised. Flick had been delighted to hear that her daughter was planning to resign from *Glitz* as soon as the *Making Mr Perfect* article was finished, but she was much less impressed by Allegra's idea of working freelance until she could find a publisher for her Derek the Dog stories.

'An illustrator?' she had echoed in dismay, and then her mouth tightened. 'This is because of Jago, isn't it?'

'No,' said Allegra evenly, 'I'm never going to be an artist like him, just like I'm never going to be a journalist like you.' She thought about her old dreams. 'I'm not a princess in disguise or a governess in a Regency romance. I'm just ordinary, and I'm going to stop trying to be anything but myself. I draw silly little pictures of animals. It's not much, but it's what I can do.'

Flick had been taken aback at first. 'Well, I *suppose* I

could introduce you to some agents,' she had offered reluctantly at last.

'Thanks,' said Allegra, 'but I've already approached one. She likes my illustrations, but she's less keen on the story. She's talking about teaming me up with a writer she knows.'

'Oh.'

Allegra suspected Flick was rather miffed by the fact that she hadn't traded on her famous mother's connections, but if Flick had talked about her to William she must have come round. As far as Allegra knew, Flick had never once told anyone that she was working for *Glitz*. The fact that she might have done something to please her mother at last gave Allegra a warm feeling around her heart for the first time since Max had left.

William was waiting for them in the lobby of the hotel, carrying off his Prince Charming costume with aplomb. Remembering how seriously he had talked the first time she had met him, Allegra smiled to herself. He really must be smitten by Darcy if he was prepared to dress up. 'I'd rather stick pins in my eyes,' Max had said.

In contrast, Dom, the photographer, stood out from the crowd in his jeans and leather jacket. He took some photos of William and Darcy together and then they all moved into the ballroom, where the ball was already in full swing.

Allegra found a place on the edge of the room. It was a classic ballroom, with glittering chandeliers and a high, elaborately decorated ceiling. One wall was punctuated with elegant long windows, open in spite of the dreary November weather to let some much needed air into the crowded ballroom. An orchestra at one end was playing a vigorous waltz, and couples in gorgeous costumes whirled around the floor.

Everything was just as Allegra had always dreamed

a ball would be. It was perfect—or it would have been if only Max had been there with her. The thought of him triggered a wave of loneliness that hit her with such force that she actually staggered. Her knees went weak and all the colour and gaiety and movement of the scene blurred before her eyes.

She couldn't bear it without Max.

Blindly, she started for the doors. It was noisy and crowded and empty without him. She would wait for Dom outside. It was too painful to be here, with the music and the laughter and the memories of how she and Max had waltzed around the sitting room, of how useless they had both been, how they had laughed together.

'Excuse me…sorry…sorry…' Allegra squeezed her way through the throng, too intent on escaping to enjoy the fantastic costumes. She kept her head down so that no one would see the tears pooling in her eyes and it was perhaps inevitable that she ended up bumping into a solid male body.

'Sorry…I'm so sorry…' Desperate to get away, she barely took in more than an elaborate waistcoat. Another Prince Charming in full eighteenth-century dress, she had time to think before she side-stepped to pass him, only to be stopped by a hand on her arm.

'Would you do me the honour of this dance?'

Allegra had already started to shake her head when something familiar about the voice filtered through the music and the chatter and her heart clenched. How cruel that her longing should make it sound so like Max's.

Blinking back her tears, she summoned a polite smile and lifted her eyes from the waistcoat and past the extravagant cravat to Prince Charming's face underneath his powdered wig.

'I'm afraid I'm just lea—' Her voice faded as her gaze

reached his eyes and she blinked, certain that she must be imagining things, but when she opened her eyes again he was still there.

'Max?' she quavered, still not sure that her longing hadn't conjured him up out of thin air.

'I know, I look a prat,' said Max.

Astonishment, joy, incredulity, shock: all jostled together in such a fierce rush that Allegra couldn't catch her breath. For a stunned moment all she could do was stare in disbelief. Max was out in the desert, in shorts and sunglasses, not dressed up as a fairy tale prince in a crowded ballroom.

'Max?'

'Yes, it's me.' Incredibly, he looked nervous.

'Wh...what are you doing here?' Still unable to believe that it could really be true, she had to raise her voice above the noise in the ballroom, and Max leant closer to make sure that she could hear.

'I've been doing some thinking, and I decided it would be a shame if we wasted all those waltzing lessons,' he told her, and he held out his hand. 'Shall we dance?'

In a blur, Allegra let him lead her onto the floor, finding a place on the edge of the other couples who were whirling around the floor in an intimidatingly professional fashion. She didn't understand anything, but if this was a dream, she didn't want to wake up.

Max swung her round into position. He held one of her hands in his, and set the other on his shoulder so that he could take hold of her waist. 'Okay,' he yelled, looking down at their feet. 'Remember the box? Let's go...*one*, two, three, *one*, two, three...'

They made a mess of it at first, of course. They stumbled and trod on each other's toes, but all at once, magically, they clicked and found the rhythm. True, they could only go round and round the 'box' but they were on the floor and they were moving together in time to the music—sort of. Allegra's heart was so full, she was crying and floating in delirious joy at the same time.

Laughing through her tears, she lifted her face to Max's. 'We're *waltzing!*' she shouted.

'Ready to try a new manoeuvre?' he shouted back and, without waiting for her answer, he lunged with her further into the crowd. This was a whole new step outside their safe box, as they had never really mastered turning, but Max had a determined look on his face and Allegra followed as best she could.

'Where are you going?' she yelled in his ear.

'Terrace,' he said briefly, face set as he concentrated on steering her through the throng of dancers.

The *terrace?* Allegra thought about the chill drizzle that was falling outside, but it was too noisy to have a conversation and, anyway, Max seemed set on the idea. He danced her grimly across the floor. They'd lost their rhythm again and kept bumping into other couples, but somehow they made it to the other side. Max took a deep breath and somehow manoeuvred them through one of the windows and out onto the terrace that overlooked the hotel's garden.

'That was harder than I thought,' he said, and let Allegra go.

Outside, the air was damp and cold, but it was blissfully quiet after the noise in the ballroom. Still gripped by a sense of unreality, Allegra shook her head slightly.

'Max, what are you doing here? I thought you were in Shofrar.'

'I was, but I told Bob that I needed to come back to London.'

She looked concerned. 'Aren't you enjoying the job?'

'The job's great.' It was. 'It's everything I ever wanted to do, and the desert is beautiful. I wish you could see it, Legs. The light is extraordinary.'

'Then why come back to London?' she asked, puzzled.

Max took a deep breath. 'Because you weren't there,' he said. 'The thing is…' He'd rehearsed this speech in his head but now that the moment had come, his mind had gone blank. 'The thing is, I missed you,' he finished simply.

'But…what about Emma?' Allegra's eyes were huge. She looked as if she was unsure whether she was dreaming or not, and Max couldn't blame her. One minute she had been heading out of the ballroom and the next she was faced with an idiot in full eighteenth-century dress.

'She told me she wanted to say goodbye to you at the airport,' Allegra went on. 'I thought she was going to suggest that you got back together.'

'She did,' said Max, remembering how long it had taken him to understand what Emma was saying. Her timing hadn't been good, to say the least. His mind had been too full of Allegra, standing on the doorstep, watching as he drove away. 'She said she wanted to try again, that she'd realised that friendship was a better foundation for marriage than passion.'

'Which was what you'd said all along.'

'I did say that and I believed it, but I've changed my mind,' Max said. 'Friendship isn't enough on its own, nor is passion. You need both. I told Emma that I'd like to be friends, but I knew that I'd never be happy unless I could be with you.'

'With me…' she echoed incredulously, but a smile lit her eyes, and he took hold of her hands.

'I love being with you, Legs. I don't care what we're doing. Even when you were making me dress up and make a fool of myself, it was fun. I missed being able to talk to you and hear you laugh, I missed you nagging about my clothes. God, I even found myself rolling my cuffs up!' he said, and Allegra laughed unsteadily.

Tears were trembling on the end of her lashes and Max tightened his grasp on her fingers, desperate to tell her how he felt before she cried. 'I missed you as more than a friend, though. I wanted to be able to touch you and feel you...I haven't been able to stop thinking about that night. It's never been like that for me before,' he said honestly. 'It was as if everything else had been a practice and suddenly with you it was the real thing. Like I'd never understood before that was how it was supposed to be. I can't explain it. With you, it just felt right...' He trailed off, seeing the tears spilling down her cheeks. 'Don't cry, Legs, please. I just wanted to tell you how I felt.'

'I'm crying because I'm happy,' she said, trying in vain to blink back the tears. 'Oh, Max, that was how it was for me too.'

The tight band around Max's chest unlocked and he released her hands to take her face between his palms.

'Allegra,' he said unevenly, 'I know I'm stuffy and I can't dance and I've got no dress sense but I love you. That's why I came back. I had to tell you.'

Incredibly, she was smiling still. 'I love you too,' she said, sliding her arms around his waist. 'I've missed you so much.'

A smile dawned in Max's eyes as his heart swelled. Tenderly, he grazed her jaw with his thumbs. 'You love me?' he repeated, dazed at the wonder of it.

'I do,' she said and her voice broke. 'Oh, Max, I do.' And she clung to him as he kissed her at last, the way he had dreamt of kissing her for so many long and lonely nights, so many bleak days.

She kissed him back, a long, sweet kiss edged with the same giddy relief at having been pulled back from an abyss at the last moment. They ran their hands hungrily over each other, a remembered inventory of pleasure. Heedless of the drizzle that was rapidly turning to rain, they forgot the ball, forgot the cold, forgot everything but the dazzling joy of being able to touch each other again, feel each other again.

Max was rucking up Allegra's skirt with an urgent hand before a splatter of rain right down his neck brought him reluctantly back to reality. Grumbling at the weather, he pulled Allegra into the shelter of an overhanging balcony and rested his forehead against hers.

'I wish you'd said something before you left,' she said, softening her criticism by clinging closer. 'I've been so wretched without you.'

'I couldn't. You made it pretty clear that night was just a one-off as far as you were concerned,' he pointed out. 'We've got different lives, you said, and you were right. I could see that. God, Legs, I only had to look at you. You were having so much fun in London. You've got a great life, doing what you want to do. You're so bright and warm and funny and gorgeous. How could I possibly imagine you wanting to be with a boring civil engineer?'

Allegra couldn't help laughing. 'Nobody looking at you dressed up as Prince Charming could possibly describe you as boring, Max!' For the first time she took in the full glory of his costume. His jacket was made of plum-coloured velvet, and he wore tight breeches and silk socks held up with garters. The satin waistcoat was the same colour as the jacket, and an intricately arranged necktie frothed at his throat. 'Where on earth did you find your outfit?'

'Dickie got it for me.'

'Dickie!' She gaped at him. 'He didn't tell me that you'd been in touch!'

'I asked him not to and, anyway,' said Max, drawing her back into him and putting on a superior air, 'I'm not Prince Charming, I'm a duke.'

'*Are* you?' Allegra tucked in the corners of her mouth to stop herself laughing.

He pretended to be hurt. 'I thought you'd have recognised a Regency duke when you saw one!'

'Hmm, I think you and Dickie might have slipped a century,' said Allegra. 'My Regency duke didn't wear a powdered wig.'

'Thank God for that!' Max snatched off his wig and cast it aside, before taking Allegra back in his arms. 'I couldn't find a time travel machine, so this was the closest I could get to your fantasy,' he confessed. 'I had this great plan. I was going to recreate it for you exactly,' he told her as her eyes widened. 'I was going to waltz you out onto the terrace, just the way you told me about, and then I was going to tell you how passionately I loved you and beg you to marry me, and bowl you over with the romance of it all. I wanted you to have the perfect proposal.

'But I made a mess of it,' he said. 'The fact is, I'm not a duke, I can't dance, I look like an idiot and it's raining. Where's the romance in that?'

'It's the most romantic thing I could imagine,' said Allegra, her voice tight with emotion. 'The duke's just a fantasy, but you're *real*.' She kissed him softly. 'Maybe you can't dance, and no, you're not the sharpest dresser, but you're perfect for me and I love you just as you are.'

'What, even buttoned up to my collar?'

'Even then.'

Max grinned, pleased. 'Hey, you really must love me,' he said and she laughed.

'I really do,' she said, and he kissed her again, pressing her against the wall until they were both breathless and shaky with desire.

'We've wasted so much time,' Max grumbled against her throat. 'I wish I'd known how you felt before I left.'

'I couldn't tell you,' Allegra protested, snuggling closer. 'You told me yourself you needed someone sensible like Emma.'

'I thought that too,' he said, as his hands slid possessively over her curves. 'But it turns out that I need fun and frivolity instead. I've asked Bob if I can transfer back to the London office. I thought even if my Regency duke impersonation didn't work, it would be easier to be in the same city. At least then I'd get to see you.'

Allegra pressed closer, loving the hard demand of his hands. 'Ask him if you can stay in Shofrar after all,' she said. 'It turns out that I don't have any fun if I'm not with you, so why don't I come with you?'

'But what about your job at *Glitz*?'

'Well, I've made some decisions since you left.' She told him what the agent had said about her drawings. 'It's a long shot but who knows? It might come off and I can always try my hand at other illustrations. I'm sure I'll be able to keep myself busy during the day, anyway,' she said. 'And you can keep me busy at night,' she added with a wicked smile.

'I'll do my best.' Max kissed her again, and that was the last they spoke for some time. Careless of the rain puddling on the terrace around them, oblivious to the music spilling out from the ballroom, they lost themselves in the heady wonder of touch and taste.

'You know we'll have to get married?' said Max eventually, resting his cheek against her hair.

Allegra tipped back her head to smile at him. 'I'm counting on it,' she said.

Max felt his heart swell until it was jammed almost painfully against his ribs. 'Allegra...' he said, shaken by the rush of emotion. 'I don't want to be apart from you again. How soon do you think we can arrange a wedding?'

'As soon as possible.' Allegra looked demure. 'I'm sure Dickie will be happy to find a flowery waistcoat for you to wear.'

'I don't mind what I wear as long as you're standing there saying "I do",' he said.

'You might regret saying that!'

'The only thing I'll regret is not telling you I loved you earlier,' he said seriously, and her lips curved under his as he kissed her once more.

Inside, the orchestra struck up another waltz, and they smiled at each other as they moved into the dance. Max's arm was around her, his fingers warm and firm around hers as they danced through the puddles, heedless of the rain.

Allegra's heart was floating. 'This is perfect,' she said, as Max twirled her around. 'Waltzing on the terrace, a proposal of marriage... What more could I want?'

'I seem to remember something about being ravished against a balustrade,' said Max, and his eyes gleamed in the dim light as he danced her over to it. Turning so that she was pressed against the balustrade, he smiled lovingly down into her face. 'You, my darling, are about to have your dream come true.'

Allegra heaved a contented sigh and wound her arms around his neck to pull him closer. 'It already has,' she said.

MAKING MR PERFECT by Allegra Fielding
Can you create the perfect boyfriend? We set one guy a modern-day quest, a series of challenges he

had to complete successfully in order to win the love of today's demanding damsels who want their man to be everything: socially skilled, emotionally intelligent, well-dressed, practical, artistic; a cook, a dancer, a handyman...

We took an uptight, conventionally dressed bloke with zero interest in the arts and a horror of the dance floor, and we asked him if he could change. Could he learn to dress stylishly and navigate a cocktail menu without cringing? Was he prepared to throw away the takeaway menu and go to the effort of cooking a meal from scratch? Could he talk knowledgeably about modern art? Could he learn how to waltz?

If you've been following Max's progress over the past few weeks, you'll know that he sailed through some of the 'tests' but crashed and burned on others, notably the exhibition of contemporary art installations. In spite of his grumbling, Max claims to have learnt something from the process. 'I learnt to make an effort,' he says. 'I learnt to think about what women really want and—more importantly, I gather—not to button my collar quite so tightly.'

But the truth is that Max didn't learn nearly as much as I did. Whether he succeeded or failed, he remained resolutely himself. Yes, he made an effort, but he didn't change. He's never going to be a snappy dresser. He's always going to prefer a beer to a fancy drink, and he's still going to have to be dragged kicking and screaming to anything remotely smacking of the arts. The tests were pointless: anyone can pretend, but what's the point of pretending? Nobody wants to fall in love with a fake.

There's no formula for a perfect man, unless it's for a man who doesn't need to pretend, a man who's happy to be himself. A man who might not be able to dance, but who makes you laugh and holds you when you cry, who makes you feel safe and gives you the strength to be the best you can be. Who will stay by your side, through good times and bad. A man who makes you feel the most beautiful and desirable woman in the world when he kisses you.

A man who sees you for what you really are, and who loves you anyway.

So let's not ask our men to be everything. Let's love them with all their imperfections, because those are what make them who they are. Max doesn't have a single one of the qualities I once thought necessary in my perfect man, and yet somehow that's exactly what he is: my very own Mr Perfect.

* * * * *

THE GIRL WHO WOULDN'T STAY DEAD

CASSIE MILES

To Annie Underwood Perry and the latest addition to her family. And, as always, to Rick.

Chapter One

She had to wake up. Someone was trying to kill her.

Her eyelids snapped open. Her vision was blurred. Every part of her body hurt.

Emily Benton-Riggs inhaled a sharp gasp. The chilly night air pierced her lungs like a knife between the ribs. Slowly, she exhaled, then drew a breath again and tried to focus. She was still in the car but not sitting upright. Her little Hyundai had flipped, rolled and smacked into the granite side of a mountain at least twice on the way down, maybe more. The car had landed on the driver's side.

Likewise, her brain was jumbled. Nothing was clear.

Even in her dazed state, she was glad to be alive—grateful and also a little bit surprised. The past few years of her life had moments of such flat-out misery that she'd come to expect the worst. And yet, recently, things seemed to be turning around. She liked her rented bungalow in Denver, and her work was satisfying. Plus, she'd just learned that she might be a very wealthy woman. *I can't give up.* It'd take more than crashing through the guardrail on a narrow mountain road near Aspen and plummeting down a sheer cliff to kill her.

Her forehead felt damp. When she pushed her bangs back and touched the wet spot above her hairline, her pain shot into high gear. Every twitch, every movement set off a fresh agony. Her hand came away bloody.

Her long-dead mother—an angry woman who didn't believe in luck or spontaneous adventure or love, especially not love—burst into her imagination. Her mom, with her wild, platinum hair and her clothes askew, took a swig from her vodka bottle and grumbled in harsh words only Emily could hear, "You don't deserve that vast fortune. That's why you're dead."

"But I'm not," Emily protested aloud. "And I deserve this inheritance. I loved Jamison. I did everything I could to stay married to him. It's not my fault that he slept with… practically everybody."

Her voice trailed off. She never wanted to relive the humiliating final chapter of her marriage. It was over.

"You failed," her mother said with a sneer.

"Go away. I'm not going to argue with a ghost."

"You'll be joining me soon enough." Unearthly, eerie laughter poisoned her ears. "Look around, little girl. You're not out of the woods. Not yet."

Mom was right. Emily was still breathing, but her survival was not a sure thing.

With her right hand, she batted the airbag. The chemical dust that had exploded from the bag rose up in a cloud and choked her. She coughed, and her lungs ached. When she peered through what was left of the windshield, which was a spiderweb of shattered safety glass, she saw boulders and the trunks of pine trees. Literally, she wasn't out of the woods.

With the car lying on the driver's side, her perspective was off. She couldn't tell if her Hyundai had careened all the way to the bottom of the cliff or was hanging against a tree halfway down. The headlights flickered and went dark. She saw steam rising from around the edges of the crumpled hood.

In the movies, standard procedure dictated that when a car flew off the road, it would crash and burn. The idea of dying in a fire terrified her. Her gut clenched. *I have to get out of this damn car.* Or she could call for help. Desperately, she felt around for her purse. Her phone was inside. She remembered tossing her shoulder bag onto the seat beside her.

She twisted her neck, setting off another wave of pain, and looked up. The passenger side had been badly battered. The door had been torn from its hinges. Her purse must have fallen out somewhere between the road and here. Through the opening where the door should have been, she saw hazy stars and a September crescent moon that reminded her of the van Gogh painting.

Trying to grasp the edge of the roof on the door hole, she stretched her right hand as far as possible. Not far enough. She couldn't reach. When she turned her shoulders, her left arm flopped clumsily inside the black blazer she'd worn to look professional at the will reading. The muscles and joints from shoulder to wrist screamed. Blood was smeared across her white shirt; she didn't know if the gore came from her arm or the head wound matting her blond hair.

A masculine voice called out, "Hey, down there."

She froze. The monster who had forced her off the road was coming to finish the job. Fear spread through her, eclipsing her pain. She said nothing.

"Emily, is that you?"

He knew her name. Nobody she'd met with in Aspen counted as a friend. She didn't trust any of them. Somehow, she had to get out of the car. She had to hide.

Carefully avoiding pain, she used her right hand to manipulate the left. The problem was in her forearm. It felt broken. If she'd known first aid, she might have fashioned a splint from a tree branch. Her mind skipped down an irrelevant path, wishing she'd been a Girl Scout. If she'd been a better person, she wouldn't be in this mess. *No, this isn't my fault.*

She cursed herself for wasting precious moments by being distracted. Right now, she had to get away from this ticking time bomb of a car and flee from the man who wanted her dead. Holding her arm against her chest, she wiggled her hips, struggling to get free. When she unfastened the latch on the seat belt, the lower half of her body shifted position. The car jolted.

With her right knee bent, she planted her bare foot on the edge of her bucket seat and pushed herself upward toward the space where the passenger door had been. The left leg dragged. Her thigh muscles and knee seemed to work, but her ankle hurt too much to put weight on it. Inch by inch, she maneuvered herself. Using her right arm, she pulled her head and shoulders up and out. The cold wind slapped her awake. She was halfway out, halfway to safety.

Her car hadn't crashed all the way down the cliff. Three-quarters of the way down, an arm of the forest reached out and caught her little car. Two giant pine trees halted the descent. The hood crumpled against the tree trunks. The back end of the car balanced precariously.

"Emily? Are you down here?"

The voice sounded closer. She had to hurry, to find a place to hide.

She hauled herself through the opening and tumbled over the edge onto the ground. Her left leg crumpled beneath her. Behind her was the greasy undercarriage. The pungent stink of gasoline reminded her that she wasn't out of danger.

Unable to support herself on her knees, she crawled

on her belly through the dirt and underbrush toward the security of the forest where she could disappear into the trees. Breathing hard, she reached a cluster of heavy boulders—a good place to pause and get her bearings. With her right arm, the only body part that seemed relatively unharmed, she pulled herself into a sitting posture, looking down at her car.

Exhaustion and pain nearly overwhelmed her. She fought to stay conscious, clinging to the rocks as though these chunks of granite formed a life raft on the high seas. She heard a small noise. Not the fiery explosion she'd been expecting, it was only the snap of a dry twig. The sound filled her with dread.

He was close.

She had to run. No matter how much it hurt, she had to get to her feet. She struggled to stand but her injured leg was unable to support her. She sat down hard on the rock. A fresh stab of pain cut through her. Before she could stop herself, she whimpered.

A silhouette of the man separated from the surrounding trees. He turned toward her. *Please don't see me. Please, please.*

"Emily, is that you?"

Quickly, he came toward her. She hoped he'd kill her fast. She couldn't take any more pain.

He sat on the rock beside her. Starlight shone on his handsome face. She knew him. "Connor."

Gently and carefully, he maneuvered his arm around her. She should have put up a fight, but she didn't have the strength, and she couldn't believe Connor wanted to hurt her.

"I already called 9-1-1," he said. "The paramedics will be here soon. I don't want to move you until they arrive with their gear to stabilize your back and neck."

He wasn't here to kill her but to save her.

She leaned against him, rested her head on his shoulder and inhaled the scent of his leather jacket. Though he felt real, she couldn't believe he was here. They'd talked yesterday. She'd been in Denver. He'd been in Manhattan. They'd both been summoned to the reading of her late ex-husband's will in Aspen, and she'd told her lawyer, Connor, not to bother making the trip. She didn't plan to attend. Why should she? She hadn't expected to receive a dime, and showing up for the reading had seemed like a lot of bother for almost zero reward.

At the last moment, she'd changed her mind. This might be her final opportunity to face the Riggs family, and she had a few choice words for them. Emily had no reason to be ashamed. Early this morning before she left Denver, she'd texted Connor about her decision to go.

"Emily, are you okay?"

"No," she mumbled.

"Dumb question, sorry," he said. "I came as soon as I could. After I got your text, I caught a direct flight from JFK to Denver, then a shuttle flight to Aspen airport, where I grabbed a rental car."

Though his deep voice soothed her, she couldn't relax until she'd told him what had happened. But her throat was closed. Her eyelids drooped.

"If I'd flown in last night," he said, "we would have made the drive together. You wouldn't have had this accident."

Accident? She wanted to yell at him that this wasn't an accident.

She heard the screech of the ambulance siren. Her mind went blank.

IN A PRIVATE hospital room in Aspen, Connor Gallagher stood like a sentry next to the railing on the right side of

Emily's bed. She lay in an induced coma after four hours in surgery. Her condition was listed as critical. The doctors and staff were cautiously optimistic, but no one would give him a 100 percent guarantee that she'd fully recover. He hated that she'd been hurt. Emily had suffered enough.

Her breathing had steadied. He watched as her chest rose and fell in a rhythmic pattern. Her slender body made a small ripple under the lightweight blue hospital blanket. Though the breathing tube for the ventilator had been removed, it was obvious that something terrible had happened to her. There were three separate IV bags. Her broken left arm was in a cast from above the elbow to the fingers. A bad sprain on her left leg required a removable Aircast plastic boot. Bandages swathed her head. Her face was relaxed but not peaceful. A black-and-blue shiner and a stitched-up wound on her forehead made her look like a prizefighter who'd lost the big bout.

Being as gentle as he could, Connor held her right hand below the site where the IV was inserted. Her knuckles and palm were scraped. The doctors had said that her lacerations and bruises weren't as bad as they looked, but a series of MRIs showed swelling in her brain. The head injury worried him more than anything else.

Bones would mend. Scars would heal. But neurological damage could be a permanent disability. She'd fallen unconscious after he found her on the ground close to the wreckage of her car. During the rescue and the ambulance ride, she'd wakened only once.

Her eyelids had fluttered open, and she gazed steadily with her big blue eyes. "I'm in danger, Connor."

Her words had been clear, but he wasn't sure what she meant. "You're going to be all right."

"Stay with me," she'd said. "You're the only one I can trust."

He'd promised that he wouldn't leave her alone, and he damn well meant to honor that vow. She needed him. Even if his presence irritated the medical staff, he would goddamn well stay by her side.

The emergency doctor who'd supervised her treatment made it clear that he didn't need Connor or anybody else looking over his shoulder. The doc had curly blond hair and the bulging muscles of a Norse god. Appropriately, his name was Thorson, aka Thor's son.

Thorson opened the door to her room, entered and went to the opposite side of Emily's bed, where he fiddled with the IV bags and checked the monitors. Connor sensed the real reason the doctor had stopped by was to assert his authority.

Without looking at Connor, Thorson said, "She's doing well."

Compared to what? Death? Connor stifled his dislike and asked, "When can she be moved?"

"Maybe tomorrow. Maybe the next day."

"Be more specific, Doctor. No offense but I want to get her to an expert neurologist."

"I assure you that our staff is highly regarded in all aspects of patient care."

Connor took his phone from his pocket. While Emily was in surgery, he'd done research. He clicked to an illustration of state-of-the-art neurological equipment. "Do you have access to one of these?"

"We don't need one."

"I disagree."

Thorson glared; his steel blue eyes shot thunderbolts. When he folded his arms across his broad chest, his maroon scrubs stretched tightly over his huge biceps.

Connor wasn't intimidated. At six feet three inches, he was taller than the pseudogod, and he seldom lost a fight, verbal or physical. Connor returned the glare; his dark eyes were hard as obsidian.

"Tell me again," Thorson said. "What is your relationship to the patient?"

"I'm her fiancé."

"There's no diamond on her finger."

"I haven't given her a ring."

Connor avoided lying whenever possible, but he'd discovered it was easier to facilitate Emily's treatment if he claimed to be her fiancé instead of her lawyer. He'd already played the sympathy card to get her into a private room in this classy Aspen facility, where she wasn't the wealthiest or most influential patient. The nurses had been touched by the tragic story of the pretty young woman and her doting fiancé.

"No ring?" Thorson's blond eyebrows lifted. "Why not?"

"I'd like to explain in a way you could understand. But there are complex issues involved in our relationship."

That was true. Emily used to be married to his best friend, and they both used Connor as their personal attorney. Her ex-husband, a hotshot Wall Street broker, had moved his business to a more important law firm. Six weeks ago, her ex died. Complicated? Oh, yeah.

Thorson pursed his lips. "I couldn't help noticing her last name, *Benton-Riggs*. Any relation to Jamison Riggs?"

Aha! Now Connor knew why the doc was hostile. The Riggs family was a big deal in Aspen, and she'd been married to the heir, the golden boy, for seven years. She and Jamison had been separated for over a year, but the divorce wasn't final until three months ago. "Back off, Thorson."

"I should inform her family."

Hearing the Riggs clan referred to as Emily's family stretched Connor's self-control to the limit. Those people never gave a rat's ass about her. Years ago, when Jamison brought her to Aspen for the first time, Connor had tagged along. Why not? Jamison was his good buddy, a fellow Harvard grad. The two of them could have been brothers. Taller than average, they were both lean and mean, with brown hair and brown eyes. They also had the same taste in women. When Jamison introduced him to Emily, emphasizing that she was his betrothed, Connor felt his heart being ripped from his chest. She should have been with him.

The Aspen branch of the Riggs family accepted Connor, assuming that because he'd gone to an Ivy League school he came from good stock. They were dead wrong, but he didn't bother to correct them, didn't want to talk to them at all when he saw how snotty they were to Emily. She didn't wear designer clothes, didn't ski and didn't know one end of a Thoroughbred horse from another. Her laugh was too loud, and her accent was a humble Midwestern twang. Connor thought one of the reasons Jamison had married her was to drive his family crazy.

Connor growled at Thorson. "Don't call the Riggs family."

"I'm sure they'll want to be informed."

"You've seen the advance directives for Ms. Benton-Riggs, correct?" In the first years of their marriage, Jamison and Emily had asked Connor to file their living wills, powers of attorney and proxy-care forms. They had named him as the decision maker, and those papers were in effect until the divorce and the dissolution of his friendship with Jamison, who had made other arrangements. Emily, however, had never bothered to make a change. "I'm in charge of her medical care, and I don't want anyone named Riggs anywhere near her."

"You aren't thinking straight."

"The hell I'm not," Connor replied without raising his voice.

There was a light tap on the door before it opened. Standing outside was a clean-cut young man in a Pitkin County sheriff's uniform. He touched the brim of his cap. "Mr. Gallagher, I'm Deputy Rafe Sandoval. I have a few questions."

"I didn't actually witness the accident, but I'm happy to help." He gave Thorson a cold smile. "The doctor was just leaving."

As soon as Thorson stormed out, the deputy entered. Rather than hovering at Emily's bedside like the doctor, the cop motioned for Connor to join him near the door. He spoke in a hushed tone. "I don't want to disturb her while she's asleep."

"She's in an induced coma."

"But can she hear us?"

Connor had wondered the same thing. While she was unconscious, did Emily have the ability to hear his words or comprehend what he was saying? Did she know he was at her side and would destroy anyone who attempted to hurt her? "I'd like to think that she can hear, but I don't know."

Still keeping the volume low, Sandoval asked, "Why were you on that road?"

"I was on my way to the home of Patricia Riggs for the reading of her cousin's will. Unfortunately, I got a late start from New York." As soon as he spoke, he realized that the deputy would need to talk to the Riggs family about the accident. As much as Connor wanted to keep them away from Emily, the police would have to contact them. "Have you spoken to the Riggs family?"

"Not yet," he said. "Why did you pull over, Mr. Gallagher? You didn't see the accident happen, but you quickly arrived at the scene."

"There are no lights along that stretch." The two-lane road that led to Patricia's château hugged the mountain on one side. The outer lane had a wide shoulder and a guardrail at the edge of a sheer cliff. "Her headlights were shining like a beacon."

"So you stopped," the deputy prompted.

"I saw the damaged guardrail. That's when I looked over the ledge."

He'd never forget the flood of panic that had washed over him when he saw the wreckage. At the time, he hadn't known that the twisted remains of the bronze Hyundai belonged to Emily. When the headlights went off and darkness consumed the scene, he'd known what he had to do. No matter who was trapped inside, Connor had had to respond.

"This is very important, Mr. Gallagher. Did you see any other vehicles?"

"No."

"You're certain."

Connor was beginning to have a bad feeling about this visit from the deputy. It was after two o'clock in the morning. What was so important that it couldn't wait? "Is there something you need to tell me about the accident?"

The young man straightened his shoulders. His nervous manner was gone. His gaze was direct. "After my preliminary investigation, I strongly suspect that Ms. Benton-Riggs was forced off the road."

"What are you saying?"

"Someone tried to kill her."

Chapter Two

Emily knew she was asleep and dreaming hard. There was no other explanation for the weird images that popped into her mind and distracted her. She needed to wake up. There was something she had to find. The object or person or place was unclear, but her quest was urgent—a matter of life and death.

But she couldn't ignore the field of psychedelic flowers that reminded her of a Peter Max poster from the sixties, and she couldn't pause as she waltzed into a paint-splattered Jackson Pollock room with a series of framed paintings on the walls. Some were classics: melting Dali timepieces, a servant girl with a pearl earring, Tahitian women bathing by a stream. Others were by the not-yet-famous artists that she was showing in her Denver gallery. The corridor took on a more formal aspect, and it felt like she was on a personal tour of the Louvre Museum, accompanied by a grinning Mona Lisa.

Swiveling, she found herself surrounded by mist. Pink clouds spun like cotton candy around her feet and knees. When she tried to push them away, her left arm wouldn't move. From shoulder to wrist, the arm was frozen. Pursing her lips, she blew, and the haze cleared.

Connor Gallagher strode toward her. This was the Manhattan version of Connor, dressed in a tailored charcoal suit with a striped silk necktie. Though neatly groomed, his brown hair was unruly, curling over his collar. His cocoa-brown eyes penetrated her defenses.

She sighed as she placed this moment in time—a memory from several months ago when she had been trying to decide whether or not to file for divorce. She'd already left Manhattan, separated from Jamison and was working hard to establish a new life in Denver, her hometown. Connor had come all the way from New York to talk business with her. As soon as she saw him strolling up the sidewalk to her bungalow, she forgot about the contracts, documents and the prenuptial agreement she'd signed.

Connor filled her mind. She liked him…a lot. He frequently starred in her erotic fantasies. In real life, she hadn't seen him without his swimming trunks, but she suspected he could give Michelangelo's naked sculpture *David* a run for his money. In addition to her appreciation for his body, she was fascinated by his moods, the sound of his laughter and the shape of his mouth.

Her memory continued. They'd met. They'd hugged. He'd smelled warm and spicy like cinnamon. And then Connor had mentioned Jamison, asking if he also favored divorce.

She didn't give a damn what Jamison Riggs wanted. Any love she'd had for him was over. She'd been living apart from him since the night when she'd found him in bed with the head partner from his Wall Street investment firm, a tall redhead with incredibly straight hair and who never smiled. Jamison had expected Emily to forgive him. He'd told her not to worry, that he was only trying to sleep his way to the top. As if that was supposed to be okay.

Emily huffed. She didn't believe a single word that spilled from his lying lips. Other people had warned her about his cheating, and it didn't take long for Emily to find evidence of other infidelities with at least three other women. Jamison had been having a wild, sexy ride. Frankly, when she asked Connor to come to Denver, she'd been hoping for a taste of the same.

Sure, there were plenty of legitimate business interests they could discuss, but those weren't foremost in her mind. She wanted Connor to embrace her, caress her and sweep her off her feet. She deserved an affair of her own. But no! Technically, she was still married, and Connor had too much integrity to betray his friend, even if Jamison was a dirty dog who didn't deserve the loyalty.

The day after Connor returned to his Manhattan law practice, she'd contacted a lawyer in Denver and started the paperwork. The divorce had taken months. So many other things had happened, a whirlwind of events.

Her unconscious mind played calliope music. *Boop-boop-beedle-deedle-doop-doop.* She was on a carousel, riding a painted pony. She hadn't known Jamison was sick until he was terminal, and she only saw him once before he died. In light of his unexpected death, her divorce seemed cold and unfeeling. Even in a dream state, she felt a little bit guilty. If she'd known he was ill, she might have forgiven him and nursed him through his final days. Or not.

Leaving the merry-go-round, she hiked up a grassy knoll to an old-fashioned boot hill cemetery. She'd wanted to attend Jamison's funeral and memorial service, but his maiden aunt Glenda, matriarch of the family, had made it clear that she was unwelcome. The family had kept her away, almost as though they were hiding something.

Jamison shouldn't be her problem anymore. They were divorced, and he had died. But there seemed to be a connection. Her car had been run off the road after leaving the Riggses' house. Someone wanted her dead, had tried to kill her. She had to fight back. She needed to wake up. *Oh, God, I'm too tired.*

Someone held her hand and comforted her. For now, that would have to be enough. She drifted back into silent stillness.

THE NEXT MORNING, Connor sat beside the hospital bed and patted Emily's right hand. She hadn't moved, but one of the monitors started beeping. A sweet-faced nurse whose name tag said *Darlene* came into the room and made adjustments to silence the alarm.

"Has she spoken?" Darlene asked.

"Not yet," he said. "But her eyelids have been moving. It's like she's watching a movie inside her head."

"Rapid eye movement, we call it REM. Nothing to worry about," she said in the perky tone of a confirmed optimist. "I'll notify the doctor. We don't want her to wake up too soon."

"Why is that?"

"They use the induced coma to protect the brain and let it relax while the swelling goes down. She needs plenty of rest."

Though he didn't know much about neurological sciences, he'd talked to a brain surgeon in New York who advised him about Denver-based referrals. His brain surgeon friend had given him an idea of all the stuff that could go wrong, ranging from stroke to seizure. Amnesia was a possibility, as was epilepsy. Head wounds were unpredictable and could be devastating.

He wished he could be as cheerful as Darlene, but Connor was a realist. "It seems like she wants to wake up," he said. "That's a good sign, right?"

"Well, I certainly think so." Nurse Darlene pressed her fingers across her mouth as if she'd said too much. "I'm not qualified to give opinions. But if you're asking me, this young lady is going to make a full recovery and come back to you."

And maybe she'll bring the Easter Bunny and Santa Claus with her. Connor forced a smile. The nurse wanted him to be happy, but she really didn't know—nobody knew, not for certain—if Emily would be all right. "Thank you, Darlene."

She patted his shoulder on her way out of the room. "Try to get some sleep, Connor. If you need anything, push the button and I'll be here in a flash."

Sleep was an excellent idea, but he didn't dare relax his vigilance; Deputy Sandoval had told him that Emily's accident wasn't an accident. Somebody had tried to kill her, and Connor needed to keep watch.

There was a lot to be done today. First order of business this morning would be to hire a private detective. He'd checked with the investigator who worked for his law firm in Manhattan and had got the name of a local guy. Though Connor didn't doubt Sandoval's competence, the young deputy might appreciate outside assistance from a PI—a guy who could do computer research and help him figure out why Emily had been targeted.

And Connor also needed to hire a bodyguard. The county sheriff and Aspen police didn't have the manpower to provide a cop who could stand outside her hospital room and keep watch 24/7. Also, Connor wasn't sure he trusted the locals. There was a high probability that the cops knew the Riggs family and wouldn't consider them to be a threat, even if they strolled into her hospital room carrying two crossbows and a loaded gun.

He squeezed Emily's hand and smoothed the dark blond curls that weren't covered by bandages. Even with a shiner and stitches across her forehead, she was uniquely beautiful. Her nose tilted up at the tip. Her bow-shaped lips were full. He brushed his thumb across her mouth. He'd never kissed those lips, except in a friendly way, and he was tempted to remedy that situation. Not appropriate. Kissing her while she was in a coma ranked high on the creepiness scale.

Besides, he wanted her to be awake when he finally expressed his pent-up longing. He whispered, "Emily, can you hear me?"

She said nothing, didn't open her eyes and didn't squeeze his hand.

He continued in a quiet voice, "There was a deputy who came in here last night. His name is Sandoval. He looks young but said he was thirty-two, and he's smart."

Her silence disturbed him. It was too passive. Being with Emily meant activity, laughter and a running commentary of trivial facts, usually about art.

"Sandoval investigated," he said. "He found skid marks on the road that might indicate two vehicles. One was your Hyundai, and the other had a wider wheelbase, like a truck. He couldn't re-create the scene perfectly, but he thought the truck bumped your car toward the edge. You slammed on the brake, but it wasn't enough. You crashed through the guardrail."

She must have been scared out of her mind. If Sandoval's theory was correct, a lot more investigation would be required. The sheriff's department would need to haul the wreckage of her Hyundai up the hill so the forensic people could go over it. And Sandoval could start looking for the truck that had forced her off the road.

"Do you remember? Why would someone come after you?"

His only answer came from the *blips* and *beeps* from

the machines monitoring her life signs while she was in the coma.

He asked, "Did you see who was driving?"

Even if it was possible for her to comprehend what he was saying, she might not be able to identify her attacker. He continued, "I don't have evidence, but the attack on you has something to do with the Riggs family. If not, the timing is too coincidental."

He could easily imagine a member of the family or one of their minions chasing her in a truck and forcing her car off the road. It would help if he knew why. There had to be a reason.

"On the phone, you told me not to come," he said. "You expected things to get ugly between you and the Riggs family, and you didn't want to force me to take sides. Don't you know, Emily? I'm on your side, always."

Jamison's dumb-ass infidelities had pretty much ended their decade-long friendship. Connor was outraged by the betrayal of Emily. He hated the humiliation she'd endured. When she left Jamison, he'd worked with her Denver lawyer to make sure that she was financially cared for. By juggling the assets she shared with her wealthy husband, he'd finagled a way for her to have enough cash to cover her move back to her hometown of Denver, rent a bungalow and set up her own little art gallery. When that money had run dry, Connor dipped into his own pocket.

He wanted her to have a good life, a beautiful life. As a friend, he'd always be close to her. It wasn't hard to imagine being more than a friend. If only Jamison hadn't met her first in Manhattan, he and Emily would have been a couple.

After he brushed a light kiss across her knuckles, he placed her hand on the blanket, went to the window and raised the shade. The mountain view was incredible as night faded into pale dawn. If the window had been open, he would have heard birds chirping while the sunlight spread across rock faces, dark green conifers and a bright golden stand of aspens.

For a long moment, he stood and drank in the spectacular landscape. Between his Brooklyn apartment and his Manhattan office, he hadn't come into contact with this much nature in weeks. This scenery knocked him out.

He checked his wristwatch. Five minutes past six o'clock meant it was after eight in New York. He pulled out his phone to check in with his assistant. Cases were pending, but there was nothing that required his immediate attention.

It was more important to deal with Emily's medical issues. Last night, he'd culled the list of reputable neurologists and neurosurgeons down to a few. He needed to talk to them, to select a doctor for her. Then, he'd arrange for transportation to the hospital in Denver.

When Sandoval opened the door, Connor pivoted away from the window. Instantly alert to the possibility of danger, he added a mental note to his list: buy a weapon. A handsome black man with a shaved head followed the deputy into the room. He extended his hand and introduced himself. "I'm Special Agent in Charge Jaiden Wellborn, FBI."

"This isn't the first time I've seen you," Connor said as he shook SAC Wellborn's hand. "You were at a memorial service for Jamison Riggs. Two weeks ago in Manhattan."

"The service was well attended, two hundred and forty-seven people. Was there a reason you noticed me?"

"I liked your suit." Connor didn't usually pay any attention to men's clothing, but Wellborn had stood out. His attire had been appropriate for a memorial service but not lacking in style. The man knew how to dress. Even now, at a few minutes after six in the morning in a hospital in Aspen, the agent looked classy in crocodile boots, jeans, a leather jacket and a neck scarf. "Your suit was dark blue, perfectly tailored."

"Anything else?"

"You weren't milling around in the crowd and seemed more interested in taking photos with your phone. That made me think you might be a reporter. Then I spotted your ankle holster. I had you pegged as a cop, Agent Wellborn."

He didn't bother denying Connor's conclusion. "Did it surprise you to see a cop at your friend's memorial?"

"I knew there was an investigation underway." Whenever a healthy, young man succumbs to a mysterious illness, suspicions are raised, especially when the victim is filthy rich and deeply involved with complex investments and offshore banking. Supposedly, the cause of death was a rare form of cancer, but Connor didn't believe it. "The medical examiner ran a lot of tests, and the police were reluctant to release his body for cremation."

"Our only significant evidence came from the autopsy," Wellborn said. "You might have heard that the real COD was a sophisticated, untraceable poison that was administered over an extended period of time."

"Is that true?" Connor asked.

"I can't say."

"Is it classified?"

"I don't have a definite answer about the poison. He didn't suffer much until the last week to ten days, and the doctors focused on treating symptoms and saving his life rather than identifying obscure poisons."

Connor glanced toward the bed where Emily lay quietly. It didn't seem right to talk about this in front of her. Though she and Jamison were divorced, they'd been married for almost seven years. "Can we take this conversation into the hallway?"

"Go ahead," Sandoval said. "I'll stay with Emily."

After being cooped up in the hospital room with all the beeping and blipping monitors, he was glad to step outside for a moment. The pale yellow corridors and shiny-clean nurses' station were a welcome relief. He led the way around a corner and down a flight of stairs to a lounge with vending machines. Though the coffee was fresh brewed and free, the vending-machine snacks were a typical array of semistale cookies and candy. The selection looked good to Connor, which meant he must have really been starving.

He fed dollars into the machine and pulled out two chocolate bars with almonds. As he tore off the wrapping, he said, "I heard the investigation centered on Jamison's Wall Street investment firm."

"And involved several agencies, including the SEC and NASDAQ," Wellborn said as he poured himself a coffee and added creamer. "I'm with the FBI's White-Collar Crime Unit. We found a couple of shady glitches in his dealings, but nothing that rose to the level of fraud or insider trading. A few people in his office hated his arrogance. There were clients who felt cheated."

"There always are."

"Bottom line, our investigation covered all the bases. We didn't find a significant motive for murder."

"Nobody contacted me," Connor said as he peeled the wrapper off the second candy bar. "Technically, I haven't been Jamison's attorney for years, but I stay in touch with Emily. Did you investigate her?"

"Not as much as we should have. The attack last night was proof of that."

"Are you implying that Emily had something to do with her ex-husband's death?" It seemed preposterous since

Emily and Jamison hadn't seen each other in months, much less had enough time together for a long-term poisoning.

Wellborn shrugged and sipped his coffee. Apparently, the feds hadn't ruled out Emily—in the role of hostile ex-wife—as a suspect.

"Why are you here?" Connor asked.

"I'm looking into the attack on Emily as it might relate to her ex-husband's death."

"As far as I know, there was very little contact between them."

"You didn't know the terms of the will. She inherited a seven-bedroom mansion in Aspen plus all the furnishings. The artwork alone is valued at nearly fourteen million."

A pretty decent motive for murder.

Connor's phone rang. The caller was Sandoval.

The young deputy's voice was nervous. "Connor, you need to get back to Emily's room. Right away."

Candy bar in hand, Connor dashed through the hospital corridors and up the stairs. Darlene the nurse beamed at him as he ran past her.

The door to Emily's room stood open.

Her bed was empty.

Chapter Three

She was gone.

The hospital machines that monitored her condition were dead silent. Connor stared at her vacant bed. Rumpled sheets were the only sign that Emily had been there. Panic grabbed him by the throat. He couldn't breathe, couldn't move. The thud of his heartbeat echoed in his ears. His fingers, white-knuckle, gripped the edge of the door.

He'd promised to never leave her. She needed his protection, had asked for his help and he had failed her. She was gone, lost.

"Son of a bitch," Wellborn muttered.

"Hush, now." Relentlessly cheerful, Darlene bounced up beside the two men and said, "This is a good thing—a blessing. Emily's family has come for her."

"The Riggs family," Connor said darkly.

"Such lovely people! Did you know our Dr. Thorson is dating Patricia Riggs? He signed Emily out."

"Where did they take her?" Connor was aware of at least three different residences, not including the one she had inherited from Jamison. "Which house?"

"I can look up the address for you." She bustled down the hall toward the main desk, talking as she went. "They hired a private nurse to take care of her at home. So thoughtful! I know Emily's in a coma, but I think she's aware of all these people who are concerned."

"The deputy that was watching her, where is he?"

"It was the craziest thing," Darlene said. "Deputy Sandoval tried to stop them."

"Why didn't he?"

"He called his boss, and the sheriff had already talked to Patricia. She told him it was okay, and the sheriff ordered Sandoval to stand down."

Connor had only been out of the room for a few moments. "How did they get this done so fast?"

"When Patricia speaks, we shake a leg."

"Ambulance," Connor said. "Are they taking Emily in an ambulance?"

"Well, of course."

He'd been with Emily when the paramedics had brought her in; he knew where the ambulances parked and loaded. If the Riggs family got her moved and settled in their home, it would be harder to pry her from their clutches. He had to act now.

He turned to Wellborn. "I've got to stop them."

"How are you going to do that?"

"Come with me and see."

"You bet I'm coming. I wouldn't miss this circus for the world."

Racing against an invisible clock, Connor flew down the corridor. Ignoring the slow-moving elevators, he dived into the stairwell, rushed down four floors and exited on the first. Wellborn followed close behind. Having him along would be useful. An ambulance driver might ignore Connor but wouldn't refuse a direct order from a fed.

At six thirty in the morning, the hallways were relatively calm. Though this was a small hospital, the floor plan was a tangled maze of clinics, waiting areas, pharmacies, shops and offices. During the four hours Emily was in surgery, Connor had explored, pacing from one end of the hospital to the other. He now knew where he was going as he dodged through an obstacle course of doctors and nurses and carts and gurneys. In the emergency area, he burst through the double doors. Outside, he spotted two ambulances.

Dr. Thorson stood at the rear of one ambulance. As soon as he saw Connor, he slammed the door and signaled the driver.

No way would Connor allow that vehicle to pull away. He vaulted across the parking lot, crashed into the driver's-side door and yanked it open.

The guy behind the steering wheel gaped. "What's going on?"

"Turn off the engine and get out."

"Those aren't my orders."

Connor had a lot of respect for paramedics and the mountain-rescue team that had climbed down the steep cliff and carried Emily to safety. Their procedures had been impressive, efficient and heroic. Not to mention that these guys were in great physical condition.

"Sorry," Connor said, "but you've got to turn off the engine."

"Listen here, buddy, I advise you to step back."

Respect be damned, Connor needed cooperation. He turned to Wellborn. "I need your gun."

"Not a chance." The fed displayed his badge and credentials. "Agent Wellborn, FBI. Please step out of the vehicle."

Further conversation became moot when Deputy Sandoval drove into the lot, his siren blaring and flashers whirling. He parked his SUV with the Pitkin County Sheriff logo in front of the ambulance. Nobody was going anywhere.

Connor stormed toward the rear of the ambulance with

only one thought in mind. *Rescue Emily.* He didn't know how he'd move her from the ambulance or where he'd take her, but he sure as hell wouldn't allow her to be carried away by the Riggs family.

Dr. Thorson stepped in front of him. "Slow down, Connor."

Some people just don't know when they're beat. "Get out of my way."

"Everything has been taken care of. I've got this."

"Beg to differ."

"I assure you that—"

"Stop!" Since the doctor didn't seem to understand direct language, Connor decided to use his well-practiced techniques as an attorney whose job required him to deal with contentious personalities. He straightened his shoulders and leveled his voice to a calm monotone. "We can handle this situation in one of two ways. First, there's the legal way, where I point to the documents that state—very clearly—that I'm in charge of all decisions regarding Emily's medical care. If you don't honor the signed and notarized advance directive, rest assured that I will sue the hospital and you personally."

Thorson's tanned forehead twisted in a scowl.

"The second way," Connor said as he dropped the lawyerly persona, "is for me to kick your muscle-bound Norwegian ass."

"I'd like to see you try."

Wellborn stepped between them. "Gentlemen, let's take this conversation inside."

"I'm not leaving Emily," Connor said as he reached for the latch on the rear door. "This facility isn't secure, and there's reason to believe she's in danger."

When he yanked open the door, he saw long-limbed Patricia Riggs scrunched into the ambulance. He hated that she was near Emily, close enough to disconnect an IV line or turn off one of the machines. Thank God the paramedic was there, keeping watch.

Patricia pushed a wing of dark brown hair off her face to reveal tears welling in her eyes and streaking down her chiseled cheekbones. "Oh, my God, Connor, I can't believe this terrible accident happened to our dear, sweet Emily."

He wasn't buying the tears. Patricia was a hard-edged businesswoman, a lady shark who knew as much about the investment game as her cousin, Jamison. The only type of tragedy that would cause her to weep was when the Dow dropped four hundred points. Still, he played along, needing to get her out of the ambulance and away from Emily. He reached into the vehicle, grabbed her manicured hand and pulled her toward the open door. "You're upset, Patricia. Let's get you a nice latte."

"Are you patronizing me?"

"Let's just say that I'm as sincere as your tears."

"You don't get it." She dug in her heels. "I need to be with Emily when we take her home for the last time."

The last time? Though Emily's condition was listed as critical, none of the doctors who had seen her thought she was terminal…except for Thorson, Patricia's boyfriend.

"No more games," he growled. "Get out of the ambulance."

"But I—"

"Emily is going to recover."

"But Eric said—"

"Dr. Thorson isn't the best person to listen to. I warned him, and I'll play the same tune for you. When you interfere with Emily's care, you're breaking the law."

"Don't be a jackass." Her upper lip curled in a sneer as she came toward him. Her tears had dried, and her dark eyes were as cold as black ice. "We want the best for Emily, even if she did divorce my cousin and tear off a big chunk of the family fortune."

Connor knew precisely how much Emily had received in settlement. Considering that she'd been entitled to more in the prenup, the amount she'd actually collected shouldn't have been enough to ruffle Patricia's feathers. "You're talking about the house Jamison left her."

"It's an estate," she snapped. "Why the hell would he leave it to her? In the past few years, they hardly ever came to Aspen. After the separation, not at all. My brother, Phillip, had to move in and take care of the property. If anyone should inherit it, it's Phillip."

"I remember when Jamison and Emily first got married," Connor said. "They stayed at the Aspen house whenever they had a spare moment. They even had a name for the place."

"Jamie's Getaway," she muttered. "Appropriate for a bank robber."

Or for a man who appreciated a place where he felt safe. Connor understood why he'd left the house to her. Jamison had been acknowledging the happier times in their marriage. His sentimental gesture wasn't enough to make up for his cheating, but it reminded Connor of why he had liked Jamison Riggs. "Here's the deal, Patricia. I make the medical decisions for Emily. If you or anyone in your family interferes, you will regret it. Jamison was once my friend, but that won't stop me from going after his family."

"You'll sue?"

"Damn straight."

Patricia stepped out of the ambulance and stalked over to her boyfriend. With her smooth dark hair and his blond curls, they made a handsome pair. Though Connor wanted to hear Wellborn question them, he turned his back and entered the rear of the ambulance. He had to see Emily, to make sure she was all right.

The paramedic was one of the men who had participated in the rescue last night. Connor was relieved to see him. "It's Adam, right? How come you're still on duty?"

"I caught a couple of z's, then came back to pick up an extra shift for a friend." He lifted a thermal coffee mug to his lips and took a sip. "Your girlfriend is looking good, considering how we found her."

He'd hooked Emily to IVs and portable machines similar to those in her hospital room, including a cannula that delivered oxygen to her nostrils. Throughout the long night, Connor had observed the digital readouts and knew what the numbers were supposed to show. He had no cause for alarm. "Are her vitals within normal range?"

"You bet. Transferring her into the ambulance went real smooth."

Still, Connor worried. "The woman who was in here, Patricia, did she get in the way?"

"You bet she did. Man, I was tripping over Riggses. There was Patricia and her bro and an older lady—maybe her mom."

"Aunt Glenda," Connor said.

"And a couple of other guys."

"Minions." The Riggs brood was a high-maintenance family, requiring many people to manage their affairs. "Did any of them touch Emily?"

"Not on my watch," Adam said. "What's got you so jumpy?"

"Just a feeling."

He was scared—an undeniable tension prickled along his nerve endings and tied a hard knot in his gut. He didn't like having emotions interfere with his actions. Not only had he grown up tough but Connor was a lawyer who had learned how to manage his behavior. That veneer of self-control was wearing thin. In addition to feeling fear, he was angry. If he'd followed his natural instincts, he would have grabbed Wellborn's gun and blasted each and every one of the Riggses who got in his way.

No doubt, one of them was responsible for running Emily off the road. If that wasn't enough, they'd snatched her from her hospital room as soon as his back was turned. He needed to get her away from here.

He tucked a blanket up to her chin and studied her face. Her cheeks glowed with a soft pink, more color than when she'd been indoors. Her full lips parted, and she almost looked like she was smiling. He couldn't wait to see her smile for real and to hear her laughter. "It's chilly out here. How can you tell if she gets cold?"

"I can take her temperature or I can do it the old-fashioned way, like your mama did. Feel her forehead. Touch her fingers and toes."

Connor's heart had been beating fast and his adrenaline pumping hard. His own temperature was probably elevated, but he did as suggested. Her forehead was smooth and cool. The white bandages protecting her head wound and the EEG sensors contrasted her dark blond hair and her complexion. Oddly, he was reminded of her snowy-white bridal veil. On her wedding day, eight years ago, she'd been so fresh and pretty and young, only twenty-two. He and Jamison had been twenty-five, just getting started with their high-power careers. Jamison had joined his investment brokerage firm as a junior vice president and had already been able to afford to buy a small apartment in Battery Park. Connor had been in Brooklyn, jumping from one law firm to another as he built his client list and his reputation.

While Jamison was furnishing his place, he'd gone to an

art gallery. That had been where he met Emily. By sheer luck, he'd found her first.

On their wedding day, Connor had forced himself to celebrate. He was the best man, after all. He had to make a toast and tell the newlyweds that they were going to be happy and their love would last forever—not necessarily a lie but not what he really wanted. He'd felt like a jerk for his interest in his best friend's bride, but he couldn't help it. He should have been the man with Emily. When it came time for him to kiss the new bride, he'd chickened out and gave her a peck on the forehead. He'd been terrified that if he kissed her on the lips, he wouldn't be able to stop.

Sitting beside her in the back of the ambulance, he took her hand, pretending to check if she was cold but hoping he'd feel her squeeze his fingers. He desperately wanted her eyes to open. There had been a few moments in her room where her lashes fluttered. REM sleep was what Darlene had called it. Emily wasn't moving now. Her face was still and serene, which he told himself was for the best. She wasn't supposed to wake up. Her brain needed time to heal.

He cleared his throat. "Is it dangerous to move her?"

"Not if I'm in charge."

Agent Wellborn poked his head into the rear of the ambulance, flashed his credentials to Adam and spoke to Connor. "I'm going to get started talking to these people before they call in their lawyers. Have you made any decisions about Emily's care?"

"I want to get her away from here. A couple of specialists in Denver have agreed to take her case. The problem is transportation." He looked toward Adam. "Can you arrange a Flight For Life helicopter?"

"I'll set it up with my dispatcher," he said. "Shouldn't be a problem, but it might take some time, an hour or more."

Connor gave a quick nod. After this incident with Thorson, he had cause to worry about the personnel assigned to take care of Emily. "I trust you, Adam. Can you come with us on the chopper?"

"Sure thing." He grinned. "I can always find something to do in Denver."

"Let's get moving," Wellborn said. "Connor, I want you to come with me when I talk to these people. You know them. You might notice something that doesn't register with me."

"I'd be delighted to do anything that might disturb the Riggs family." He glanced back at Adam. "While I'm with Special Agent Wellborn, you need to keep everyone away from Emily."

"You got it."

"One more thing," Connor said. "Patricia suggested that Emily wasn't going to wake up. Is there something I haven't been told?"

"I don't know all the details," Adam said, "but the screen on the EEG monitor shows normal brain activity for an induced coma. Seriously, dude, as long as we keep an eye on the monitors, she'll be okay. She's a fighter."

Connor agreed, "She looks like a delicate flower, but she's tough."

It seemed impossible that someone would want to murder this gentle but courageous woman. Somehow, he had to keep that fact at the front of his mind. She was in danger. It was his job to keep her safe.

EMILY COULDN'T TELL where she was, but she sensed a change in surroundings. Through her eyelids, she was aware of the light fading and then becoming bright and fading again. The calliope music still played—*boop-boop-beedle-deedle-doop-doop*. But the tone was different. And she heard a man's voice.

"She looks like a delicate flower," he'd said.

It was Connor...or had she imagined the smooth baritone? She tried with all her might to listen harder and wished she had one of those old-fashioned ear trumpets with a bell shape at the end to vacuum up sound. *Speak again, Connor. Say something else.*

There was something important she needed to tell him. At the reading of the will, there were details she wanted Connor to know.

When she'd arrived at Patricia's super-chic, nine-bedroom mountain chalet for the reading of the will, an avalanche of hostility roiled over her. Patricia hated her. Aunt Glenda had always looked down her nose at Emily. Phillip and his buddies, some of whom were good friends of Jamison, eyeballed her with varying degrees of suspicion and contempt. If Connor had been there, the atmosphere would have been different. He would have called them out and shamed them.

Though she was capable of standing up for herself, Emily didn't really want to fight with these people. Seeking refuge, she'd locked herself into the bathroom—an opulent, marble-floored facility with three sinks, gold-tiled walls, a walk-in glass shower big enough for four adults, a toilet and a bidet. She'd actually considered spending the rest of the night in there.

Staring in the mirror, she'd given herself a pep talk. *You have every right to be here. You were called to be here, for Pete's sake. You can tell these people that they're mean and interfering. After tonight, you never have to see them again.* She'd lifted her chin, knowing that she looked strong and healthy. She'd been doing renovations at the gallery and was probably in the best physical condition of her life. During the past few months in Denver, her chin-length, dark blond hair had brightened. Natural highlights mingled with darker strands. There were women who paid a fortune for this look.

She'd applied coral lipstick and given herself a smile before she opened the bathroom door. Voices and laughter had echoed from the front foyer and bounced off the ornate crystal chandelier. The sound had been disproportionately loud. She'd recoiled and covered her ears. Not ready to rejoin the others, she'd slipped down the corridor to a library with a huge desk and floor-to-ceiling shelves of leather-bound books.

The cream-colored wall opposite the curtained windows had displayed framed photos of various shapes and sizes. Many were pictures of Patricia with celebrities or heads of state or family members. None had showed Patricia's ex-husband, a man who she and Jamison had referred to as "dead to her." *Do I fall into that category?* She'd searched the wall for a sign of her relationship with Patricia. There had been several photos of Jamison, but Emily saw none—not even a group photo—with her own smiling face. Patricia had erased her from the family. So typical!

The door had opened, and a woman had stepped into the library.

Embarrassed to be caught looking at photos, Emily had taken a step back. "Are they ready to start?" she'd asked.

"Not quite yet," the woman had said. "I thought I saw you come in here. I wanted a chance to meet you before the reading."

Emily's gaze had focused on the Oriental carpet. She hadn't been really interested in mingling or meeting people. With trepidation, she'd looked up. The woman's legs were a mile long, and she was dressed in the height of Aspen chic. Her hair was long, straight and a deep auburn. Her face had had a hard expression that Emily would never forget.

"We've met," Emily had said.

"I don't think so." Not even a hint of a smile. This woman had been as cold as a frozen rainbow trout.

The first time Emily had seen her, she'd been preoccupied—tangled in the sheets and having sex with Jamison. "You're Kate Sylvester."

"Do you mind if I ask you a few questions?"

Emily hadn't refused, even though she doubted she'd be much help. She hadn't talked to Jamison in months, and she'd heard that Kate was living with him. Why had she wanted to ask so many weird questions about Jamison's finances?

In her unconscious state, she heard the distant sound of alarm bells. At Patricia's chalet, she'd been more preoccupied with keeping her equilibrium after the Riggs family's open contempt had thrown her off her game. She hadn't given Kate a second thought.

But now? After the attempt on her life?

Everything about the will reading took on a much darker tinge.

When she woke up, she had to remember to tell Connor about this connection that spanned the country from Aspen to Jamison's New York investment firm.

Chapter Four

In a vacant office near the emergency exit, SAC Wellborn assumed the position of authority behind the desk. Patricia and Aunt Glenda sat opposite him while Connor remained standing with his back against the closed door. The only thing keeping him awake was a fresh surge of adrenaline, and he thoroughly resented that the Riggs women held coffee mugs from the hospital cafeteria in their manicured hands.

He hadn't seen Aunt Glenda in four or five years. She hadn't aged, which was a testament to plastic surgery and stringent maintenance procedures. He knew for a fact that she was in her late seventies. Her straight hair—solid black without a trace of gray—was pulled up in a high ponytail, showing off her sharp features. Though the never-married matriarch of the Riggs family might be described as a handsome woman, Connor thought she looked like a crow with her black hair and beady eyes.

"Where's Phillip?" he asked.

"Dealing with another matter," Patricia said. Her upper lip curled in a sneer. She really didn't like him.

The feeling was mutual. Connor couldn't resist baiting her. "Your baby brother should be here. Whatever he's doing can't be more important than talking to the FBI."

"Phillip is accompanying Dr. Thorson." Her hostility

flared. "Because of your absurd accusations, Eric is in trouble with the hospital administration. Phillip went with him, hoping to smooth the waters."

Reading between the lines, Connor figured that Phillip would get Thorson off the hook with a big fat juicy donation to the hospital. Not only was the Riggs family wealthy, but they'd been in Aspen for a long time and wielded a lot of influence. Some of the cousins were on the city council, and Phillip had considered running for mayor. Their uncaring manipulation of power made Connor want revenge. Suing them wasn't enough. He wanted blood.

Wellborn placed a small recording device on the desk. "I'll be making a permanent record of this conversation." He stated the date, the location and the people in the room.

Before he could proceed, Patricia rapped on the desktop. "Excuse me, should we have a lawyer present?"

"That will not be necessary," Aunt Glenda pronounced. "We wish to do everything possible to be helpful. I feel partially responsible for Emily's accident. When she left, I should have sent someone along with her or had her followed."

"Why is that?" Wellborn asked.

"Isn't it obvious? After hearing about her inheritance, she was so thrilled and excited that she couldn't keep her little car on the road." Glenda spoke with absolute confidence. "We'll do whatever we can to take care of Emily. That includes opening my home to her and hiring a nurse to watch over her."

Patricia backed up her aunt with a barrage of commentary, describing the facilities at Glenda's sprawling cattle ranch, which included a barn, a bunkhouse and a hangar for a small single-engine airplane—none of which seemed pertinent to the care of a woman in an induced coma. But Patricia was on a roll, babbling about how much she liked Emily and how much they had in common and many, many, many other lies.

Wellborn interrupted, "Why didn't you consult with Mr. Gallagher before moving the patient?"

Glenda held up a hand to silence her niece. "It simply never occurred to me. I don't know what Connor has been telling you, but he has no relationship with Emily."

Wellborn looked toward Connor. "I thought you were her fiancé."

"No."

Patricia took her shot. "You lied. So pathetic! You've always been insanely jealous of Jamison. You envied his success, his style and now his wife. What's the matter, Connor? Can't find a girlfriend of your own?"

Rather than going on the defensive and trying to justify his lying, he sidestepped. "Aunt Glenda is right. My relationship with Emily is irrelevant. However, her advance directive documents give me durable power of attorney and appoint me as the decision maker for her medical care. I'll be happy to show you the paperwork."

"Which brings me back to my initial question," Wellborn said. "Why not talk to Connor before transporting an unconscious woman to your ranch?"

Glenda looked down her beak. "How would I know he was responsible?"

"Thorson knew," Connor said. That fact was indisputable.

"But I didn't." Glenda sniffed as though she'd caught a whiff of rotten eggs. Apparently, she had no problem throwing the blond doctor under the bus, blaming the whole incident on him.

Patricia leaped to his defense. "My fiancé saved Emily's life. He's—"

"You're engaged to Dr. Thorson," Wellborn said.

"Yes, I am." Proudly, she stuck out her left hand so they could admire her flashy Tiffany-cut diamond. "We'll be married next year."

"Or sooner," Aunt Glenda said. "Patricia mustn't wait too long, doesn't want to add any more wrinkles before the wedding. She's fourteen years older than the doctor, you know."

"Please, Aunt Glenda." Patricia pinched her thin lips together. "The FBI doesn't need to know about my personal affairs."

"Agent Wellborn might want to watch out," Aunt Glenda continued. "He's a very attractive man, and he's wearing a Burberry scarf."

"You'll have to excuse my aunt," Patricia said.

"It's no secret that you prefer younger men. You're a cougar, my dear, and a successful one. You should be pleased with yourself."

"How dare you!"

"Cougar."

Their infighting made him sick. Connor hated that Emily had wasted some of the best years of her life in the company of these harpies, and he vowed to never again complain about his huge Irish family in Queens. Sure, the Gallaghers did a lot of yelling. But there were also hugs, apologies and tears. Under all their blarney and bluster, there was love.

"Ladies," Wellborn said, "I'd like to get back to the central issue. Did you move Emily on the advice of Dr. Thorson?"

"We wanted to take her to the ranch," Patricia said before her aunt could throw another barb at her fiancé. "You must have forgotten, Aunt Glenda, but we spoke to Eric about our plan, and he told us there might be a problem with the paperwork."

"I didn't forget," Glenda snapped. "My mind is as sharp as it ever was."

"Of course it is." Patricia's voice dripped with condescension, and she rolled her eyes. Not a good look for a bona fide cougar. "We were so concerned about Emily that we didn't pay enough attention to Eric's advice. It was for the best, we decided, to avoid a confrontation with Connor. Emily needs to be home and surrounded by family before she passes on."

"She's not dying," Connor said.

Patricia schooled her expression to appear sympathetic. "I understand the denial. But, Connor, you must be aware that Emily flatlined on the operating table. It happened twice. She was technically dead. Her heart stopped."

He hadn't heard this before. Though he wouldn't put it past Dr. Thorson to make up a story like this if it suited his purposes, there had been other doctors present. No one had told him that Emily was so near death. "You're lying."

"Think what you want," Aunt Glenda said. "That girl is hanging on by a thread."

It wouldn't do any good for him to explode. Connor threw up a mental wall, blocking their innuendo and deceit. Glenda and Patricia wanted Emily under their control; they'd admitted as much. But why?

"If Emily died," he said, hating the words as soon as they passed his lips, "what would happen to the house she inherited?"

"You seem to be acting as her attorney," Patricia said. "You tell us."

It was an interesting question—one he needed to research. As far as he knew, Emily had no living relations. She'd been an only child. Her parents were older when they had had Emily, and they'd died from natural causes when she was a teenager. He doubted she had a current will reflecting her divorce. There were documents he'd drawn up when she and Jamison were first married, but that was a long time ago.

A further complication when it came to ownership of the house she'd inherited was the actual transfer of property. Emily didn't have a deed. The probate court would surely step in. He handled transactions like this on a regular basis, and the paperwork was intense.

While Patricia launched into another diatribe about how her brother had been taking care of the property and deserved compensation, Wellborn leveled an assessing gaze in her direction. Connor had the sense that the good-looking black agent was accustomed to dealing with self-obsessed rich people who wouldn't stop talking. He maintained an attitude of calm. The only sign of his annoyance was the way he tapped his Cross pen as though flicking ashes from a Cuban cigar.

"Last night," Wellborn said, "was the reading of the will for Jamison Riggs. Start at the beginning and tell me everything that happened."

Patricia settled back in her chair and sipped her coffee. "I should probably start with the list of individuals who had been invited. My assistant has a copy, as does our family attorney."

Inwardly, Connor groaned. This conversation or interrogation—whatever Wellborn called it—could take hours. He couldn't spare the time. Emily needed to be moved to Denver, where he could make sure she was safe.

When Adam, the paramedic, texted him to let him know that they were ready to transfer Emily to the helicopter, he was relieved to get away from the Riggs women.

With a wave to Wellborn, he opened the door to the office. "I'll stay in touch."

IMPRESSED WITH THE efficiency of Adam and the other medical emergency personnel, Connor watched as they carried Emily on a gurney into the orange-and-yellow Flight For Life helicopter. They moved slowly and with extreme care but couldn't help jostling her.

Though she showed no sign of being disturbed, every bump made Connor think he might be making a mistake. Transporting her to Denver, where she could get the best care, seemed rational and prudent. He'd spoken to Dr. Charles Troutman, a neurologist with a stellar reputation who had taken a look at Emily's brain data and had agreed to take her case. Connor's instincts told him he was doing the right thing, getting her away from the place where she'd been threatened. But what if moving her caused her condition to worsen?

With the big cast on her left arm and the plastic boot on her left leg, she was hard to handle. But Adam and his associates managed to transfer her onto the bed where they readjusted the IVs and monitoring equipment. Connor stared at the wavy lines and the digital numbers on the screens. The emergency medical transport was equipped with all the equipment in the hospital and more. The crew included a pilot, an EMT copilot, a nurse and Adam, who vouched for the others.

Connor couldn't take his eyes off Emily. Even when she was being moved, the monitors showed very little change. Though that was what the doctors wanted—a smooth transition—he longed to see a reaction from her or to hear her speak—just a word. He wanted some kind of sign that she was all right.

When she was safely secured, belted himself into a jump seat and watched her as the chopper swooped into the clear blue skies. Through the window, he glimpsed snowcapped mountains. Soon, it would be winter. The golden leaves of autumn would be gone, and snow would blanket the tall pines and other conifers.

"You'll be better by then," he said to Emily.

"What?" Adam looked up from the equipment he'd been monitoring.

"I was talking to her," Connor said without shame. Even if she couldn't hear him, he felt the need to reach out to her and reassure her. He unbuckled his seat belt and moved closer to her. With the back of his hand, he caressed her cheek. Taking full responsibility for her, making life-and-death decisions, was the hardest thing he'd ever done.

Adam bumped his arm as he reached across her bed to slide a pillow under the plastic boot on her ankle. "Sorry, Adam, I need to step away. I've got a couple more things to check.

"We've got everything under control."

Not only did Connor appreciate the skill and competence of this young man but he trusted Adam. "You're doing a great job. If there's ever anything I can do for you, name it."

"Well, let me think." He grinned. "I'm already hooked up with a season ski pass, my rent isn't too bad and I've got a kick-ass girlfriend. All in all, my life is good."

"I'll get out of your way."

Back in his jump seat, he flipped open his laptop. He envied Adam's simple but fulfilling lifestyle. Connor had never been a laid-back guy. He had needed to fight to win a partial scholarship to Harvard, and when he was there he took on the role of a super achiever. The struggle hadn't ended with graduation. He'd worked his way through several law firms until he'd found the perfect match at Shanahan, Miller and Koch, where he was well on his way to partnership.

Lately, his fire had dimmed. During these hours he'd spent rescuing Emily, he'd felt more alive than he had in years.

Using his computer, he contacted his assistant at the law firm. Last night, he'd hired a security firm, recommended by the investigator who had done work for him in New York. The bodyguard—a former marine—was scheduled to meet them at the airport before they continued on to the hospital.

If all went smoothly, Dr. Troutman would be waiting for them at the hospital. He was associated with one of the top neurosurgeons in the country, a woman who had developed techniques to treat stroke victims. Troutman hoped Emily's condition wouldn't require an operation, but they should prepare for the possibility.

During the flight, Connor texted back and forth with his assistant—a fresh-from-law-school junior partner who was capable of handling most of Connor's caseload with minimal direction from him. Projecting that he wouldn't be back to work for at least two weeks, maybe longer, Connor suggested which cases could be postponed and which should be reassigned to other attorneys in the firm. A few years ago, when his ambitions had been burning brightly, he never would have passed on these projects. But he didn't hesitate now. He'd proven himself to be a hard worker, so that wouldn't be in question. Plus, Emily's well-being was more important.

Adam called to him, "Connor, you should come over here."

Immediately, he disconnected his laptop and went to Emily's bedside. She lay motionless, breathing steadily. The machines that monitored her vital signs hadn't changed, but the EEG monitor showed flashes of brain activity. "What's going on?"

"I'm not sure."

"Could it be the altitude?" Tension sent Connor's heartbeat into high gear. "Maybe it's the movement."

"All I know," Adam said, "is that she's waking up. The nurse wants you to put in an emergency call to the neurologist in Denver. He'll tell us what to do."

While Connor punched in the phone number, he asked, "If she wakes up, what happens?"

"Maybe nothing," Adam said. "There might be no problem at all."

"Worst-case scenario?"

"She could have a seizure. There might be an internal bleed or a clot that would cause an aneurysm."

An aneurysm and internal bleeding could lead to irreparable damage or death. As soon as Connor had the doctor on the phone, he handed it to the nurse, who rattled off a barrage of medical terminology. Sitting as close as possible, Connor held her small delicate hand and watched her face, trying to read what was going on inside her head. She looked the same as she had a few hours ago at the hospital in Aspen, except her eyelids were twitching. Her breathing became more emphatic. He saw variations in the rhythm of her heart and her blood pressure.

Keeping the desperation from his voice, he said, "If you can hear me, Emily, I need you to listen. You need more sleep, more rest. Don't wake up, not yet."

He felt the tiniest squeeze on his hand. Had he imagined it? Though he wanted to see her awake, talking and interacting, that wasn't the best treatment for her. "Stay asleep, Emily."

Gently, he caressed the line of her chin and her stubborn jaw. She'd never been a woman who blindly followed orders or instructions. Being asleep and unable to react would never be her first choice. He tried to reassure her, telling her that there was nothing to worry about. "I've arranged for your medical care and hired a bodyguard because... You know."

Though she knew that someone had run her off the road, he probably shouldn't talk about it while she was in a coma. Her brain might pick up the threat and become alarmed, pumping out spurts of adrenaline that would cause her to wake up. He should be talking about better times, evoking positive thoughts. One topic always made her happy: art.

"There's a special exhibit at that little gallery you always liked in Brooklyn," he said. "It features posters, and they even have a couple from Toulouse-Lautrec."

While the nurse unhooked one of the IV bags, Adam said, "We've got a solution."

"What does the doctor think?"

"It's got to be the sedation. It's not keeping her in the coma. I changed the IV bag on the ambulance ride to the airport." And now the nurse changed the bag again. "It's possible that the one I used didn't have the correct dosage to keep her asleep."

Connor doubted the wrong dosage was an accident. Patricia and Dr. Thorson had been near Emily in the ambulance. Either of them could easily have switched the bags. "Don't throw that bag away. There might be fingerprints."

"You got it." Adam stepped aside as the nurse prepared a hypodermic needle. "She's going to give Emily a shot that should keep her calm until we get to Denver. We're only about a half hour away."

The chopper shuddered. "Is it safe to do that while we're bouncing around?"

"Trust me," Adam said. "I'm usually in the back of an ambulance racing around hairpin turns at a million miles an hour. This chopper ride is smooth."

When a needle was jabbed into Emily's arm, Connor

stared at the monitors. It was probably unreasonable to expect immediate results, but he needed some kind of reaction. How long would it take for the sedative to enter her bloodstream? When would he see the change? He needed to know.

Adam was back on the phone, talking to the doctor. He, too, watched the screens. The EEG showing brain activity continued to flare in multicolored bursts—green, red and yellow. Connor held his breath, waiting for a sign. After a few tense moments, her blood pressure and pulse gradually started to drop.

Adam reported the numbers to the neurologist, and then he gave Connor a thumbs-up. "This seems to be working."

Relief breezed through him. He lifted her hand and brushed a kiss across her knuckles. "You scared me, Emily."

Her lips parted. Faint words tumbled out. "Handsome... Sleeping... Kiss."

He leaned closer. "What is it?"

Her eyelids separated. Through the narrow slits, she stared at him. And she whispered, "Snow White... Kiss."

Adam shoved his shoulder. "You heard the lady."

With a smile, the nurse concurred, "Kiss her."

Leaning over her, he planted a light kiss on her lips. This brief contact wasn't meant to be the least bit erotic, but he felt a jolt of awareness. His senses heightened. He'd been in the dark, and now a light bulb had come on.

That momentary kiss made him feel alive. He knew what had been missing in his life.

Chapter Five

He kissed me.

In every fairy tale, the sleeping beauty needed the kiss of a heroic prince to wake her, and then they lived happily forever. Emily knew better than to count on that rosy ending, but she was glad to have the magical kiss. It was a wake-up call. Now she could find the person who wanted her dead.

Hoping to bring her vision into focus, she blinked a couple of times. Connor's features became clearer. Looking at him was always pleasing—now more than ever because he was officially her hero.

His brown hair was disheveled as though he'd just got out of bed. Not that she'd know what that looked like. She and Connor had never gone to bed together. Once, on a group trip to the Caymans, they had been the first ones up and had shared a first cup of coffee before strolling across the pristine sand to wade in the shimmering blue sea. She remembered the sense of wonder and intimacy that surrounded them. Maybe she felt closer to him than any of Jamison's other friends because she and Connor didn't come from a richy-rich background. She trusted him. He was on her side, and she needed allies to help her figure out who was trying to kill her.

It was about time for her to wake up. She had a lot

to tell Connor, but the poor guy looked like he hadn't slept all night. Was it only one night she'd been asleep? Was it two? She wanted to ask but got distracted as her gaze roamed over his features. Though his chin was covered with stubble and his chocolate-brown eyes were red-rimmed, he was as handsome as Prince Charming. Maybe he'd kiss her again, this time with more pressure. She remembered how he'd looked on that beach in the Caymans. He'd been wearing low-slung board shorts and nothing else. His wide shoulders and lean, muscular chest had tantalized her. Though she'd been a married woman at the time, there was no rule against looking.

And now they had no reason to stay apart. She wanted him to kiss her like he meant it. If his tongue happened to slip inside her mouth, she wouldn't mind too much.

Her lips tingled. When she tried to reach up and touch her mouth, her left arm wouldn't move. Her gaze flickered toward her left hand, and she saw a massive cast that went from her wrist all the way up past her bent elbow. It looked bad. Then she noticed an ugly gray plastic boot on her left leg. She had many injuries, but they didn't seem to hurt. Floating on a wave of euphoria, she was feeling no pain. Her eyelids drooped.

"That's good," Connor said in his soothing baritone. "Let yourself go back to sleep."

"No." She roused herself. There were things that needed to be done, wrongs to be righted and bad guys to track down. She flexed her right arm and tightened her grip on Connor's hand. "Don't want to sleep."

"I understand," he said, "but the doctor advised that you rest."

"What doctor?" She lifted her head off the pillow to scan her surroundings and saw lots of medical equipment and windows filled with clouds and sky. This wasn't like any hospital she'd ever been in. "Where am I?"

"Helicopter," Connor said. "We're on our way to Denver, where we'll meet with a neurologist—Dr. Charles Troutman."

Her head lowered to the pillow. The edges of her vision were getting hazy. "Somebody tried to murder me."

"The police are looking into it."

"Sandoval," she said. "Deputy Sandoval."

"Wow." His fingers tightened on hers. "I didn't think you heard me talking about him. I thought you were asleep."

And she didn't remember the conversation, but the words were in her head. Deputy Sandoval had noticed skid marks on the road and the shoulder. He'd deduced that there had been two vehicles, one with a wide wheelbase.

"Forced off the road," she said, "by a truck."

"That's right."

"Did he find it?"

"Not yet, but he's looking. Do you remember anything about the truck? Did you see who was driving?"

"No."

A different speaker said, "Hey, Emily, no need to worry. Just relax. Let it go."

"Who are you?"

"I'm a paramedic," the voice said. "My name is Adam."

"I know you, Adam." His voice was familiar, and she had memories connected to him, recent memories. She parroted his words. "You said, 'Trust me.'"

Under his breath, he said, "Damn, she hears everything."

"I do." And she took satisfaction in her ability to comprehend what was happening. "Somebody gave me a shot."

"That was a nurse, and the shot was a sedative. Dr. Troutman wants you to stay asleep."

"Induced coma," she said.

They might as well be accurate in what they were saying. She wasn't taking a little catnap but had been sedated. And the doctor she'd be seeing was a neurologist, which meant she had some kind of head injury. A particularly visceral memory played in her mind. After touching a wound on her head, her fingers had been sticky with blood. More blood smeared her white shirt. Her hair had been matted.

For some reason, she'd come out of the coma. "Why…" Her awareness was fading, and she realized it was due to the sedative. She forced herself to string words together. "Why'd I come around?"

"I'm not going to lie to you," Connor said, "or hide the real circumstances. You need to know the truth so you can understand that the danger is real."

Oh, I know all about the danger. The proof was in her busted arm, her messed-up leg and God knows what other injuries. "What truth?"

"Here's what we think happened. You've been receiving a steady stream of sedatives through an IV line. When we loaded you onto the helicopter, Adam changed to a fresh bag. The medication wasn't enough. You started to wake up."

A mistaken dosage didn't seem so dangerous. As far as she was concerned, it was a minor error. She was glad to be awake, even if it was only for a few minutes. Through barely open eyelids, she studied Connor's expression. His jaw was tight and stubborn. She suspected there was something more he wasn't telling her.

The inside of her mouth tasted like the Sahara. "More. There's more to the story."

He started with a complicated description of a chase

through an Aspen hospital with Thor carrying her away. *Thor? Really?* Patricia Riggs wanted to take her home to Aspen, which didn't make any sense to Emily. There was only one reason she would want to become her caretaker: to pull the plug.

Her grip on the conscious world was slipping. Vaguely, she heard Connor say something about Aunt Glenda. In *The Wizard of Oz*, Glinda was a good witch who helped Dorothy return to the people who loved her in Kansas. Not so for Glenda Riggs. She'd never helped anybody— not even her nephew Jamison after his own parents died. Her only true love was for her horses.

Emily reined in her free association and tried to understand what Connor was telling her. He said something about a sack or a bag.

"I guess I should explain," he said. "*SAC* is an acronym for *Special Agent in Charge*. His name is Jaiden Wellborn, and he works with the White-Collar Crime Unit."

As soon as he mentioned New York, her mind zoomed off on another tangent. She recalled her conversation with Kate Sylvester before the reading of the will. Jamison's former lover had wanted information from her. She'd hinted that Emily might know something about a secret account— just the sort of details an agent who worked in white-collar crime would want to know.

Kate Sylvester.

Emily felt like she'd spoken the name aloud, but Connor didn't respond. She tried again, louder this time.

KATE SYLVESTER.

Without a break, he continued his narrative, explaining how someone had switched the IV bags before takeoff. "They tried to kill you," he said, "again."

He made his point. Cutting down on the sedative dosage would cause her to come out of the induced coma, which might lead to brain damage, seizure or an aneurysm. The switch seemed like something that could be easily proved.

Who had access to the IV bags?

"We'll turn the bag over to Wellborn." Connor hadn't answered her statement, which she probably hadn't spoken aloud. Still, he'd given her a sort of answer. "The forensic people can check for fingerprints, but this evidence won't be of much value in court. It's too circumstantial. The doctor has a built-in excuse for handling equipment. And the back of the ambulance was crowded. Anyone could have touched it by accident."

But it wasn't a dead end. If changing the bag could be considered a threat, the person who was after her was one of the people in the ambulance or the hospital. Concentrating hard, she tried again to speak. *Who was in the ambulance? The hospital? Are there security tapes? Was Kate Sylvester there?*

"The good news," Connor said, "is that you don't seem to be affected by the change."

Except now I can't talk. Listen to me. You need to talk to Kate Sylvester. Mentally, she yelled the name over and over. *KATE SYLVESTER. KATE, KATE, KATE!*

Her voice was gone. What if this was a permanent condition and she was never to speak again? If she was able to hear the whistles of birdsong and music and other voices, her own silence wouldn't be much of a sacrifice. Vision was the sense she prized the most. Her greatest pleasure came from appreciation of art or by watching a sunrise. She couldn't imagine a life without ever seeing Connor again. He was well on his way to becoming an essential part of her world.

"We're here," he said, "coming in for a landing."

I can tell. When the chopper dipped, her world shifted. Being supine on an aircraft was very disorienting.

"This helipad is close to the hospital," Adam said. "I can see the ambulance at the edge of the landing circle, waiting for us."

"Will you come with us?" Connor asked. "I want to make sure her transfer goes smoothly."

"Me, too. And I'd like to meet Dr. Troutman."

That's a funny name, Troutman. Wonder if he looks like a fish.

Underwater images played in her mind. She'd always liked *The Little Mermaid*. Rational thought faded from her mind.

NOT ONLY WAS the ambulance waiting at the edge of the helipad, but other people were there to greet them. A man and a woman, both wearing aviator sunglasses, stood beside a black SUV with heavily tinted windows. The man wore a dark gray sports jacket and loosely knotted necktie. The tall blonde woman was dressed in a black pantsuit with a white blouse. Her rigid posture and intense attitude made Connor think that she'd been in the military.

They both looked tough, and Connor hoped they'd been sent by the security company he'd contacted. He could use some muscle on his side. While Adam and the other ambulance driver transferred Emily from the chopper to the ambulance, he approached the SUV.

The man in the suit made the introductions. "Connor Gallagher? We're from TST Security. I'm Robert O'Brien, and this here is T. J. Beverly. She's your bodyguard."

Connor shook hands and listened while O'Brien did a snappy run-through of his credentials, which included computer skills and twelve years as an LAPD detective. Beverly's resume was six years as a bodyguard and nine as a marine, honorably discharged.

When Connor led them to the ambulance and introduced Adam, the paramedic bonded immediately with the tall blonde woman. They exchanged salutes. He murmured, *"Semper fi."*

"Oo-rah," Beverly said under her breath.

An interesting development. Connor hadn't suspected that the easygoing Adam was a former marine, but that background made sense. When Adam wasn't skiing, he was still in the business of rescuing people in danger.

Connor paused beside the gurney where Emily lay still and calm—a gentle presence in the midst of all the medical equipment. "This is Emily Benton-Riggs. She's in an induced coma. We're taking her to Crown Hospital, where she'll be under the care of Dr. Troutman."

"I'm going to need a whole lot more information," O'Brien said. "I heard there was a fed assigned to the case."

"As soon as she's settled in her hospital room, I'll fill you in."

"Sure thing," O'Brien said.

Connor's concern was, first and foremost, for Emily's well-being. All this shuffling around couldn't be good for her. He nodded to Adam, giving him the signal to load her into the ambulance and turned back to the team from TST Security. "I have an unusual request. Whenever possible, I want our conversations about the investigation to take place in Emily's presence. She looks like she's unconscious, but she hears more than you'd think. And she wants to keep informed about what's happening."

"Have you had a chance to question her?" O'Brien asked.

"Not really," Connor said. "She was awake for a few minutes but didn't say much. I had the feeling there was something more she wanted to tell me."

When he climbed into the rear of the ambulance, he was

surprised to find Beverly right behind him. She pulled off her sunglasses. "From now on, I stay with Emily."

Though Connor appreciated Beverly's dedication to duty, the back of the ambulance was seriously crowded. "It's okay. I can take care of her."

"No offense, sir. But this is my job. I know what's best."

In usual circumstances, Connor would have ceded control to someone with more expertise, but he was tired and irritable and didn't want to be crammed into the ambulance. "It's only twenty minutes—a half hour at most—to the hospital. What could go wrong?"

"There's potential for a naturally occurring problem, such as a malfunction of the ambulance or a collision." Without breaking a smile, Beverly continued, "If someone is deliberately trying to hurt Emily, this vehicle could be targeted by a sniper. We could be carjacked. There are a number of places along the route that could be rigged with explosives. Do you want to hear more?"

Horrified and fascinated, Connor nodded. "Tell me."

"You can't trust anyone. For example, how much do you know about the ambulance driver and the paramedic?"

The ambulance service had been arranged by the hospital, but Connor got the point. "You're saying that I can't trust anyone."

"Correct," Beverly said. "For your information, we ran computer checks on these men before your arrival. They're clean."

"I'm glad you're working for me."

"In my six years as a bodyguard, I've never lost a client. Never had one injured."

Connor believed her.

On the drive to the hospital, Connor and Adam explained the switch in IV bags to Beverly, who thought that technique seemed too sophisticated when compared to running Emily's car off the road with a truck. Were two different people trying to kill her?

Connor pointed out the similarity. "If either of these attempts had succeeded, her death could have been considered accidental."

"True." She frowned. "You suspect the family. Why?"

"Just last night, Emily inherited a mansion in Aspen, complete with furnishings—millions of dollars' worth of property and artworks."

"That's a motive," Beverly agreed.

In spite of the many dire possibilities, they arrived at the hospital in one piece. While Beverly scanned the unloading area, searching for potential threats, Connor kept his eye on Emily. She looked much the same, beautiful and unconscious.

In the hope that she could hear him, he whispered, "We're almost there. You're doing great."

When he looked toward the hospital staff who took over Emily's care, he noticed a woman in scrubs with straight red hair. She caught his eye and then quickly looked away. He'd seen her before, but couldn't remember when.

Before he had the chance to approach her or to alert Beverly, the monitors attached to Emily changed in rhythm and pitch. The sound touched a nerve in Connor. Panic rushed through him. Noise became a blur. His field of vision zoomed in on Emily.

Her jaw clenched as she threw her head back. Shivering and twitching, a convulsion racked her body. Adam and the other paramedic went into action.

How the hell could this happen? Why? Why now? They'd been so close to safety. Connor had almost allowed himself to relax. He jogged beside the gurney as they charged through the doors into the ER.

Chapter Six

While the ER staff went into high gear, a sense of helplessness paralyzed Connor. He couldn't think, couldn't move. There was nothing he could do but stand and watch as Emily's monitoring equipment fluctuated, flashed warnings and crashed. ER personnel swarmed the gurney, and Beverly inserted herself into the mix, making it her business to limit their numbers.

Connor allowed himself to be shoved out of the way, but he didn't leave. He found a position where he could remain in visual contact with her, just in case she looked for him. It pained him to see her struggle. Her lips drew back from her teeth. Her eyes bulged open. Straining, she stared at the ceiling. Her chest rose and fell in rapid gasps. Her limbs shuddered.

Desperately, he wanted her pain to stop. If he'd been a praying man, he would have dropped to his knees, begged forgiveness for past sins and promised to be a good person henceforth. He ought to be able to do something like that—to make a deal with God. Drawing up contracts was his special expertise. He'd gladly offer the moon and the stars. He'd give anything to make her well.

But life didn't work that way. He didn't know what had triggered her seizure, didn't know how long it would last or how to control her muscle spasms. His only certainty: it wasn't fair. She'd done nothing wrong, didn't deserve this.

Gradually, the episode passed. The tension left her face. Her jaw relaxed. The lines on her forehead smoothed. The sense of urgency faded as she was moved into the intensive care unit to recover. At Beverly's insistence, she was placed in a tight little room with curtains across the front.

A tall, lean man wearing a white lab coat escorted Connor away from her bed and introduced himself as Dr. Charles Troutman. His narrow face, deeply etched with wrinkles, seemed intensely serious, until he smiled. The doctor had an infectious grin.

"Some people call me Fish," Troutman said. "I'd rather you didn't."

"Whatever works for you," Connor replied. "How is she?"

Troutman glanced over his shoulder at the bed. He'd left the curtain open so they could see her. "Emily doesn't appear to be someone who gives up easily. She's a survivor."

Though Connor took comfort in that description, he wanted more. "Give me your medical diagnosis."

"Brain trauma. That's all I can say right now. Our first order of business is to get her stabilized."

Though Connor knew next to nothing about medical procedures, he'd consulted with an East Coast neurologist he often used as an expert witness. "You were highly recommended."

"Thanks." Troutman's smile dimmed. "According to Emily's advanced directives, you're the decision maker when it comes to her treatment. Correct?"

"That's right." Connor had a bad feeling about what might be coming next.

"I want you to be prepared. After examination, we might determine that Emily needs brain surgery, which is, of course, a life-threatening operation. I'll need your authorization for that procedure."

His gut clenched. This responsibility was too much. "Can you guarantee she'll be okay?"

"I wish I could make you an ironclad promise," he said, "but I'm a doctor, not a psychic."

Connor hedged. "You don't need an answer right now."

"No, I don't. But it's wise to consider all possibilities." Troutman gave him another gentle smile. "You look tired, Connor. I've scheduled her examination for four o'clock. You might try to get some sleep before that."

Not a bad idea. If Emily was okay, it wouldn't hurt for him to step away. He slipped behind the curtain into her ICU cubicle and moved into the spot next to the bed railing where he could hold her hand. The machines and monitors played their familiar symphony. Her breathing seemed normal. Her color was good.

He glanced over at Beverly. "I'm going to find a bed and catch a couple hours' sleep."

"Where?"

"It's a hospital. One thing they've got here is beds."

Beverly pulled out her cell phone and tapped in a number. "I'll tell O'Brien to arrange a place for you to rest."

"Don't bother." He didn't even need a bed. As soon as Connor had started thinking about sleep, the exhaustion he'd held at bay nearly overwhelmed him. "I can flop down on one of the couches in the waiting room."

"This isn't about your comfort."

"Then what's it about?"

"Don't be an ass, Connor. You're in danger."

What the hell was she talking about? "Me?"

"I'll put it bluntly. Somebody wants Emily dead, and you're in the way."

Connor hadn't thought of himself as being vulnerable, but Beverly was right. "I'll do things your way."

"Damn right you will."

"I didn't even know O'Brien was at the hospital."

"He's been busy on his computer. We need background checks on all the personnel who have contact with Emily. It's too easy to slip into a pair of scrubs and get into a hospital. If they haven't been cleared, then don't get close."

Connor appreciated the hypervigilance. Hiring this security company was probably the smartest move he'd ever made. While they were in charge, nothing bad would happen to Emily or to him. Not on their watch.

IN THE MEDICAL building adjoining the hospital, O'Brien directed him to a private office with a door that locked. Better yet, there was a back room with a cot and a bathroom with a shower.

Connor got comfortable on the bed. He should have been asleep in a minute. Instead, his brain was wide-awake, doing mental calisthenics as he considered the central question: Why had someone tried to kill her?

Depriving her of her inheritance from Jamison made a solid motive, but it seemed too obvious, too easy. No matter what he thought of the Riggs family, they weren't idiots. They had to know they were suspects. If the truck that had run her off the road was found, the driver would be tied to the crime. For a moment, Connor was tempted to bolt from the cot and put in a call to Sandoval for an update on his investigation. Not now. He needed to sleep—to reboot and refresh his thinking.

Breathing deeply, he replayed what had happened from the moment she'd called him in New York until a few moments ago. So far, Connor was okay with the major decisions he'd made. Getting her away from Aspen was smart. His security team was top-notch. Troutman seemed competent.

Doubt arose when Connor considered what came next. He might have to give the green light on her brain surgery, a dangerous operation. How could he do that? So much could go wrong. He held Emily's future in his hands. If he made the wrong call, she might die or be paralyzed for life or lose her memory or any number of other negative outcomes. The blame would be laid at his doorstep. Somehow, he had to get this right.

Still not comfortable, he shifted position on the cot. In his work, he was accustomed to taking risks into account and advising people about life-changing decisions. But those people weren't Emily. What was best for her? If she was awake and alert, would she want the surgery?

There were other decisions as well, a lot of balls in the air. When the medical procedures were over and done, she was going to need help. In the worst-case scenario, she might never awaken from the coma and would require full-time nursing. A shiver stiffened the hairs on his forearms. He hated to think of Emily—a vivacious, energetic woman—being physically limited. Whatever she needed, he'd arrange for her. And he'd replace her car. And her art gallery would need overseeing.

None of those tasks were as important as nailing the person who was responsible for the three attacks. The first had been on the road. The second was on the Flight For Life chopper when her sedation had been altered. And now the seizure. It had to be connected to the other two attempts and had scared the hell out of Connor.

Her survival was his number one concern.

There were a million reasons why he wanted her to recover. Though they'd been friends for years, there had always been a chasm between them. She'd been his best friend's wife, and Connor had no right to interfere with that relationship. Now that barrier was gone. Actually, she'd been divorced for months, and he could have made his move sooner. He'd been on the verge of contacting her when Jamison died. That set him back. But not again, nothing else would stand in his way. Finally, he could act on the physical attraction that had always simmered between them.

He thought about gathering her into his arms and kissing her, gently at first and then harder while he stroked her lightly freckled shoulders and combed his fingers through her hair. He'd seen her in a bikini and loved her breasts—they weren't too big, but round and full. When he and Emily finally rolled into bed together, he didn't think she'd need coaxing. She wanted him, maybe not as much as he wanted her, but enough. He imagined her smooth, slender legs entwined with his. Her firm torso would rub against his chest. For years, he'd dreamed of these sweet, sensual moments.

His sleep on the cot was filled with fantastic dreams. It felt like only a minute had passed when O'Brien tapped his shoulder and announced, "Fish is almost ready to start the neurological exam."

"Fish?"

"Troutman," O'Brien clarified. "It's almost four."

Connor had been asleep for five hours. "Coffee?"

"Yeah, I'll grab some. Why don't you take a shower?"

Connor dragged himself from the cot to the small bathroom with the even smaller shower. This was definitely a no-frills cleanup, but the steaming hot water felt deluxe. He stuck his face under the showerhead and washed away the grime and sweat.

While sleeping, his brain had been super productive. Not only had he engaged in wild, intense fantasies about sex with Emily but he'd also remembered something Jamison had mentioned before he got sick.

The timing of his last face-to-face meeting with Jamison had been odd. A few weeks after the divorce was final, Jamison had showed up at Connor's office, saying that he was in the neighborhood and they should have a drink. They hadn't been close for some time, but he went along for old times' sake. Trying to avoid a drawn-out conversation at a bar, Connor had opted for coffee. Their conversation had turned to Emily.

"The divorce is almost final," Jamison had said. "Good news for you."

Guardedly, Connor had replied, "I'm not sure what you mean."

"You've always had the hots for my wife and—"

"Ex-wife," Connor had corrected.

Jamison had glared at him over the rim of his coffee mug. "You can make your move, buddy boy. Plead your case. With your working-class background, you have more in common with her than I ever did."

He'd almost sounded jealous, but Connor hadn't credited his former friend with that level of sensitivity. Jamison had betrayed and disrespected Emily. He hadn't deserved her. "I don't need your permission."

"Let me give you a little warning. She thinks she's done with me, but she's not. I'm still calling the shots." He'd looked around the coffee shop. "They'd all do well to remember that. I hold the purse strings. I'm in charge."

At the time, Connor had chalked up Jamison's thinly veiled threat to a shout-out from his ego, letting Connor know that he had a hold on Emily. But maybe the warning had had a wider implication. Jamison's reference to purse strings might have applied to the property in Aspen, or it might be part of the FBI investigation undertaken after Jamison's death by Agent Wellborn.

After his shower, Connor slipped into a fresh shirt that O'Brien was considerate enough to bring for him. He nodded to the security man. "Thanks for the change of clothes."

"I learned to carry extra shirts when I was LAPD." He looked up from his tablet computer. "There's nothing worse than smelling your own stink, especially when there's blood."

"Did I have bloodstains on my shirt?"

"You rescued Emily from a car wreck. I'm guessing the blood belonged to her."

It had been one hell of a day, not even twenty-four hours. When he took a good, hard look at his leather jacket, Connor saw it was in serious need of dry cleaning. "What are you searching for on the computer?"

"Filling in background on the Riggs family and poking around into Jamison's finances—the stuff that has Wellborn involved."

"The FBI couldn't dig up anything on him," Connor said.

"Which doesn't mean it's not there."

"Have you been in touch with Sandoval?"

"He's a good man, doing the best he can. Most of his day was spent by dragging her Hyundai up the cliff."

"What about the truck?" Connor asked.

"He found black paint chips stuck on the rear fender, suggesting that she was hit and forced off the road. He put out an alert to all the local law enforcement and vehicle repair places. Nobody saw the truck."

Connor followed him through the medical building and into the hospital. On the far end of the first floor, they entered a suite of offices, examination rooms and operating theaters for the neurology department. He and O'Brien looked through an observation window at a large room with dozens of machines with dials, gauges and screens.

Still unconscious, Emily sat in a chair that resembled a recliner. Her head was immobilized with a contraption that reminded him of headgear his youngest sister had worn when she had braces. Emily's good arm was strapped down. Like a kick-ass guardian angel, Beverly kept watch, hovering near the door. Troutman and three other doctors buzzed around the room, hooking and unhooking various pieces of equipment. When Troutman spotted Connor in the window, he came out to talk to him.

"The exam is going very well," he said. "She's already undergone a series of X-rays and MRIs. The swelling on her brain has gone down. We found no clots, blockages or aneurysms. Also—I can't stress how positive this is—she has no tumors."

"What about the seizure? Could she have been attacked again?"

"I can't say for sure, but we'll be doing blood tests. My best guess is that she had a reaction to other medication, perhaps the sedative. I see no indication that she'll have another event."

All this positive news made Connor suspicious. Things were going too perfectly. Gazing into the examination room, he looked for signals of impending disaster. "And what are you doing now?"

"A thorough analysis of her brain activity. Would you like a detailed explanation?"

"Give it to me in layman's terms."

"So far, everything is within normal range. She might have some short-term memory loss, might need some physical rehab, but there doesn't appear to be any serious damage."

"No need for an operation?" Connor held his breath, waiting for the answer.

"None." Troutman charmed him with a smile. "We don't need to keep her in a coma anymore. As a matter of fact, it's better if she's awake for some of our testing. We're bringing her around right now."

"You're waking her up?"

"That's right."

Connor had to restrain himself before he gave Troutman a high five. This was the best news ever. Emily was coming back to him.

O'Brien spoke up. "I've got a question, Doc. How come the people in the examination room aren't wearing masks and operating clothes?"

"These examinations are external. We're wearing scrubs because they're as comfortable as pajamas and these exams take a long time. As you can see, your friend Beverly didn't change from her street clothes."

"Is it okay if I come into the room?" Connor said.

Troutman hesitated for a moment before he nodded. "You need to be quiet and stay out of the way."

"You've got my word."

He tiptoed into the room behind Troutman and stood beside Beverly. Troutman didn't bother to introduce him as he rejoined his colleagues, which didn't matter in the least to Connor. He was focused—100 percent—on Emily. He noticed a slight movement of her right foot inside a heavy sock. The fingers of her right hand twitched.

She was waking up, coming back to him.

Not more than ten minutes later, he watched in awe as her eyelids fluttered. With a gasp, she opened her eyes, looked directly at him.

Desperately, he wanted to speak, to tell her that everything was taken care of. He wanted to cross the room in a single bound and kiss her again.

Her lips were moving. She was trying to talk.

Though he'd promised not to get in the way, Connor took a step toward her. He spoke softly. "What is it, Emily? What do you want to say?"

Her voice was little more than a whisper. "Find Kate Sylvester."

Chapter Seven

Seated in the medical version of a recliner chair, Emily struggled to be alert and coherent, and could only mumble a few odd words. *Find Kate Sylvester.* Explaining Kate's involvement would take an effort that was, for the moment, beyond Emily's capability. At least she'd alerted Connor to the problem.

Though her vision was hazy, she watched as he came closer. She blinked, trying to bring him into sharp focus. The lighting in this room—an examination room?—was intense, and she could see every detail of his face from the character lines lightly etched across his forehead to the stubble outlining his jaw. His dark eyes compelled her to gaze into their depths and find comfort. When he captured her right hand in his grasp, her heart took a little hop. She tried to turn toward him but found herself unable to move her head.

His smooth baritone cut through the other voices and the mechanical sounds of monitors and other equipment. "It's good to have you back, Emily. I missed you."

"Me, too."

"I'm guessing that you want to get up and run around."

"Good guess."

"You'll have to wait awhile longer. These medical people have questions they need to ask and more tests to run."

Testing was okay, but she wanted to tell him that she did not, under any circumstances, want to be put back into a coma, not that she was in a position to make demands. "What questions?"

"Do you remember when we talked about Dr. Troutman?"

"Fish," she said.

A tall, pleasant-looking, older man in turquoise scrubs and a white lab coat stepped into her field of vision. "If *Fish* works for you, I'll answer to that name."

"Nice Fish."

Her mouth felt like she was grinning, but she wasn't sure what her muscles were actually doing. Apart from an occasional twinge, she seemed disconnected from her physical self. The only real sensation came from Connor's gentle pressure on her fingers.

When Fish asked him to move away, she tightened her grip and protested, "No."

"Emily, I know you've had a rough time," the doctor said, "but I'm in charge. You need to do as I say."

"Please, Fish. I just need a minute with Connor."

Reluctantly, he took a step back. "Make it quick."

Connor leaned down. "Is there something you need to say?"

"About Kate." Concentrating hard, she forced herself to put together a sentence. "I saw her when I was being brought out of the ambulance. She was there."

Connor swore under his breath. "She has red hair, doesn't she?"

"Yes."

"I saw her, too. At the time, I didn't know who she was, but she was there. She's here." He straightened up. "I'll make sure she doesn't get close to you again. Right now, you need to cooperate with the doctor."

"Don't leave me, Connor."

"I'll stay nearby."

He went across the room and talked to a man with a buzz cut and square shoulders. She'd seen this man before. Somehow, she knew he was a friend.

The doctor started in with his coordination and reflex questions, having her look to the right, then to the left. Upon his instruction, she wiggled her toes and fingers. Though these seemed like basic kindergarten exercises, she was proud of her success. When she glanced toward Connor, his expression was encouraging and kind without being patronizing.

The clouds of confusion that had obscured her thinking faded and gradually disappeared. She was nearly awake. The world began to make sense to her. The downside of regaining consciousness was the realization that her body had been badly injured. When she took a deep breath, her ribs ached. Her left arm was immobilized from biceps to fingertips in a massive cast, and the lower portion of her left leg was encased in a plastic boot.

She interrupted Fish to ask, "My leg. Is it broken?"

"According to your chart, you have a sprained ankle."

"Can I walk?"

He gave her a steady, assessing look. "Why do you ask?"

"I need to get out of the hospital so I can figure out who's trying to kill me."

His grin was charming. "You're joking."

"Am I laughing?"

"In due time, Emily, you'll recover."

"It needs to be sooner than later." She didn't know how long she'd been out of commission. Whether it had been a week or only a few hours, she needed to get in gear and investigate before all the clues dried up and the trail that led to the truth went cold. "What time is it? As soon as we're done here, I could get started."

The doctor glanced toward Connor. "You want to handle this?"

Connor stepped up, and her spirits lifted. Surely, he'd understand, and he'd be able to explain to the doctor. "Tell Fish," she said. "Tell him that I need to go after the bad guys."

"Here's the deal, Emily. There's a full-scale investigation underway with a deputy in the mountains and an agent from the FBI. Also, I hired a private detective. And I want you to meet Beverly." He gestured toward the tall woman who stood at the door. "She's your full-time bodyguard. For now, we need to let them do their jobs."

While she'd been unconscious, Connor had covered the bases. Skilled people were solving the crime, and she was protected. Though she was grateful, she didn't intend to sit quietly in the corner and watch.

While she was with Jamison, he'd always told her to sit back and relax because he had taken care of everything. Following that particular direction hadn't turned out well for her, and she didn't want to be a bystander anymore. This was her life. She'd been threatened and needed to take part in the investigation, to point them in the right direction. "There are things I know that nobody else does. That's why they're coming after me."

"I believe you," he said. "And you'll be able to investigate after you recover. You survived one hell of a crash."

"My car?"

"Totaled."

"That's enough," Dr. Fish said as he nudged Connor toward the door. "Emily, I need for you to pay attention to me."

"Please don't put me back into a coma." Though tired, she didn't want to sleep anymore. "I've got to stay awake."

"So far, your progress is encouraging," he said. "After we're done here, we should be able to move you from ICU into a regular room. Maybe we can bring you some food."

An enchilada with guac on the side. The thought of melted cheese and mashed avocados made her mouth water, even though she doubted that the hospital kitchen would be able to whip up spicy food. She was definitely hungry. Anything would taste good.

Before they got back to the tests, she heard a commotion at the door. Angry voices argued with each other. She couldn't see clearly but thought there was some shoving.

Dr. Fish appeared to be an extremely patient man, but this was the last straw. He pivoted toward the door and snapped, "What the hell is going on?"

"It's me. It's Phillip."

"Phillip Riggs," she mumbled under her breath. He had a lot of nerve showing up here. Typical of the overprivileged Riggs family, he thought it was okay for him to barge into a room where she was undergoing a medical procedure. She ought to have her bodyguard throw him out on his ass, but his sudden arrival made her curious. "What are you doing here?"

"I was worried about you."

Liar! They'd never been close. More the opposite, he spent all his time skiing and sneered at her for not being interested in a sport she'd never been able to afford when she was growing up in Denver. Patricia's younger brother was more childish than any grown man had a right to be. "Give me another reason."

Fish stepped between them. "This is unacceptable. Get out."

"Wait," she said. "Let him answer. Why are you here, Phillip? Is it about the will?"

"Not now," Fish said. "When I've finished my examination, you can play detective, but this is my facility, and I'm in charge."

"Yes, sir," Beverly said. "I'll remove Phillip and hold him until he can be interrogated."

"But I drove all the way down from Aspen," Phillip said. "If I can just get a signature from Emily, I'll be on my way."

The bodyguard muscled Phillip out the door with a comment about hospital security and the cop who was stationed at the front entrance. Emily was glad to see that Connor had stayed behind to be with her. She looked up at the doctor and said, "I'm sorry."

"Let's finish up here."

Though anxious to find out what was going on with Phillip, Emily did her best to behave like a model patient, while Fish and his team went through more tests and monitoring. At one point, she was rewarded by having the headgear removed and the other restraints that held her in place unfastened. Her tension relaxed. She lifted her right arm—just because she could—and flexed her fingers. What did Phillip want her to sign?

He was nuts if he thought she would help him out. Emily didn't consider herself to be a vindictive person, but she wasn't inclined to do any favors for the Riggs family.

Vaguely aware of her surroundings, she was loaded onto a gurney and moved from the examination room to another location and then another. She closed her eyes and rested while she was transported on the medical version of a magic carpet ride. Visions of Aladdin danced at the edge of her consciousness, but she didn't allow herself to dive into a full-blown *Arabian Nights* fantasy. Emily needed to be alert.

Every time she looked up, Connor was there, hovering at her side. He didn't look like Aladdin, and there was no way she could imagine him wearing flowing pants and shoes with turned-up toes. But he was clearly her hero.

Throughout all her troubles and her divorce, Connor had provided the shoulder for her to lean against. He'd held her hand. Most of all, he'd listened. Even though Jamison had been his best friend, Connor had sided with her. Before she drifted off to sleep, she reminded herself to tell him about the secret account Kate had mentioned in Aspen.

EMILY WAS SITUATED in a private room on the fifth floor with a partial view of the mountains west of town, and she was sleeping. Connor stood by her bed and gazed down at her. Most of the monitoring equipment had been removed. Apart from the obvious casts, she looked mostly normal. Though the wound on the left side of her forehead near her hairline was stitched and the swelling had gone down, her left eye was still black-and-blue.

His preference would have been to talk to Phillip himself and send the little jerk back to Aspen, but Connor knew Emily would be furious if he deprived her of an opportunity to be part of the investigation. She was so adamant about Kate Sylvester, who had managed to blend in by wearing scrubs. What was the Wall Street broker up to?

Beverly and O'Brien had been in the hallway talking. They returned to the room together, and O'Brien spoke up. "I'm wasting my time in Denver. I should be in Aspen, following up with Sandoval and talking to the Riggs family."

Connor shuddered at the thought. "Not a fun job."

O'Brien shrugged. "Somebody's got to do it. Before I

head out to the mountains, I wanted to check out Emily's house for clues."

"I'll come with you."

Troutman wanted to keep Emily in the hospital for observation and physical therapy with her sprained ankle. He'd suggested picking up some of her clothing from home—comfortable stuff, like pajamas and sweat suits. "When she wakes up, I'll find out where she keeps the spare keys," said Connor.

"Or I can pick the lock," O'Brien offered.

"That works for me. Also, I'd like to get my hands on a weapon."

Connor noticed when O'Brien and Beverly exchanged a glance. Was it that obvious that he wasn't a marksman? "Is there a problem?"

"We'd need to get you a concealed carry permit," Beverly said. "Do you know how to handle a firearm?"

"My cousin is a cop in Queens. I've fired a Glock before, but you're right," Connor said. "I'd appreciate if you could take me to a shooting range for practice."

A small voice rose from the hospital bed. "Me, too."

Connor went to her side. "What is it, Emily?"

She aimed her forefinger at him and fired an imaginary shot with her thumb. "I could use some time on a practice range."

He wasn't sure if the world was ready for Emily Benton-Riggs, armed and dangerous. But he decided it was best if he humored her. "Sure thing."

After a bit of fumbling around, they adjusted her bed so she was sitting up. Her blue eyes were bright. Her smile was surprisingly alert as she greeted Beverly and O'Brien.

"I'm ready," she said. "Let's get Phillip Riggs in here."

Connor didn't bother arguing. He glanced at Beverly and asked, "Where did you take the little weasel?"

"I left him in a waiting area and told him I'd call if Emily wanted to see him."

"And I do," she said.

She whipped out her phone. "I'm on it."

While Beverly made the call, Emily said to Connor, "My spare house key is hidden under the plastic garden gnome on the porch. Since you're going by the house, I'd really like for you to bring me the blue bathrobe and the moisturizing lotion in the pink container."

Under his breath, O'Brien commented, "Hard to believe she heard us talking. That lady has a great set of ears."

"My vision is pretty good, too."

"You're an art dealer," Connor said. "You've got to be able to see."

"Finding a great piece of art requires more than an ability to discern brushstrokes," she said. "It's more about the emotions evoked. Art can make you cry or laugh or shrink inside yourself to find the truth. There's a woman I'm working with who's a genius. I can't wait to launch her onto the scene in New York."

Emily's commentary on the world was something Connor had always enjoyed. With very little provocation, she could go on and on—a talent she attributed to being an only child who didn't have siblings to babble with when she was young. The words had been building up since she was a baby, and she welcomed any opportunity to let down the floodgates and talk.

Her cheerful demeanor transformed as soon as Phillip stepped into the room. He gave her a sheepish grin, pushed his sun-streaked brown hair off his forehead and bobbed his head. "Hey, Emily, it's good to see you sitting up."

She wasted no time getting to the point. "Why are you here?"

"I don't know much about finances." He almost sounded

proud of his ignorance. "But I'm supposed to get your signature. Aunt Glenda said we needed to make sure the inheritance was all figured out. On account of you not having any living relatives and the property might get stuck in probate or something."

Emily looked toward Connor. "What's he trying to say?"

He cut to the venal truth. "He wants you to sign a legal document that would give him possession of the house in Aspen in the case of your death."

Phillip winced. "I didn't want to be blunt about the whole dying thing."

"Yeah, you're a real sensitive guy." Connor didn't know the exact terms of the will but could guess at the provisions that Jamison would have employed. "If Emily had died before she had the deed to the house, I'll bet the property reverted to his estate and, therefore, went to whoever inherited the bulk."

"That's what Jamison would have wanted."

"You can tell Aunt Glenda that the inheritance is safe from the probate courts. Emily and I intend to update her will. Isn't that right?"

"Absolutely." She beamed a smile at Phillip. "Everything I own goes to my executor, Connor Gallagher."

Phillip stammered, "B-b-but if you don't get the deed transferred, the will won't be valid. Right?"

"Don't you worry," Connor said. "I'll file the paperwork first thing tomorrow morning."

"You can't do that. You can't cheat me out of my property. Forget it." His stumbling confusion turned into rage. Roughly, he shoved Connor's shoulder. "That house is mine. I took care of it for years."

"Wrong again, Philly."

"You can't make me move." He threw a clumsy jab that went wide.

Connor knew better than to retaliate but couldn't stop himself from shoving hard enough to rock Phillip back on his heels. "You'll be lucky if moving out is your only problem."

Phillip sneered. "What's that supposed to mean?"

"It's suspicious," Connor said. "Emily's car is forced off the road. She almost dies. On the very next day, you show up with documentation for what needs to happen if she's dead. It almost seems planned. When did you have those papers drawn up?"

Phillip made a sharp pivot and stalked out the door.

Chapter Eight

The next morning, Emily took an awkward shower, sitting on a chair with her cast wrapped in plastic. An aide washed her hair. A blow-dry was out of the question, which was probably for the best. When she caught sight of her bruised face in the mirror, she figured that no amount of hairstyling was going to make her look cute. The swelling around her eye had faded to dull mauve, and there was a bruise on her jawbone that she hadn't noticed before. Still, she didn't feel too bad—probably a result of pain meds and the pleasure of exchanging her hospital gown for a pair of lightweight pink pajamas that Connor and O'Brien had brought from her house.

Sitting up in the hospital bed, she sipped a cup of herbal tea from the downstairs coffee shop and admired the get-well bouquet of orange daisies and yellow roses from Connor. The man himself sat beside her bed, nursing a cup of coffee. He'd set up his laptop on a table with wheels and was scanning the screen. Though he'd assured her that his office could manage without him for a couple of weeks, she felt guilty for taking him away from work.

"Phillip doesn't seem like the type," she said. "He's a jerk and a spoiled brat. But a murderer? I don't think he's got the nerve."

"It doesn't take courage or smarts to be a stone-cold killer."

"I guess not." She liked the way Connor picked up on her rambling train of thought without reason or explanation. Clearly, they were on the same wavelength.

"Running your car off the road sounds like the kind of dumb plan Phillip would come up with."

She nodded. "True."

"And he has plenty of idiot friends with trucks who he could talk into ramming your car." Connor closed his computer and gave her a smile. "Change of subject. I like your hair."

"You're kidding." She self-consciously tugged at the chin-length bob that would have looked much better if she'd been able to operate a blow-dryer.

"You've got more blond streaks than when you lived in Manhattan. The Colorado sun is good for you."

"It's a healthy lifestyle…if nobody is trying to kill you. Tell me more about Phillip."

He leaned on the railing beside her bed. "He has more to gain than anybody else. With you out of the way, he might get his greedy paws on the house he's been living in, not to mention the furnishings and the artwork."

She scoffed. "What a waste! He knows nothing about art, can't tell a Picasso from a doodle by a second grader."

"Sometimes," Connor said with a wink, "neither can I."

She didn't mean to be snobby, but she'd spent years studying art. It hurt her when true genius wasn't properly appreciated and cared for. While married to Jamison, she'd spent a lot of time and effort curating their art collection and had managed to procure a number of world-famous works. Those works should be shared with people who'd enjoy them. "When all the terms of the will are satisfied, I want to loan several pieces to the Denver Art Museum."

"Phillip will hate that."

"He might change his mind if I can get Aunt Glenda on my side."

"And how are you going to perform that miracle?"

Glenda had hated her from the moment they met. The older woman considered Emily to be common and not worthy of Jamison. However, Glenda would be delighted to promote the Riggs family name. "I'll tell her that the art on loan will have a plaque and be designated as part of the Jamison Riggs collection."

"Excellent plan! If you didn't have that arm in a cast, I'd give you a high five."

Though their buddy-buddy relationship felt comfortable and safe, she wanted more from Connor than high fives and slaps on the back. She tilted her chin toward him and pointed to her cheek. "How about a kiss?"

"Gladly."

When he leaned in close, she turned her head. No doubt, his intention had been to give her a friendly peck, but their lips met. He didn't move away. His mouth pressed firmly against hers, and he deepened the kiss, pushing her lips apart and penetrating with his tongue. A sizzle spread through her body. She wanted to take it further, but they weren't alone. Beverly stood guard by the door, and she heard people moving and talking in the hallway.

Reluctant to separate from him, her tongue tangled with his. She tasted the slick interior of his mouth. Though their bodies weren't touching, his nearness aroused her. Outer distractions faded into nothingness as she surrendered to the fiery chemistry between them.

A knock on the door interrupted their kiss. Beverly answered, allowing Dr. Fish and two other medical people in white lab coats to enter. After Fish greeted Connor, he gave her a long, steady look and asked, "How are you feeling?"

After that kiss, her blood pressure had to be up. Her heart fluttered. Her breath came in excited little gasps, and she suspected that she was blushing. "I'm good."

"You seem to be tense."

"Not a surprise, considering that my former relatives are trying to kill me." She noticed that Fish's companions exchanged a disbelieving glance. They were probably wondering if they needed to call in a psychiatric consultant. "How are you doing, Fish?"

"A little bird told me that you own an art gallery," he said. "I'd like to buy a piece for my office, something by a local artist."

"I have just the thing. It's from a retired guy who paints incredible landscapes of Grand Lake. We might even be able to talk him into adding a leaping trout."

"Perfect." He introduced the two people who accompanied him. One was studying neurology with Fish. "And Dr. Lisa Parris is here to take a look at your broken arm, the cracked ribs and the sprained ankle."

"Pleased to meet you, Dr. Parris." When Emily turned in the bed to shake her hand, she experienced a stab of pain from her ribs but forced herself not to wince. "How soon can I get out of the hospital and go home?"

"That depends." With her bouncy ponytail and lack of makeup, Dr. Parris looked so young that even Emily—who was only thirty—wondered about her level of experience. The doctor pushed her glasses up on her nose and said, "Before I can release you, I'll need to look at more X-rays, and you'll have an evaluation from a physical therapist."

"Dr. Parris was a PT for eight years," Fish said. "There's nobody better for getting you back on your feet."

Which was exactly what Emily wanted. "When do we get started?"

"Not so fast." Fish stepped up. "I get first crack."

She listened with half an ear as he rattled off a series of MRIs and scans and so forth that he and his associates would be using on her brain. Glad to be alive, she didn't complain but was anxious to move on. All of this medical effort wouldn't be worth much if someone managed to kill her.

When Fish wrapped up, she said, "If possible, I'd prefer using a wheelchair instead of a gurney to get transferred from one test to the next."

"Shouldn't be a problem," Parris said. "If you'd be more comfortable, we can move you into this recliner chair right now."

Emily threw off the covers. With the cast, her left arm had limited mobility, and she was grateful for the support from Parris and Fish as she stood. Though the plastic boot protected her sprained ankle, Emily avoided putting weight on it. Hobbling, she made it into the chair where she tried to relax her sore muscles.

After the others departed, she looked up at Connor and let out a sigh. "Everything hurts."

"Should I call the nurse? Get more pain meds?"

"Don't want them." After her time in the induced coma, she was willing to put up with the natural aches and pains. "I'll be okay. It's just that moving around is harder than I thought. The bandages around my ribs are as tight as a corset."

"Can I get you anything?"

"I wish I could wear my blue bathrobe, but there's no way the sleeve will fit over my cast."

"We could cut off the sleeve."

"But I love the robe." She rested her back against the recliner. "It's a shame I can't wear it, especially after you and O'Brien went to so much trouble to get it for me."

"Right." He went across the room to pick up his coffee cup.

"You never told me," she said. "Did you have any trouble getting in?"

"Not a problem. We found the key under the gnome."

When he raised his coffee cup to hide his expression, she had the distinct impression that he wasn't telling her everything. "I guess I should take better care of my home security."

"You need an alarm system," he said. "I already made a note."

She couldn't tell if he was being cagey or if she was too suspicious. "What did you think of my house?"

"It's nice."

Nice? Was that the best description he could come up with? She loved her little two-bedroom cottage. Though the neighborhood was in the middle of the city, the trees around her house—peach, pine and Russian olive—created an aura of privacy. Her garden displayed a bevy of bright pansies and late-blooming roses. She'd replaced two of the front windows with reclaimed stained glass. It was adorable. "Is that all you have to say?"

"I like your giant claw-foot bathtub. Three people could swim laps in there."

Before she could question him further, the physical therapist bounced into the room and ran through a series of exercises Emily could do without leaving the chair or the bed. Working together, they maneuvered her into a wheelchair. And she was whisked away, still wondering if Connor was being evasive.

HE DIDN'T LIKE keeping secrets from her, but Connor feared her reaction to the truth. Late last night when he and O'Brien had entered her house, they found the place ransacked. The only real damage had appeared to be a broken windowpane in the back door where the intruder had reached inside to turn the handle. The details of the search had told a tale to former LAPD detective O'Brien, who had immediately contacted the local police so they could look for fingerprints and other forensic clues.

"But don't get your hopes up," O'Brien had warned him. "Everybody knows enough to wear gloves, and this was a careful, calculated search."

Connor hadn't thought the intruder had been particularly cautious. In the kitchen, plates and glasses had been taken off the shelves. In the upstairs master bedroom, drawers had been pulled open and the contents of the jewelry box dumped on the dresser. "You call this careful?"

"No unnecessary destruction. The intruder wasn't tearing up the place for revenge. And the point of the break-in wasn't burglary. Most of her electronics and jewelry are still here."

"The sparkly stuff in the bedroom is costume jewelry." He knew that Emily had wasted no time in selling the expensive jewelry that Jamison had given her. She hadn't wanted reminders of her marriage. "It's probably not worth much."

In the home office on the first floor, O'Brien had pointed out details. "Here's where the search focused. You got files strewn across the floor. And paintings lifted off the walls, probably looking for a wall safe. Over there on the desk, there's an open space."

"And a hookup for a laptop," he'd said.

"But no computer." O'Brien had paced around the room, being careful not to touch anything. "Here's what I think. The intruder was looking for something small, like a computer flash drive or a code number. Anything come to mind?"

Connor had drawn a blank. "I don't know."

"How about an engagement ring?" O'Brien had asked. "A big shot like Riggs probably spent a small fortune on a giant diamond."

"She doesn't wear it. If she still has it, she probably keeps it in a safe-deposit box."

"That's what I need to hear," O'Brien had announced triumphantly. "A safe-deposit box requires a key and an access code. Who knows what else could be stashed in there? This break-in and search could be about finding that number."

Connor hadn't been convinced last night, and he was equally skeptical this morning. His primary suspects were the Riggs family, and they were too rich to bother with an engagement ring. As for other documents, he was familiar with Emily's business dealings and doubted that she'd been hiding financial secrets from him. Her late, great ex-husband was another story. Jamison had frequently skirted legal boundaries in his investment business.

Outside the hospital X-ray room, Connor and Beverly sat in a waiting area while Emily was treated. He thumbed through a magazine that featured healthy recipes. As usual, Beverly was silent.

Connor cleared his throat. "I should put through a call to O'Brien."

"Suit yourself," Beverly said. "He'll contact us if he has anything to report."

Connor knew that O'Brien was busy with the local cops, checking alibis for Phillip and whoever he had brought with him into town. Maybe Phillip had connected with Kate. Plus, O'Brien would follow up with Sandoval and make sure the rest of the Riggs family had stayed in Aspen last night. "I'm not complaining, but I'm anxious to get results."

Beverly gave a quick nod of acknowledgment.

"O'Brien is doing a good job. So are you." He fidgeted. "I want to take a more active part in the investigation."

She raised her eyebrows and pursed her lips. There was no need for her to speak. He knew what she was implying.

"I know," he said. "I sound like Emily."

"You have your assignment."

It was supposed to be Connor's job to talk to Emily and see if she knew what the intruder had been searching for. He was reluctant, scared that as soon as Emily heard that her cute little house had been broken into, she'd want to go and see for herself. Somehow, he had to discourage her. In the hospital, she was relatively safe.

Beverly stepped away from the waiting area to take a phone call. Her posture was erect, and her movements crisp. Last night, she'd taken a break, using another bodyguard to fill in for her, so she wouldn't get too tired to do her job. When she returned and sat beside him, she said, "You have to tell her about the intruder. The cops are almost done, and TST Security is standing by. We're ready to install the new locks and a top-of-the-line alarm system, but we've got a problem. Either we replace the back door or repair it. That should be Emily's decision."

"I meant to tell her first thing this morning."

"But you didn't."

"As soon as she hears about somebody breaking into her house, she'll bust out of the hospital. There'll be no stopping her."

"That's what I'd do," Beverly said. "A break-in is personal. It's a violation."

Beverly was a former gunnery sergeant in the Marine Corps. She could take care of herself, but Emily was vulnerable, untrained in self-defense. "What if the killer is waiting for her to show up? Even if her doctors agree to release her, it's not safe."

"It's unlikely for the intruder to hang around while the cops are there," Beverly said. "But I agree with you. Less exposure is better."

He was glad they were on the same page. T. J. Beverly was careful to maintain a cool, professional distance, but Connor sensed a budding friendship between them. "Are you any closer to getting me a gun? If the intruder had been at the house last night, I could have used a weapon."

"It's not going to happen, Connor. The best I can do for you is a stun gun."

"I'm okay with that."

Any advice he could get when it came to protecting himself and Emily was welcome. Though he didn't have formal training in self-defense and never went looking for trouble, he'd grown up in a tough neighborhood. Other guys told him that he was a good man to have on your side in a barroom brawl.

"A suggestion," Beverly said. "Tell Emily what's going on with her house as soon as you get a chance. Otherwise, she'll never trust you."

"I'm not sure how much she trusts me now."

She hadn't hesitated to sign over the authority to make life-and-death medical decisions for her, but he didn't think she'd blindly trust him to pick out a new door for her house. During the months when she'd talked to him about her disintegrating marriage, she'd listened to his opinions but had done whatever the hell she wanted. The moment when he really felt her lack of confidence in his advice came when he offered her a place to stay in New York, namely in the guest room at his apartment. Instead, she'd packed up and moved to Denver.

When Emily was wheeled out of the X-ray room, Connor and Beverly trailed her through the corridors to her room. He mentally rehearsed what he was going to say to her about the intruder. Gradually, he'd reveal what had happened. He'd hold her hand. Maybe he ought to arrange for lunch to be delivered. She was easier to handle when her belly was full.

In her room, Special Agent Wellborn was waiting. He'd changed from jeans into a suit and tie but still wore the crocodile cowboy boots. The guy was a Manhattan fashionista, but his posture and bearing echoed Beverly's style. There was a mutual respect and recognition, almost as though they were wearing uniforms. When they shook hands, he saw the bond between them.

Wellborn approached Emily in her wheelchair. "It's nice to actually meet you. The last time I was in your hospital room, we weren't formally introduced."

"You're with the FBI, right?"

"Yes."

"You were part of the investigation into my ex-husband's death."

Connor heard the edginess in her tone. Though she was obviously tired, with her shoulders slumped and her hands folded listlessly in her lap, she wasn't ready to accept her exhaustion and sleep.

Politely, Wellborn answered, "I'm with the White-Collar Crime Unit. We looked into the death of Jamison Riggs."

"You questioned me," she said.

"Yes."

"And I talked to one of your colleagues on the phone," she said. "He drew a couple of obvious conclusions. Number one was that I hadn't spent any time with my ex-husband in months and didn't have the opportunity to poison him—if, in fact, he was poisoned. Number two, I wasn't in love with him anymore."

They were entering dangerous emotional territory, and

Connor wanted to warn Wellborn to tread lightly, but there was no need. This federal agent was smooth.

"I wish I'd had the opportunity to interview you in depth. Working together, we might have come to more useful deductions. I'm inclined to believe the attacks on you are connected to Jamison's death. I believe you've spoken to Kate Sylvester."

"I have."

"Are you feeling well enough to talk about what happened at your house?"

She sat up a bit straighter in her wheelchair. "My house?"

"The intruder was searching for something small," Wellborn said. "Do you have any idea what he or she was after?"

"Intruder?" She turned her head and glared at Connor. "You knew about this."

"Yes."

Flames shot from her eyes and charbroiled the well-meaning excuses he'd been prepared to offer. His motivations had been good: he hadn't wanted her to get excited, demand to be involved and put herself in harm's way. His intention had been to protect her.

At the moment, he felt he was the one who needed protection...*from* her.

Chapter Nine

Outrage exploded her exhaustion and weakness. Emily forgot about the twinge in her ankle and the aching from her bruised ribs. Still staring at Connor, she asked, "Was there a lot of damage to my house?"

"According to O'Brien, it was a careful search. The intruder didn't tear your place apart seeking revenge."

"Doesn't make me feel better," she growled.

"A pane of glass in the back door was broken, and it looks like your laptop might have been stolen."

"But you don't really know," she said, "because you're not familiar with the stuff in my house. Maybe I had a million-dollar sculpture on the table in the entry. And what if I had a cat, a sweet little calico cat named Taffy? What if the intruder kicked Taffy and she was hiding under the house, meowing in pain?"

"I didn't see any food bowls or litter boxes."

"Because I don't have a cat." She wished she hadn't hopped down this rabbit hole, but she was making a point. "Bottom line, I'm the only one who can give a true inventory of what was in my house, whether it was a cat or valuable artwork."

"You're right."

"I can't believe you didn't tell me right away."

"A mistake," he said. "I apologize."

Adrenaline fueled her anger, but she knew better than to unleash her unbridled fury on Connor. He'd meant her no harm. The opposite, in fact. He had been trying to do the right thing. The warmth in his eyes deflected her rage, and she reminded herself that this wasn't his fault. She muttered, "It's all right."

"I didn't hear you."

"You're forgiven, okay? And for your information, my laptop wasn't stolen. I took it with me to Aspen. The poor thing was probably smashed to bits in the crash. Let's move on." She stared at the FBI agent, who looked like he'd stepped from the pages of a men's fashion mag. "How can I help your investigation?"

"This might be a long conversation," he said. "Would you like to lie down?"

Being in bed seemed like a position of weakness, and she wanted to appear strong so she'd be taken seriously. Her powder puff–pink jammies put her at a definite disadvantage when compared to Wellborn's designer clothes. "I'd rather sit in the chair. Also, I'd like more tea. And I think I ordered a sandwich."

In moments, her demands were met. One of the aides provided a light blanket to cover her lap. Someone found a pot of hot water for tea and a container of ice water with a bendy straw. A freshly made turkey sandwich she'd ordered for lunch from the hospital kitchen appeared before her, which meant it must be noon. Already? She was anxious to get moving, ready for action.

In one sense, the break-in at her house was good news. Local law enforcement had a whole new area to search for clues. In the crime-solving shows on television, a single hair or a fiber could be used to identify and track the criminal, but she couldn't count on forensics. Lots of people—including local artists and workmen—came into and out of her house, and all of them left traces behind. Unless they found something that pointed to the Riggs family or some other direct suspect, the best kind of clue would be if the intruder had stolen something significant. And the only way they'd find out about such a theft was for her to go to the house and look around.

Before she started her talk with Wellborn, Dr. Parris interrupted. She had good news. After a consult with a podiatrist, Emily's ankle injury was downgraded to a light sprain, which meant she'd be up and around, possibly using a cane, in a few days. Also, her arm cast could be replaced with a smaller one.

"From wrist to elbow," Parris said. "I don't know why the ER doctors put on such a giant cast in the first place."

Emily had many other doubts about the hospital team led by Dr. Thorson, but she didn't criticize. Thorson sounded like a jerk, but the surgeons in Aspen had saved her life when she'd flatlined on the operating table. "I have only one question. When can I go home?"

"Dr. Troutman has the final say," Parris said. "As far as I'm concerned, you can go tomorrow if you have someone to take care of you."

Connor spoke up. "I can have your house cleaned before that."

"I'd rather you didn't," Wellborn said. "I'd like Emily to walk through and see if she notices anything unusual."

"I'd like that, too," she said. "A walk-through would be great. Can I do that this afternoon, Dr. Parris?"

"I wouldn't advise walking on that ankle," the doctor said, "but you could take a field trip in a wheelchair if Dr. Troutman gives the okay."

Emily's spirits lifted. Finally, she'd be involved, taking charge of her own life. Beaming a smile, she turned to Wellborn. "You said the intruder was looking for something small. Do you have an idea of what that might be?"

"A flash drive, a ring, a key," he said, listing possibilities. "Do you have a safe-deposit box?"

"Yes, it's for documents like the loan papers for my house, my car title and stuff like that. Nothing of value to anybody else."

"Jewelry?"

"Diamond earrings from my mother, a couple of gold chains." She concentrated, trying to envision what was in there. And then she blushed. There was an encouraging card that Connor had sent when her divorce was final. He'd signed with *I love you*, and she remembered reading it again and again, rubbing her thumb across the print and telling herself that she was making too much of a casual sign-off. "There's a smaller box inside, filled with mementos, and a notebook with a list of my passwords."

"Do I have your permission to access the box?"

"I'd like to come along when you do." She was reluctant to allow unrestricted access to her personal possessions. It was bad enough that the police were at her house, poking around her things. "What if the intruder already found the key? It's not really hidden. I keep it in my jewelry box."

"Give me the name of your bank," Wellborn said. "We'll put a Stop and Seize on anyone attempting to impersonate you."

While he dealt with the bureaucratic issues, she sank back in the recliner and nibbled at the edges of her turkey sandwich. When she mentally reviewed the contents of her house, she wasn't aware of anything that merited breaking and entering. Her home wasn't a showplace like the massive house she and Jamison had furnished in Aspen, and she wasn't a secretive person. Jamison had been a hundred times more enigmatic than she, and he continued to surprise her from the grave. Never did she think he'd leave that beautiful house to her. And the art!

The idea of seeing those paintings and sculptures again gave her chills: the small Renoir of a girl on a swing, a couple of wry lithographs by Banksy, a Georgia O'Keeffe calla lily and so much more. One of her big regrets in the divorce was losing access to these wonderful artworks. By the end, she'd been ready to give up almost anything. Not that she hated Jamison, but she desperately wanted her marriage to be over.

Connor pulled a plastic chair up beside her. "Do you really feel well enough to go to the house?"

She nodded. "And I'd appreciate if you'd back me up with Fish."

"I'm not in love with the idea, but I understand why you want to go. We'll make sure you're well guarded."

She reached toward him and was glad when he clasped her hand in his familiar grasp. Forgiveness went both ways. "I'm willing to cooperate, Connor, but you've got to keep me in the loop and let me make my own decisions."

"Done."

"As soon as possible, I want to go to my gallery in the art district," she said. "I'm not too worried about a break-in there. I've got decorative iron grillwork on the doors and windows, plus a security alarm that screams for twenty minutes and calls the cops."

"Do you need to be open for business?"

"I wish!" She grinned. "It's not a problem if I'm closed for a couple of days. I don't get a lot of walk-in traffic. Most of my sales come from personal contacts and from showings. I have an event scheduled for next week."

"A wine-and-cheese thing," he said in a world-weary tone that indicated he'd attended too many of those *things*.

"Get your mind out of Manhattan," she said. "This

showing is all about Southwestern art and sculpture. We're having chips, salsa, tequila and a mariachi band."

"I'm in."

Wellborn rejoined them. "Your safe-deposit box is secure. If anyone tries to use the key, they'll be detained."

"Thank you." She nodded her approval. "I'd probably have my own problems with the bank if I tried to access my accounts. I've got no ID. My handbag and wallet went flying out of the car when I crashed."

Wellborn placed his briefcase on the foot of the hospital bed, flipped it open and took out her bronze leather purse, which was much battered but still intact. "Deputy Sandoval found this when they were hauling the remains of your car up the cliff. Also, here are your keys."

"My phone?"

"They didn't find it. That's treacherous terrain."

"I'm glad to have my handbag." She was gradually reassembling the shattered pieces of her life. Shoving the remains of her sandwich out of the way, she unfastened the clasp on her purse. Inside was her wallet with her driver's license, an insurance card, credit cards and twenty-seven dollars in cash. The contents were so pleasantly normal that she wanted to cheer.

"Before we get started," Wellborn said, "do you have questions for me?"

"I do," Connor said. "How much can you tell us about the people in Aspen? We know Phillip is in Denver. What about the others?"

"Patricia and Glenda admit to nothing and have pretty much barred the door. The family attorney refuses to allow law enforcement to enter any of their homes without a search warrant, and we don't have enough evidence to get a judge to sign off."

"Technically," Connor said, "the house that Jamison

owned now belongs to Emily. As soon as I have the deeds and paperwork filed, she can open the door to a search."

"I'd appreciate it," Wellborn said.

"What about Thorson?" Connor asked.

"The doctor is taking three months' unpaid leave while the hospital administration decides what to do about him. They aren't real happy after the incident with the ambulance."

Until now, Beverly had been standing quietly near the door. She cleared her throat. "This incident, can you tell me about it?"

"No big deal." Aware that he'd behaved badly, Connor tried to wave it away. "Thorson and the Riggs family attempted to abduct Emily—who was unconscious—and we stopped them."

"You're leaving something out," Wellborn said. "If we'd followed the rules, Thorson would have been fired. The administration extended leniency because they doubted you'd sue after you'd been so aggressive."

"They deserved worse."

"You tried to grab my gun."

"Not good," Beverly said. "You are so not getting a weapon."

"Fine," Connor said. "Let's get back to the subject. What else is going on with Thorson?"

"Patricia is angry with him, threatened to kick him out of her life."

Though Emily had been in a coma through most of the ambulance drama, she was glad Thorson was being punished. "He's still in Aspen, right?"

"He was at his apartment last night," Wellborn said. "The only person of interest whose whereabouts were unaccounted for during the time of the break-in is Kate Sylvester. From what I understand, you talked to her before the reading of the will."

"That's right. And Connor said he saw her when we first arrived at the hospital."

"I think so," he said, "but I don't really know the woman."

Agent Wellborn glanced between them, reading their expressions. His features were arranged in a professionally neutral expression, neither happy nor sad nor enthusiastic. But she had the impression that Kate's appearance in Denver was significant to his investigation. She asked, "Have you interviewed Kate before?"

"Extensively," he said. "She was close to Jamison, both professionally and in other ways."

"That's putting it nicely," she said. "At the investment firm, she had seniority over him. In their personal relationship she worked under him. Or maybe not. She strikes me as a woman who likes to be on the top."

"I want you to tell us—in detail—about your conversation with her. Don't leave anything out."

Emily inhaled a deep breath, then exhaled and started talking. "I ran into her after I left the downstairs restroom at Patricia's chalet, which is a crazy-opulent room with tons of marble and gleaming gold tiles. A little excessive in my opinion. I mean, what kind of person needs all that glitter and shimmer to go to the bathroom? Anyway, I went down the hall from the bathroom and ducked into a library. Kate followed me in."

She vividly remembered the moment when she recognized the stunning auburn-haired woman who'd slept with her husband before he was an ex-husband. Emily wasn't one for slut shaming, and she had struggled to find the politically correct words to let Kate know that her behavior was despicable. Before she could unleash her tirade, Kate had said, "He dumped me, too."

That simple statement gave Emily a burst of smug pleasure because she was the one who had dumped Jamison and not the other way around. Sure, he'd had an affair with Kate, but Emily was the dumper. He was the dumpee.

Emily shot a glance toward Connor. "Kate thinks we have something in common, but I don't. Apart from both of us having had sex with the same man, we're very different."

"How so?" Wellborn asked.

"I'm into art. She's into numbers. We both have good taste, but she goes for the classics and I like to try new things. As far as I can tell, she has zero sense of humor. Oh, and she's way more competitive than I am. With her Wall Street job, I guess she needs to be fierce and ambitious."

"Was this the first time you talked with her?" Wellborn asked.

"We'd met at company dinners and work-related events, but we were usually part of a group. She's not the type of woman who hangs out with female friends."

"Why do you think she sought you out?"

"At first, I thought she wanted to talk about Jamison. Being in Aspen reminded me of him and the good times we'd had. He loved the mountains."

And he'd died too young. His death saddened her. In spite of their divorce and their final angry arguments, he held a place in her heart that no one else would ever fill. It felt like she'd never mourned him, that she didn't have the right to that sorrow.

Connor squeezed her hand and whispered, "Are you okay?"

"I'm sorry he's gone."

"Me, too."

She turned toward Wellborn. "Kate said something

about how nobody knew Jamison better than the two of us—the ex-wife and the ex-girlfriend."

"Do you agree with that?" Wellborn asked.

"We both knew him well, but he was different with Kate." She glanced over at Connor. "You know what I mean, don't you? Kate was a good match for the man he had become. They were both consumed by their work. I'm surprised they had time for, um, anything else."

Wellborn pointed her back toward her conversation with Kate before the reading. "What else did she talk to you about?"

"She wanted to compare memories of Jamison. Where had we gone to dinner? Who did we go on double dates with? What kind of gifts did he give me for Valentine's Day? She wanted to make it a competition where he gave her better gifts and introduced her to more important people. Kate is the kind of person who goes to an art gallery and takes selfies next to the paintings rather than actually looking at them. She creeps me out."

Emily remembered the uncomfortable sensation when Kate had started adding up their time on vacation. The red-haired woman seemed to have a calculator for a brain. "And then she switched gears and wanted to be my friend. She offered to come to my house and check out anything Jamison might have given me to see if it was valuable."

"Such as?"

"She talked about a portfolio, investments and a secret bank account." Emily raised an eyebrow, giving Wellborn a meaningful look. "Interested?"

"I am," he said. "Did she mention specific names of companies and investments?"

"I don't remember. The whole situation—Jamison's death, being at Patricia's home, the woman who slept with my husband acting like we should be besties—it was all so surreal. If I'd known what was to come, I'd have committed every single word to memory." Emily shook her head. "But she kept stressing that I might not be aware of how much Jamison's financial gifts were really worth."

"Ironic," Connor said. "A few minutes later, Emily learned that Jamison had bequeathed her the Aspen house, complete with furniture and art—a multimillion-dollar gift that outstripped anything he'd ever gifted to Kate."

"And she's real familiar with the house," Emily said. "She told me that she was staying there with Phillip. That's why she was at the will reading in the first place."

Wellborn held up his hand, signaling a halt. "Are you saying that Kate Sylvester and Phillip Riggs are close?"

"They aren't lovers if that's what you mean. At least, I don't think they are. Who knows? They hang out together, go to the same places, see the same people." She shrugged. "That whole bunch—the family and Jamison's friends—are as thick as thieves."

"An apt comparison," Wellborn said. "What did Jamison leave to Kate?"

"A designer briefcase and a Rolex."

"Versus a house in Aspen," Wellborn said. "I'd say you won the competition for best gift from Jamison."

That wasn't a game Emily wanted to play. If she'd married Jamison for his money, they would still be together. Something more important had been lost—their love.

Chapter Ten

Tucked into her wheelchair and dressed in loose-fitting lavender sweats with the left arm slashed open to accommodate her cast, Emily gazed through the windows of the ambulance van at the late-afternoon sunlight. She loved autumn. In the mountains, the foliage had already turned, but in town the process was belated. Only a few of the trees showed their September colors of orange, gold and scarlet. She inhaled a deep breath. Even in traffic, the air smelled crisp. She was glad to be out, so glad to be alive.

The main reason Fish had agreed to let her leave the hospital to check out the ransacking at her house was that Special Agent in Charge Jaiden Wellborn had told him that her observations might aid a federal investigation. An outstanding negotiator, SAC Wellborn radiated authority but was also respectful to the doctor. And it helped that her brain scans were positive. No doubt Fish would have insisted that she stay on bed rest if she hadn't been on the mend.

Ever since she'd got to the hospital, they'd been running tests, scans and MRIs. Fish and the other neurologists hadn't been able to pinpoint the cause of her seizure. Though there was still a bit of swelling, they hadn't found clots, tumors or other brain damage. Fish diagnosed her with a simple concussion resulting from a blow to the head.

Also, he'd suggested that her seizure might have been due to exposure to a poison or an allergic reaction, and he had ordered tox screens along with other blood tests.

Poison? Was it coincidence that Connor had seen Kate moments before she went into anaphylactic shock? It seemed impossible that Kate would attempt to poison her in a hospital with so many witnesses, but stranger things had happened. Nobody had believed that a healthy, young man like Jamison had contracted a mysterious illness and died at the height of his career.

Emily added attempted poisoning to the list of murderous attacks. First, there was the truck forcing her off the road, and then her IV bag had been switched on the flight from Denver, and now she might have been poisoned. She was using up her good luck faster than a cat runs through nine lives.

In the back of the van with her, Connor asked Beverly when she could get him a stun gun that wouldn't require a special permit. She told him that there was no reason for him to have a weapon while she was on duty.

"Let me do my job," she said.

"I can be your backup."

"To chase down ambulance drivers?" She'd obviously taken note of the incident when Connor had been ready to shoot first and ask questions later.

"Here's an idea," Emily piped up. "Connor can use my Beretta M9."

They both turned toward her, gaping like a couple of surprised goldfish. Beverly spoke first. "Where do you keep your weapon?"

"It's locked in a metal box in the back of my closet, along with a half dozen other boxes. I should have mentioned it to Wellborn, but I didn't think of it. I hardly ever take the Beretta out of the box."

"Are you trained to use the gun?" Beverly asked.

"Absolutely." After her parents passed away, her uncle had given her the Beretta when she was sixteen. His reasoning had been that if she was capable of protecting herself, he could leave her alone for long periods of time. He'd thought it was a really nice present, which said a lot about his fitness as a father figure. He was her mother's brother and shared her fondness for booze. Also, he got a kick out of teaching her how to handle the weapon. "I know how to lock and load, how to clean the M9, how to take it apart and how to aim."

"Have you ever shot anything?" Beverly asked.

"Nothing human."

Connor finally closed his gaping mouth. "Why didn't I know about the Beretta?"

"It's not a big deal. Do I have to remind you that I grew up in Colorado?" She gave him a smile as she pointed through the side window. "This is the corner to my street."

"Nice neighborhood," Connor said. "Quiet."

In this older part of town, the trees were tall and well established, the houses were brick and the design of the homes varied from three-story Tudor houses to cozy cottages like hers, which was set back a long way from the front sidewalk. A driveway extended all the way to the garage in the back, and it was filled by two police vehicles parked end to end. The medical van squeezed in behind the DPD police cruiser and the driver came around to the side so he could operate the lift for her wheelchair.

"I don't really need that," she said. "I can stand on my good leg and hop."

"Use the lift," Connor and Beverly said in unison. At least they agreed on something.

Grumbling, she stayed in the chair and descended from the van on a square platform operated by hydraulics. The real problem would come when they got to her side door. Two steep stairs led to the porch, and there wasn't a ramp. An even bigger problem: her bedroom was on the second floor. With the driver and Beverly accompanying them, Connor pushed her chair along the edge of the driveway past three peach trees.

"Stop," she ordered.

He halted so quickly that she almost spilled forward. "What's up?"

"I want a peach." She pointed to the branches where luscious, ripe fruit dangled beyond her reach. The season was almost over. Leaves on the tree were tinged with yellow.

He reached up and picked two. "One for you and one for me."

As she rubbed her thumb over the peach fuzz, she wished they'd been visiting her home under different circumstances. "Let's go around to the back so I can see the broken door."

He rounded the corner and went between the house and the garage, where he parked her wheelchair on a small concrete patio. Four lawn chairs circled a glass-topped table, and there was a comfortable chaise with a striped cushion. A long low redwood box held a display of petunias and pansies in varying shades of pink, yellow and purple. The landscaping—with all the trees—had been one of the features that had sold her on this house. She liked the shrubs along the back fence and the climbing red roses on two arched trellises.

"It's nice out here," he said. "You aren't going to be happy about what you find inside the house."

"I know." She realized that she'd come into the garden to avoid the moment when she had to confront the reality of having had an intruder. "I love this house. It's the first place where I've lived alone."

Growing up, she'd been with her parents, of course. When they died, she lived with her uncle. In college and her first years working in New York she'd needed roommates to help pay the rent. Then she'd been married.

"Do you miss having other people around?" he asked.

"Not a bit."

"I know what you mean," he said. "When I finally got my own place, I loved the peace and quiet. My mom said I'd get bored."

"Did you?"

"Not yet," he said. "I love my big, loud family, but sometimes I wish I'd moved farther away from Brooklyn."

"Could you ever go back to living with someone else?"

"That depends on the someone."

Sensing a change in the atmosphere between them, she looked up into his chocolate-brown eyes and saw an enticing heat. When he mentioned living with *someone*, he wasn't referring to a new roommate or family member who needed a place to stay. Connor was taking a frank look at his life and considering a major life change—having a girlfriend move in with him to share his home and his life. At least, she hoped that was what he'd been thinking.

Though they'd never been anything more than friends, the chemistry had been bubbling between them ever since her divorce. She asked, "Are you looking for this *someone*?"

Inside her head, she chanted, *Pick me, pick me, pick me.*

"I'm not ruling out any possibilities, except for not dating anybody I work with. There are blind dates and online dating. Maybe I'll see someone on the street. Or maybe I've already met someone and don't know it yet." Quickly, he changed the subject. "You know, Emily, you don't have to go inside the house. We can return to the van right now. I'll arrange for somebody to come in and clean up the mess. And when you come home, your house will look like it's supposed to."

His offer was tempting, but she'd spent most of her life avoiding conflicts and having other people solve her problems. Maybe Kate had been correct when she'd said that Emily didn't understand what she'd had and what she'd lost. "I have to do this for myself. I'm ready."

He wheeled her to the concrete stairs leading to the back door with the busted window. "There are two ways we can get you up the stairs. The driver and I can lift the chair or I can carry you. Your choice."

"Let's do a carry," she said. "It can be practice for hiking up the staircase to the second floor."

"And we need to go there because…"

"My bedroom is upstairs."

"And?"

"It's where I keep my Beretta."

As soon as she rose from the wheelchair, he scooped her into his arms and cradled her against his chest. Her good arm was closest to his body, and she slipped her hand up and around his neck. Her intention had been to make it easier to carry her. The effect was different—warm, sensual and intimate.

She'd known Connor for years, which meant plenty of hugs and casual physical contact. Once or twice, they'd danced together. Other than the few kisses they'd shared, nothing had felt as extraordinary and personal as this moment. Though they were surrounded by other people—the ambulance driver, Beverly, uniformed officers and forensic technicians—it seemed like they existed in a bubble that was their own special world.

She jostled against him. Two layers of fabric separated them: her velour sweatshirt and his black V-neck cashmere sweater. And yet their touch started a friction that thrilled her. *Was it possible for her to hear his heartbeat, or was she imagining the steady, strong thump?* Despite her injuries, she couldn't help responding to his nearness. If she'd been able to read her reaction on a brain scan, Emily knew that her pleasure centers would be blazing. She was utterly, totally, happily aware of him as a man.

Inside the house when he returned her to the wheelchair, the real world came back into sharp focus. One of the CSI investigators offered a pair of latex gloves, Emily turned him down. Her fingerprints would be all over her house. The others had to wear plastic bootees to cover their shoes. This space wasn't her home anymore. It was a crime scene.

Her charming kitchen looked like it had been taken over by an army of destructive raccoons. Drawers hung open. Shelves had been emptied. Her cute retro canisters for flour, sugar, coffee and tea had been overturned and the contents were spread across the polished granite countertop.

"Seriously," she muttered, "did they think I'd hide my valuables in a sugar jar?"

"You'd be surprised," Wellborn said. "People stash things behind the sink, inside the light fixtures and in the freezer."

She glanced at her fridge, noting that the contents were strewed across the floor. An unpleasant smell emanated from a container of leftover *moo shu* pork. "Not much real food in there. I was a New Yorker so long that I picked up the bad habit of grabbing takeout rather than cooking."

Accompanied by her little entourage, she wheeled from the kitchen to the front room. The afternoon light shone multicolored through the two stained glass windows onto a scene of clutter, which, thankfully, didn't show much permanent damage. A chair was overturned but not broken. The intruder had yanked the pillows off the sofa but hadn't torn them apart. Several books had been pulled from the built-in shelves and flipped through. *Smart move*, she thought. A lot of people hid things in hollowed-out books; she wasn't one of them.

"He didn't touch my flat-screen TV," she said. "Does that mean the intruder isn't a burglar?"

"I'm going to say yes." Wellborn strolled around the room with his hands in his trouser pockets. "This search seems to be targeted to a specific item. Are you getting any ideas about what they were looking for?"

"Not really."

They made quick work of the downstairs closets and bathroom. Her small office had taken the worst hit. Files were scattered like a manila leaf storm. The contents were personal and mostly outdated because she kept track of her bills on her computer. "I'm glad I keep all the invoices, receipts and consignment papers for my business at the gallery. I wouldn't want an intruder to have access to that information."

"What's going on over here?" Connor gestured toward the blank wall between the door and the closet. "It's not like you to leave an open space."

She visualized the way the wall had looked last week: a plain white background for three sharp graphic prints in black and white. "I had simple art so I wouldn't be distracted when I sat at the desk. The intruder must have taken it down looking for a wall safe."

"Do you have a wall safe?" Wellborn asked.

"I didn't think I needed one. There's a fireproof vault at my gallery."

The usually clean surface of her desk was cluttered with the contents of the drawers. Carefully, she picked through the array of pens, notepads, paper clips, business cards, rulers and scissors. "I can't say for sure, but I think I'm missing a couple of flash drives. And I don't see the spare keys for my house and my car."

"You won't need the house keys," Connor said.

"Or the keys for my poor, dead Hyundai."

"You'll have new locks. The people Beverly works for are upgrading your security. As soon as the CSI people are done and you choose the style of door you want to replace the one that got busted, they can get started."

"What about keys for your gallery?" Wellborn asked.

"I use a secure keypad."

"You might consider the same treatment for your home."

The need to turn her charming little cottage into a fortress angered her, but she couldn't hide behind rose-colored glasses and pretend nothing was wrong. Somebody was trying to kill her. "I wish I could find some more useful clues."

"Try to put yourself in Kate's position," Wellborn suggested. "What would she want? It might possibly be an object that belonged to your ex-husband."

What would a woman like Kate really want? Emily didn't think her foe valued a sentimental treasure or a thing of beauty. She wanted power, and the route she'd chosen was through money.

At the staircase, they decided that she and Connor would be the first to go up to the second floor, and the others would follow. Unlike the first time he had lifted her, there was an awkward pause before she tumbled into his arms. They'd both been somewhat aroused and neither of them wanted to look foolish. As he maneuvered to pick her up, her movements were as floppy as a rag doll.

But when he held her against his chest, nothing else mattered. She didn't care how she'd got into the position but was happy to be there. Tilting her head, she looked up at him. They were so close. Her breath mingled with his.

"Hang on," he said. "I don't want to bump you against the wall."

She wouldn't have minded too much. What was one more bump? But she welcomed the invitation to tighten her grasp around his neck. To keep her arm cast from dangling, she angled her left wrist across her belly and turned her body toward him. As he climbed the staircase, her breast rubbed against him, and the pressure aroused sensations she hadn't experienced in quite a while. He smelled clean and fresh like sandalwood soap. In the V-neck of his sweater, she glimpsed a sexy tuft of hair that made her want to plunge her hand inside and caress his muscular chest. The black cashmere was unbelievably soft against her cheek. Giving a small moan of satisfaction, she burrowed into the hollow below his chin.

At the top of the stairs, they were nearly alone. Everybody else was on the first floor.

"We made it." She gazed up at him. "My bedroom is on the right."

Leaning down, he kissed her forehead. "I wish we had something more suggestive planned for your bedroom."

"Not yet."

"But soon," he promised as he carried her into the bedroom and set her down on the bed, where the white duvet had been tossed aside, revealing smooth lavender sheets. He lingered, and she thought he might kiss her again, but then everybody else piled into her bedroom.

Connor stood up straight. "Let's take care of first things first. Where's your Beretta?"

"It's inside a Doc Martens shoebox at the back of my closet."

"If it's there," Connor said. "I can't believe the intruder would leave a weapon behind."

Her gaze flicked around the cozy bedroom with blond

Swedish modern furniture and accents of purple and yellow. Apart from some of her clothing that had been tossed around, the biggest mess was on top of the dresser, where her jewelry box had been dumped. From where she sat on the edge of her bed, she could see the sparkle and shine. None of her costume jewelry was worth more than a couple hundred bucks, but she liked each piece, and she hated that a stranger had been touching them, rifling through her house, invading her privacy.

She looked away from the dresser. The wall opposite her bed was decorated with dozens of snapshots of places and people who were special to her, ranging from coffee with friends to the house in Aspen to the most beautiful sunset she'd ever witnessed. This wall hadn't received the same treatment as the one in her office downstairs; none of these photos were large enough to hide a wall safe. Still, as she gazed, she noticed that a couple of the snapshots were askew, and the pattern she'd arranged them in was unbalanced.

One was missing.

Chapter Eleven

Connor emerged from the closet, shoebox in hand. Unlike the kitchen and the office, the clutter in the bedroom wasn't too bad, and the closet—where dozens of shoeboxes were stacked—looked like it had barely been touched. He placed the box labeled Doc Martens on the bed beside her and lifted the lid. Inside was the locked metal container that held her Beretta M9.

"Not the first place I'd go looking," he said, "but if I was searching, I might dig through the boxes. I'm surprised the intruder didn't discover the gun."

"I think I know why," Emily said. "By the time the intruder got to the closet, she'd already found what she was looking for."

"*She?* As in Kate Sylvester?"

"I'm afraid so."

Emily had everybody's attention—Wellborn, Beverly, the ambulance driver and two plainclothes officers. "Explain," Connor said.

"When Kate and I were talking in Aspen, she mentioned Jamison's habit of leaving cute little personal notes on the backs of photographs."

"He did that when we were in college," Connor said. "He'd take a photo on a first date, make a note and send it to his latest girlfriend. Women thought it was sweet."

"Jamison was good at courtship. In the long term? Not so much." She pointed to the wall opposite her bed, where twenty or more framed snapshots were clustered in groups. "Tell me what you see."

The first thing he noticed was that his smiling face appeared in two photos: a group shot on a ski slope in Aspen and a touristy pose on a bridge in Central Park. He recognized several other people: friends in New York, people she'd worked with and artists whose work she'd displayed. Noticeably absent were photos of family events, like birthdays or Christmas. Emily had no siblings and her relationship with her uncle wasn't something she talked about. Her in-laws and Jamison had also been deleted from her life.

"Do you get it?" she asked. "Anything odd?"

Connor studied the photos more intently, trying to decipher her meaning. He figured that Emily had taken most of these pictures, and the composition showed her natural artistic sensibility in terms of balance and light. Each shot captured a glimpse into the character of the subject, whether it was beauty, humor, joy or poignant sadness.

Beverly was the one who spotted the anomaly. "This group of three photos on the far end seems lopsided. Was something removed?"

"There was a fourth picture," Emily said. "It was a friend of mine feeding a banana to a blue iguana."

"In the Cayman Islands," Connor said. He remembered that group trip very well, especially the sunrise morning when he and Emily had got up early and walked along the beach. "Your friend Liz Perry was fascinated by the iguanas and earned herself the nickname of *Lizzie Lizard*."

"The Caymans," Wellborn said. "I have a bad idea about where this is headed."

"While we were there," Emily said, "Jamison had me open an account in this strange little bank with a small lobby and a floor-to-ceiling safe. I signed a bunch of documents and let them take my photo and fingerprints. It wasn't the first time Jamison guided me through a business transaction."

"I advised you not to sign anything without letting me review it first." Connor hadn't wanted her husband to take advantage of her easygoing nature. "I was right there. On the island. You could have called me over."

"Jamison gave me a logical reason for setting up the account, and I believed him. He was my husband." Her voice quavered, but she held her emotions in check. "He kept the account number, and I didn't really think about it again."

"And Jamison didn't mention this account in the divorce proceedings." He figured they were onto something. Jamison had a mysterious stash in the Caymans.

"Like Kate said, I don't pay much attention when it comes to financial dealings. And by the time our marriage ended, I was more concerned with getting out than finances."

Her self-critical tone bothered him. He wanted to tell her that she had nothing to be ashamed about. Her mistake hadn't been careless or stupid. The reason Emily slipped up was that she'd trusted the wrong man.

Wellborn asked, "Can you give me the name of the bank?"

"I don't remember. There can't be many."

"Actually, there are," he said. "Offshore banking is a big business, and there are well over a hundred institutions in the islands. Did Jamison use your name to open the account?"

"My hyphenated name—*Benton-Riggs*."

Her account would be filed under *B*, distancing her from her husband in case the White-Collar Crimes Unit managed to get a peek inside the records of this unnamed, offshore bank. This investigation would be complicated and might not yield results.

SAC Wellborn appeared to be up for the challenge. He whipped his phone from his pocket, ready to call in the reinforcements—CPA investigators armed with actuarial tables and calculators. "Is there anything else you can tell me, Emily?"

"There's a reason that Kate took the photo." Twin frown lines appeared between her eyebrows. "There were numbers scrawled across the back. Jamison must have written them."

"What kind of numbers?"

"I thought it was an international phone number, but it could have been a bank account. Jamison was always scrawling numbers, notes, whatever on anything he could find. I really didn't think much of it." She shook her head. "It's amazing how an attempt on your life changes the way you see things. If Kate has that number, will she have access to whatever is in there?"

"Not immediately," Wellborn said. "You usually need the account number and a password or code. Do you remember a password?"

"I think I typed something into a keypad. Who knows what it was? I've got dozens of passwords, ranging from a yogurt store to my retirement account." Clearly frustrated, she threw her good hand in the air. "I keep lists of them on my computer and in a notebook stored in my safe-deposit box."

Wellborn checked the time on his phone. "It's too late for us to go to your bank today. We'll have to follow up tomorrow. In the meantime, I'd like a list of as many different passwords as you can remember."

She groaned. "I'll try."

"Your computer is still missing. If my tech people

know your passwords, they can tap into the files from long distance."

"Good luck with that," she said. "My computer was a gift from Jamison before the divorce. He set up the encryption."

Clever move. Her ex-husband had been thinking ahead. He didn't expect investigators to look to his ex-wife for information, and if they did, he'd installed firewalls and the best cyberprotection money could buy. But SAC Wellborn wasn't about to give up. After he jotted down several passwords from Emily, he thanked her and headed out the door with his phone already pressed to his ear. The other law enforcement people followed him.

Connor glanced over at Beverly and asked, "Could you give us some privacy?"

"I'll wait outside."

When the door closed and they were alone, Emily slumped forward like a marionette whose strings had been cut. Her voice was ragged. "He played me for a fool."

"You're not the only one," he said. "Jamison betrayed a lot of people, many of those who invested money with him. He sure as hell conned me into thinking he was a good guy. That's not supposed to happen. I'm a lawyer. I should have known better."

"He used me."

Connor couldn't deny the painful truth. He sat on the bed beside her. When he touched her back, she cringed as though human contact was painful. But he didn't move away. Slowly, he massaged the knots of tension in her shoulders. "It's not your fault."

"I'm not so sure of that." She turned her head and looked up at him. Her blue eyes welled with unshed tears. "My mother would have told me that I deserved every bad thing that happened to me."

"Was she judgmental?"

"Worse, she was judgmental and drunk."

"And she was wrong." His hand slipped lower on her back to her jutting shoulder blades. Below that point, he felt the bandage supporting her injured ribs—a reminder of the hell she was going through. "You didn't do anything to deserve this."

"I thought I loved him, and I turned a blind eye to what Jamison was doing. I've heard that expression all my life and never really understood what it meant until now."

"Don't blame yourself, Emily."

"He purchased millions of dollars of artworks, and I helped him. I did the bidding at auctions and never worried about where the money was coming from."

A long time ago, Connor had questioned his former friend's good fortune. Sure, Jamison had come from a wealthy family and was doing well at his job, but he was spending almost as fast as he was earning and buying big-ticket items. There had been a trust fund, but Connor wouldn't have access to that until his thirty-fifth birthday, so the spending didn't make sense. Shortly after Connor had suggested they do an audit and set up a budget, Jamison shifted his business to another attorney. That should have raised a red flag.

"My vision wasn't twenty-twenty," Connor said. "I never expected him to do anything wrong or illegal."

"Illegal?" Alarmed, she sat up straight. "Did Jamison steal from people? Did he cause them to lose their life savings?"

It seemed really likely to Connor. The reason for a mysterious offshore account was to hide money—ill-gotten gains. "We won't know for sure until after Wellborn is done with his investigation."

With a surge of energy, she struggled to her feet and balanced on her good leg. "I have to get busy."

He maneuvered quickly to support her and make sure she didn't put weight on her sprained ankle. "First, you need to get better."

"Help me, Connor." Her right hand clung to his arm. Her gaze implored him. "As soon as the paperwork is in order, I want you to sell that house in Aspen. The proceeds can be used to set up a fund for the relief of Jamison's victims. I need to fix this mess."

Her heart was in the right place, but it wasn't going to be easy to determine who was a victim and who was complicit. "I'll take care of the sale. What about the art?"

"For now, it can be on loan to schools and art museums. Later, I might sell that, too."

He encircled her in his arms and pulled her into an embrace. In spite of her energetic plans, her slender body felt as fragile as a baby bird. She rested her head on his shoulder and went silent. Her injuries had damaged her physically, but the wound of her latest betrayal at the hands of her ex-husband caused a far deeper pain.

"We'll take care of this," he said. "You can trust me."

"Can I?"

"I would never knowingly harm you, Emily."

She looked up at him, and he tightened his hold around her waist to keep her from falling. "Connor, I'm scared."

"Understandable. Somebody is trying to kill you."

"That's nothing compared to the hurt I'm feeling inside. How could I have been so wrong about Jamison? Why didn't I see him for what he really was?" Her lower lip trembled. "How can I ever open my heart again?"

There was no straightforward answer to that question. All he could do was hold her close and hope the hurt would go away and she would look around and see him standing beside her, ready and willing to give her all his love. He couldn't promise that their relationship would be perfect or that they'd never argue. But when he did make a promise, he wouldn't betray her. She could trust him with her battered heart.

Gently, he kissed her forehead beside the bandage covering her head wound. Her skin was hot, not feverish but heated. Lower, he kissed the tip of her nose. And then he slowly tasted her lips.

Passion raced through his veins, but he held back. Right now, she didn't need a lover. She needed a friend. And he was a patient man.

BACK IN HER hospital room, Emily kept her eyes closed, even though she wasn't sleeping. She was humiliated by the way she'd been conned and deeply regretful of the trouble she might have inadvertently caused her ex-husband's investors. When nurses and technicians came in and out of her room, she responded to their physical instructions. But that was the extent of her interaction. The only person who noticed her silence was Connor.

Beverly never did much talking. And Agent Wellborn had disappeared into his investigation. Only Connor stayed at her side. Steady and supportive, he held her hand and brought her things before she knew she wanted them. He encouraged her to eat her dinner even though she wasn't hungry because she needed to recover, to get her strength back.

In the physical therapy gym, she concentrated on her workout, using equipment that wouldn't put weight on her sprained ankle. Later that night, the lights were finally turned out, and it was as quiet as it ever got in a hospital. She asked for a sleeping pill and sank into a heavy slumber.

The next morning, her depression lessened when she

gazed through the window at a pink-and-purple Rocky Mountain sunrise. She told herself that a new day meant new hope. As soon as she'd adjusted her bed to a sitting position, Connor gave her a little peck on the cheek. He'd already been awake for a while, long enough to wash up, if not to shave.

"You smell good," she said.

"Soap and water."

Part of her wanted to close her eyes and never confront the mess her life had become. The more practical side knew that action was required. "This is hard to deal with."

"You've had a whole series of life-changing shocks." He ticked them off on his fingers. "You got the inheritance, learned of the betrayal by Jamison and survived three murder attempts, which reminds me…there's something I wanted to ask about the operation you had in Aspen. The doctors—not Thorson but other docs—told us that you flatlined twice. Do you remember anything about it?"

"Like did I see white light and angels?"

"Or something else."

She'd always enjoyed the vision of the afterlife that included a welcoming party standing at the pearly gates. How could that possibly work? When her parents were alive, they hadn't really got along. In death, would old hostilities be forgotten? Emily couldn't imagine her distant father and her hostile mom with her endless resentment toward a daughter who demanded too much attention. Even their good times were tinged with ugliness. If she hadn't been able to escape into art, she didn't know how she would have survived.

And if her near-death experience didn't include her parents, who would be there? Surely not Jamison. She shuddered. "I don't think I want to remember."

"How come?"

"Let's just say that most of my guardian angels are carrying pitchforks." And she didn't want to be welcomed into their company. "We need to start making plans. There's a lot to do today. The number one, most important thing—I might get released."

"Dr. Troutman said it's a good possibility."

"I like Fish."

"And everything at the house should be ready for you," he said. "The security system complete with new door will be done by lunchtime, which is also when the housecleaning crew will finish up. Also, I've arranged for a part-time nurse and a physical therapist to come to the house twice a day to help with workouts."

"Damn, you're good. How would you like a permanent job as my assistant?"

"Sure, if you're willing to pay my rate for billable hours."

"Probably not." She was so accustomed to seeing him as a friend that she forgot he was really a highly paid New York attorney. "I really want to go to my gallery today. Maybe this afternoon."

"We can make that happen." He went toward the door. "I'm going for your tea and my coffee. When I come back, we can talk about the rest of your day. Wellborn needs to schedule a time to get into your safe-deposit box."

While he was gone, Emily summoned the nurse's aide to help her into the bathroom, where she did the basics of brushing her teeth and splashing water on her face. Hesitantly, she looked into the mirror and was happy to see that the bruises were fading. The worst of the swelling had gone down. With makeup, she might pass for human.

Back in the bed, she pulled up the covers. "I should warn you, Beverly, about my Beretta. I'm not a very good shot."

"Are you planning to carry your weapon?" she asked.

"Not really." Her left arm was still in a cast, and the physical therapist hinted that she'd be using a cane with her right. Or she might be stuck in a wheelchair for another day or so. "I don't even know how I'd carry it."

"That's what I figured," the bodyguard said. "There's only one safety lesson you really need to learn."

"What's that?"

"Don't get shot." She stepped up to the bedside, unbuttoned the collared white shirt she wore under her suit jacket and pulled it open to show her undergarment. "This is a lightweight, breathable, bulletproof vest."

"It looks like a T-shirt."

"I hardly notice I have it on."

The door opened, and Emily craned her neck, expecting to see Connor. Instead, Phillip Riggs and his sister, Patricia, sauntered into her room.

Beverly reacted swiftly, pivoting and blocking access to the bed. Her tone was authoritative. "I have to ask you to leave."

Patricia stood her ground. She looked the bodyguard up and down. "You're a big one, aren't you?"

"Big enough to handle you," Beverly said as she took a step toward them. "Wait in the hall until Connor returns and gives the okay."

"Fine." Patricia sneered as she looked around the bodyguard. "I have a bone to pick with little missy here. It's not enough that she caused so much trouble for poor Phillip. Now she's destroyed my personal life."

"Hold it," Emily said. "What are you talking about?"

"Because of you, my fiancé, Dr. Eric Thorson, was forced to take a leave of absence. All he was trying to do was help you. And now he might lose his position at the hospital."

As far as Emily was concerned, Thorson deserved a

much worse punishment. "You really can't blame me for what happened. I was in a coma."

"He's gone," she said. "He's not at his apartment and isn't answering his phone. And it's your fault."

You'll thank me later.

Emily pressed her lips together to keep from blurting out her opinion. Some things were better left unsaid.

Chapter Twelve

Connor exited the elevator carrying a tray with three beverages from the custom coffee shop in the lobby: a tea for Emily, black coffee for him and a latte for Beverly. As he walked, he mentally ran through the day's agenda and added a visit to her gallery to the list of things that needed to be done. He rounded the corner and saw Patricia and Phillip pacing the hallway outside Emily's room.

In a low, rasping voice, Connor demanded, "What the hell are you doing here?"

"No need to be rude." Patricia was cold and obnoxious. "May we have a word?"

"In a minute."

Beverly opened the door for him, and he entered Emily's room. As he handed out the beverages, he asked, "Did they tell you what they want?"

"I'm not sure," Emily said. "I think it's something about Thorson."

He raised his hot, aromatic coffee to his mouth and took a sip. "You don't have to talk to the Riggs family if you don't want to. They have no hold on you."

"I feel like I owe them an apology." She struggled with the cardboard cup, balancing it on her lap and flipping open the hole in the lid with her right hand. "I thought they were the ones trying to kill me, but now I'm almost certain that Kate is behind the assaults."

"Don't be so sure."

Being a lawyer had taught him to expect the unexpected. Kate looked like the number one suspect, but her motives didn't add up. When she first talked to Emily, she wanted information. The search at the house had been about finding the bank account number and the password. He couldn't see what Kate had to gain by having Emily dead.

There was a sharp rap at the door. "Let us in," Patricia said harshly.

"It's okay," Emily said with a sigh. "We might as well get this over with."

When Beverly opened the door, Patricia and Phillip spilled inside. Connor took a closer look at them. The unflappable Patricia wasn't put together perfectly. Her straight brown hair was askew. A wig? He never knew she wore a wig. Her clothes looked like she'd slept in them. And her makeup had smeared into raccoon eyes. Any sympathy he might have felt for her vanished when she opened her mouth.

"I demand to know," Patricia said. "Where is my fiancé?"

"The police are looking for him," Connor said.

"Whatever for? He's done nothing wrong."

"He's a witness. That means he's involved."

She tugged on her hair. "This is all a terrible misunderstanding. When he moved Emily into the ambulance, he was only trying to help me."

"To what end?" Connor asked. "Kidnapping?"

"Never." She stiffened her spine. Beside her, Phillip mimicked her posture. Clearly, he was the follower in this family dynamic.

"Be honest," Emily said from the bed. "We've never been close. Why did you want to take me to your home?"

"My primary concern was, of course, your well-being," Patricia said. "And I will admit that because you had just inherited a valuable piece of our family property, I wanted to make sure you did the right thing."

"By *the right thing*," Connor said, "you mean giving the house back to the family."

Phillip piped up, "It's a great house. I've lived there for years."

"You have," Emily said. "Exactly how long?"

"At least six years," he said. "I took care of the place when you and Jamison weren't there. When you came to town, I moved in with Aunt Glenda so you'd have your privacy. I love that house. I don't want to leave. Jamison knew that."

"I'm sorry," Emily said.

An expression of concern crossed her face, and Connor was amazed by the depth of her compassion. The Riggs family—every last one of them—had been bitchy toward her from the moment she first said hello. He couldn't believe she'd cut them any slack.

"I've got a solution," he said to Phillip. "Emily is going to sell the house. If you want it so much, you can buy it."

Patricia laughed out loud. "Phillip doesn't have that kind of money."

Other people in the family, including Patricia, could finance the purchase for her hapless younger brother, but Connor didn't want to squabble. "In a few weeks, it'll be on the market."

"What about the art?" Phillip asked.

Emily brightened, as she always did when discussing the subject that was nearest and dearest to her heart. "I'm planning to loan most of it to museums. Are there any pieces you especially like? The Degas? The Banksy lithographs?"

After a moment of hemming and hawing, he said, "I like the cowboy picture."

"The Remington," she said. "Good choice. Maybe we can figure out some way that you can keep it."

"Yes, yes, lovely," Patricia drawled. "Let's get back to what's really important—my missing fiancé. What do you intend to do about him?"

He sensed a symphony of false notes in this romance. Patricia had never been a warm person, and Thorson was a narcissistic jerk. "How did you two meet?"

She wrapped her black knee-length cape more tightly around her and shrugged her bony shoulders. "I don't really remember. It was one of those hospital fund-raisers."

"So he didn't sweep you off your feet," Connor said drily.

"We're adults." She spread her cape like a vampire bat. "Our relationship is built on mutual goals and desires. Eric appreciates my financial abilities. And I respect his talent. He's more than an ER doctor, you know. He has a world-class reputation as a virologist."

"Has he cured anything I might have heard of?"

"He's been an integral part of teams in Central Asia and Africa. After we're married next year, I plan to set up a research center for him."

"Next year?" Emily questioned.

"It would have been sooner, but I decided to wait for a decent interval after Jamison's death."

"To see how you fared in your cousin's will," Connor said.

"A sensible plan."

Not exactly a starry-eyed declaration of love, but these two were, in their own way, made for each other. Patricia got to call herself a doctor's wife and parade around her Norse demigod husband while Thorson received funding for his virus research.

"If we hear anything about him, we'll let you know," he said. "Let me ask you a question. How well do you know Kate Sylvester?"

"She's an acquaintance."

Not according to the scant information he had. "She was staying with Phillip."

"Hey," he said, "I've got a girlfriend. But Kate is an excellent snowboarder. When she comes to town, I let her use one of the bedrooms and—"

"That's enough," Patricia said. She looked down her nose, an expression that failed to intimidate, given her smeared makeup. "Why are you interested in Kate?"

Not wanting to show his hand, he brushed her question aside. "I wondered why Jamison left her a Rolex in his will."

"Don't ask me. I don't understand half the things Jamison did."

When the breakfast tray from the hospital kitchen was delivered, Connor chased Patricia and Phillip from the room. He settled into the chair beside Emily's bed and watched with approval as she dug into the scrambled eggs and bacon. She looked healthier today. In spite of yesterday's painful revelations, she continued to recover.

The visit from Patricia and Phillip caused him to reconsider some of their conclusions about Kate. "Did they seem suspicious to you?"

"With the Riggs family," she said, "there's usually an ulterior motive. I'm pretty sure that they weren't whisking me away from the hospital because they were concerned."

"Patricia admitted that they wanted to keep an eye on you."

"Why? At that point, nobody knew how bad my injuries were. I could have been in a coma for months."

Keeping Emily under their thumb would have worked well for the Riggs family. They could have maintained her coma, supposedly for her own good, while they manipulated the property away from her. "We need evidence," he said.

She nibbled on a piece of bacon. "You could talk to Adam, the ambulance guy."

As soon as she said the name, he pulled his cell phone from his pocket and put through a call to Adam. When she had started waking up prematurely, he and Adam had supposed it was due to a changed dosage in the sedative that she'd been given. Connor had seen the switched IV bag as a threat, designed to bring her around to consciousness too soon.

Adam answered quickly. "Hey, Connor, how's our girl?"

"She'll probably get out of the hospital today or tomorrow," he said. "Thanks again for everything you did."

"Anytime you need somebody for a free helo ride to Denver, give me a call."

"Did you ever get the switched IV bag tested?"

"I brought it back to the Aspen hospital," Adam said. "The lab people told me the dosage wasn't what had been prescribed."

"What about fingerprints?"

"I gave the bag to Sandoval. Check with him." Static noise interrupted their call. "I've got to roll, Connor. Good to hear from you."

He disconnected the call. The assumptions he and Adam had made were correct. Somebody had tried to tamper with her treatment. As far as he could tell, Kate hadn't been involved while they were in Aspen. It wasn't until they had got to Denver that he spotted her at the hospital wearing scrubs. Wellborn and the DPD had been looking for her, but she'd disappeared.

His suspicions shifted back toward the Riggs family and Patricia's doctor fiancé. Thorson would have understood how the IV was used and the danger it might be to Emily.

"This is going to sound crazy," he said, "but I find myself agreeing with Patricia."

Her blue eyes opened wide. "About what?"

"We need to find Thorson."

The doctor had some explaining to do.

INSTEAD OF TROOPING along with Wellborn to the bank, Emily opted for medical care. Fish and his team did a few more tests and were pleased with her progress. Her seizure continued to puzzle them, and the blood tests failed to identify any foreign substance that might have caused that reaction. There was no evidence, but she'd suffered a seizure after Connor had seen Kate Sylvester in scrubs at the hospital. Could Kate have somehow infected her with an untraceable toxin? Though she didn't want to take the next logical step, Emily couldn't help wondering if a similar poison had been used to cause Jamison's fatal illness.

His mysterious death loomed at the center of everything and caused the threats to her life. Kate would go to great lengths to get the account number and the password that she thought Emily knew. The Riggs family was trying to thwart Jamison's will and reclaim her inheritance.

She was angry at him for putting her into this situation. But how could she rail at a dead man? He didn't deserve to die so young.

She perked up when Dr. Parris removed the cast on her arm and replaced it with a much smaller version that covered the back of her hand and stopped below her elbow. Moving her arm to different positions was sheer pleasure.

"How long will I have this cast?" she asked.

"Less than a month," Parris said. "Now, let's take a look at that ankle."

As she removed the plastic boot, she issued a series of instructions. "You need to keep icing it, elevate it when possible and use compression."

Emily looked down at her sprain. Bruised and swollen, her ankle was not a pretty sight. "Can I walk on it?"

"If you use the boot, you can put weight on it as long as it doesn't hurt. But I don't trust you with that solution. You're a woman who pushes herself. You might overestimate your mobility and worsen the injury."

"Yeah, I do that. Trying to run when I shouldn't even be walking."

"Let's keep you in a wheelchair for as long as possible. You need to recover slowly. We can start with a splint and a cane."

"Cool." She glanced toward the backup bodyguard, a square-shouldered guy with a beard, who was standing in for Beverly. She asked him, "What do you think, Schultz? Can you get me a cane with a sword inside?"

"I'm pretty sure Beverly wouldn't go for that."

"We don't have to tell her," Emily said.

"No swords," Dr. Parris said. "Don't strain the sprain. Get it?"

"Got it."

In the physical therapy gym, she learned how to use a cane and practiced walking the perimeter of the area. When her leg was tired, she dropped into a wheelchair and allowed the therapist to whisk her back to her room, where she took her time with a long shower and had a change of clothes. Only a few garments required help from a nurse's aide. On top, she wore a short-sleeved T-shirt under the lavender velour sweatshirt with the cut sleeve. Her new cast was smaller but still too bulky to fit neatly inside a sleeve. Her slacks were khakis. She had a purple sock on the injured ankle and a purple sneaker on her good foot.

Back in her room, she was seated in the comfortable recliner, with her ankle elevated on the footrest. She waved Schultz toward her. "Do you like to draw?"

"I'm no artist." Behind his trim brown beard, the corners of his mouth turned down. "My three-year-old daughter makes prettier pictures than I do."

"No problem," she said. "I have a set of markers in my purse. Grab one and sign your name on my cast."

After gathering a few more scribbles and signatures from hospital staff, she was beginning to feel restless. This was more than enough time in the hospital. She wanted to go to her gallery and was anxious to show Connor the work she'd done, transforming a simple storefront into a warm, inviting space. As soon as possible, she needed to meet with her part-time staff. There was work to be done before the scheduled showing of Southwestern art. She needed to curate, to plan and to finalize her contract with the mariachis.

Connor strode into the room accompanied by Beverly. When he saw Emily, he stopped in his tracks. "Well, look at you," he said. "A smaller cast on your arm and no plastic boot."

His complimentary tone matched her upbeat energy. She pointed to her forehead. "And Fish took off the big bandage."

"With your hair combed over, I can't even tell you were whacked." He placed the box he'd been carrying on one of the small tables with wheels that he whipped across the floor and parked beside her. "You're almost back to normal. Not that you've ever been normal or average. You're way above. Top-notch."

She pointed to the box. "A present?"

"I should have brought you something beautiful. Hang on a minute. I can run down to the lobby and get more flowers."

His enthusiasm warmed her inside. This man—this very handsome man—thought she deserved bouquets and beauty. If he got this excited about clean hair and a velour sweatshirt, she wondered what would happen if she dared to put on a filmy, lacy negligee. The thought made her blush, and she pushed the image to the back of her mind to be savored later. "What's in the box?"

"The contents of your safe-deposit box. I did like you said, piled it all in here without looking at anything."

"Does Wellborn need to be here before I open it?"

"I promised to contact him if you find a password." He scooted a chair across the room and sat beside her. "His tech people got access to your files that were saved onto the cloud but haven't uncovered anything significant."

"If Jamison didn't want it to be found, he knew how to keep stuff secret."

She lifted the lid and peeked inside. Mostly, her safe-deposit box had contained documents. There were a couple of small velvet jewelry boxes for special pieces, letter-sized envelopes with mementos tucked inside, a diary from her teen years and a five-by-seven notebook with a hot-pink cover. She plucked out the notebook and started flipping through pages, looking for the right password.

"What happens," she asked, "if I can't find it?"

"I asked Wellborn about that. Worst-case scenario, he'll take you to the Caymans, where you can find the bank and use your fingerprints to get whatever is in there."

"Another trip to the island doesn't sound too terrible." She wiggled the fingers on her right hand at him. "All I have to do is leave my prints."

"There is a downside."

"Of course." She braced for the inevitable downer.

"If Wellborn is able to get into the offshore account and Kate isn't, she'll need to prevent his access. She'll want to stop you from helping the feds. It's another motive."

"That's just what I need—another reason for somebody to want me dead." It seemed like every time they uncovered a potential clue, they found nothing but a dead end. She went back to the beginning. "Have you heard anything about the truck?"

"The last thing I heard from Sandoval was that he hadn't found the truck or your laptop. Are you sure you had it with you?"

"I remember thinking I should take it in case I was too tired to drive home and had to spend the night in the mountains. I figured I could catch up on emails." She frowned at the numbers scribbled in her pink notebook. "I can't swear that I actually put the computer in the car."

"You're calm about it," he said. "If I get separated from my laptop or my phone or any of my electronic devices, I go a little crazy."

She liked to think that long ago, when she'd jotted everything in notebooks, was a simpler time, but that just wasn't true. Her electronics made it easy to keep track of virtually everything. She pointed to a page in the pink notebook. "This is the number for a savings account. Not the one in the Caymans, but I might have used a similar password."

"What is it?"

"Warhol," she said, "because Andy Warhol did that painting of a one-dollar bill."

He tapped the keys on his phone and made a note. "Anything else?"

Her little notebook was filled with page after page of

notations. Some were important, like the account number, while others were reminders or recipes or phone numbers. "It's hard to believe I scribbled all these details. Now I keep everything on my phone and my computer."

"It's safer that way. Your information is stored with a long-distance server, right?"

"Supposedly." Though she seldom had reason to contact the cloud, where her files were stored, she trusted that the system was effective as long as she kept the account paid and current. She closed the notebook and looked up at him. "I'll set this aside for later. Right now, I'm ready to go to my gallery."

"And I'm ready to see it."

He leaned over and gave her a friendly kiss on the cheek that both pleased and annoyed. She liked their familiarity but didn't want to continue on the platonic path. As a bosom buddy, he ought to pay more attention to her breasts. She wanted their sizzling chemistry to ignite into a full, luscious blaze.

Mobilizing to leave the hospital was a complicated operation, and Beverly took charge, ordering Schultz to bring the van around to the front exit and arranging with the hospital staff to keep the stuff from her safe-deposit box in a secure location.

Less than a half hour later, Beverly turned to her and Connor with further instructions. "Schultz will drive. Connor and I will ride in back. Emily is in the passenger seat. I've arranged for O'Brien to meet us at the gallery. He has information from the DPD and from his trip to Aspen."

"Evidence?" she asked hopefully.

"I don't know," Beverly said. "Solving the crime isn't my job."

"Maybe give it a try," Emily suggested. "I'll bet you'd make an outstanding detective."

"I would. But it doesn't interest me."

Connor pushed her wheelchair through the corridors, into the elevator and down to the first floor. When they went through the double doors at the front of the building, she turned her face toward the bright sunshine and reveled in the caress of a September breeze. In a landscaped area near the parking garage, the leaves on five slender aspen trees had turned to gold. She'd only been out of commission a few days, but it felt like a lot longer.

Instead of the ambulance cab, they were able to use a regular van. At the passenger door, Connor helped her inside. He took her wheelchair, folded it up and stowed it in the rear of the van. Beverly made sure she was safely inside before she closed the door.

Emily put on her safety belt, glanced toward the street and froze. Fear smacked her right between the eyes. She blinked wildly but still saw it. A black truck turned right at the corner.

Chapter Thirteen

Emily held her breath and stared straight ahead through the windshield. She wanted to scream but held back. She couldn't allow herself to burst into hysterics every time she saw a black truck. This was Colorado, where lots of people drove trucks, even in the city.

She heard Connor's voice. He sounded hollow as though calling to her from the bottom of a well instead of the back seat of the van, and he seemed to be asking if she was all right.

"Fine," she said quickly. "I'm fine."

"You look startled," he said.

Had he always been so talented at reading her mind? Though she was hoping the two of them would get close, she didn't like being so very transparent. Glass was fragile, easy to break. And she needed to be strong.

Determined to hold it together, she changed the subject. "You're going to like my gallery."

Trying not to sound like a tour guide or a real estate agent, she described the five-block area in an older part of town near Etta Morton Elementary. Most of the rundown businesses had been renovated into art galleries, craft stores, cafés, tapas bars, yoga studios and more. Every first Friday of the month, the Morton Merchants' Association sponsored an open house. On holidays, they threw street fairs. "I checked out a lot of neighborhoods all over town and worked at other galleries before I found the perfect space."

"And you call it Calico Cat," he said, "but not the imaginary calico named Taffy."

"Not imaginary."

"Why that name?"

While the van crept through afternoon traffic, she watched the vehicles around them and behind them, looking for the black truck. Though she told herself there was no way he'd ambush them on the road in front of all these witnesses, she couldn't erase her fear.

"Calico Cat," she said. "I never had pets when I was a kid. My mom hated the mess. But I found a mangy stuffed animal—a calico cat. I whispered my secrets to the calico and told her my dreams, but that's not why I chose the name. The Japanese think a calico cat is good luck."

"Excellent reason."

When they turned off Downing Street, the traffic lessened. Since it was too early for the dinner crowd, the Morton neighborhood wasn't too hectic. Her shop was around the corner from a clothing store that specialized in woven organic-hemp purses and loose-fitting shirts. The sign hanging over the door of her gallery was shaped like the namesake cat. Decorative ironwork covered the front window and the door.

From the back seat, Beverly issued an order to Schultz. "Drive down the alley to the back. I want to check out the security."

"It's solid," Emily said. "Before I moved in, this storefront was a pot dispensary. Those guys really know how to guard their product."

After Beverly gave the okay on the back door, they circled around the block and returned to the street in front of the store. Schultz found a parking space on the other side of the alley, less than fifty steps from the door.

"Give me your keys," Beverly said. "I'll unlock the door."

"You'll also need the code to deactivate the alarm system." Emily rattled off the code numbers. "The box is to the left above the light switches."

"I'll find it. After I open up and take a look around inside to make sure it's safe, I'll signal to the boys. They'll get your wheelchair and bring you inside."

"I brought my cane," she said. "I could walk."

"We'll do this my way." Beverly was calm but authoritative. "I want you to stay in the wheelchair until we get inside. Then you can hop, skip or jump. Fair enough?"

The precautions seemed extreme, but Emily didn't argue. Her bossy bodyguard was an expert. If the black truck showed up again, she wanted to be with somebody who took control and kicked butt. And so, they sat in the van and waited for Beverly's signal.

As soon as she waved, Schultz and Connor went into action. Their moves were efficient, almost choreographed. Connor brought the wheelchair to the passenger side and opened the door so she could climb out and get seated.

Schultz walked next to her on the street side.

Beverly had taken a position in front of the gallery. Like Schultz, her hand rested on the butt of her holstered weapon.

Emily heard the *pop-pop-pop* of muffled gunshots.

A heavy impact slammed into her upper chest. She jolted backward in the chair.

Everything went black.

CONNOR THREW HIMSELF in front of her. Too late, he was too late. Emily was unconscious. She'd been hit.

He wouldn't give up. Not now. Not ever. *Move fast. Get her to safety!* He scrambled to drag her limp body from the wheelchair. Throwing her over his shoulder wasn't an option. Not with her bruised ribs. He held her under the arms and knees.

Schultz stood in front of them both. He scanned the area. His gun was drawn.

"Over here," Beverly yelled as she held the shop door wide open. "Connor, bring Emily inside. Schultz, go after the shooter."

Connor staggered through the door, taking care not to bump her head or any other part of her body. He avoided looking down at the woman in his arms. If she was bleeding, he didn't want to see it. He couldn't bear to watch her die.

Inside the gallery, Beverly turned off the overhead lights and rushed him toward an antique door near the back of the gallery. She twisted the brass knob and yanked it open. "Stay in this storage room. Keep the door closed."

"Wait," he said. "I should call 9-1-1."

"No," a small voice objected.

He was stunned. "What?"

Emily wiggled in his arms. "Don't call 9-1-1."

"You're not dead."

"Not yet."

Beverly turned on the lights in the storage room, and he looked down into Emily's clear, wide-open eyes. There were no discernible smears of blood on her body. He didn't know how or why, but she appeared to be all right.

"Put me down," she said, "and go after that son of a bitch."

"That's my job," Beverly said. "Connor, stay in this room, and keep an eye on her."

"Why here?"

"No windows," she said.

Beverly dashed from the room and closed the door behind her. Connor couldn't think of what he was supposed to do next. His usually organized mind was overwhelmed by a tsunami of adrenaline. His pulse was racing. Too much had happened in a very short time span. He was off balance, unable to get his bearings.

"Connor, are you all right?"

"I should be asking you that question."

She'd been attacked…again. And he had failed to protect her…again.

He had to get it together, starting now. He set Emily down on a folding chair near the door, hunkered down beside Emily and patted her knee, reassuring her and himself at the same time.

"I don't understand what happened. I heard the shots. You slumped forward." Trying to calm himself, he exhaled slowly. "I thought you were hit."

"I was."

"You're telling me that you were shot."

"Correct, but I'm pretty much okay."

For sure, he was glad. But he had to admit that her ability to survive against all odds was beginning to get spooky. "I'm going to need more information."

She unzipped her sweatshirt and pulled the boatneck of her light blue T-shirt down to reveal an undergarment. "Bulletproof vest," she said. "Beverly said I had to wear one whenever I went outside."

"Where were you hit?"

"Here." She winced as she rubbed at her upper chest below her left shoulder. "It feels like I got punched really hard."

"Let me take a look."

When he eased her casted left arm out of the sweatshirt, she winced. From the little he knew, a bulletproof vest wasn't like a suit of armor. The bullet didn't pierce the skin, but the impact was still felt. He reached inside her T-shirt and unfastened the strap for the vest, which he carefully pulled away from her shoulder. A reddish-purple bruise marred her smooth pale skin.

She twisted her neck, trying to see the area. "How bad is it?"

"Bad enough that you need to get it checked out by a doctor."

"I'll do that," she said. "I didn't want to call 9-1-1 right now because I wanted Beverly and Schultz to focus on going after the person who shot me. Did you see him? Maybe it wasn't a man. Was it Kate?"

"I don't know." He replaced the strap on the vest. As long as she was out in public, she needed all the protection she could get. "I saw a couple of people milling around at the street corner outside the hemp shop. If one of them had been pointing a gun, I sure as hell would have noticed. Maybe he was in a car."

"Or a truck," she said.

For the first time, he looked around the storage room and saw a giant papier-mâché skull decorated with bright flowers. Four skeletons, wearing sombreros and serapes with orange, yellow and green stripes, danced across the back wall, where a decorated coffin leaned ominously. "What's going on in here?"

"Dia de los Muertos," she said. "The Day of the Dead is next month, and I'm storing some of the artwork. My gallery is sponsoring a float for the parade on the weekend before. It's not a holiday I usually get excited about, but I keep thinking about how Jamison died so young."

"You miss him."

"Oh, no," she said, "that's not how I feel about my ex-husband, especially not after the past couple of days. They say that on *Dia de los Muertos*, the veil between life and death is lifted, and you can communicate with the dead. I'd like the chance to tell him how I hate being used and manipulated."

"Or you could ask him for the password."

She gave a short laugh. "I don't like being angry like this. I'd rather stick to the Day of the Dead tradition of dancing with death to celebrate life."

"I have another idea for celebrating. It doesn't involve skeletons or skulls or floats or parades." His gaze mingled with hers. He was fascinated by the many facets of her sapphire eyes. "I'd like to throw a private party for just you and me. Maybe we could have a bottle of wine, listen to some music."

Her slight, subtle grin told him that she was on the same wavelength and had also been thinking about time they could spend together. Soon, they'd have their chance.

The door at the front of the store crashed open, and he jumped to his feet, ready to defend her.

Beverly called out, "It's me and Schultz. O'Brien is with us, too."

Emily stood and grasped his arm for support. "I want to hear what they found out."

"Are you supposed to be walking around?"

"It's okay as long as I don't strain the sprain. You can help by putting your arm around my waist and matching your steps to mine. I want to go to my office at the back of the shop. Beverly will approve of that space. There's only one small window."

He followed her instructions. Wrapping his arm around her gave him pleasure. At six foot three, he was at least eight inches taller, but they fitted together nicely. Her body rubbed against him as they shuffled slowly across the slate-tiled floor.

Beverly had turned on the overhead lights, and he had a chance to view some of the pieces on display. Her shop was three times as long as it was wide, and Emily had added several partitions to add more hanging space. The art ranged from photography to watercolor to oil, and many different styles were represented. Though the walls were mostly white, she'd used wood and plastic trim to give texture and contrast.

"You did a great job in here," he said.

"Thank you."

She sank into the swivel chair behind an L-shaped desk with a sleek black acrylic top. Her office at the farthest end of the shop was open to the rest of the gallery but set apart with strategically placed partitions to give privacy. A break room with a kitchen counter, microwave and sink was on the opposite wall.

She waved toward the fridge. "Help yourselves. There's wine, beer and soft drinks."

Connor greeted O'Brien. He hadn't spoken to the detective in person since they discovered Emily's ransacked house together. "Beverly said you have information."

"Not enough," he muttered. "I'll fill you in."

"Something to drink?"

"I wouldn't mind a beer."

Since Emily was laid up, Connor played host, serving craft beers to O'Brien and Schultz. Beverly got herself a glass of tap water. And Emily wanted an orange soda. He took the same and then sat at a round table with four chairs. O'Brien joined him. Schultz sprawled on the long Scandinavian-style sofa while Beverly remained standing, ready to leap into action at any given moment.

"Tell me about the Denver PD," Connor said. "The CSI team was all over Emily's house. Did they find anything?"

"No witnesses. They interviewed neighbors and other people who might be in the area." O'Brien raked his fingers through his graying hair. "There were fingerprints. When they ran them through the system, nothing popped."

"What does that mean?" Emily asked.

"Nothing showed up in criminal databases for Colorado or for the FBI. Others fingerprints could be logically explained, like your neighbor and a woman who works for a professional cleaning service."

She asked, "How soon will my house be ready for me to move back in?"

"I just came from there," he said. "It's been cleaned, security added and the door repaired. It's ready now."

That had to make her happy. Connor knew she was itching to get home, which seemed strange, given everything that had happened to her—including someone breaking into her house and going through her things. Maybe she found strength in her own space and felt less vulnerable.

He turned to the detective. "You've been in Aspen. Find anything useful?"

"It's so damned pretty." He took a long pull from his beer bottle and loosened his necktie. "That mountain scenery is why I moved to Colorado. Glenda Riggs is not a charming woman, but her ranch has got to be one of the most beautiful sights on earth. That's the kind of place where I want to retire. I'm getting close to that age. I know I don't look it, but I'm fifty-six."

"No kidding." Connor said with a teasing grin, "I would've guessed seventy-seven."

"Wise guy."

Actually, it would have been difficult to pinpoint O'Brien's age. He was in good physical condition, but the lines in his face showed a lifetime of experience. "While you were admiring the peaks, did you get a chance to talk to Deputy Sandoval?"

"I did. He and his crew are working over Emily's smashed-up Hyundai. They haven't located her laptop."

"Did he tell you about the switched IV bag?"

"Pitkin County Forensics found smudges on the bag that might indicate someone handled it with gloved hands. The only distinct prints belonged to you and the ambulance driver."

Emily exhaled a frustrated sigh. "So we struck out in Aspen and in Denver."

"It's not a total loss. I've got a long list of names to check out, including people who were at the reading of the will. I broke them into two groups. First, there are those loyal to the Riggs family. Second are Jamison's business associates, who would also know Kate Sylvester."

The investigation wasn't a blazing success, but Connor could see progress. Various directions were taking shape. "We should talk about what just happened here—the shooting."

"I caught a glimpse of the shooter," Schultz said. "Somebody in a hooded sweatshirt stuck their arm out of the passenger side of a car and fired. I heard three shots. I think he was using a silencer."

"A good marksman," Beverly said under her breath. "Only three shots to get a direct hit."

"They drove off fast," Schultz said.

O'Brien asked, "Did you get a license plate?"

"The last two numbers were seven and three, Colorado plates. They were gone before I could read more."

While Beverly and O'Brien peppered Schultz with questions about whether the shooter used a silencer and the escape route of the vehicle, Connor took a moment to digest this significant bit of information. There was a driver and a shooter—two people. Either Kate Sylvester was working with a partner or Patricia and Phillip Riggs had jumped back to the top of the suspect list.

"Excuse me," Emily interrupted. "I have to know. What kind of vehicle was it?"

"A dark gray Chevy sedan," Schultz said. "Why?"

"I saw a black truck at the hospital."

Chapter Fourteen

Aware that she'd dropped a bombshell, Emily swiveled in her desk chair and glanced around the room, looking from one person to the next until she confronted Connor's hard gaze. She explained, "I couldn't tell if it was the same truck that ran me off the road. I didn't notice dents or damage. It pulled away after we'd all loaded into the van."

"They were watching," Beverly said. "That explains the coincidence of a shooter who appeared outside your shop as soon as we arrived."

"But the shooter wasn't in a truck," Emily said.

"There's a second vehicle," Connor said in measured tones. "A shooter and a driver. There are at least two people involved."

Though he didn't yell and wave his arms, she knew he was mad at her. Her inclination was to apologize and avoid conflict. But why should she? She'd done nothing wrong. "I didn't point out the truck because I wasn't sure. I didn't want to set off a false alarm."

Instead of reassuring her, he turned toward O'Brien. "Can the truck and the sedan be tracked through traffic? In Manhattan, there are enough security cameras on stoplights and ATMs and buildings for the police to follow the camera feeds and do surveillance, especially when they know what kind of car they're looking for."

"I can arrange something, maybe not through law enforcement. I have my own channels." O'Brien took his phone from his pocket. "Still, before we do anything, we should make a report to the police."

"You'll find us at the hospital," Connor said as he stood. "Emily needs to be checked out by a doctor. Beverly, you'll come with us."

"I'm all right," Emily protested. The bruise where she'd been shot throbbed, but she could handle the pain. "I can stay and talk to the police."

"It's not necessary," he said as he strode the length of the gallery and grabbed her wheelchair, which one of the bodyguards had left at the front door. "Beverly, which is more secure, the front door or the back?"

"Back," she said. "I'll pull the van around."

He whipped the wheelchair up beside her, put on the brake and took her arm to help her move from her swivel chair.

She jerked her arm from his grasp. "I don't need help."

"Suit yourself."

Balancing on her good leg and putting very little weight on the sprained ankle, she maneuvered her way into the chair. A full-scale eruption was building inside her, and she sealed her lips so she wouldn't snap at him or Beverly as they shuffled her around like a sack of potatoes. In moments, they were in the van with Connor behind the steering wheel.

So what if he was angry? That didn't give him the right to order her around and refuse to listen to her. After she'd been married awhile, Jamison had started treating her the same way, like a child who was incapable of making her own decisions. When she'd objected to her ex-husband's controlling attitude, he had placated her with gifts and had told her that he enjoyed taking care of her. Sometimes she liked being pampered, but there were occasions when she chafed under his condescending pats on the head. She hoped Connor wouldn't turn out to be more of the same.

Sure, he respected her as a friend. But what if their relationship turned into something more? He already felt obliged to protect her. Too easily, protection could become control. She didn't want him to watch over her every move, to dictate her life.

She wasn't helpless—far from it. Emily had pretty much raised herself after her parents' death. She'd escaped her annoying uncle and put herself through school on scholarships. At age twenty-two, she'd found a job in the highly competitive art market of New York. To top it off, she'd married a rich man. Her life should have been a success. Why did she feel like such a disaster?

In the driver's seat beside her, Connor was silent.

An apology was out of the question, but she hated feeling so distant from him. "Is there something you want to say to me?"

"I'm not buying your false-alarm excuse."

"I don't care if you do."

He stared through the windshield at the bumper-to-bumper traffic. Though it wasn't even four o'clock, rush hour had already begun. "I don't get it. Why didn't you say something? You know we're all searching for the black truck. Did you think we wouldn't believe you?"

"Maybe."

His jaw clenched. "You've got to trust us, Emily. Trust me. I'm on your side. You don't have to handle this alone."

"I was scared." The words jumped out before she could stop them. Even worse, she felt tears flooding her eyes. She didn't want to be a crybaby. Her mom had taught her better; she sneered at those who wept.

At a stoplight, he turned his head and studied her. His

dark eyes softened. He reached across the center console and rested his hand on her arm above the cast. "I'm sorry."

His sensitivity melted the hard core inside her. Her guard dropped. Was there anything more macho than a man who could admit when he'd made a mistake? She swabbed away her tears before they slipped down her cheeks.

"You were right about one thing," she said. "I'm glad we're going back to the hospital. Even with the vest, I'm feeling the pain."

From the back seat, Beverly said, "The bruise will go away in a couple of days. You're lucky you weren't hit in your cracked ribs."

Her ribs were feeling good in comparison to the new contusion. "Have you been shot before?"

"Half a dozen times," she said casually. "Only once without the vest. I was in the hospital for two weeks, and that was when I decided to leave the marines."

"But you became a bodyguard. That's not exactly a nonviolent profession."

"A life without risk isn't worth living. Charles Lindbergh said that."

When they parked at the emergency entrance to the hospital, Beverly was hypervigilant as they traveled the short distance from the van to the door. Rather than going through the ER doctors, Connor put through a call to Troutman and Parris.

Dr. Parris arrived first. She dashed into the waiting area with her ponytail bouncing from side to side. "A gunshot? Really?"

"I like to keep you on your toes," Emily said. "It's starting to hurt."

"This way." She'd been involved with Emily's case long

enough to know that Beverly would follow them wherever they went.

Before they swooshed through the first set of doors, Emily waved to Connor. "I'll meet you back at the room."

She wasn't angry at him anymore. And she hoped he felt the same.

CONNOR STAYED IN the waiting area outside the ER until Troutman arrived. After he greeted the doctor, he said, "I wasn't sure if I needed to call you to handle a gunshot wound."

"Was she shot in the head?"

"No."

"You don't need me." Troutman's expression turned thoughtful as he stroked the line of his narrow jaw. "But I'm glad you called. I'll walk with you back to her room."

They fell into step together as they went down the first-floor corridors leading to the elevators. At the gift shop, Connor paused, wondering if he should run inside and grab a bouquet of roses to underline his apology. "I probably owe her some flowers."

"You did something wrong," Troutman deduced. "White tulips mean *I'm sorry* in the language of flowers. I always give my wife a bouquet when I've forgotten an anniversary or messed something up."

"I wasn't wrong." He was right to demand that she trust him and tell him everything, but he should have realized how frightened she was. "It was a mistake."

"She'll forgive you," Troutman said as they boarded the elevator. "I see how you two look at each other."

"It's that obvious?"

"You bet," the doctor said as they boarded the elevator. "But that's not why I wanted to confer with you."

At her floor, Troutman said hello to several of the staff.

It wasn't until they were in Emily's private room that he got to the point.

"I know you've been working with the FBI, which means Emily's case is more than a hit-and-run car accident. I'm concerned about the results from her blood tests. The lab found a small amount of a toxic substance that appears to be organic in nature. Before I turn this information over to our toxicology technicians, I wanted to know if I should consult with the FBI."

"Is this substance a poison?"

"That's the simple explanation. It appears to be quickly absorbed into the body, which makes it untraceable." He shrugged his shoulders and flashed his charming grin. "It's not my field. I'm not an expert."

But Connor knew someone who was. Patricia had bragged about her virologist boyfriend, Dr. Eric Thorson. "I'll put you in touch with Special Agent in Charge Wellborn."

"Is this something I should keep to myself?"

"That's probably best."

"The FBI." The doctor's grin got even wider. "Kind of exciting."

Connor could do without any extra drama, but this merry-go-round wouldn't stop until the bad guys were caught. "On a different subject, Emily wants to go home tomorrow."

"If you've arranged for a nurse, I don't see any reason why she shouldn't be released. My office will schedule a follow-up in about a week."

When the doctor left, Connor sat in the recliner chair that he'd come to think of as Emily's throne. He popped up the footrest, stretched out his legs and leaned his head back, enjoying this moment of quiet before he put in a call to Wellborn.

With every new piece of information, the trail of evidence got more twisted and complex. He tried to put Troutman's mystery toxin into perspective. Right before Emily's seizure, he'd seen Kate Sylvester. It was possible that Kate had infected her with the toxin, either with an injection or some airborne method. A similar exposure might have led to Jamison's death. But how would a Wall Street broker get her mitts on an organic poison—a substance so exotic that it had Troutman baffled?

An expert like Thorson, who had a background in virology would know about complex toxins. Connor had instinctively disliked that guy from the moment they'd met. He'd questioned Thorson's competence, but it was hard to think of an ER doctor as a murderer. Also, Thorson was Patricia's fiancé. Why would he help Kate?

For the money.

The answer came quickly. Thorson obviously enjoyed an elite lifestyle in one of the most expensive little towns in the world. The doctor could be bought. Kate might have tempted him with a fast fortune, citing Emily as the only obstacle to getting the funds in Jamison's offshore bank account.

Connor put through a call to Wellborn, who had told him that he'd be at the Denver headquarters for the FBI. He hadn't sounded happy about spending so much time with research and computers.

As soon as he answered, SAC Wellborn got right to the point. "Please tell me you have some kind of new lead."

"How about a disappearing truck, a near-fatal shooting and trace evidence of a mystery toxin?"

"Busy day."

Connor launched into a description of what had happened at the gallery and asked if the FBI could help O'Brien track the vehicles through a network of cameras.

"Send O'Brien over here," Wellborn said. "I've got a couple of techie computer guys he'd love to compare notes with. Give me more about this toxin."

Connor relayed Dr. Troutman's information. "I told him you'd be in touch."

"I'll do better than call. I'd like to go over this information in person."

"It's after five o'clock," Connor pointed out. "The doctor might not be in his office."

"Which makes it the perfect time for us to prowl around in the labs," Wellborn said. "While I'm at the hospital, I'll stop by Emily's room. I need to talk to you about her house in Aspen."

Transferring the inherited property should have been a simple matter of paperwork that Connor's assistant could handle long-distance from New York. But nothing was easy. The Riggs family lawyer was contesting her claim. "I have the property attorneys at my firm working on it. Ultimately, Emily will get what's coming to her, but it might take a while."

"And I still don't have enough evidence for a search warrant," Wellborn said.

Connor ended the call. Wellborn was right about one thing. This had been a busy day, and it wasn't over yet.

Hoping to grab a catnap, he closed his eyes. His first thought was Emily, which was getting to be standard operating procedure. Whenever he slept, he dreamed of her. This vision wasn't the usual silky, sensual image that both plagued and delighted him. In his mind, he saw her face after she'd admitted to fear. A tear spilled from her sweet blue eyes. Her lower lip trembled. He wished with all his heart that he could promise a happy ending, but that might not happen. She might never get the house in Aspen. The offshore bank account might provide proof that her ex had been an embezzler, and she'd have to face that guilt. Plus, he had a bad feeling that there would be more murder attempts.

When he heard the door open, he was surprised. He hadn't expected Emily's emergency care to be finished so quickly. His eyelids lifted, and he saw Patricia Riggs coming at him like an ancient, evil harpy. Her manicured nails were sharpened into claws.

"How dare you?" she snarled.

"Hey, Patty, have you found your fiancé?"

"Don't call me Patty. The only person who ever did was Jamison."

"And we all know what happened to him."

While she launched into a tirade about how she shouldn't be involved in any of these unseemly and terrible plots, Connor recalibrated his thinking. Patricia and Thorson might have been working together to poison Jamison with the mystery toxin. But why? The answer was, as always, money. All along, Patricia's plan might have been to inherit the Aspen house and artwork. But Jamison outsmarted her by bequeathing the property to his ex-wife. Getting Emily out of the way was the only way to make sure the property stayed in the family.

"Do you have any idea how embarrassing this is?" Patricia leaned over the recliner, literally hovering over him. "Phillip and I are staying with one of the wealthiest families in the whole damn state while we're in Denver. These are my friends—influential people. I simply can't have the local police showing up and asking to talk to me."

"Back up, Patricia."

"Why should I?"

"You have crazy eyes. You look like you're going to rip open my gut and tear out my liver."

"This is your fault. The detective you hired—that

O'Brien character—sicced the cops on us. How can they think I'm a suspect in this sordid affair?"

"I asked you nicely to back up."

"I don't take orders from the likes of you, Connor Gallagher."

"You had your warning." He leaned forward, snapped the footrest down and rose in a single swift move. Though he didn't lay a hand on her, his chest bumped her.

With a shriek, she staggered back and repeated her mantra. "How dare you?"

He looked toward the door, glad to see that several of the staff stood watching this encounter. He might need witnesses. "I asked a question. Where's Thorson?"

"I don't know." She turned away from him. "I take it Emily has been attacked again."

"She was shot." Their audience in the doorway gasped in unison, and he spoke more to them than to Patricia. "But she's going to be okay."

"I left the house before the police talked to me. Do you think I should go back?"

Was she really consulting him? He couldn't believe the nerve. "Are you asking for my professional opinion?"

"I have my own lawyers," she said with a sneer.

"So I've heard. My office has been dealing with them all day. You and Phillip and probably Glenda are contesting the will, trying to keep Emily from taking possession of the property."

"It's only right," Patricia said. "If Jamison had been in his right mind, he would have left the house to his family. He loved us."

Not her. Not Phillip. There was no love lost among them. But Patricia was right about one thing. Jamison had cared deeply for his parents. Their deaths within a few months of each other—his mother from cancer and his father in a private plane crash—had shattered him. He'd been in high school, and Aunt Glenda had shipped him off to boarding school as soon as she could. He'd told Connor that he'd never forgiven his aunt. "He didn't owe you a thing."

She tossed her head, sending a ripple through her smooth brown hair. "Aunt Glenda raised him."

And she'd made it clear why she'd never had children of her own. Jamison hadn't hated her, but he'd been distant. Connor always thought that one of his attractions to Emily had been that she was—like him—without the joy that came from having a mother and father. Seen in that light, it almost made sense for him to leave the house and the art to her.

"You're not getting the house," Connor said. "Neither you nor Phillip."

"We'll see about that," she huffed. "I'm going back to Aspen to protect my interests."

"By the way…" He casually pulled the pin and dropped his grenade. When the law went his way, he thoroughly enjoyed his profession. "You and Phillip are no longer allowed in the house. Until the inheritance is settled, the doors are locked."

"You can't do that."

"Oh, but I can," he said. "If Phillip needs to remove some of his belongings, contact the sheriff's department. A deputy will accompany him."

"Where's he supposed to live?" said the woman with the nine-bedroom house.

The hospital staff who had been unabashedly watching from the doorway stepped aside as Emily was wheeled through in her chair. Connor could tell that her examination had included an extra portion of painkillers because she actually smiled at Patricia.

"What are you doing here?" Emily's words were slurred.

"How can you be so rude? After all I've done for you?"

"You're trying to grab my inheritance." Emily's grin belied her words. "Connor says we're not going to let you. We're going to bar the door. And don't think you can sneak in the back door and steal the art, not even that small framed sketch Picasso did on a dinner napkin that I never really liked." She tapped her temple. "I have a catalog of every painting and sculpture and photo in my head. After all, I helped pick most of them out."

"These treasures belong in my family."

"Or not." Emily waved. "Goodbye, Patricia. I'll see you in Aspen."

Under her healthy tan, Patricia paled. A threatened visit from Emily scared her, and he had to wonder what she was hiding.

Chapter Fifteen

The next morning, Emily ached from so many different injuries that she couldn't pinpoint which was the worst. She didn't like to rely on medication, but the painkillers prescribed by Dr. Parris were her best friend. Those lovely pills took the edge off the hurt. And yet, she realized, the relief came at a cost. Her brain was sluggish as if she'd had a sleepless night.

She was glad to have something positive to look forward to. Today, Fish said he'd release her. She could go home to her house. Even better, Connor would be with her. Except for the bodyguards and security people, they'd have some alone time.

For the past couple of months, she and Connor had been dancing around each other with phone calls, texts and emails. They tried to connect and tentatively considered how they could get together without being too lawyer-client or too buddy-buddy or too focused on Jamison.

She exhaled a weary sigh. Relationships were hard. It had taken a handful of murder attempts to change her dynamic with Connor. Now she had a better idea of what she wanted with him. Her sigh turned into a contented purr. They definitely weren't stuck in the friend zone anymore.

She gazed across her hospital room to where he stood at the window, looking out and talking on his cell phone.

She liked the way his navy sports jacket emphasized his shoulders. Connor had a lean, rangy build with narrow hips, but he wasn't skinny, and he had the don't-mess-with-me posture of a man who'd grown up scrapping with several brothers and sisters.

He ended the call and pivoted to face her where she sat in the recliner with her ankle elevated on the footrest. "Wellborn is going to stop by in a little while," he said.

"Promise not to talk to him until I get back from my physical therapy. I hope this will be my last session at the hospital."

"After that, we'll be home."

He'd said *we*, and she liked it. *They* were becoming a *we*.

"The therapist recommended some equipment I might need."

He nodded. "I passed the list to Beverly. Rehab isn't part of her job, but she knows a lot about physical conditioning. She'll work with the people at her company to take set up a minigym at your house."

"I could have handled that," she said.

"Excuse me for denying you the thrill of talking to sales departments and delivery people," he said with a full measure of sarcasm. "Nobody questions your self-reliance, Emily. You get a free pass to goof off on the day after you're shot."

"I had a bulletproof vest."

"It still counts," he said. "According to Dr. Parris, the impact of the bullet against the vest had enough force to stop your heart for thirty seconds. You were dead again."

"But I'm back." She didn't want to be dead again, not even for half a minute. "And, by the way, physical therapy can hardly be counted as goofing off."

"Agreed, and that's the kind of effort you need. You

can focus on healing and getting stronger. Let me take care of the rest."

Though she knew he was right, she couldn't help being frustrated by her lack of control. This was her life. She needed to be the captain of her little ship. As the therapist helped her transfer into the wheelchair and zipped her off toward the therapy gym, Emily floated around in her muddled brain, imaging a lazy rowboat on a mountain lake. That would be her ship, and the inheritance might indicate that her ship had come in…whatever that meant.

In the physical therapy gym, she focused on the exercises, practiced walking with a cane, stretched and flexed and pedaled on a recumbent bike. Though Fish hadn't given a specific time for her departure, she hoped it would be before lunchtime, and they could order out for Chinese food. The wall clock showed it was approaching noon. She was tired and hungry and a little bit disappointed by the idea of another lunch from the hospital kitchen.

Wrapping up her exercises, she got into the wheelchair and settled back for the ride up the elevator and down the hall to her room. With her eyelids drooping, she hardly noticed when the person pushing the wheelchair zipped past the three elevators and continued down the hall.

"Where are we going?" she asked.

"You'll see."

The wheelchair swiveled into a room at the end of the hall. The door closed.

"Listen to me, Emily. I need to talk fast."

She looked up into the cold jade eyes of Kate Sylvester, who had covered her trademark red hair with a curly blond wig. For a disoriented moment, Emily wondered if she was imagining the woman who stood before her wearing aqua scrubs. "Stay away. I'll scream."

"Then you'll never hear what I have to say." Kate

wheeled her to the farthest corner of the room behind the bed. "I'm guessing I have less than five minutes before your bodyguard realizes you're missing."

"Talk," Emily said.

"This has to end. Please believe me when I say that I never meant for you to be hurt. The truck banging into your car was my idea, but I never wanted him to force you off the road."

"What was your plan?"

"To make you stop and do whatever it took to convince you to tell me what I needed to know."

Taken aback, Emily realized that her plan made more sense than a murder attempt. "You needed me alive so you could get the bank numbers and the password."

"Jamison swore you were the only one who knew. He taunted me with how much he trusted you and claimed you were an old-fashioned note taker."

"He lied." She sat up straighter in her wheelchair and tried to get her brain to work. "He was a liar, just like you. Did you try to poison me?"

"It was a tiny dose—a pinprick. It was supposed to relax you and help you remember."

"What about the shooting yesterday?"

"That had nothing to do with me." Her hand was on the doorknob. "My partner has gone crazy, and he scares me. I'm getting the hell out of town."

"Call the police," Emily said. "Or the FBI. They'll protect you."

"Or they'll arrest me," she said darkly. "I came here to warn you. Don't go back to your house. It's dangerous. Look in the basement."

"The security people have checked it out. It's safe."

Kate whipped open the door and peered out into the hall. Over her shoulder, she said, "I loved Jamison, you know."

"Did you kill him?"

"Goodbye, Emily."

She was gone.

"No, no, no," Emily muttered to herself as she tried to get her wheelchair turned around. She couldn't let that woman escape. Even if Kate wasn't the killer, she had information that would lead to the guilty person.

Giving up on the wheelchair, Emily stood. Putting as little weight as possible on her sprained ankle, she hobbled to the door and pulled it open. At the other end of the corridor, she spotted Beverly and waved.

The bodyguard was at her side in a moment. "Where did you go?"

"Kate Sylvester was here. She grabbed my chair and zipped me down the hall before I knew what was happening."

Beverly held her shoulders and peered into her face. "Are you all right?"

"I'm fine, just feeling like an idiot. I should have been more alert."

"You need to be checked out."

She was about to protest when she remembered that Kate had admitted to giving her a shot of poison. Had there been another pinprick? She didn't want to risk another seizure. "Help me get back to the wheelchair."

As soon as she was seated, Beverly whipped her down the hall to the elevators. In seconds, she was in her room where Connor stood with Wellborn. This was a conversation Emily didn't want to miss, but her news took precedence. She spoke up. "I was just with Kate Sylvester. It was only a few minutes ago. She was wearing aqua scrubs and a blond wig."

"I'll check it out," Wellborn said. "Beverly, stay with them."

She looked up at Connor. "It might be smart for me to

have some blood tests to make sure she didn't poke me with a mystery toxin."

While he put through a call to Fish, she transferred herself into the recliner chair and elevated her ankle on the footrest. If this visit from Kate messed up her chances to go home, Emily was going to be royally enraged.

"Before we go to my house," she said to Beverly, "I should tell you that Kate came to me with a warning. She said we should check in the basement, but that doesn't make sense. I don't really have a basement."

"The crawl space," Beverly said. "I'll take care of it."

Connor braced himself on the arm of her chair and leaned down to kiss her cheek. "Dr. Troutman promised to expedite the blood tests himself. How are you feeling?"

"Tired. Hungry. Light-headed from the painkillers. And really dumb for letting Kate escape."

"I heard what you told Beverly. Is that why Kate showed up? To warn you?"

Emily concentrated, trying to get past the mush in her brain and understand what had just happened. An undercurrent of emotion had given Kate's words a certain depth and significance. When she'd said that she loved Jamison, Emily sensed that she was asking for some kind of absolution. "I think she wanted me to forgive her. She said she never meant to hurt me."

"That gunshot was no accident."

"Kate claimed that she wasn't responsible for the shooting. She was working with a partner, and he had gone off the rails."

"Did she mention his name?"

She shook her head, wishing she'd done something to keep Kate in that room. "I should have knocked her unconscious with my cast. Then we'd have answers."

"I have something that'll cheer you up," he said.

"Oh, good. I need some happy thoughts before Fish rushes in here with a technician to draw more of my blood."

He went to the table beside the bed and picked up a photograph from a traffic camera. He carried it back to her and placed it in her lap. "We found the truck."

CONNOR NOTICED THE gleam in her eye as she ran her fingers over the photo of a black pickup truck with a banged-up fender on the passenger side. She cooed, "It's beautiful."

"I guess you know art."

"Artistically, it's nothing special. It's not even high resolution. But this photograph is proof that I'm not crazy. I didn't imagine the truck and freak out. I really saw it. Or did I? Where was this picture taken?"

"It came from a surveillance camera at a construction site two blocks from here."

"Yes!" She raised her good arm to cheer. "I was right! Were there other photos?"

"None that Wellborn could find." He pointed to the photo. "*See, right here.* If you look close, you can see the driver. It looks like they were wearing a baseball cap."

"It's blue." She held the photo up to her eyes and squinted. "I can't tell if it's a man or a woman. How about a license plate?"

"Not even a partial. Wellborn also did camera searches for the car with the shooter and found nothing."

Troutman charged into the room with his posse of assistants. Yesterday, Connor remembered, the doctor had been enthusiastic about talking to the FBI and being part of a real-life investigation. Today, he was wearing a necktie with a fingerprint pattern. While he ran through the standard examination procedures with Emily, Connor stepped back and stood beside Beverly.

The bodyguard spoke quietly. "I wouldn't blame you

if you fired me. I wasn't paying attention. Emily was in danger, and it was my fault."

"No need to fall on your sword," he said. "You're not the only person to get tricked by that woman. She's been playing all of us. Think of Wellborn. He's known for months that Jamison's death was suspicious, but he never got evidence."

"Was Kate involved in Jamison's death?"

Connor realized that he shouldn't be discussing mystery toxins in front of these witnesses, but the connections to Jamison's death were undeniable. Kate had admitted to poisoning Emily. Jamison could have been her first victim. "I wouldn't be surprised if she fed him the toxin, one bite at a time."

"She claims to be innocent."

And yet she refused to turn herself in to the police. He wasn't ready to buy her so-called apology to Emily. Though he didn't know Kate well, she hadn't risen to a prestige position in a highly competitive Wall Street investment firm by being an innocent, fluffy lamb. She was a clever manipulator. If Jamison had been involved in money laundering and embezzlement, Connor would bet that Kate was right there at his side with her hand in his pocket. She'd gone to incredible lengths to get the account number and password.

"Bottom line," he said, "I don't trust Kate. She's the opposite of you, Beverly. I'm glad we're working together. You're loyal, moral and efficient."

"That's enough. I'm an ex-marine, not a Girl Scout."

But he wanted to let her know he liked her. Beverly wasn't the sort of woman who he felt comfortable giving a little peck on the cheek to. Shaking hands was too formal. He ripped off a salute. "I appreciate what you do."

She saluted back. "Thanks."

Troutman was just finishing up when Wellborn came back into the room. In a low voice, he said, "We caught her on camera at one of the exits, then she dashed across the street and disappeared into the neighborhood. I called in local law enforcement, but I don't expect we'll find her since I couldn't give them a model of car or license plate. And she might be a redhead or a blonde."

"She's a regular chameleon," Connor said. "Reptilian, slimy and sneaky."

"The description fits." Wellborn took off his designer sunglasses and glanced at the several people in the room. "Come with me, Connor. We'll find a place to talk, then come back here."

Two doors down, they found the necessary privacy. Connor ran through the important points Emily had told him. His greatest concern was Kate's supposedly crazy partner.

"She sounded anxious to throw him under the bus."

"Of course," Wellborn said, "she wants to divert all the guilt onto him."

"It makes sense that she has a partner. We know there were two people in the car outside Emily's gallery—the shooter and the driver."

"Also, Kate had an alibi for the time when Emily was forced off the road. Emily was one of the first to leave Patricia's house. There had to be another person involved—the driver of the black truck."

Connor didn't know if that driver was brilliant or a complete idiot. On one hand, he'd hidden the truck so well that Deputy Sandoval and all the cops in and around Aspen couldn't find it. But then he'd driven the vehicle into Denver without fixing the dents. "We should be able to nail this guy."

"Or woman," Wellborn said grimly. "I remember my interview with Patricia and her aunt. Both of those women are capable of murder."

"They have alibis," Connor reminded him.

"I would expect them to hire an accomplice. And I can also believe that a none-too-bright accomplice wasn't supposed to cause Emily to go hurtling over the cliff."

A none-too-bright accomplice sounded a lot like Phillip, but he had an alibi. There was somebody else who fitted the bill, somebody who hadn't been at the reading of the will. "Have you located Dr. Thorson?"

"Not yet. But I've put out a BOLO. At the very least, he's a witness."

"But we can't prove anything until we have evidence."

"That's why I want to find that truck. There'll be fingerprints or trace DNA or an object left behind that will identify the driver. After that, it's game over."

When they returned to Emily's room, Dr. Troutman was waiting. He cheerfully reported that his initial analysis of Emily was positive. "We won't know if she was infected until we have the blood tests back from the lab, but she's not showing any troubling symptoms."

"And I can go home after lunch," Emily said. "Right?"

"Absolutely." He flashed her one of his brilliant smiles and then sobered as he looked toward Wellborn. "Do you have information for me?"

"I've referred the lab results you gave me to the toxicology lab at Quantico, which is one of the most advanced, well-equipped forensic facilities in the world. Now that they know what to look for, they can check this against Jamison's blood for trace elements. It'll take at least a week or more to have definitive results."

Troutman nodded. "I understand."

"I need to ask a favor, Doctor. Because we need to limit the number of people who know about this mystery toxin, I'd appreciate if you would be our point person in Denver."

"Dealing with Quantico." He couldn't hold back his grin. "I'd be honored to work with the FBI. I can tell my wife, can't I?"

"You can tell her, but no details."

"She's a mystery buff, and she's going to love this."

After Troutman left the room, Wellborn approached Emily. "We need to talk about your house in Aspen. I'm working on a legal arrangement that would designate you as the person responsible for the property before you have the deed."

Connor added to his explanation, "That means you wouldn't be able to sell the house immediately, but you could agree to open the doors to an FBI investigation without a search warrant. As soon as the paperwork is ready, you can sign."

"We'll talk about it this afternoon," she said, "after we're at my house."

Not the response he'd expected. She had every reason to advance the investigation. It didn't make sense for her to pull back. "Is there something you're not telling me?"

"I want to be there when they search. Patricia was right when she referred to the artwork as a treasure. I want to protect it. I want to be there when they search."

Another trip to Aspen wasn't his idea of a good time. And it was dangerous. As long as the killer was on the loose, Emily wasn't safe. She needed protection, not field trips. But she sounded determined. He might need to spend the rest of the day convincing her. "Before we make any plans, let's get you home."

"I can't wait. It'll be nice to have some quiet time."

He agreed. A full day of normal activity, unmarred by attempted murder, sounded like heaven.

Chapter Sixteen

Emily hobbled up the back stairs, opened the brand-new security door and entered. Inside her home, she experienced a profound sense of relief. Her tension eased, and the weight of heavy stress lifted. Her injuries seemed less painful. Being home was more effective than painkillers, with the added benefit that she wasn't dopey and disoriented.

The chaos had been tidied up, allowing her to appreciate the decorative touches she had carefully selected and placed. Living alone for the first time in her life, her home reflected her taste and no one else's. The violets on the windowsill above the kitchen sink reminded her of a kind neighbor woman who had watched her when she was a child and her mom was drunk. The sofa pillows in the front room that depicted famous paintings amused her. She'd rescued the small dining room chandelier with dangling prisms from her first New York apartment that she'd shared with two roommates. Jamison had hated that chandelier. He'd thought it was too girlie.

She felt safe in her house, even though the security company had discovered not one but two explosive devices in the crawl space. She owed Kate a thank-you for the warning. Destroying her charming little house would have been a shame.

At the foot of the staircase, she paused.

Connor stepped up beside her. "Can I give you a lift?"

Though she thoroughly enjoyed being carried in his arms, the physical therapist had been working with her on stairs. "I want to try it myself, but I'd like for you to follow close behind in case I get tired or stumble over my own feet."

"You won't trip," he said. "You've been walking like a champ. We brought the wheelchair just in case, but you're doing fine with the cane."

"Thank you for getting the place put back together."

"I can't take credit. Beverly's employers contacted the cleaning crew. They specialize in crime scenes."

"Don't tell me more. I have enough grisly details of my own to think about."

She slowly ascended the staircase, leaning on the banister and not putting too much weight on her ankle. With the compression wrap, the injury hardly looked swollen. But she still felt the tightness. The therapist had warned her about not doing too much and frequently repeated the acronym for the care of a sprain: RICE. It stood for *Rest*, *Ice*, *Compression* and *Elevation*. Rest was probably the most important.

She made it into her bedroom, sat on the edge of her bed and ran her hand across her clean white duvet with the eyelet trim. Connor followed. Like her, he seemed more relaxed. He'd taken off his sports jacket, and the sleeves of his blue oxford cloth shirt were rolled up to the elbows. Though there were other people in the house, she felt like they were alone. They had no pressing need to talk about the investigation or her physical condition or any other kind of business. In this moment, it was only the two of them.

Kicking off her shoes, she scooted around on the bed until her back was supported by pillows and her legs stretched out in front of her. Though comfortable enough, she didn't like this position. "I'm not really a bed person. I don't like breakfast in bed, don't like to lie around. If I read in bed, I just fall asleep. But I know that I need to rest."

He went to the west-facing window and pulled up the shade, allowing the afternoon light to spill across the small square table with a center drawer and matching blond wood chairs on each end. "We could bring a comfortable chair up here."

"I don't have one with a built-in footrest." She didn't want to turn her bedroom into a replica of her hospital room, but she needed somewhere to sit where she could put her leg up. And a breakfast table might be nice.

"There are places that rent chairs like that."

"I definitely don't need more furniture in the house," she said. "Where did Beverly put the exercise equipment?"

"Guest bedroom. With the recumbent bike, the step machine and a couple of other contraptions, there isn't much room for the bed."

"Beverly did a good job setting up my home gym. But where will you sleep?"

A slow, sexy grin stretched the corners of his mouth. "I'll figure something out."

She had a couple of her own ideas on the interrelated subjects of where he should go to bed and how she should get her exercise. There were lots of creative ways they could get hot and sweaty together, and she wouldn't mind trying them out.

With a quick knock, Beverly and the part-time nurse entered her bedroom. Protection was her bodyguard's primary concern. She outlined the security systems that were currently in place, including an alarm system and hidden cameras. An additional bodyguard would be on duty downstairs. Beverly preferred to have Emily stay on the second floor because there was only one way to get up there—the staircase.

The part-time nurse chimed in. She seemed nice enough but had a singsong voice. When she started listing reasons why her patient shouldn't be climbing up and down the stairs, Emily's interest faded. She was tired. All she really wanted was dinner and a nap.

Connor read her mind. He herded everyone else from the room and sat beside her on the bed. "How about a bath?"

"Oh, I hadn't even thought about that, but it sounds great. A bubble bath."

He led the way into the white-tiled bathroom adjoining her bedroom, and he locked the other door that opened onto the second floor. When he turned on the water in the tub, he commented approvingly, "Massaging water jets. Nice."

"This was the only room I remodeled when I moved in. The toilet converts into a bidet, the shower can be used as a sauna and the tub, well, the tub is wonderful."

He helped her take the compression wrap off her ankle and brought in extra towels—fluffy lavender and yellow—to rest her casted left arm upon. Though he was more than willing to stay with her, Emily threw him out. His assistance was not required to get undressed, and removing the bulletproof vest and the wrap around her ribs was the furthest thing from a sexy striptease. She didn't want him to think of her as a patient.

She added scented bubble bath to the swirling water and carefully climbed into the tub. The hot water and massaging jets were sheer bliss. With a moan of pleasure, she lay back, closed her eyes and let the pulsating water soothe her battered body. She hadn't indulged in a luxurious bath like this in quite a while. There never seemed to be time. Her gallery kept her busy. When the attacks were over and her life returned to normal, she vowed to take advantage of this fantastic tub on a more regular basis.

There was a tap on the door. Connor peeked inside and said, "I brought you an iced mint tea."

Her favorite! She arranged the bubbles so nothing was showing. "Come in."

He carried a tray with her tall glass of tea and a plate of sliced peaches, and he placed it on a towel on the floor. "Fresh-picked fruit from the trees by your driveway."

Kneeling beside the tub, his eyes were level with hers. Neither of them looked away. They'd waited nearly a decade for this privacy and intimacy. She knew him so well.

His gaze lowered and lingered on her wet, bare shoulders and arms. He cleared his throat. His voice was hoarse. "I should go."

"Wait," she said. "Would you set up some candles for me? In the second drawer by the sink, there are votive containers and matches."

He did as she asked, lighting the flames on half a dozen candles, which he placed around the bathroom. "They smell good."

"Now I want you to pull down the shade." She sipped her iced tea and licked her lips. "Now turn out the light."

The bathroom wasn't pitch-dark. A bit of sunlight crept around the edge of the shade. But the flickering illumination of candlelight created an atmosphere of warm sensuality. Shadows outlined his brow and cheekbones. He hadn't shaved since her first day in the hospital, and his stubble was heavy.

In a barely audible whisper, she said, "Now take off your shirt."

Apparently, he heard her loud and clear because he unfastened the buttons with lightning speed. The shirt was gone. She wanted to run her fingers through the swath of dark hair on his chest, but her cast was in the way. Trying to get her right arm into position, she twisted in the tub. A sharp jab in her torso reminded her that her ribs were injured. Nonetheless, she tried again. The bubbly, scented water splashed and churned.

"Let me help," he said.

"Try not to get the casts wet."

He reached into the water, leveraged his hands under her arms and lifted her up and out. Water streamed from her body as he placed her on the edge of the tub.

"I know what you're doing." She pushed her wet hair off her forehead. "You just want to see me without my clothes."

"I could give you a towel."

He crouched in front of her, still holding her upper arms so she wouldn't lose her balance and topple backward. His gaze was brazen and demanding as he stared at her naked body. She should have been embarrassed. But she liked the effect her nudity was having on him.

Shoulders back and chin lifted, she stared back at him. "I don't want a towel."

"You're beautiful, Emily."

He wasn't half-bad himself. "The first time I saw you, I had second thoughts about Jamison. I've always—"

"Stop." He placed a finger across her lips. "Let's not talk about the past. I want to start working on a future, our future."

Turned sideways, she embraced him. His bare chest rubbed against her slippery, wet breasts as his arms encircled her. Their lips joined.

As their kiss deepened, their position changed. She slid against him. He lifted her. Their arms tangled and somehow she found herself lying on a towel on the tile floor.

"I'll try to be careful," he said. "Tell me if I hurt you."

She was willing to put up with a little pain for what she imagined would be a great deal of pleasure. He trailed soft kisses down her neck, where he nuzzled and nibbled. He took a sharp nip at her throat, and she gave a startled yelp.

Immediately, he backed off.

"Don't stop," she said. "I'm not hurt."

He rose above her, supporting himself on his elbows and knees. She could tell that he was trying not to put too much weight on her, and she appreciated his concern. But she didn't want to be treated like she was helpless.

She pressed her good hand against his chest. "I have an idea."

"I'm listening."

Her index finger trailed down the center of his chest, following the line of dark hair until she tugged at his belt. "Take off the rest of your clothes and lie down. I'll be on top."

He bolted to his feet and stripped off his belt and jeans. After he stretched out on the floor, she braced herself against him. At first, she took her time. With her right hand, she traced light circles on his chest and torso.

She straddled him, and then lowered herself so they were touching from head to toe. His body absorbed the moisture from hers. She kissed him with the passion she'd suppressed for all these years when they were friends, only friends. Her tongue plunged into his mouth. Her fingernails scraped against his skin. How had she found the courage to be so aggressive? Maybe it had something to do with being near death on a regular basis.

She wanted him and couldn't hold back. Instead of a slow, subtle seduction, she was all over him. Her arm cast made her clumsy, but he wasn't complaining. His erection pressed against her. She wanted him inside her.

"Emily, slow down. We need a condom."

"Don't you have one?" Nearly overwhelmed by need, she sucked down a huge lungful of air. Her chest heaved. "What are you saying?"

"We have to stop."

"No." She stared down into his dark eyes and shook her head. How could she control this hunger? "I want you."

"Oh, baby, I want you, too."

He held her face in both hands and kissed her hard. A fierce need throbbed through her veins. With a groan, she collapsed onto his chest.

He held her there. His hand slipped between them and descended her body, gliding past her stomach to the juncture of her widespread thighs. His fingers massaged her sex, accelerated her nascent passion to an unbearable level. He fulfilled her.

She rolled off him, not apologizing when her cast bumped his chest. She still wanted the full treatment, but she was happy with what he'd given her. Sensual tremors radiated outward from her groin. Her pulse raced at an urgent speed. "That was good."

"I know."

She wanted to believe there would be plenty of time for them to further this relationship and have even more sex, but the constant murder attempts reminded her that life was fragile. She needed to seize every opportunity that presented itself. She doubted there would ever be another man who was as right for her as Connor.

He lurched to his feet and gathered his clothes. "I'll help you get dressed."

"I'm not ready to move." She wanted to savor the thrill. "You go. I'll be out in a minute."

In spite of the great orgasm, she was a little bit mad at him. He should have been prepared. Wasn't it a man's duty to carry a condom at all times? She supposed it could be argued that a woman had the same responsibility. Really, it was nobody's fault.

Taking her time, she brushed her teeth, used a blow-dryer on her hair and put on makeup for the first time in days. She slipped into a silky pink robe with kimono sleeves. When she was done, she looked through the window. The sun had gone down, and the streetlights were glowing. Almost time for bed, and she wondered if he would join her under the covers. If so, he'd better have a condom with him.

When she stepped into her bedroom, she saw that a minor transformation had taken place. A chaise longue from her living room had been moved up here. It was an old-fashioned design but actually comfortable and perfect for elevating her ankle. The table beside it was the perfect height for her to recline and dine. On the table, a fresh glass of tea awaited her along with a big green salad and a slice of pepperoni pizza.

Connor took her arm to escort her. "Dinner."

Pizza from Luciano's was a treat, and she didn't want to be ungrateful. But it was irritating that he hadn't asked her before placing the order…or moving her furniture around. If he was Mr. Prepared, why hadn't he thought ahead and bought condoms?

She arranged herself on the chaise. "I want to get my ankle wrapped before the nurse leaves for the night."

"I'll get her," Connor said. "She put the pills you'll need before bed into this paper cup on the dresser."

Before he went out the door, she spoke up. "Listen, Connor, I appreciate everything you're doing, but I don't want you to get the wrong idea."

"Explain."

"You're making all the phone calls and arrangements, hiring people to take care of me, rearranging my furniture and you even ordered dinner without asking me what I want. Never mind that pizza is probably what I would have ordered. I want to make my own decisions."

"I understand."

"This is important. I don't want you to think you're running the show."

He forgot about calling the nurse and took a seat on the other side of the table. His expression was serious. "Don't confuse me with your ex-husband. I know what Jamison was like. He was a master manipulator. He's been dead for months, and he's still got us jumping through hoops."

"I would never confuse you with him."

"When I do things for you, it's not because I'm trying to control you," he said. "I want to support you in doing what you want."

She took a sip of her iced tea and cocked her head to one side. This might be the right time to test his motivations. "I want to get this straight. You are not trying to control me."

"Not at all."

"Suppose I said I wanted to go to Aspen, to be there when the FBI searches the house. Would you be okay with that?"

He threw up his hands. "That's not a fair question."

"Why not? Is it because you don't think I'll like the answer?"

"It's not safe for you to go there," he said. "Here, in your house, you're protected. Nobody is going to get in here and hurt you. I don't want you to take the risk."

"That's not your decision, Connor." She'd made her point, but the victory was hollow. "I don't want to argue with you. There are so many other ways—better ways— we can use our time."

The air in the room seemed to vibrate. In an instant, everything changed. There was a massive explosion. The windows rattled in their frames.

Chapter Seventeen

Connor rushed to the window at the front of her bedroom. The explosion had come from that direction, and his first instinct had been to confront the danger and protect Emily. He raised the window shade and looked past the tree branches to the street outside her house. At the curb, a vehicle was on fire. Fingers of yellow flame clawed their way across the hood and roof. Smoke gushed. There were other cars on the street. He didn't see any witnesses.

Beverly charged into the room. "Step back from the windows," she ordered. "Standing there in the light, you make a clear target."

"What's going on?" Emily asked.

"I'm guessing it was a car bomb."

He pivoted to face the bodyguard. "It was the truck, wasn't it? The black truck."

"We won't know until the police investigate."

Already a chorus of sirens from fire trucks and police cruisers echoed through the night. Emily's house was near central Denver, and response time was quick. Connor wanted to run downstairs and tell the cops that this fire wasn't an accident. They needed to fan out and start a search, question witnesses, check cameras. They had to find him…or her…whatever. They had to arrest this psycho. Blowing up the truck in front of Emily's house was a choreographed attack, designed to send a message. The psycho was thumbing his or her nose at them.

Connor strode toward the exit, but Beverly blocked his way. "Stand down," she said. "Let the police do their job."

"I could help."

"You need to stay here and take care of Emily. Don't go near the windows. I'll let you know as soon as I have information."

She closed the door behind her.

Emily remained on the chaise with her ankle elevated on a pillow. "I don't get it," she said. "Why blow up the truck?"

"Potential evidence."

"Of course! The dents on the bumper were proof that I was run off the road. And there were probably fingerprints."

"The fire will obliterate any trace," he said. "Unless the police pick up Kate Sylvester and she agrees to talk or confesses, we've got nothing."

The trip to Aspen became even more imperative. The house that had belonged to Jamison was the last, best place to uncover any sort of clues. Connor had already made plans to go there tomorrow with Wellborn. The only question was whether they'd drive or take a police helicopter.

The commotion from the street in front of her house grew louder and more chaotic. It took willpower to keep from going to the window and watching the fire department in action. The smoke—a stinking combination of gasoline and burning rubber—permeated the air. From downstairs, he heard doors slamming and loud conversations. The alarm hadn't gone off, so Beverly must have given the okay for someone to enter.

He had his hand on the doorknob, ready to find out who

was in the house, when Emily spoke up. "Connor, wait. You were told to stand down."

"I'm not a recruit in Beverly's army. She doesn't get to give me orders."

"Believe me," she said, "I understand how you're feeling. Nobody likes being on the sidelines, but there's nothing you can do. If they need you, they know where to find you."

"You're right," he said.

"I know."

"Don't gloat."

He returned to the chair opposite her chaise. For lack of anything better to do, he folded the pizza slice and took a bite. The twirling red and blue lights from emergency vehicles flashed against the window. He was dying to rush outside and join them.

"There must be other evidence," she said. "Ballistics on the bullets they used?"

"They need a weapon for comparison."

"How about this?" she said. "Wellborn said that his tech guys didn't find anything when they hacked into my computer files, but they aren't me. If I could take a look at the stuff they've dug up, I might notice something."

"Can't hurt," he said. "I'll arrange for someone to come here."

"I could go to the local FBI headquarters, unless you think it's better for me to sit here and do nothing."

Her smile had an ironic twist. He knew what sort of game she was playing. By comparing her situation with his, she intended to show him that he was being unreasonable. "You're not real subtle," he said.

"It doesn't matter as long as I'm convincing."

She wiggled her eyebrows, and he noticed that she was

wearing makeup that made her eyes even more blue and beautiful. Her streaked blond hair covered the bruise and stitches on her forehead. She looked strong, healthy and full of energy.

"If you didn't have that cast on your arm," he said, "I wouldn't know you were in a car crash. You're healing fast."

"I still have bruises."

He had just seen every delicious inch of her body, and he thought she looked good. "The worst is the area near your shoulder, where the bullet hit."

"Tomorrow," she said, circling back to the topic, "I can stop by the FBI offices. Or I could go to Aspen."

Or none of the above. He couldn't order her what to do and couldn't physically restrain her, but he refused to put her in a dangerous situation. Her house was well protected. She needed to stay here.

Beverly came into the room. "It's going to be tough to figure out who owns the truck. The VIN number and all the other identifiers have been removed."

"No surprise," he said. "What else?"

Her lips pinched together. "There was someone inside. A woman. There's not much left of her, not enough for immediate identification."

"Kate Sylvester," Emily whispered. "That's a heinous way to die. She didn't deserve it."

Connor wasn't so sure. Kate sure as hell deserved some form of punishment. She'd admitted having been involved in the attacks on Emily, and it was likely that she'd administered the mystery toxin that killed Jamison. He remembered seeing her on Jamison's arm at cocktail parties and events. They'd been a dazzling couple. Now both were dead. The ill-gotten money in the offshore bank account—no matter how much—wasn't worth this cost.

THE NEXT DAY, Emily felt better, even considering everything that had happened. After consulting with the nurse, she'd reduced her painkiller dosage to just a little more than aspirin. And her emotional wellness was improved, having been given a substantial boost after last night in bed with Connor, who had been resourceful enough to rustle up three condoms. They used them all. In future, she thought, they should consider buying in bulk.

For the first time in days, her mind was clear. She could see that the obstacles to taking charge of her life were of her own making. Connor told her—emphatically—that he didn't want her to leave the protection of her house, and he was entitled to that opinion. He didn't dictate her actions and didn't control her life. Whatever happened, it was her decision.

Sitting downstairs at the dining table with the prism chandelier casting shards of sunlight around the room, she gazed at the man who had been her friend for a very long time and was now something more. Before he'd come to her bed last night, he'd shaved. Though the stubble was trendy, she liked his smooth, stubborn chin. Sipping her coffee, she said, "I've decided not to sign Wellborn's document. Unless you take me along, the FBI doesn't have my permission to search the Aspen house."

"Fine."

She'd expected more resistance. "I'm serious."

He dug into the cheese omelet that he'd served up moments ago with bagels on the side. Since everybody in the house was on a different schedule, they cooked and ate whenever convenient. "You can tell Wellborn yourself. He ought to be here in a couple of minutes. Then I'm leaving with him. We're taking a police chopper."

"You're still going to Aspen? But you can't get into the house."

"I'm a lawyer, and he's a fed." Connor shrugged. "We'll figure out something."

She stabbed the yellow omelet with her fork. Just like that! Her leverage was gone. They could work around her, and she couldn't force them to take her along by withholding her signature. "Smooth move."

"Whatever you might think, I'm not trying to manipulate you. I have concerns about your safety, and I don't want to put you at risk."

"It's my choice whether I crochet doilies or swim with sharks."

He reached across the table and took her hand. "I care about you, Emily. So do plenty of other people. After the explosion last night, your phone has been ringing nonstop."

She frowned. "How do you know? My cell phone was lost in the crash."

"These calls are on your landline. People left dozens of messages. Last night, Beverly worried that the entire mariachi band would show up on the doorstep, so she talked to one of your part-time employees, Julia."

"Julia Espinoza. She's a terrific help."

"She agreed to get the word out, and suggested you get a new cell phone as soon as possible."

The outpouring of concern touched her. "The mariachis were coming here?"

"And a mob of artists and your book club and more." He gave her fingers a squeeze. "They care. And I care. That means you have a responsibility to us. We don't want to lose you."

He was persuasive. Perhaps Connor was manipulating

her, but she was beginning to think that she should do as he suggested. His concern seemed sincere. But so was her desire to take charge and do things for herself.

Wellborn arrived, cool and collected as always. After asking Beverly to join them, he sat at the end of the table. "Here's the update," he said. "We know the year, make and model of the truck. None of our suspects own a vehicle that matches the description. Deputy Sandoval suggested that it might be stolen, although the sheriff's department hasn't received a report for a missing truck."

Emily had an explanation, "People who don't live full-time in the mountains might leave a vehicle behind while they aren't at their home, especially a truck."

Wellborn continued, "We believe the body in the truck was Kate Sylvester. It'll take a while for DNA analysis and reconstruction, but she was carrying a passport in a silver case that protected it from the explosion."

Emily pushed away the mental image of a body that had been burned so badly it couldn't be recognized. Only a few hours earlier, she'd spoken to Kate.

Connor said, "Our main suspect seems to be Phillip. Does he have an alibi for last night?"

"He claimed that he was on the road, driving back home to Aspen. His sister was with him."

Not a very solid alibi in Emily's opinion. Phillip and Patricia wouldn't hesitate to lie for each other. "What about her fiancé?"

"I haven't been able to reach Dr. Thorson." He set his briefcase on the table, popped open the lid and took out a document. "If you'll sign these papers, Emily, we'll be on our way."

She made one last attempt. "I'd like to be with you when the house is opened."

Wellborn glanced at Connor, who looked down and

shook his head. His gesture irritated her far more than his rationalizations. She really didn't like the way these two men were deciding the limits for her. Now was the time to do a *carpe diem* and take matters into her own hands. She had a plan, and it didn't include them. Without a word, she picked up the pen and signed on the line where Wellborn had marked an X.

The lawyer and the fed could do whatever necessary.

And she would do the same.

After Connor had left with Wellborn, she moved forward, confident that she could handle the arrangements. Taking a landline phone to her bedroom, she closed the door and got busy. Using various friends and contacts, it had taken her less than an hour to schedule her own helicopter flight to Aspen, hiring a charter service that she and Jamison had used before. The hard part was convincing Beverly. After much debate, she worked out a compromise, allowing Beverly to accompany her.

Walking with her cane, Emily boarded a motor home driven by an artist friend who was somewhat paranoid and had outfitted his home on wheels like a fortress. Beverly approved of the triple-pane windows, reinforced walls and four guns stashed in various places. It seemed to Emily that Beverly also liked the artist, who was six feet seven inches tall and built like Paul Bunyan. The bodyguard sat in the passenger seat as they drove south to a private airfield, pulled onto the tarmac and parked outside hangar fourteen, where a red-and-white helicopter was tethered. So far, her trip to Aspen was working out precisely as planned.

When she climbed out of the motor home and walked toward the chopper, a tall blond man wearing a down vest and sunglasses came toward her, moving fast. He enveloped her in a bear hug that was much too familiar and much too tight.

"Great to see you," he said.

She pulled her head back. "Do I know you?"

"I'm the guy who saved your life." A hard-edged object poked at her injured ribs. "It's me. Eric. You remember. Dr. Eric Thorson."

Chapter Eighteen

Emily had never actually seen Dr. Thorson. While in his care, she'd been in a coma. Twisting her arm, she struggled to escape his grasp. "Get away from me."

"Don't fight it. You're coming with me." Still holding her with one hand, he faced Beverly and the artist. Thorson held open his vest to show them an array of explosives attached to the inner lining. "Gunnery Sergeant T. J. Beverly, with your military experience, I believe you're familiar with suicide vests."

Another bomb. Emily's heart jumped into her throat. She couldn't scream if she wanted to. Escape with her sprained ankle was impossible. She'd organized herself into an ambush.

"Nobody has to get hurt," Beverly said.

"Exactly what I'm thinking," Thorson said. "In my left hand, I'm holding the kill switch. As long as I keep this button pressed down, we've got no problem. But if I release—because maybe you shot me—we'll all be blown sky-high. Just like the truck last night."

Beverly said, "I won't let you hurt Emily."

"Not my intention. All I'm after is information. As soon as she tells me what I need to know, she's free to go. Simple."

Drawing on a reservoir of courage she never knew she

had, Emily squared her shoulders. "It's all right, Beverly. I'll go with him."

"Good girl." Still holding the kill switch in his left hand, Thorson wrapped his right arm around her midsection and pulled her backward to the helicopter.

When Beverly started toward them, he waggled the kill switch. "Don't move."

Inside the chopper, he shoved Emily toward the rear and pulled his handgun, which he aimed at a gray-haired man, who was handcuffed to a metal strut. His name was Steve; she recognized him from a few years ago. "I'm so sorry," she said to him. "I had no idea this would happen."

"My fault," he muttered. "I let this jerk get the drop on me."

"No need for name-calling," Thorson said as he tossed Emily a set of keys. "Unfasten his cuffs. We need to take off."

After she unlocked the cuffs and the pilot moved forward to his seat, Thorson sat in the copilot position. He directed her to sit in a seat behind the pilot so he could keep an eye on both of them.

Through the windshield, she watched Beverly, who was gesturing emphatically and talking on her cell phone. Who could she call? Who could possibly change this turn of events?

"Let's go," Thorson said. "I want to get the hell out of here."

When the pilot turned the ignition, the engine roared and the rotor slashed through the air. It was too loud to talk, but she had to have some answers.

"How did you know?" she shouted. "How did you know I was going to be here?"

"You can thank Kate for that," he yelled back. "When she visited you at the hospital, she attached a bug. Over the past couple of days, I've been listening to every word you said."

"Impossible." There was nowhere Kate could have hidden a bug. Emily had changed clothes several times. She'd been naked and washed her hair. "Where did she hide this bug?"

He reached over with the gun and tapped her cast. "She slipped it in here. Call it microtechnology. It's tiny, miniscule. You never even felt it, did you?"

She'd had an itch but nothing painful, nothing compared to the wrenching agony in her gut when she'd realized that Thorson had been listening to her intimate conversations with Connor. That violation disgusted her more than she could ever express in words. Seething with impotent anger, she jammed her finger into the cast and dug around at the edges until she found the tiny disk. She ripped out the microtechnology, threw it on the floor of the chopper and crushed it with her foot as they lifted off.

Swooping through clear blue skies toward the mountains west of town, she tamped down her rage. It wouldn't do any good to explode. More than ever before, she had to play this smart. "Where are you taking me?" she yelled.

"None of your business," he said. "It's going to be a nice, smooth ride. I've explained to the pilot about the kill switch. And he's not going to be putting through any calls to airfields. We're on our own."

She didn't know how the airborne communication systems worked but was certain that Beverly would have alerted authorities. Someone would be tracking them. Thorson was seriously delusional if he thought he could get away with this.

He manipulated the mechanics on his kill switch so he could set it aside without triggering an explosion. Then he passed her noise-canceling headphones with an attached microphone so they could talk to each other without yelling. Still keeping the gun aimed at her, he handed her two other items: her computer and her cell phone.

She clenched her jaw when she saw the laptop and her battered phone. "Did you grab these when my car crashed?"

"That wasn't supposed to happen." His voice was easier to hear over the headset. "I barely nudged your car. If you weren't such a bad driver, you could have kept it on the road. Kate and I could have asked questions then, and none of this would have happened. I never intended to hurt you."

She pressed her lips together to keep from shooting off her mouth and telling him that he wasn't making sense. Logic told her that he and Kate would have killed her when they had what they wanted. But it wouldn't do any good to quibble with a psycho.

He continued, "Open your laptop and check your documents."

"I can't believe they still work."

"And they still get internet. Find me the name of the bank and the password."

He didn't need the account number. Kate had already got that from the iguana photo in her bedroom.

"Dr. Thorson." She addressed him using his title, hoping to remind him that he was more than a mindless thug. He was an ER doctor and virologist. "You must know that the FBI already hacked into my laptop. They didn't find a list of passwords."

"They weren't familiar with Jamison the way you were. Kate was sure you knew."

"And look where it got her."

She watched him for a reaction. He'd admitted to blowing up the truck, and he certainly knew about the woman inside. The expression in his slate blue eyes was unreadable. She couldn't tell if he was sad or angry or just plain confused. What was his relationship with Kate?

"I'll miss her."

But he must have killed her. "I understand. You have regrets."

"Shut the hell up."

Don't poke the bear. Long ago, her mom had offered that advice when Emily wouldn't stop teasing one of the guys she was dating. When he'd hauled back his meaty fist and smacked Emily, Mom gloated and told her that she deserved to be hit. Just like now. Emily should have stayed at her house.

Looking out the side window, she saw that they'd left the densely packed houses of Denver behind. The chopper seemed to be following the route of a highway, winding deeper into the foothills.

She guessed the trip to Aspen would be a little over an hour. Was Aspen their destination? If they went to the house, Connor and Wellborn would be there. Somebody might be able to stop Thorson.

"I loved her," Thorson mumbled. "Kate was beautiful and smart. When we accessed the funds in the offshore account, we would have had enough money to disappear and live like royalty for the rest of our lives."

"But you were engaged to Patricia."

"That was over. She found me and Kate together. You know, doing it."

Emily had lived a similar scene. She had to wonder if Kate engineered these moments when a wife or girlfriend would walk in and catch her having sex with their husband or lover. Kate was competitive. Stealing another woman's man probably gave her a thrill.

"She wanted to turn herself in," Thorson said. "I told her it was crazy, that we'd end up in jail, but she wouldn't listen. We argued. I was so damn mad. I went storming off. That's the last time I saw her alive."

She noticed that he hadn't confessed to murder. "Then what happened?"

"That's all I'm going to say. You start reading the documents."

"What if I can't find anything?"

"We move to plan B. You and I go to the bank in the Caymans and use your fingerprints to withdraw all the money in that account."

There was no way in hell she'd allow that to happen. Thorson sickened her. She'd almost rather die than go to the Caymans with him. "I'll find something."

With her laptop balanced on her knees, she brought up the familiar screen with her many icons and documents. There was one icon she'd been thinking about from the first moment she heard about her inheritance. Before they had broken up, Jamison had created a file on her computer that contained photos of all the artwork they'd purchased.

She clicked, and it opened. The screen showed a remarkable Kandinsky abstract. She flipped through the pictures—not sure of what she was looking for, but knowing there was something important hidden in those works. Most of their art collection was modern or postmodern, but she paused on a painting by an unknown artist who painted in the style of Edward Hopper. Not a particularly brilliant picture, but there was a haunting loneliness to the scene of a young woman sitting at a desk in front of a window with bleak gray light shining down on her hands as she wrote. The title of the painting was *The Note Taker*.

Emily remembered that Kate had referred to her as a note taker. Jamison had made that comparison as well, teasing her about her notebook, where she wrote down reminders rather than keeping them on her computer.

"I've got the answer," she said. "We need to go to Aspen."

"Tell me why."

She explained about the painting. "Do you remember how Jamison wrote the number for the bank account on the photo that I hung in my bedroom? Well, I think he did the same thing with a painting in Aspen. It's called *The Note Taker*."

When she held up her laptop so he could see the picture, he laughed out loud. "I've walked past this picture a million times. Your ex-husband was a crafty bastard. I guess we have to go to Aspen."

While he was distracted by talking to the pilot, she turned on her phone. With only one bar left, it was almost out of power. Even with her clumsy right hand, she managed a quick text to Connor's phone: J's Aspen home. ETA: 1 hr.

Though unsure of what Connor could do, she trusted him. The realization struck her with belated force. *Trust!* It had always been an issue with her, and she deeply, honestly trusted him more than any other person in her life. Even in the early years of their marriage, she hadn't felt this way about Jamison. Her mother had never been in the least trustworthy. Connor was different. He found ways to protect her. He'd stayed at her bedside, had hired a security firm with a bodyguard and had advised her to stay safe at home today. She should have listened to him.

Okay, sure, she'd made wrong decisions, but she wasn't about to give up. She wouldn't let Thorson win. Somehow, she had to figure out a way to deal with his suicide vest. Or did she? Was he really crazy enough to detonate the device, killing himself and everyone else around him? She knew he didn't want to be taken into custody, but death was a terrible solution.

She considered physical action. No way could she overpower him. The doctor was a big athletic man who could pick her up and bounce her off the windows of the chopper without breaking a sweat. There might be something she could do to separate him from the explosives. Right now, he had manipulated the kill switch so it was deactivated. Could she grab the switch and throw it from the chopper? Not likely—he wouldn't let her near the switch.

If not physically overpowering him, she had to convince him to let them go. To open a dialogue, she asked, "Where did you learn about explosives?"

"I did an internship in western Africa, where militants were fighting the established order. One of the rebels took a shine to me. I wasn't involved with his cause, but I learned about firearms and explosives."

"Is Africa where you studied virology?"

"I wish I'd never learned about those poisons and diseases."

The pilot interrupted, "Excuse me, but the way I understand the doctor's instructions is fly to the house where I used to take Emily and Jamison."

"That's right," she said. "What was your prior destination?"

"He doesn't exactly know," Thorson said. "I have a hideout near Glenwood. My plan was to have you give me the numbers, go there and transfer the money from the offshore account to another untraceable account that Kate set up for me."

She had a feeling that Kate had been the one who plotted and made plans. "What were you going to do with us?"

"I'd go on the run and disappear. And I'd let you go free." He focused on her. "Pay attention, Emily. I told you before, I'm not a killer."

Even if she accepted his excuse for running her off the road, there were other incidents. "What about messing with my medication when I was in a coma? And giving Kate something to infect me in Denver? And shooting me?"

"The stuff with the meds never put you in danger. As for the shooting? Not me."

Why should she believe him? "What about Kate's death?"

"God, no, I didn't hurt her. I stormed off after our fight. When I came back, she was dead. Shot with impressive skill through the heart."

"And then you put her in the truck?"

"We'd already discussed blowing up the truck to erase the evidence, and I decided it would be her funeral pyre. Like for a warrior princess. It seemed appropriate. She deserved a fierce send-off."

Emily found herself buying into his story. She desperately wanted to believe that Thorson would allow her and Steve, the pilot, to go free. "If you really haven't committed murder, you should take Kate's advice and turn yourself in. The FBI might even make a deal with you in exchange for information about Jamison's account."

"They've got stuff to charge against me. I didn't kill him, but I provided the toxin Kate administered to your ex-husband over a period of months. I always thought he'd recover, but I was wrong. That makes me an accessory—a common criminal. Also, if I turn myself in, I'll be flat broke. And they sure as hell won't let me practice medicine."

She had to agree that his future sounded bleak. Her arguments weren't doing much to change his mind.

Her cell phone, which she'd left turned on, trilled. She looked down at the screen. Caller ID showed it was Connor. She held it so Thorson could see. Without asking his permission, she answered.

"Connor, it's Emily. You're on speaker. We can all hear you."

"Thorson," Connor said. "If you plan to come to the house in Aspen, we need to make arrangements so nobody will accidentally shoot you and blow up the chopper."

"I want a deal," Thorson said. "I want to talk to the FBI agent."

"We can do that."

"I don't want to set off another explosion." Thorson's smile was cold. "But if I don't get what I want, somebody is going to die."

Emily shuddered. That threat sounded more honest than anything Thorson had said before. Maybe he actually was innocent of murder, but she sensed that he'd do what he deemed necessary. If that meant she and Steve got blown sky-high, so be it.

Chapter Nineteen

The red-and-white helicopter piloted by the grandfatherly man named Steve hovered outside the spectacular mansion Emily had inherited. Such a beautiful setting, the meadow property was surrounded by forest and vistas of distant snowcapped peaks. She had enjoyed much of the time she'd spent here with Jamison—the long hikes, watching the sunset behind the Rockies, wading in the creek that ran through the property. The downside was the unfortunate proximity to his family.

"You struck it rich," Thorson muttered.

Though she couldn't bear to live in a house paid for by illegal schemes that hurt the investor, she had to admit that the house was remarkable. "The best part is the artwork inside. I snagged a couple of true masterpieces."

As the chopper descended on the flat area to the south of the house, she looked around for the police helicopter. It was nowhere in sight. Nor did she see police cruisers. Thorson had taken the phone for a private conversation with Connor, so she didn't exactly know what they had worked out.

"Where is everybody?" she asked.

"No cops," he said. "I told Connor. No cops."

"I thought you were going to turn yourself in."

"I haven't decided, but I knew for sure that I didn't want

to take a chance on some trigger-happy deputy shooting me while I walk up to the house."

"Neither do I." If Thorson was shot and took his thumb off the kill switch, they'd all die, unless... "Are you still going to be wearing the suicide vest?"

He frowned. "Connor didn't want me to, but I need the insurance."

The chopper landed, kicking up a curtain of dry dirt and leaves. She peered through the window and saw Connor approaching. Alone, he walked without hesitation, showing no fear. Not many men would take this kind of risk, and it was especially unexpected from an attorney from Brooklyn. He wasn't trained to fight psychos and didn't even know how to handle a gun, but he stepped up.

She was grateful and proud of her man.

Did he know how much she valued him? Did he realize how the passion they had shared last night had deepened their connection? She hadn't told him that she loved him. Instead, she'd got up this morning with a chip on her shoulder, demanding to take care of herself. Her self-reliance wasn't wrong, and she wouldn't apologize for it. But she also trusted him.

By the time the rotors stopped churning, Thorson had the kill switch reengaged and clutched in his left hand. The gun was in his right. He nodded to her. "Open the door."

Connor climbed inside. His gaze fixed on her. "Are you all right?"

She nodded and whispered, "I love you."

His dark eyes flashed. Her message had been received.

"Here's what's going to happen," Thorson said. "We go to the house together. I get the password and transfer funds from the offshore account. When my deposit has cleared, I'll take another ride on the chopper."

"You don't need to drag along Emily or the pilot," Connor said. "I'll be your hostage."

Thorson barked a short, ugly laugh. "Are you trying to negotiate? Don't you understand that I could kill us all with one flick of my thumb?"

"You don't want to die," Connor said. "Not when you're so close to cashing in."

"Okay, the pilot can stay here, but Emily comes with you and me."

Before Connor could object, she spoke up. "I'll do it."

"Good girl," Thorson said. "You two go first. I'll follow."

Climbing down from the chopper, she felt a twinge from her ankle. This much activity wasn't good for the sprain, but she managed to walk fairly well. As they approached the house, she glimpsed a flash of light among the pine trees on the hillside. Was it the reflection of sunlight off the lens of a rifle scope? She suspected there were several cops and deputies hiding in the forest and possibly inside the house.

The front door flung open, and Patricia Riggs stood there with her fists on her hips. She glared at the man who had once been her fiancé. "You bastard, how could you do all these terrible things?"

Under his breath, Thorson muttered, "I'd rather face the SWAT team."

"Step aside," Connor said. "We're coming in."

They rushed into the house, and Patricia closed the door behind them. In the foyer, Phillip had taken a proprietary position, leaning against the carved-oak banister at the foot of the staircase. He presumed to greet them like the lord of the castle. *Jerk!* Emily paused and looked around, taking in her surroundings.

She hadn't been inside this house for over two years,

and her first impression was that Phillip hadn't changed much of anything. The decor was the same, as was the arrangement of furniture. He'd left the small Renoir in the elaborate frame hanging on the back wall of the foyer. It was one of the first things a guest would see upon entering—a sun-dappled pastel of a child in a garden. During the good years of her marriage, she used to think that little girl was her own. Today, the painting failed to charm her. The atmosphere in the house was totally different.

"You know what I want," Thorson said.

"What about me?" Patricia demanded. "What about what I want?"

Connor confronted her directly. "This man is wearing a suicide vest. If he lifts his thumb off the kill switch, we're all dead. I advise you to stay back and keep quiet."

Moving as quickly as possible, Emily crossed the front room, circled past the grand piano and stopped in front of a small desk. Above the desk was *The Note Taker*. "Connor, would you take that painting off the wall?"

"Hey," Phillip said as he stepped forward. "What do you think you're doing?"

"You've been warned to stay quiet. Nobody needs to get hurt."

Connor lifted the painting down and carried it to a glass-topped coffee table. As she gazed down at the simple picture, her heart beat faster. What if she was wrong? Thorson said he wanted to deposit the money before he'd let them go. If she couldn't give him the password, she wasn't sure what he'd do.

"Turn it over," she said to Connor. "I need to see the back side of the canvas."

The notation she'd hoped for was readily visible. Scrawled in Jamison's messy writing was the name of a bank, the password and the account number.

"Good work," Thorson said as he pushed her out of the way and sat on the sofa beside the coffee table. "Everybody, stand back. And don't try anything. I'm going to set down my gun, but I still have the kill switch."

While he sent a text on his phone, she noticed Patricia and Phillip conferring with each other. They were up to something, but Emily didn't care what kind of plot they'd hatched. As soon as this house was sold, the Riggs family would no longer be her problem. She wouldn't miss the luxury, but she loved the artwork. She wandered to the fireplace and looked up at the Remington painting of a mustang herd charging across the plains. Whenever she looked at this vivid picture, she could almost hear the pounding of hooves and the whinny of the horses. Not today. The color seemed muted. The proportions of the central horse were off. The artist never would have made a mistake like that.

Thorson leaned back on the sofa. "My message was sent. Now we wait until I have confirmation."

"I should contact Wellborn," Connor said.

"Not yet." Thorson held up the kill switch to remind him.

They were in more danger than Connor knew. Emily had figured out what was wrong with the house, why it was uncomfortable. Patricia and Phillip were the ones to fear. She looked down, not wanting to betray her suspicions.

In less than ten minutes, Thorson's phone rang. They waited in suspense while he answered and talked. When he disconnected the call, he allowed himself a satisfied grin. "You're looking at a very rich man."

"Deactivate the switch," Connor said.

"With pleasure." Thorson fiddled with the mechanism. He released it. No explosion. "If anything goes south, I can reactivate in a few seconds. For right now, I can't wait to get out of this vest. It's too hot."

He peeled it off, set the explosives aside and rose to his feet.

Phillip aimed his handgun and fired.

Thorson hardly had a chance to look down and see the blood spreading across his muscular chest. The bullet had been lethally accurate—straight through the heart. Dr. Thorson was dead before he hit the floor.

Phillip stared at her. "You figured it out."

"This Remington over the fireplace is a copy. I'm guessing you sold the original."

"Good guess," he said. "Now you know why I couldn't let you into the house. Nobody else noticed, but you're an expert."

"How many others have you sold?"

"Enough to support me in style. I started making substitutions when Jamison was still coming here. He never appreciated the art."

"And you do?"

"I appreciate what it can do for me." Almost casually, Phillip sauntered across the room. "This is working out just the way I wanted. Thorson is out of the way. Now I take care of you two. And I'll use the doctor's gun. Patricia and I will corroborate each other's stories about how Thorson shot both of you. Then I shot him."

"You and Patricia provided alibis for each other before," Emily said, "when you killed Kate."

"That bitch had it coming," he said. "She wanted to blab to the cops."

Thorson hadn't lied to her. He was more of a dupe than a villain. "And you shot at me outside my gallery."

"That was a difficult shot," Phillip said. "Three attempts from a moving vehicle, and I got you in the chest. When you slumped, I thought this was finally over. Damn you, Emily! Why wouldn't you stay dead?"

He reached down to grab Thorson's gun, but Connor was faster. He yanked the weapon into his hands and pointed the barrel in Phillip's direction.

But Phillip hesitated. His plan had been disrupted. She guessed that he didn't want to shoot them with his own weapon because the ballistics would be hard to explain.

Emily took advantage. She grabbed a Navajo wedding vase from the mantle and hurled it at Phillip. The earthenware vase bounced off him and crashed to the floor, but it was enough of a distraction for Connor to charge forward and unload a roundhouse right on Phillip's aristocratic chin. He followed up with three hard gut shots.

Phillip's knees buckled, and he fell to the floor. Connor took his gun and handed it to Emily. "You're a better shot than I am," he said.

"How do you know? You've never seen me take target practice."

"You've got that gunslinger vibe," he said. "Keep an eye on Patricia. I should put in a call to Wellborn."

The phone call was unnecessary. At the sound of Phillip's gunshot, Wellborn and all the other cops who had been lurking at the perimeter of the property converged. They poured through the front door and the patio doors and dashed down the central staircase. While they arrested the Riggs siblings and started all the forensics associated with Thorson's murder, Emily allowed Connor to lead her down the hallway to a library.

He closed the door, holding back the sounds of the investigation coming to a close. And she meandered around the room, staring at the art on the walls. "It breaks my heart to see copies instead of originals."

"We'll take care of it." He pulled her into an embrace

and lightly kissed her lips. "You said something important to me when I saw you on the chopper."

"I did." A wonderful warm sensation spread through her.

"I never had a chance to respond," he said. "I love you, too."

She had a very good feeling about what would happen next. For one thing, people would stop trying to kill her. For another, she had the best of reasons to stay alive.

* * * * *

COMING SOON!

We really hope you enjoyed reading this book. If you're looking for more romance be sure to head to the shops when new books are available on

Thursday 27th March

To see which titles are coming soon, please visit
millsandboon.co.uk/nextmonth

MILLS & BOON

LET'S TALK
Romance

For exclusive extracts, competitions and special offers, find us online:

- **f** MillsandBoon
- **X** @MillsandBoon
- **◉** @MillsandBoonUK
- **♪** @MillsandBoonUK

Get in touch on 01413 063 232

For all the latest titles coming soon, visit
millsandboon.co.uk/nextmonth